THE GETAWAY

By Hope Anika

Copyright © 2016 Hope McKenzie
All Rights Reserved

Other books by Hope Anika:

The Bequest
Aequitas
In Plain Sight

For The Survivors

PROLOGUE

"He's going to kill you."

Lucia Sanchez said nothing.

"Did you hear me? You're *dead*."

Her gaze flickered to the rearview mirror. The boy sat in the middle of the Nova's sagging back seat, his features schooled into the remote mask she'd come to expect. Pale green eyes stabbed into hers, as hard and opaque as the jade they resembled.

"I am not afraid to die," she told him softly.

"Everyone is afraid to die."

How dismissive he sounded. How callous. It never failed to appall her.

"Even the ones who pull the trigger themselves," he added cruelly, purely for spite.

A direct, piercing hit, but Lucia didn't flinch. The boy was like a shark in bloody waters; any weakness would be devoured. No matter the chaos that churned within her, she must be unwavering. *Steadfast.* And so she only turned her gaze back to the hypnotic, dotted line of freeway. The vibration of the uneven pavement made the steering wheel shudder in her hands, an echo of her fiercely pounding, terrified and angry heart.

Thud-thud. Thud-thud. Thud-thud.

Be calm, she told herself. *Destiny is not for the weak.* But deep within, she knew better. Deep within—*ay, yai, yai, chica, what have you done? Muy estupido! You should have waited, should have planned, you will pay—they will pay—and now there is no going back*—because four hours and three hundred miles lay behind them, and the lights of the city had faded long ago. To the east, the first rays of sunlight were creeping across the desert scrub brush, and the wheels she'd set in motion were spinning far beyond her control. But the panic that sat in her chest like a lead weight was nothing compared to the fury that burned in her veins, so hot and caustic and volatile she knew she could not allow it escape. *Enough damage has already been done.* She had jumped; it was too late to worry about landing now. No matter the furious, frantic beat of her heart.

"You know he'll come," the boy continued, and his tone might have been flat with resignation, but his eyes...they glittered at her in the mirror, a bright, dizzy sheen of fear he couldn't hide.

She had pushed him with this action, right to the edge. He stood beside her now.

"*Sí*," she acknowledged.

He growled, a low, rumbling sound few would believe him capable of. "Then why are you doing this?"

Lucia took him in: chiseled bones, hinting at the man he would become, a strong jaw and stubborn chin. Pale, jade green eyes lashed with thick ebony crescents; a tiny beauty mark kissing his right cheek. Only ten years old, but already so beautiful that sometimes just looking at him hurt.

"Because someone must, *mijo*."

"Not you," the boy said, and there was something in his voice that made her squeeze the steering wheel until the worn plastic abraded her skin. He looked down at the small form sprawled across his lap. "You aren't...*enough*."

An infuriating—if accurate—assessment. But it changed nothing. She would have to be enough. A grim reality, and not something she could change. She'd tried.

"You can't win," he added, as though it were fact. *What goes up must come down.*

Which only fed the fury that threatened to blind her, so toxic and unstable, something she *must not* allow to control her. But Lucia was sick to death of being told her limits, her place, of being relegated to someone else's definition of her existence. It had taken years to carve a path out of the madness of her childhood; blood, sweat and tears to travel that path. No one would tell her what she must accept, what she must *allow*. Not any longer. Because the monstrous present had raised the equally grisly past, and she would not stand idly by as it repeated itself before her.

No.

Perhaps this rash, dangerous act would change nothing; perhaps the evil men did was already written, something no one—her least of all—could change. But she refused to be complacent, to be silent. *To watch it happen again.* Others might turn away, but she would not. Because for her, evil was not merely an idea. A stranger she had never met. No, malevolence was an old enemy, one with whom she had been long acquainted. One she was introduced to in childhood, whose shape and form and scent she knew intimately.

One she recognized as if it were family. *Family.* Something she had not had in over a decade. Something that same evil had taken from her.

And now it will take even more! Your future, your dreams, your life—

But that would not stop her. She would not run and hide, not again. Not ever again.

No matter the specter of death Alexander spoke of.

"You underestimate me, *mijo*," she replied finally, darkly. "You should never underestimate anyone."

"You're nothing," the boy said, certain.

A roar filled her throat, begging for escape. She wanted to pound her fists against the ancient dash and make him understand. But that would only egg him on and—probably—crack the dash in half.

"Everyone is someone," she told him, calm, hard, equally as certain. "And anyone can change the world."

"Is that what you're doing?" he derided, his mockery honed to knifelike precision. "Changing the world?"

She met the sharp glitter of his eyes. "Your world," she said.

His gaze dropped. He looked out the window, to where the sun was steadily rising in a fiery arc of orange and pink. Fingers of light speared across the road before them, highlighting the tar lines that held the pavement together.

Thud-thud. Thud-thud. Thud-thud.

The old Nova sliced through the cold morning air at eighty miles an hour, shuddering in effort to meet the demands of her lead foot. The car smelled of aged vinyl and cigarettes, and a long crack arced along the windshield, shearing the pane in two. Traffic was light, the road littered with garbage and the occasional animal carcass.

But no police. *No Ivan the Terrible.* Not yet.

"When he catches us..." The boy shook his head. "Do you know what he'll do?"

Lucia knew; she didn't care. Not anymore. That fear was useless, a waste of time she no longer had. "*Sí.*"

"No, you don't."

But she did. She knew exactly. And even if the knowing woke terror in her heart—because the man who would come, he would want blood, he would *enjoy* her pain—such a thing would not stop her.

Nothing would stop her.

"Some things," she told him, "are worth the risk."

"Not this. Not to me."

Her heart fluttered painfully in her chest, like a panicked bird fighting its cage. She only ignored it and watched the boy in the mirror, her resolve like steel, no matter his doubt. Her own. "No?" Her eyes fell to the child he held. "What about to him?"

The boy wanted to hit her. She could see it flaring in his eyes, the suppressed violence that always simmered there, just below the surface. The hate and rage that lived within him like a second self.

It had taken her eight months to understand. Eight months too long.

"You can make choices for yourself," she said. "But

not for him."

"I can't, but you can?"

Such fury, like a whip snapping through the air, but she said only, "*Sí*, I can, *mijo*. I *am*."

The boy looked away. The stoic line of his profile and the hard, unforgiving line of his jaw where a muscle ticked uncontrollably made Lucia want to do violence. She'd known horror and pain and devastating loss; blood so thick it would not run, the sickening stench of death. The dreams still *were*, as they had always been, and she would not have believed it would become something she would embrace.

Something she would use.

She'd been wrong.

A child should not know this pain.

But Alexander wasn't a child. He hadn't been for a long time, certainly longer than she'd known him. His decade might as well have been a century. There was nothing at all child-like about him.

That had been her first clue.

"You don't understand," he muttered, a small crack in his cold reserve.

"What don't I understand, *mijo*?" Lucia asked. "What he will do to me? Or what he will do to you?"

The weight of her question filled the car like a thick, sulfurous cloud. But she knew he wouldn't respond.

He never did.

She had only her own conviction, the proof evidenced by her own eyes. The sickening truth she could not—*would not*—deny. Not even for him. She'd been too young the first time, too weak. Too ignorant and naïve and *stupid.* Not so now. And while she understood the boy's silence, it wouldn't stop her. Nothing was going to stop her—nothing but the death of which he spoke. No matter her mistakes, her panic, the regret eating at her, berating her for allowing her fury to control her, she would stop at nothing.

She would save him. Save them both. No matter the odds against her, the men who would come, the army that would hunt them. Because the alternative was unthinkable, and not something she could live with. Not again.

Never again.

She'd abandoned all that she was, all that she could ever hope to become for this mission. The phoenix that had risen from the ashes of her childhood would die a sudden and brutal death, buried as effectively as any corpse, its grave barren and unmarked. All she'd fought for would be anted up on the alter of this sacrifice: every precious, hard-won day of survival, the life she'd built brick by painful brick, the education she'd worked nearly into the grave for, the future of which she'd dreamed. *Gone.* All gone. And part of her screamed at the injustice, mourned profoundly the loss, but what drove her was unconcerned with that loss. Life *was* loss. Sacrifice and pain were nothing new. If the tradeoff was their future, she would happily make it. Because it was not death she feared, it was failure.

"*You'll just make it worse*," Alexander hissed, another fissure forming in his diffidence.

"No," Lucia disagreed quietly. "There is no shame in truth; there is only strength."

"Truth." The boy's mouth twisted. "Yours or his?"

"There is only one truth, *mijo*."

He shook his head again. The muscle in his jaw quivered. He wanted so badly to deny it. Lucia could see the words trembling on his lips, the cry welling in his thin chest.

But he wouldn't. He couldn't. They both knew the truth intimately, even if they did not speak of it. She had tried, more than once, but he would not be swayed. He was too ashamed—the burden of which no victim should carry—and no matter what she said, he wouldn't accept that he wasn't responsible, that he'd never been in control. A victim, not a participant.

He couldn't seem to tell the difference, which only enraged her more.

So many casualties. She hadn't expected it to find her again. More fool her.

"What will we do?" Alexander demanded tightly. "Run forever?"

A valid question.

Lucia's gaze flickered to Benjamin, who slept fitfully in his brother's arms, his ruddy cheeks flushed. She wanted so many things for them both, so many wonderful things…things she would never be able to give them. These children, who had come so unexpectedly into her life, whom she hadn't expected to change her. *To love.* And Alexander was right: they deserved more than the nomadic existence she was damning them to, more than a life driven by uncertainty and a constant fear of discovery. A life spent running instead of living.

Because the one who would come for them—*for her*—

would not stop. Not until she was dead. But the alternative was worse, and one she could not allow. No matter the price.

Destiny is not for the weak.

"He's going to find us," Alexander said coldly, his belief absolute. "And then he's going to kill you."

Lucia's hands tightened on the steering wheel until her knuckles ached. "He is going to have to."

CHAPTER 1

Fuck.

"Thank you."

"Don't tell me thank you," snarled Sam Steele, Deputy U.S. Marshal and—at the moment—ornery son of a bitch. "I haven't said yes."

"Yet."

They'd been friends for thirteen years. Together they'd survived Army Ranger training, covert ops in the dank green hells of Columbia, several near-death experiences in the mountains of Afghanistan, and one hellish divorce. But in that moment, Sam didn't particularly give a shit. He was tired, hungry and sick of pretending. It was his first goddamn day off in over three months, and he'd had less than four hours to enjoy it.

Christ.

"I need you on this, Sammy. This is a fucking disaster. The feds are on their way, and once they're here, it's over. I have to move now. She's heading north, an hour, maybe two behind you—

"How do you know that?"

"One of the cameras picked her up."

Sam pinched the bridge of his nose.

"I just need her intercepted. Stopped, the kids secured. Held until I can get there. Easy as pie."

Yeah. Right. "Then call the locals, and have them do it."

"I don't trust the locals. I trust you. Cruz has political influence from here to DC; he's probably got the damn CIA out looking for her. I need to get my hands on her before he does."

Sam scowled. His fucking head hurt, his belly was growling, and exhaustion filled his skull like cotton batting. The wound left by the bullet he'd taken in Baja was still oozing pus and blood, and this call—this *favor*—was the last goddamn thing he needed. Or wanted.

The very last.

"Why?" he demanded. "She's a felon at this point. You do the crime, you do the time. What's the problem?"

The man on the other end of his cell phone hesitated, and Sam felt the fine hair at his nape bristle in warning.

"What?" he repeated, straightening in the seat of his rented Land Rover.

"Lucia is…an old friend." Anthony Malone, detective with the Las Vegas Metropolitan Police Department, hesitated. "And I don't think things are what they seem."

Sam stiffened. "How do they seem?"

"Cruz is claiming she's been abusing them."

Perfect. "And what makes you think different?"

"She came to see me several weeks ago and made the same claim about him."

Even better. "Did she have evidence?"

"Nothing that would hold up against a guy like Cruz," Tony replied grimly.

"So it's he said/she said. Even better." Sam rubbed his aching skull. "What did you tell her?"

Silence fell.

"Tony?" he pressed sharply.

A sigh. Regret, Sam thought.

"I told her she was imagining things," Tony said.

"Good call," Sam grated, unable to ease the bite.

"Yeah. Not one of my better moments."

"And now you believe her?"

More silence.

"Or you *want* to believe her?" Just what the fuck he needed.

"I don't know what to believe," Tony admitted.

Jesus H. Christ. Sam growled softly to himself and wondered why in the hell he'd bothered to answer his phone.

"She might be telling the truth," Tony muttered. "But it might be…something else."

"Something else?" Sam repeated softly, his tone dangerous. "Like what?"

"Like the past."

Better and better. "Don't tell me she's an old girlfriend."

"No. We were…childhood friends. It's a long story."

"I'm listening."

Another heavy sigh. Definitely regret. "It was a long time ago—Jesus, the feds just walked in. I have to go. She's in a '78 blue Chevy Nova, headed northwest on US84. Call me when you have her—and thanks."

The dial tone sounded in his ear.

Goddamnmotherfuckingshit.

Sam squeezed his phone and valiantly fought the urge to smash it against the pavement. He should have never answered the fucking thing, but Fieldstone was still in intensive care, and he couldn't afford to miss any news that might come his way—good or bad. He'd spent the last three months undercover, protecting the worthless ass of a drug runner who'd reluctantly agreed to testify against the cartel that employed him, and because they'd hopped around every few weeks like a damned jackrabbit, they'd managed to stay under the cartel's radar.

Until Baja. When all hell had broken loose.

And now, when he was finally back on US soil, when he could finally take the break he so badly needed, there was this: a runaway nanny and her kidnapped charges. And not just any charges—no, they just had to be the two sons of international businessman Donovan Cruz, Las Vegas gazillionaire and budding politico heavyweight.

Double fuck.

Sam was tempted to call Tony back and tell him forget it. This shit was the last thing he wanted to deal with. He was totally burnt out, fried to the edges of his desiccated soul. He felt as if he were turning to dust.

He wanted his hammock, his Rainier view and a six-pack. He wanted three months of sleep in an empty alpine meadow and his fly fishing pole. He wanted, if only for a small space of time, some fucking peace and quiet.

He needed it. Or he wouldn't be any use to the Marshal Service, or to the witnesses he was sworn to protect.

He wouldn't be anything but dead.

An old friend.

Fucking perfect. An old friend—an old childhood friend, at that. One who'd pitted herself against a man who could crush her like a bug.

Why? Because she truly believed he was abusing his children? Or because she was the abuser and hoped to shore her defense by becoming the apparent champion?

Just what kind of abuse were they talking about?

Not that Sam cared. Not really. He supposed he should; his lack of regard for the entire situation only proved how badly he needed to step away from the world at large and forget. If only for a little while.

For a long while. He didn't want to do this. This was Tony's problem, not his. This was the feds' problem, not his. Donovan Cruz's problem—not his.

He looked over to the Flying J where he'd been headed for breakfast and felt the acid in his stomach bubble like a frothy hot tub. He wanted chicken fried steak and eggs, a cup of strong, hot coffee and a cigarette.

He glanced at his watch. 9:23.

So, was he going to call Tony back? Or was he going to park his ass at the next pull out and wait for a blue 1978 Chevy Nova to pass by?

Son of a bitch. He should have just flown home. But he'd thought—mistakenly, idiotically—that the drive would do him some good. What were the odds, he wondered darkly, that his chosen route would intersect with the path taken by Tony's runaway?

Christ, his head hurt. Like someone had taken an ax and buried it in his temple. He shouldn't be going anywhere but home. He knew that.

So why was he hesitating? What the fuck was his problem?

Tony would recover. He had other contacts, other people he could call for help. Other people he trusted.

But Tony was a friend, and for a man like Sam, who didn't have any family, the handful of friends he could lay claim to were precious and few. Not to mention that Tony had saved his ass on more than one occasion.

I just need her intercepted. Stopped, the kids secured. Held until I can get there. Easy as pie.

How much trouble could it really be? But the hair at his nape was still bristling, always a bad sign.

A portent of things to come.

Still, he was a Deputy U.S. Marshal, grizzled and lean from his work in the field, armed with a Glock, a twelve-inch serrated combat knife, and, at the moment, a bad fucking attitude. Lucia Sanchez was a runaway nanny driving a thirty-seven-year old beater, too foolish to realize she couldn't outrun the law, or a man like Donovan Cruz.

The odds were in his favor. Hell, she didn't stand a chance.

Sam reached down and started the Land Rover.

CHAPTER 2

Boom!

Lucia thought it was a gunshot.

The steering wheel jerked in her hands, and the Nova swerved violently toward the ditch that lined the right side of the road. A startled cry sounded in the backseat, and even though she wanted to slam her foot down onto the brake, she forced herself to downshift into neutral instead, which made the Nova lurch in protest, throwing her against her seat belt. Immediately they began to slow, bobbing like a boat in rough water as she wrenched on the wheel and fought to keep them from the ditch.

The car rolled to a sluggish stop on the side of the freeway. Lucia sat for a long moment, her hands white-knuckled around the steering wheel, her heart hammering in her chest. Rain beat down against the roof in a torrent. The clear sky that had dawned just a handful of hours ago was gone. In its place was a line of churning thunderheads, and a cold rain that hit the Nova's metal roof so hard it sounded like a spray of bullets.

Ay, yai, yai. Further proof of your stupidity.

Because as getaway vehicles went, the Nova left much

to be desired. The fact that the old relic—her sole inheritance from her mother—was barely roadworthy had not been an issue on the rare occasions she drove it. Biking was her preferred method of travel through the city in which she lived, and the only reason she'd even driven the vehicle to work the day before was because her bike had a flat.

As the Nova now had. Which was almost funny.

Almost.

"Awesome," was Alexander's derisive murmur from the back seat.

But Lucia had not expected to flee into the night with the aging car. That, however, was little excuse for the situation in which they now found themselves. *Muy estupido!*

What else could go wrong?

Do not ask such a foolish question. Because the Universe would surely answer.

"I don't suppose there's a spare?" the boy inquired scathingly.

Lucia met his cold, pale gaze and fought the urge to make a face. Next to him, Ben sat up, rubbing his eyes, looking around in interest. "What happened?" he wanted to know, yawning hugely.

"Flat tire," Alexander told him. "This car is a piece of shit."

Lucia couldn't argue, so she only took a deep, steadying breath and eyed her mirrors. Still no police. *No Ivan.* Who was surely behind them somewhere, as inescapable as the tide. Still, they'd made it nearly two states away from the city they'd fled with no sign of trouble, which—considering she'd absconded with the two male heirs of one of the most influential and wealthiest men on the planet—was nothing short of miraculous. But she knew it was only a matter of time before her free-fall ended.

Gravity was an inevitability.

"I needs me some grub," Ben announced.

Lucia's belly growled in agreement, but Alexander said nothing. She knew he was hungry, too, but the boy never complained, stoic in the face of every circumstance: hunger, pain, fear. He was completely self-contained, as though he had no human needs. She'd finally come to understand he construed such things as weakness, and he wouldn't allow himself any weakness—not even hunger. He was determined to endure.

She understood that fear lay at the root of that control, that Alexander believed giving into those things which might undermine him could undo him entirely. But he was not alone in that, and she found it bitterly ironic, that it had taken her so long to understand the simple, gut-wrenching truth that lay beneath the cold, caustic bearing he so carefully cultivated. A shroud she had seen before, one she should have known instantly.

One she should have recognized.

"I will change the tire, and then we will eat," she told Ben. She met his curious brown gaze and tried to smile. Sweet Ben. He was the smartest, funniest, most charming five-year-old she'd ever met, the very antithesis of Alexander, which told her he had been spared his brother's fate. *So far.* But she had no hope such a blessing would continue, and neither did Alexander.

Or he never would have let her take them.

"Can we have some McDonalds?" Ben asked, excitement lighting his features.

"*Sí*, monkey." Lucia glanced out her window at the downpour and sighed. *If we can get to one.*

A big if, dependent upon many things, the first of which was the existence of a spare tire. Because her mother, a woman who hadn't known oil from antifreeze, had rarely driven, and in all of the years Lucia had owned the Nova, she'd never paid much attention to the state of its tires—*Idiota!*—and she had a feeling that the likelihood of a decent spare being on board was right up there with bovine flight. But she wouldn't know until she looked, so she turned on her hazards and, bracing herself, stepped out into the rain.

The wind blew ferociously; in an instant she was soaked through. Passing traffic sprayed her with waves of dirty, stinging water as she strode back to the trunk and opened it. Their backpacks sat nestled in one corner; her tent, first aid kit and two old sleeping bags were shoved into the other. She pushed everything to one side and lifted the lid of the spare tire compartment and found deliverance: bald, black and beautiful.

A Goodyear miracle.

"Hot damn," she said, simultaneously both relieved and hotly furious with herself.

Because this was *her* fault. She was not the stupid, rash, thoughtless, *crazy* woman she'd been behaving as for the last ten hours, but there was no evidence of that to the contrary. Not in this rickety old car and its warped, treadless spare tire. Not in the state of their current condition, which was stuck on the side of the freeway as the skies opened above them and released a deluge of icy, punishing rain…*dios mío*. Her fault. For finally snapping completely; for allowing her rage and terror and the past she'd never escaped full, disastrous reign. Such agonizing fury that her common sense had fled, her brain had shrunken to the size of a pea, and she'd done everything—*everything*—wrong.

So much stupid. You should get a prize, chica.

A big, gleaming idiot award to replace her now defunct medical degree.

Because it was not what she'd done—something she refused to regret, no matter the consequences—but *how* she'd done it that would determine her level of success. And so far the only thing she'd done right was, apparently, head in a direction no one thought she would go. Everything else was a big, fat *fail*.

As Alexander continued to point out.

She sighed and reached down to lift the spare out, stumbling a little beneath the weight. It was a regular tire, not a donut, but it looked serviceable—so long as they didn't go far. The jack stand was there, too, along with a rusting tire iron. She leaned the tire against the car and removed the stand and iron and tried to remember the fundamentals of tire changing.

The rain was cold, big, fat drops that slapped her like angry words. Traffic flew past, making the Nova sway. She set up the jack, put a couple of large rocks in back of the front tires and managed to get the car several inches off the ground. But when she tried to loosen the lug nuts with her tire iron, the tire simply spun, making it impossible to remove them.

She stared at the tire through the thickening rain, shivering, fury at herself growing.

Mierda! She should know how to change a damn tire. Why had she never learned such a basic skill? It was not rocket science, and yet it might as well be. And she supposed she deserved this—*moron!*—but the children did not. She had been foolish and impulsive—blinded by rage—and now here they were. Worse, she couldn't figure out what she was doing wrong, and they didn't have time—

A large black Land Rover suddenly pulled up behind the Nova.

Lucia watched it slow to a halt, her grip tightening on the tire iron. It had California plates—*not Ivan, not the police*—but her heart kicked into overdrive anyway, and unease spread through her like a stain. She waited, motionless, as the driver's side door swung open, and a large man climbed out. He strode toward her, seemingly unconcerned with the rain that instantly soaked his black t-shirt and faded jeans.

She rose from her crouched position, the tire iron heavy and cold in her hold. There was an old .22 stuffed into her purse, but her purse was in the front seat of the Nova, and there was no hope of reaching it before he did her. Not that she truly needed the weapon; she'd learned long ago how to put a man down, and they never expected it of her: petite, fragile, *female*. Still, it was not a skill she particularly cared to put into practice unless absolutely necessary, and there was nothing to say she would need to do so, nothing but her own chilling, rampant paranoia, born of blood and experience.

Perhaps he just stopped to help.

But chivalry had been dead a long time.

The man halted before her, water slicing down the hollows of his jaw. Startlingly bright, blue-green eyes met hers, as luminous and translucent as the Caribbean waters they resembled. "Trouble?"

Lucia stared at him through the rain. He towered above her, the width of his shoulders easily twice her own. His voice was deep, rasped from the depths of a broad chest, and the sodden t-shirt he wore clung to the rope of muscle that covered him. The faint golden beard that lined his jaw did nothing to soften the sharp bones that carved his face into hard angles and planes. A wicked looking scar cut his left eyebrow in two.

"No," she said, watching him. "No trouble."

He looked at the jacked up car and scowled. "Looks like trouble."

"Looks can be deceiving," she told him.

He transferred that scowl to her. "You need help."

"No," she said again.

He snorted and held out his hand, presumably for the tire iron she held, but Lucia didn't hand it over. He was a very big man and a stranger—something she never trusted—and the dark look on his face…he appeared annoyed. *Angry.* Which was a mystery she didn't understand, didn't care to solve, and was not about to arm with a large steel tool.

"I can help," he said shortly and motioned impatiently with the hand he held out. "Give me the tire iron."

But Lucia only stared at him, unmoving, her grip on the iron tightening.

"Let me change the tire for you." He ground out the words as if she were a village idiot, something for which he clearly had no patience. A muscle leapt in the hard, bristled line of his jaw, and in his gaze she saw something she didn't understand: contempt.

The rage within her suddenly burst to life. Lucia tried to talk it down; this man, he was no one. *Not worth the effort.* But the disdain in his startling eyes abraded her, rousing the anger she was trying so hard to contain.

"Thank you for stopping," she bit out. "But I have it under control."

The man's features drew into an ominous visage, and her heart fluttered. His scar whitened, his mouth thinned, and he took an aggressive step toward her. "I can do it, or you can wait until the Highway Patrol comes along, and they can do it."

Her heart fluttered again, stronger. Because this man was an unknown, and part of her thought that clobbering him over the head with the tire iron was a good idea. *Safer than accepting his help.* But that was not a reasonable solution, and her saner self heard his words—*or you can wait until the Highway Patrol comes along*—and thought, no, she really couldn't. Because if the police found her, this entire misadventure would have been for naught, and she wasn't willing to give up. Not even for this man…this unpleasant and inexplicable angry man…from whom she wanted nothing. And yet he was right. If she could not get the tire free, eventually the police *would* find them—

"Goddamn it," the man growled and reached abruptly for the iron, catching one end to pull rudely against her hold. "Give it to me."

But Lucia didn't let go. She simply couldn't. He was glaring at her through the rain, his unhidden dislike a brutal slap in the face. Perhaps she should be frightened, but she wasn't. She was furious.

Maldito cabrón! What the hell was his problem?

Because she hadn't asked for him to stop. To help. And while she might have appreciated some advice—like a clue as to why the damn tire wouldn't come off—she had no need of his wrath.

"No, *thank you*," she repeated—hissed—and pulled futilely at the tire iron. "I will get it off myself."

"Just let me help you," he snarled in return.

"You do not want to help me." Lucia tugged at the iron, irate. "You want to growl at me like an angry dog."

He blinked and reached up to scrub his free hand down his face, sluicing the rain away. "No."

"Yes," she argued. "You are confrontational and belligerent."

He stared at her, unspeaking.

"Please let go of my tire iron," she said through clenched teeth.

That luminescent gaze narrowed on her. "Stubborn."

"Rude," she countered.

His brows rose. He looked at the tire, and his grip on the iron seemed to tighten, tugging her infinitesimally closer. "Did you loosen the lugs before you lifted it?"

"Should I have?" she demanded, trying not to yell.

"Only if you want to get the tire off."

She yanked again at the iron, unimpressed with his

sarcasm. "Then you have solved my problem. *Gracias.* You may go now."

"I don't think so, sweetheart."

The urge to kick him was very tempting. "You—"

"Those nuts are rusted on," he continued, talking over her. "No way you're getting them off."

Which Lucia took as a personal challenge. She was going to get them off if it was the last thing—

Lightning shattered the sky above her, a blinding flash followed by a violent crack of thunder that shook the ground beneath her feet. Her heart leapt, and her grip slipped, and before she could protest, the man was yanking the tool from her and moving to crouch before the tire.

She wanted to protest, to take the tire iron from him and shove him rudely aside, into the dirt. Instead, she ground her teeth as rain ran down her cheeks and forced herself to watch in silence as he efficiently lowered the Nova, loosened the lug nuts, and then lifted it again. He removed the nuts and pulled the blown tire off. As he studied it, he shot her a veiled look.

"This thing is a piece of shit," he said, echoing Alexander. "Do they all look like this?"

"No." *Yes.*

He stared at her through the rain. His eyes slid down her, taking note of her worn flannel shirt, her sodden, threadbare jeans and cheap, battered hiking boots. His gaze flickered back to hers, but she could read nothing there, not even the annoyance that echoed in his voice.

"Hand me the spare," he ordered.

Barely resisting the urge to salute, Lucia rolled the miracle tire toward him. She stepped back when he lifted it onto the bolts as though it weighed nothing.

"Is everything okay?" Alexander asked suddenly, making her start. The boy was leaning out the back window of the Nova, his pale eyes locked on the man changing their tire.

"*Sí, mijo,*" she said. "Nothing to worry about."

"Are you sure?" His tone was careful, his attention focused unwaveringly on the man next to her.

That man looked up at him. They stared at one another for a tense moment.

"I needs me a Happy Meal," Ben called through the window.

"In a minute, monkey." The man and Alexander were having a chilly stare-down contest, and Lucia's gaze flitted between them, trepidation worming its way through her.

"What about you?" the man asked Alexander. "Are you okay?"

Alexander only blinked, his face molded into its cold, arrogant cast, and ducked back into the car. The window rattled in protest as he rolled it up.

Lucia said nothing, and the man looked at her over his shoulder, a piercing look that made her belly tighten. She only stared back at him, unblinking.

He released the jack and lowered the Nova. The tire made a soft, keening whistle and deflated, leaving the weight of the car on the tire's bent, rusting rim.

"No good," the man said, his voice hard.

Lucia wanted to kick it. "*Mierda*."

He stood, the tire iron gripped loosely in one hand. "You'll have to come with me."

"Oh, no," she said. "I do not think so."

His mouth thinned into a hard line. "I can take you to get a tire—or two."

His mockery plucked at her last nerve, and no matter their dire situation, she wanted nothing more from this ornery jackass of a man. Lucia drew herself up and reached out to take the tire iron. "That is unnecessary."

The man lifted the iron out of reach and took a step toward her, so close she could feel the immense heat he emanated. "Those are funnel clouds, sweetheart. Is the side of the freeway really where you want to be if they touch down?"

Lucia tore her gaze from him and looked at the sky. *He was right.* A wall of black moved steadily toward them, so thick and opaque it looked impenetrable, and clouds churned overhead, twisting into a dangerous, cone-shaped mass that was slowly arcing toward the earth. The wind had grown stronger while they argued, powerful enough now to make her sway on her feet, and lightning forked across sky, followed a heartbeat later by thunder so loud and violent, she felt it vibrate through her bones. Ben cried out, a sharp, piercing cry that made her heart slam into her ribs.

"At least think about your kids," the man growled, taking another step toward her. His shadow slid over her like dusk falling, and the urge to step away was strong, but Lucia held her ground. His heat pressed against her through the wind and rain, and the force of his will was palpable. He smelled like peppermint.

Peppermint?

"What's going on?"

She nearly jumped out of her skin. Alexander stood just behind the man, motionless, soaked to the bone. Watching tensely.

The man turned to look down at him. Again their gazes collided, and they eyed one another warily, as if they were animals vying for territory.

"Get back into the car, *mijo*," Lucia told him. "I will be right there."

"The tire's still flat," he pointed out unhelpfully, watching the man closely.

Thunder chose that moment to crack violently above them, making her jump.

"We need to go," the man said. He moved around her and tossed the jack and the tire iron into the Nova's trunk. "This your stuff?"

He didn't wait for an answer, but gathered their packs, the tent, the first aid kit and the sleeping bags and turned to head toward his Rover.

"Stop!" she protested, but thunder boomed again, drowning her out.

"What's he doing?" Alexander demanded.

She didn't know. "We need a new tire."

"We need a new car."

A wild laugh caught in her throat.

"We can't go with him," the boy said seriously. "It isn't safe."

Lucia knew that. The man was a stranger—a contrary, belligerent stranger, perhaps even dangerous—who'd already proven to be trouble. Trusting him was out of the question. He'd made her angry, and she was already angry enough. *She'd already been foolish enough.* She didn't need him to make everything worse. But her options were few and far between. Because at the moment, her status as an abductor—*a fugitive*—meant nothing; the storm raging around them took precedence. No matter that following this man could prove disastrous—for him should Ivan or the police descend, and for them if he really was as furious as he seemed—this hellacious storm was—

Thunder boomed; lightning flashed. Sand and gravel blasted her, and Ben cried out again. Above her, the clouds rolled and billowed into monstrous shapes, and around her, the Idaho desert watched with disinterest.

Ay, yai, yai. From the frying pan into the fire. You had to ask what else could befall you. You had to ask.

Destiny—bah.

Because no matter the danger their unwilling champion presented—or how much he provoked the rage that churned within her—she couldn't leave the children behind in the Nova while she went in search of a new tire. It was only a matter of time before someone found the car, especially now that it was slumped uselessly on the side of the freeway. And the difficult, cross man who'd just commandeered their belongings didn't appear to be willing to leave without them. Even if she got him to leave, Lucia had a feeling he would call them in to the authorities, if only to make sure they were safe.

There were no good choices here.

"Lucia?"

She headed toward the car. "Get your stuff; we are going with him."

Alexander halted, watching her through the rain. "No."

"We cannot stay with the car. Look!" She pointed up at the funneling clouds, rolling and dark and splintered by jagged lightning. The wind howled; dirt and sand peppered them, mixed with the driving rain. "We have to get out of here. Now."

Alexander scowled up at the sky. "It's a sign."

"Get your stuff," she repeated and turned away, toward the Nova. She gathered her purse and coat from the front seat.

"Did ya hear the thunder?" Ben wanted to know as she swung open the back door. "I screamed like a girl."

Alexander was already unbuckling him, his mouth set in a hard, unforgiving line.

"We shouldn't do this," he warned softly.

The hair at her nape bristled, as if in agreement. But she didn't know if it was portent or fear, and fear could not stop her.

"We have no choice," she said. "We cannot chance the storm. The next town is only a few miles away; he can drop us somewhere we can get a tire and be on his way. It will be fine."

She hoped. *So unforgivably stupid.* It was not destiny that had come up short. And she could only hope this decision—to follow a man she would just as soon smack with a tire iron—was not the final nail in her coffin. Or in his.

"And if they find the car?" the boy persisted.

"Then we will take a bus," she told him. "Or we will rent a car. We will work it out, *mijo*."

"You really won't give this up?"

His voice was tight, his eyes glittering wildly. Lucia stilled, aware of the inner battle that waged within him. Ben looked between them and began to chew on his thumb.

"No," she said softly, with finality. "I will not."

Alexander blinked and pulled Ben into his arms. "It's your funeral."

But there was something beyond the indifferent, cutting tone he had so perfected. It was small, wavering, uncertain.

She couldn't have said for sure, but Lucia thought it might have been hope.

CHAPTER 3

"Do you mean to tell me you still don't know where she is? What about the APB? Jesus Christ, there aren't that many goddamn roads in this state; how the hell far could she get?"

Detective Tony Malone watched as the baby-faced Fed who'd introduced himself as Special Agent Austin Kent paced furiously back and forth within the small confines of Tony's office and wondered how much longer he was going to be able to stall them.

The feds were a pain in the ass. Always late to the game, always thinking they could cut in line. Always counting their chickens.

Tony was a cop because the process of investigation—of crime solving—fascinated him. He liked collecting clues and amassing the missing pieces; he enjoyed trying to fit them together. The psychology of his suspects, the idiosyncrasies of the criminal mind, the recognition of reason within chaos—those were the reasons he'd joined the force.

He had no respect for someone who rode the race piggybacked and then showed up at the finish line and expected a medal. If they wanted a goddamn medal they had to run the goddamn race.

This was no different. It might have been a fucking mess, but it was his fucking mess.

"No one's reported seeing her? In this entire city? What about the camera footage? We were told there was a possible sighting north of the city. Is that true? Was there a sighting?" Kent halted in front of Tony's desk, his eyes narrow, his tone demanding. Kent, who was young—too young, in Tony's opinion—and impetuous, his impatience only serving to highlight his inexperience. One had to be patient to be a good investigator. Rushing just got people killed. "Have you issued an Amber Alert?"

"Of course." There had been no choice. An Amber Alert was standard operating procedure when they had a description of the abductor and vehicle, and he hadn't been able to justify not issuing one. Not even for Lucia. "Just like the book says. But we've been unable to confirm from the video footage that it's her."

The slender woman who'd accompanied Special Agent Kent into Tony's office suddenly cleared her throat. Her name was Isabel Bjorn, and she stood next to the only window in Tony's office, her pale hair and skin illuminated by the misty gray light that filtered into the room. Her gaze was oddly dark in her face, as if somewhere in her genes a swarthy ancestor had skewered her pure Nordic lineage, and as she lifted that gaze to him, Tony felt a streak of heat skewer him just as effectively.

"These allegations of abuse...have you looked into them?" she asked. A faint drawl pulled at her words, slowing the cadence of her speech. Her head cocked to the left as she waited for his response.

"Yes."

Kent halted in his pacing and turned to look at him. Agent Bjorn's brows rose. "And?"

"And I think Donovan Cruz is full of shit," Tony told them bluntly.

Kent's gaze narrowed on him. "Why?"

Because Tony had known Lucia Sanchez his whole life. Because he knew exactly what she was capable of—and what she wasn't.

Because what they'd survived together made it impossible.

"You think Mr. Cruz is lying," Isabel clarified.

Tony focused on her. Her face betrayed nothing, not even the typical derision the feds displayed toward anyone who wasn't on the federal payroll. She only watched him calmly, her stillness a telling juxtaposition against her partner's restless movement. "Yes."

"Why?"

"Because Lucia Sanchez spent the last three weeks trying to convince the Clark County Health and Welfare Department to open an investigation on Donovan Cruz. And when they refused, she went to the Las Vegas chapter of Child Protective Services, who were also reticent to rock the Cruz Boat." His mouth twisted in self-disgust. "The LVMPD was no better."

"Those agencies require physical evidence," Isabel murmured. "One woman's word is never enough, especially against a man like Donavon Cruz."

"Lucia Sanchez kidnapped those boys," Kent said with a

sharp shake of his head. "Right now, that's the priority. We can figure the rest out later." He swung away and began, once again, to pace back and forth. "Cruz is certain she's our perp. She's gone, they're gone. The mother's dead, no other living relatives. So it has to have been Sanchez, right? Has to be. But I'd be surprised if she went north. I think she's far more likely to head for the southern border. Her father was from Belize; it's a good bet she has family down there. We need to find out if—"

"She's alone," Tony said and knew he sounded as angry as he felt. Isabel's speculative gaze touched him, but he looked at Kent instead. "No family."

"That'll make things easier," Kent said. "She won't have anyone to help her."

A soft growl welled in Tony's chest. *He* should have fucking helped her.

If he'd listened when she'd come to him, none of this would be happening. But that damned name—Donovan Cruz—had thrown him badly. Had shaken him. And when Lucia had spelled it out to him…

Jesus Christ.

Talk about dropping a fucking bomb.

"Alone?" Isabel repeated, one sleek silver brow arching at him.

"No family," he repeated.

"And no friends?"

Her question was indirect, but he heard it. And ignored it. "None that we've been able to hunt up."

"A loner, then." Kent nodded as he paced. "That'll

make things harder. Still, chances are, she'll head to her homeland. Somewhere she feels safe."

Tony said nothing. America was Lucia's 'homeland,' which the dumb fucker would know if he'd done his homework. But Special Agent Kent could make all the ignorant assumptions he wanted. Tony wasn't going to correct him. If Kent wanted to embark on a wild goose chase to Central America, Tony was more than happy to help him pack.

But Isabel…she was going to be another matter. Her dark gaze pierced him like an X-Ray. Perceptive. Intelligent.

Trouble.

"You believe Lucia," she said, watching him closely. "Why?"

Tony felt a flush touch his cheeks. It made him scowl. "I don't know what the hell to believe."

"But you think Cruz is lying," she pointed out, her melodic voice rising above the cacophony of phones and raised voices outside the office door. "Which means you must believe that Lucia Sanchez is telling the truth. Why is that?"

He stared at her. Hard. He let his gaze fall to the square toes of her black leather shoes, up the slender line of her legs encased in a stylish, severely cut black suit, over the gentle swell of her breasts, along the long graceful line of her throat to that dark, unwavering gaze. The thick web of her lashes flickered, but she didn't otherwise respond to his perusal.

She just waited.

Tony eyed her, annoyed by the tension that tightened the

muscles lining his spine as he looked at her. Bad enough she was on top of the game. Worse that he wouldn't mind playing along with her.

"I think Cruz is a corrupt, dirty son of a bitch who I wouldn't let walk my dog," he retorted. "And until I have physical evidence—either way—I don't believe anything anyone says."

Agent Bjorn only stared at him, silent.

"We need to *move*." Kent continued to pace. "Too much talk, not enough action. I thought she'd go south, but if that *was* her going north, we need to follow up. Now. "

Tony was ready to tie him to a chair. Punk fed. Just a fucking kid—

The phone on Tony's desk burst suddenly to life. He answered it with a scowl. "Malone."

"This is Donavon Cruz. I want to talk to the FBI. Put me on speaker."

Tony stiffened. *The big man himself.* "Mr. Cruz—"

"Now, Detective."

He snarled softly and stabbed the speakerphone button, annoyingly aware of Isabel Bjorn's unflinching gaze. "You're on."

"I want my children back." Sharp words that fell like glass shattering. "Where are they?"

"We're working on that now, sir." Kent halted abruptly in his furious pacing and rubbed at the back of his neck, his features tight. He looked at Isabel, who only blinked at him. "We have an APB out, and an Amber Alert has been issued."

"And?"

"And we're compiling resources, mobilizing local law enforcement, and getting the word through social media."

"And?"

Tony shook his head.

"And she may have been spotted heading north, out of the city. We're going to try and confirm the sighting but—"

Goddamn it.

"Try harder."

"With all due respect, sir, until we get more information—"

"You have what you need. *Find them.* Or I will."

Kent looked alarmed. "Sir, you shouldn't—"

"You will bring them to me within twenty-four hours," Cruz cut in, his tone like granite, the laconic, Louisianan accent he was known for barely in evidence, "or I will act."

Kent took a step toward the phone. "Sir—"

"You've been warned."

The dial tone sounded, and a heavy, steady pulse began in the back of Tony's skull.

Jesus Christ, what the hell else could happen?

As if in answer, his office door suddenly opened, and Detective Bob Peabody stuck his head through the open doorway. "Start your engines. Someone spotted the car."

CHAPTER 4

A real man does for others before he does for himself.

Sam turned aside that thought and focused on the stretch of road before him; wind blew ferociously, dirt, gravel and debris battered the side of the Rover. Ahead, the clouds were churning right along with his gut. He had a bad feeling, one that had nothing to do with the fact that he was currently aiding and abetting a kidnapper.

No, right now he was more worried about the massive thunderheads that were gathering overhead. Having been raised on a cattle ranch in Oklahoma, Sam knew tornado weather intimately, and every one of his instincts was screaming at him to get off the road and find shelter. Never mind that this part of the country rarely experienced tornados—the politicians could pontificate all they wanted, but the earth was changing, and as far as he was concerned, all bets were off.

"There it is! Holy cow, holy cow, holy cow, it has a *Play Land!* I love Play Land!"

Sam glanced in the rearview mirror. The youngest son of Donovan Cruz had his face pressed against the Rover's window, his excited breath creating a sheen of fog across the glass. He didn't seem at all upset about having been kidnapped. But then, he couldn't have been more than five. What the hell did a five-year-old know?

He probably didn't even understand what had happened to him. He probably thought they were taking a goddamn field trip.

But the other one, the older one, he was a different matter.

"*Sí*, monkey," said the woman next to Sam. "I know."

Her voice was shaped by a Spanish accent Sam couldn't place, and she was tiny, no more than five-two, with warm, golden brown skin and a thick, braided rope of dark, chocolate-brown hair. Amber eyes flecked with green continued to shoot him wary, annoyed looks, and her delicate, exotic features were drawn into a scowl. The lush red bow of her mouth was flat. A slim, worn leather watch with a scratched face and slender, silver hoop earrings were her only accessories. She nearly vibrated as she sat next to him, her hands clasped tightly in her lap, her head turned away as she glared out at the gathering storm. Sam watched her gaze flit to the side mirror, they away again, back and forth, as if she was watching for someone, and he could feel her anxiety and her irritation, and no matter how hard she tried to hide it, her fear, which was sharp and ripe, like the cold rain that battered them. Lucia Sanchez was afraid.

She fucking should be.

But far more potent was the emotion that pulsated from her, uncontained and electric, sparking against his nerve endings like a live wire; it was a sensation Sam would know blind and gagged in a dark room: *fury*.

Which was the last thing he'd expected. His fault, for having expected anything at all.

But he couldn't afford to assume Tony was right in his belief of this woman's innocence; there was history there, muddy waters, and Sam understood it was his job to be the neutral one, to render an impartial assessment of the situation, and the woman who'd created it. No matter her claims of abuse, the Cruz kids were worth a small fortune, and it was Sam's experience that most people were assholes, so he operated under that assumption until they proved him different. *Guilty until proven innocent.* Because it was just easier that way.

That being the case, he'd fully expected a manipulator and a criminal, the same kind he dealt with on a daily basis. He was always assigned the hardest witness protection cases, usually the turncoats who were only saving their own asses, because he had an intrinsic understanding of human behavior and an uncanny ability to predict that behavior. Reading people had always come easy to him—their thoughts, their fears, their motives. Deciphering good from bad, truth from lie was instinctual for him, something he did without much thought. He just *knew*.

It had saved his life—and those he protected—more than once.

So when he'd come across the broken-down Nova and its stranded fugitives, he figured he'd stop, and Lucia Sanchez would jump at the chance for help. She'd bat her lashes and make use of his Rover—and him—and she'd do what she could to get the most mileage out of him. Either that, or she'd come at him armed and ready. Instead, she'd told him to go fuck himself and almost brained him with that damn tire iron. He'd had to strong-arm her into accepting his help, and he knew in his bones she would take the boys and hightail it the first chance she got. She clearly had no use for him and was only occupying the seat next to him out of necessity. And maybe she feared he would uncover her secret—because she feared *something*—but Sam got the feeling it was more a matter of his irritating the hell out of her. Which shouldn't have bothered him—he knew he could be an abrasive son of a bitch—but did.

He had more questions than answers, and that pissed him off. Because he really didn't want to care about who Lucia Sanchez was or what her motives were. Sam knew himself well enough to know he was in no condition to deal with it—not physically and sure as hell not mentally. It was unfortunate, then, that the thought of dumping her and the kids at the closest police station, *or* handing her over to Tony—before he understood exactly what the hell was going on—was not something he was now willing to do.

A real man does for others before he does for himself.

Christ.

The echo of his uncle's voice wasn't helping matters any. Magnus Steele had been a hard man, strong, and he'd considered it his responsibility to share that strength—to lend it—to anyone who needed it, regardless of consequence. He'd drilled that belief into Sam early and had never yielded in it.

You're strong, boy. On the inside, where it counts. Someday others are gonna need that strength, and you gotta be there for 'em. It's your duty.

Sam knew his duty. He'd spent seven years as an Army Ranger doing his duty to his country and the last five as a Deputy U.S. Marshal, laying his butt on the line, taking whatever was meted out so those he protected didn't have to.

He knew all about duty, and he didn't particularly appreciate the reminder now.

"What's your name?" he demanded brusquely, because the woman beside him hadn't offered it, and he didn't expect her to.

"Lucia," she muttered, surprising him, but then her mouth tightened, and she looked away and shook her head, and Sam could almost hear the mental slap she gave herself.

But she couldn't take it back, and her lack of foresight needled him. As did the piece of shit Nova. The bald tires, the tent, the sleeping bags. Her lack of planning was obvious. It made no sense to Sam. If he was going to kidnap the children of a billionaire, he sure as shit would have a plan. A decent fucking car. Hell, even an accomplice. *Something* other than what was sitting next to him. Nothing about her jived with what he'd been prepared to find, and that needled him even worse.

"I'm Sam," he said and thought *fuck*.

He didn't need this. The questions niggling at him, the doubt they gave life to, this stupid ruse. The enigma that was Lucia Sanchez and her endgame. He simply didn't want to care.

Not about anything. *But damn it, she wasn't who she should be.*

She smelled like spicy vanilla and rain, and washing his

hands of her—and this entire mess—would've been simple, if she'd used that delicate beauty and lush body and tried to handle him. But she hadn't. Hell, the storm was the only reason he'd won the tussle they'd had over the damned tire iron. Even though she clearly needed some help, because she hadn't even known to loosen the goddamn lugs before lifting the car.

Then you have solved my problem. Gracias. You may go now.

Cold words delivered with a furious, heated glare. Damned if some part of him hadn't responded to that impossible mix—which didn't fucking help matters.

At all.

If he'd sensed—even minutely—that she was the woman Cruz claimed, an abuser, an opportunist, a *threat,* busting her ass and walking away would have been easy. But Sam's gut insisted there was more to the story, and he trusted his gut. Even if he didn't trust her.

Double fuck.

A gust of wind shook the Rover, and he swerved hard to stay on the road. The vehicle rattled violently; a sharp cry sounded from the backseat. Next to him, Lucia clung to the dashboard, her knuckles bloodless. Gravel and sand blasted the Rover's roof.

"We should stop," she said.

"Not until we find shelter," he replied grimly. "Otherwise, we're sitting ducks."

She glanced back at her two charges, tried to smile and failed miserably.

Goddamn it. No doubt about it, Lucia Sanchez was a

dark horse. Unpredictable, which made her dangerous, but the fury Sam felt rolling from her was something he couldn't ignore. That simmering rage, an echo of his own volatile state. In taking off with the kids—neither of whom appeared upset they'd been stolen—she'd gone completely off the reservation, so either she was crazy—which Sam had yet to see any evidence of—or she was driven by something so important, consequences didn't matter.

Desperation? Or greed?

She sure as hell didn't look like an abuser, but Sam knew better than anyone that what appeared on the surface was rarely a true reflection of what lay beneath.

Another gust of wind nearly blew them off the road. The steering wheel vibrated in his hands; the entire Rover shuddered in effort to stay upright. Hail was beginning to fall, pea-sized chunks of white ice that beat against the Rover like a slot payout.

"*Ay, yai, yai,* it is getting worse." Lucia turned and looked at the boys. "*Mijo*, you must put something dry on."

Sam met the older boy's pale green gaze in the mirror. The shock of those eyes hit him again, like a sharp, quick blow to the solar plexus. They were so cold they chilled him. Remote and empty, the same soulless look worn by men he'd often fought next to, men who'd spent their lives killing other men.

What the fuck had been done to him?

When the boy had appeared outside the car while Sam was changing the tire, he'd been ready to intervene. Sam could feel the kid's suspicion, his adrenaline, his aggression. The determination to *do* something, if necessary, without fear or hesitation. How old was he? Nine? Ten? What kind of kid confronted a stranger without batting an eyelash?

He'd obviously believed Sam was the threat—not Lucia.

"I'm fine," the boy muttered, lifting his chin, his eyes still holding Sam's.

"No. You will get sick." Lucia leaned over the seat and wrestled with something. Sam watched in the rearview mirror as she pulled a shirt from one of the backpacks and thrust it at the boy. "Put it on, *mijo*. Please."

The kid's chin lifted mutinously, but he snatched the shirt from her. His icy gaze narrowed on Sam. "Don't you look at me," he snarled. "Don't you even think about it."

"*Alexander*," Lucia said sharply.

"I mean it," he hissed, and the fine hair at Sam's nape started to bristle again.

Sam was no expert on children; hell, they were all like little aliens to him, but he knew *fucked up* when he saw it. He bit back the virulent words that rose in his throat and fought to keep the Rover on the road. "What the hell is his problem?"

Lucia looked away, the lush curve of her mouth hardening. "He is fine."

Sam's patience, which had been paper-thin to begin with, was beginning to rapidly disintegrate. "Bullshit."

Lucia flinched and shot him another blazing, golden glare, and Sam knew he sounded as angry as he felt. Angry—at her, at Tony, at the storm bearing down upon them. At fucking life.

"If you could just drop us off at the McDonald's up

ahead," Lucia said in a biting, cold tone that rubbed against him like sandpaper, "that would be fine."

"Chicken nuggets and fries!" crowed the youngest son of Donavon Cruz.

Sam's gaze again slid to the rearview. The older boy watched him, his stare unwavering, his eyes hard with hate and distrust as he threw his damp t-shirt into his backpack.

Jesus.

"Can I have two happy meals?" the little one wanted to know, making circles in the steam he'd left on the window. "And a chocolate shake?"

"One Happy Meal is enough, monkey," Lucia replied. "And we will share a shake."

The kid groaned. "But I *love* McDonald's, and we *never* get to go there...." He trailed off, and Sam didn't miss the glance he sent his older brother. "Are you gonna be okay now, Zander?"

Lucia stiffened.

"Shut up, Ben," Alexander muttered, glaring at Sam in the mirror.

Ben looked back out the window and fell silent. Lucia turned and leaned across her seat to brush back his hair. "It will be fine, monkey. Do not worry."

"But what if he comes?" Ben's voice fell to a whisper. It was lucky, then, that Sam had sharp ears. He watched them in the mirror, his three fugitives, their heads bent close. They looked far more like co-conspirators than captor and abductees. "What if he finds us? He might..."

"Kill you," Alexander said, his voice low.

"He will have to," Lucia replied, her tone like steel.

Sam's hands tightened on the steering wheel. Thunder boomed violently from above; wind lashed against them with hurricane force. Lightning broke apart the sky and sheared down toward them. The green Exit sign they were approaching exploded in a burst of fiberglass and metal; the sound was deafening. In the backseat, Ben screamed.

Sam wrenched the wheel; the Rover squealed in protest as it swerved wildly around the chunks of fiberglass and steel that rained down around them. The hail was the size of golf balls now, denting the Rover's hood. They pelted the windshield like cherry bombs, and he knew their time was up.

They had to stop. He pulled over.

"What are you doing?" demanded Alexander, his eyes locked on Sam in the mirror.

Another crack of thunder sounded from above; the Rover swayed unsteadily in the wind.

"There's a culvert running beneath the road." Sam released his seatbelt. Adrenaline speared through him, a heady rush of current and white heat, like a shot of Tennessee moonshine. "It's safer than the underpass."

"We cannot go out there!" Lucia protested. "The hail—"

"It's either the hail or that goddamn tornado," he snapped, his tone sharp. He pointed out the twister on the horizon that was churning toward them, surrounded by a violent whirl of dust and debris. "Your choice."

Ben started to cry.

"Shhh, monkey, no tears." Lucia took a deep breath.

"Okay, take off your seatbelts. We are going to go to the culvert."

"I don't think that's a good idea," Alexander said, but his eyes were wide as they surveyed the black vortex of wind and debris headed toward them. "Maybe it will miss us."

"Maybe is not good enough." Lucia unbuckled her own seatbelt. "Get ready."

Sam climbed from the Rover; the wind slapped him in the face, dust, gravel, sand stinging his eyes and scouring his skin. The door wrenched against its hinges, and hail fell like hellfire, pummeling him. He wasted no time, collecting the bags, tent and his own large backpack from the back of the Rover, then went and swung open the passenger side door next to Alexander.

"*I'm scared!*" Ben wailed, but when Lucia reached for him, he went, wrapping himself around her like a second skin. She tucked his head into her neck, murmuring something Sam couldn't hear. He met her gaze briefly before she lifted Ben from the seat and turned away. Alexander stared up at him, unmoving, his pale eyes wide and wild, his hands clenched into fists.

"Don't you touch me," he growled.

"Don't flatter yourself, kid," Sam told him. "Out. *Now.*"

The kid's eyes flared and violence simmered for a moment between them, but thunder cracked like sudden gunfire and effectively shattered the moment. Sam stood back, and Alexander climbed out, giving him wide berth, hurrying around the side of the car to stand so close to Lucia they were nearly touching. But not quite.

Sam said nothing, just headed for the large cement culvert he'd spotted. Hail battered him like falling rock, and he moved closer to Lucia, trying to shield her and the kids as best he could from the brutal downpour. The ditch that housed the culvert was steep, shifting desert scrub and slick rock, and he slid down it, gritting his teeth against the pain that immediately twisted through his left leg. *Damned bullet wound.* He'd taken knives, bullets, hell even a little shrapnel from a roadside bomb in Kandahar, but nothing had hurt worse than the last 9mm round he'd taken in his thigh. *Too fucking old for this shit.*

Lucia scrambled down beside him, Alexander glued to her side like an errant shadow. The culvert was only four feet in diameter, barely big enough for them to crowd into; water rushed over their feet with enough force to make Alexander sway. Sam reached to steady him, and the kid reared back, hissing like a feral cat.

"Christ," Sam muttered. The wind was getting stronger, louder, and pressure was welling, pressing against his lungs and making his eardrums pop painfully. Debris swirled around them like earthen confetti as he shoved Lucia and Ben in and glowered at Alexander until he followed. Sam climbed in behind them. Lucia curled up against one wall, Ben buried in her arms, Alexander beside her, his mouth trembling, water streaming down his pale cheeks like salty tears. The sudden roar that sounded shook the concrete around them; rain and grit and rock flew sideways, into the culvert, pelting them with vicious force. Sam moved to brace himself over Lucia, urging her closer, until Ben was securely between them. He slid an arm around Alexander, ignoring the boy's violent protest, and pulled him close.

Hail and debris hammered at Sam's back, eating through his thin t-shirt to bite at his skin. Alexander squirmed and fought with bony fists and kicking feet. Lucia tried to calm him, but Sam only pulled him closer, the boy's struggle no match for his own brute strength.

An explosion sounded, followed by several violent *pops*, and the wind whirled and screamed. The pressure built until all Sam could hear was the pulse of his blood throbbing in his ears. Beneath him, Lucia shook violently, and Ben's tiny shoulders vibrated against his chest. The bags he held strained against the call of the wind; next to him, his pack lifted and he barely caught it before it flew out of the culvert. The water beneath them rose, until the current nearly reached his knees and he had to brace himself against the ceiling of the culvert to stay on his feet. His thigh felt like it had split wide open.

Above them, the twister snarled and howled like a caged animal seeking freedom. Sam could almost track it as the pressure swelled around him, pulling at his body, whipping and ripping his clothing, tugging at his hair and skin and bones until he groaned. The wind shifted without warning, wrenching his feet from the solid cement, threatening to suck him from the culvert. Lucia cried out and grabbed the waistband of his jeans, her small hand curling around it for dear life, knuckles digging deeply into his belly in an effort to pull him back down. Between them, Ben screamed with ear piercing intensity.

He hovered for just a second, maybe two, but it felt like eternity.

The cement tube trembled and cracked; water was rushing above their knees now. *Survived a tornado only to drown,* he thought, just before a shuddering rush enveloped them, like the thunderous roar of Niagara Falls, and he fell back to earth, landing against Lucia and Ben, nearly crushing Alexander beneath him. The wind slowed, whistled and keened; gravel and sand and dirt floated like dust motes around them. And then silence, abrupt and surreal.

Sam's heart beat like a jackhammer in his chest. He dragged his feet beneath him, growling low in his throat as his leg screamed in protest. Beneath him, Lucia still held his waistband, and Alexander was shaking so hard his teeth were chattering.

The water was nearly at his thighs now, flowing over Lucia's lap, engulfing Alexander. Sam forced his arms to unlock from around them and pushed back, but Lucia's hold on his pants stopped him. He looked down at her hand—small, but strong, fine boned and delicate. Something heated and shocking and completely inappropriate stirred within him.

She made a soft sound, drawing his gaze, and color rushed into her cheeks, two bright rosy spots that glowed within the pallor of her skin. She uncurled her hand, fingers bloodless, and released him.

Alexander stirred, pushing at his weight, and Sam leaned back, until he lay against the opposite wall of the culvert. For a long moment, all he could do was breath.

"Out," he rasped.

"Is it safe?" Lucia asked, her voice hoarse.

"Hell if I know," he muttered. "But we can't stay here. The water's rising too fast."

He reached down and hauled her up, pushing her out of

the culvert. Alexander struggled to stand; he was pale and shaken and flinched when Sam lifted him up, but he didn't fight. He followed Lucia, staggering in the water, and climbed up the ditch on hands and knees.

Sam followed, dragging the bags, the tent and his pack. His leg pulsed with pain, and the skin on his arms, his hands and back was raw and bleeding. He was soaked to the bone; his t-shirt hung from him in dirt-streaked tatters.

The sun was the first thing he saw, shining down brightly from a newly washed, crystal blue sky. Fluffy white clouds floated lazily across the atmosphere, as if the twister had been nothing more than an aberration. Or imagination. Water flowed through the culvert, gaining speed and volume, and climbing back up the ditch made him hiss as his bad leg shifted beneath him. Lucia stood waiting for him, Ben held tightly in one arm, the other around Alexander's narrow shoulders. They stared at the horizon, looks of horror and shock stamped across their faces.

Sam didn't want to look. He really didn't. He'd had enough, more than enough. *Too much.*

But he wasn't a man to turn away; the easy path was rarely the one he chose to travel. He understood there was no escaping most things, that it was better to face them head on. So he wiped at his face with a hand that shook faintly, sighed heavily, and followed their gaze.

CHAPTER 5

"Here."

Tony looked down at the coffee Isabel Bjorn held out to him. The smell of the dark, rich brew mingled with the faint scent of cinnamon that emanated from her skin, and he couldn't do a damn thing about the urge that gripped him, the one that demanded he step closer and take more than just the coffee she offered.

Son of a bitch.

She was just too much. Too aware, too smart. *Too goddamn beautiful.*

He could eat her up, swallow her whole in one luscious bite. A fucking fed, of all things. Christ, whoever ran the universe had a sick sense of humor.

"You're worried," she murmured, watching him with those dark eyes.

He said nothing, accepted the coffee, and turned away. They'd headed north, toward the second sighting of the ancient Nova Lucia was driving, but hadn't gotten any farther than the little shit-hole town of Yellowgrass, Utah before they'd had to stop because of the storm—the same storm that had just laid a huge chunk of the Idaho countryside open like a gaping, bloody wound.

Were Lucia and the Cruz kids in the middle of that goddamn mess?

Was Sam?

Tony's heart thudded heavily in his chest. In spite of the sighting, they hadn't found the Nova; according to the old man who'd spotted it, it was just south of the storm path, jacked up on the side of the freeway, but because of the storm no one had been able to get there to confirm it was, indeed, Lucia's Nova. The man hadn't seen Lucia or the boys, just the car. In point of fact, no one had seen Lucia or the Cruz boys, and Sam's cell was going straight to voicemail. Tony didn't have any fucking clue what had happened to them, and FBI Special Agent Austin Kent was pacing around the tiny gas station they'd stopped at like a rat in a cage.

Then there was Isabel.

"Detective," Isabel said, as if she could hear the chaos of his thoughts. "Talk to me."

But he couldn't. Not that he wasn't a little tempted—he had a feeling she was a damned good listener. Probably too good. But spilling his guts wasn't really his style. He forged his own path and held his cards close. He might not object to a round of hot, sweaty sex, but his secrets were his own.

Besides, she was the last person he could trust with the truth, with his suspicions of one of the country's wealthiest and most influential people. The FBI was no more immune to political manipulation than any other law enforcement agency; hell, that was the entire reason they were here, because Cruz played with the big boys.

You've been warned.

The fuckhead.

No, telling Agent Bjorn anything would only endanger Lucia. Endanger those kids. And fuck things up more—if that were possible, which he was beginning to doubt.

Nope, he was on his own. He had to figure this thing out. And fast.

Guilt and gut-churning regret ate at him, as caustic and unpalatable as the acid currently brewing in his belly. *He should have listened.* Lucia wasn't a liar, and she didn't overreact. He should have realized that the state she'd been in, the claims she'd made—the things she'd *said* were real. If only in her head. And he wasn't even sure they *were* in her head. There was every possibility that they were real.

Fear, he thought, disgusted with himself. That's what had shut him down. Goddamn fear. Fear of remembering. Fear of returning to a time he'd never fully exorcised. Fear of the truth. And instead of listening—instead of doing his damn job at the very *least*—he'd treated her like an idiot and an inconvenience and slammed the door in her face.

He deserved everything he was getting. But not Lucia. Not if she was telling the truth. And somewhere deep inside himself, in a place he rarely visited, a place dark and damp and musty with disuse, certainty of her stirred. Unquestioning. Unrelenting.

Inescapable.

"I can't help if you won't talk to me," Isabel said from behind him. Her patience was wearing thin; he could hear it in the tightening of that sweet, southern lilt. "I can't help you, and I can't help *her.*"

Tony turned around and took a sip of the coffee she'd handed to him. Her arms were crossed, her head tilted as she studied him with that piercing black gaze. He got the uncanny feeling she knew he was full of shit. That she saw everything no one else thought to look for.

Why was that?

"Her?" His brows arched; he couldn't contain the mockery that edged his voice, although he knew he should. "Why would you want to help her?"

"I'm not the enemy, Detective."

Tony only snorted. At this point, *everyone* was the fucking enemy. Even his own men. "You're only here because Cruz is rich as Croesus and just as well connected. If those kids were anyone else's, the FBI wouldn't give a rat's ass about them. So let's not confuse the issue here: you want those kids back, no matter the price."

Her sleek silver brows rose, and she took a step toward him. When she spoke, her voice was low. "Is that what I want?"

Tony blinked. Something wove through her tone, a low, vibrant anger that stung him like the finest nettle. Her eyes glowed, nearly black.

"Don't you?" he murmured, firmly squelching the urge to rub his knuckles along the ivory edge of her cheekbone. She stood so close, her scent flooded into his nostrils, sinking into his skin, his blood, his bones, and his mouth watered.

Jesus. Get a fucking grip, man.

"I want the truth," she said, still in that hushed, intense tone, and his skin prickled in sudden, uncomfortable awareness. "What is it you want?"

So many things came to him that he couldn't speak. What he wanted...he looked away, out at the clouds that churned across the sky like a vast army marching to war, unable to face those knowing eyes. "Truth is subjective, relative to position. I want them safe. *All* of them."

Now it was Isabel who snorted. "A pretty speech for such a plain-spoken man. Tell me, Detective, what are we doing here? Who are we helping? There are a hundred men out there looking for Lucia Sanchez and those kids. But no one is looking for the reason why it's necessary in the first place. Why is that? Because the truth is subjective and relative to position, or because they fear it?"

He flinched. Took another sip of the coffee. "Whose truth? His or hers?"

Isabel stepped into his line of sight. "Exactly."

His breath wedged in his lungs. Chest tight, he stared down at her. "What are you saying, Isabel?"

She blinked, and Tony realized he'd used her first name. A mistake, probably, but not his first. And inevitably, regrettably, not his last.

She flicked a glance at Kent, who was arguing into his cell phone, then to Bob Peabody, who stood next to the donut display, chewing slowly on a glazed bearclaw as he took in the approaching storm. Then she stepped closer, until Tony could see the tiny golden flecks that speared from her pupils and her breath, warm and moist, brushed his chin. "You know Lucia Sanchez—no, don't bother to deny it, I can *see* it, and you believe her. So what the hell are we doing here? Why are we wasting time on retrieval when we should be *investigating*?"

He told himself to step away. Distance. He needed distance.

Perspective.

Instead he stood motionless next to her, absorbing her scent, her heat, letting the lilt in her voice wash over him like a soothing summer rain. And called himself a thousand kinds of fool.

"Investigate," he repeated, and his heart jerked like a hooked fish. "Christ."

He strode to Bob, turning the older man away from the oncoming path of Austin, who was still pacing, scowling into his cell phone.

Investigate.

What a dumb bastard he was. He'd given Lucia the only chance he could: Sam. Short of apprehending her himself and stashing her somewhere safe until he had this whole mess sorted out—which would be impossible with the FBI riding shotgun—this was as good as it was going to get. And Sam would keep her safe. There was no one he trusted more. When he reached Sam again, he would tell him to hold onto her. Keep her hidden—just for a little while. Just long enough to do exactly what Isabel had suggested.

Find some goddamn proof—one way or the other.

Hell, it would take a miracle. But it was more than he had right now.

"Some storm," Bob mumbled around his bearclaw, motioning out at the hail beginning to pelt against the glass store front. "Hope they ain't out in it."

But they were, somewhere. Only the thought that Sam might have found them gave Tony any real hope. "I'm heading back," he told Bob, motioning toward Austin. "I need you to stay with Boy Wonder and check out the car."

Bob's bushy brows furrowed, and he gave Tony a look. Bob was four months from retirement; he'd seen more shit go down in Vegas than the local sewer plant, and despite his bland countenance and benign appearance, he was sharp as a tack.

"Why?" Bob asked idly, taking another bite of his claw. "You got somewhere you gotta be?"

For a long moment, Tony said nothing. He glanced at Isabel who stood next to the door, arms folded, waiting.

"There's a reason she ran," he said finally. "I'm going to find it."

Bob's eyes narrowed. "Cruz ain't no one to mess with. Best be careful."

"He's not above the law," Tony said flatly.

"Law don't exist to a man like Cruz. Pays to be careful when you deal with someone like that. Doesn't mean you don't do your job—you just do it real quietly." Bob looked at Austin and sighed. "Sure you don't want some help?"

"Agent Bjorn will assist."

Bob looked over Tony's shoulder, his avid gray eyes taking in Isabel's slender golden form. "She's a Fed. Best not forget that."

Tony met his gaze. "I won't."

Bob nodded. "I'll give a buzz if we find anything in the

Nova. Still can't believe she drove a Nova. Ain't exactly the ideal get-away car."

"She was desperate," Tony said. "I need to know why."

"True enough," Bob said and finished off his bearclaw.

Tony headed for Isabel.

Kent was watching, his baby blues narrow with suspicion. He wore a dark gray Brooks Brothers suit and a double breasted wool overcoat; his blond hair was thick with something that gleamed wetly in the overhead lighting. Even his shoes shone. He was pretty and slick and full of youthful hubris. Tony detested him.

Worse, Kent was ambitious and determined and teeming with the urgent need to prove himself.

At any cost.

"Isabel?" Kent said sharply, and Tony had to check the urge that gripped him, to slap the kid down like an annoying insect. "Where are you going?"

Tony opened his mouth, but Isabel overrode him, giving Kent a cool smile and murmuring, "Having both of us wait around is a waste of resources. Detective Malone and I are going to head back to the city and see if Miss Sanchez left us any clues as to her destination. I'll be in touch as soon as I find something."

Kent stared at her for a long moment. "If she left anything, it's probably in the car."

Isabel only shrugged. "Perhaps. But I'm tired of waiting."

He flicked a look at Tony, then back at her. "You sure?"

Again, Tony had the desire to smack him silly. But

Isabel stepped neatly between them. "Quite." She gave Bob a sympathetic glance. "Detective Peabody will stay and accompany you."

Bob nodded. He met Tony's gaze, rolled his eyes and helped himself to another bearclaw. Outside, thunder rumbled and lightning arced sharply down from the sky, a blinding glint that outlined them all like a sudden camera flash. Rain poured down in a torrent.

"Ready?" Isabel asked him, her face a perfect mask of calm. Tony admired that. But her ability to lie to her partner so smoothly bothered him. There was nothing to say she wouldn't do the same to him. Nothing at all.

He might come to like Isabel, and God knew he wouldn't mind a long weekend in her bed.

But he didn't trust her. Not for a minute.

CHAPTER 6

"Everything is just...*gone*."

Lucia didn't respond. She knew if she opened her mouth, the horrified scream lodged in her chest would escape.

They'd abandoned the Rover, which had been crumpled and tossed aside like a flattened beer can, and headed toward the closest town. It had taken nearly an hour to walk the half-mile into town, down the broken freeway, up the ruined exit, where chunks of asphalt and earth and bent metal guard rail lay twisted and exposed, as if a giant mixer had tried to blend them into one creation. They'd trudged down the narrow, ruined highway as the sun disappeared into another wall of dark, churning clouds, and found nothing but death.

The tornado had wiped Canyon Falls, Idaho from the map.

Debris littered every square inch of the demolished town: sheets of scarred metal, two-by-fours turned into toothpicks, a carpet of jagged, glittering glass that coated every surface like coarse sand. Paper, insulation, cardboard; appliances lay battered in the middle of what had once been a road. Overturned cars, broken telephone poles, electrical wires strewn about like unpredictable serpents. The ground had been scoured down to earth and rock, leaving a scar that disfigured the landscape as far and wide as the eye could see.

Bodies lay like mangled dolls, old, young, furred and feathered; a foot sticking out here, an arm there. Lucia stared in disbelief, overwhelmed by the sheer devastation and cut to the bone by the human toll. Her heart felt huge and hollow, and no matter how hard she strove for control, tears slid silently down her cheeks.

"Everyone's dead," Alexander said dully.

"Not everyone," Sam replied as he surveyed the destruction. "There're always survivors."

Which seemed unlikely from where Lucia stood, but she knew he was right. Even if it was not a sentiment she would have expected from him—hope—and even if the idea of sorting through the carnage in search of those survivors seemed impossible.

"We need to look," he added and turned to level that brilliant aquamarine gaze on her.

Alexander immediately shook his head, but Lucia only nodded in agreement. She was a healer—that was a truth she'd known since she was a child hiking through the jungles of Belize at her grandmother's side as they'd ferreted out those too frail—or superstitious—to seek treatment from the local *el medico*. She'd worked her butt off to earn her medical degree, and that she hadn't quite made it—and never would—mattered little here and now, where she could use the skills and knowledge she'd sacrificed so much for to help others. It was, in fact, her duty to do so. Because if

Sam hadn't stopped and bullied her into letting him help them, it was quite possible they would be as ruined as the town around them. It hardly mattered that he was not a happy man—or an easy man, something that was more apparent the longer she spent in his company—he'd saved them, and for that, she was immensely grateful.

Even if he lit her temper like a match to flame, and part of her was still tempted to give him a good shove.

The situation was, after all, temporary, and she would figure out how to get rid of him soon enough, because they could not stay together. No matter how helpful he'd been, she could not trust him. Not with the truth. No one had believed that truth when she'd tried to tell them—not even those who should have—and he would be no different. He would hear that name—*Donavon Cruz*—and he would run and hide, as they all had. And that would be just one more betrayal, something Lucia simply couldn't face.

"*Sí*," she said finally and brushed away her tears with her wet sleeve. "We will look."

Alexander turned to stare at her. His cold mask had been torn violently away; he looked pale and shaken and afraid. "No," he said harshly.

Lucia only arched her brows at him. "*Sí, mijo*. We must."

"We can't. There's no time."

He's coming.

As if she would forget. As if every heartbeat didn't seem a loss of time and distance, irretrievable and disastrous. As if the knowledge of what he would do to her when he found them wasn't even now eating at her like some kind of fatal, infectious disease. There was a reason she'd christened him *Ivan the Terrible;* she knew exactly what he was capable of. She'd known enough monsters; she recognized the makings. But she couldn't sacrifice anyone else on the altar of their escape. *She wouldn't.*

"We will make time," she told the boy, aware of Sam watching with a gaze that was sharp with intelligence and far too perceptive. She'd seen that acute intellect from the first moment he'd glared down at her through the pouring rain, and if she'd had any doubts about his acumen, his response to the tornado had disassembled them. Smart, observant; a man who took charge. Who shielded others and used his strength to bear the brunt of whatever storm descended.

Military, she surmised. Or law enforcement—which was, truly, a horrifying proposition. But there was nothing to be done. At least, not at the moment.

"No," Alexander said again, more forcefully. "We have to *go.*"

Lucia only blinked at him. In her embrace, Ben hiccupped a small sob. Her arms ached, bones, tendons and joints locked into place beneath his weight. Her shoulder was throbbing from grabbing Sam in the culvert, and her skin burned from the numerous cuts and scrapes that covered her. It hadn't escaped her notice that Sam was limping as well, his left thigh bleeding through his jeans. He'd changed out of his shredded t-shirt, but she'd seen his back when he pulled off the tattered remnants, broad, muscled, scraped and raw, bloody and badly bruised. But he said nothing; he hadn't even flinched, and now he walked beside them, his backpack lodged over one shoulder, filled with whatever mysterious objects he carried, plus their sleeping bags, packs, and the tent. Ben's Snoopy bag dangled from his right hand.

Around them, nothing stirred but the wind. No sirens, no screams. No signs of life other than their own. On the horizon, clouds continued to gather, another violent storm that crept ever closer.

"This is what I have trained to do, *mijo,*" Lucia said quietly. "I must do it."

"I don't care." Alexander glared at her. His hands fisted, his entire being vibrated, and his voice rose. "We have to go now. *We have to save ourselves.*"

"Really? You would leave them buried in that rubble to die?"

"Yes!"

"No, you would not. You are not…"

"*Him.*" Tears glazed the boy's eyes, and Lucia took a step toward him, her heart squeezing tight in her chest. "Are you sure?"

"Quite," she said.

Sam watched, too observant to be ignored. But there was nothing to be done for that, either.

"You said we wouldn't stop," Alexander hissed. "You promised you wouldn't give up. *You lied to me.*"

His eyes glittered; he looked desperate and wild, but Lucia only stared back at him, unable to sacrifice one for another. Ben clutched at her, his fingers digging into her arms like claws.

"Please," Alexander said, his voice cracking, and the plea in him made her throat fill. "Please, Lucia. We have to *go.*"

His panic was so piercing, it felt like a blade between her ribs. "*Mijo*—"

"No!" he yelled and took an abrupt step toward her, his gaze so turbulent Lucia knew he wanted to hit her. *Again.* He never had—not yet—but he was damaged and despondent and filled with rage. Sometimes it was all he knew.

She drew herself up, but suddenly Sam was there, his large hand landing on Alexander's shoulder, stopping him in place.

"Easy," Sam barked, an order that made Alexander jerk violently. He tried to wrench away, but Sam held tight. "Get a hold of yourself, son."

"I'm not your son," Alexander snarled, his body trembling, his hands clenching, unclenching, clenching again.

"For which you should thank your lucky stars," Sam retorted. "Because if my boy ever raised his hand to a woman, I'd tan his goddamn hide."

Alexander shuddered. Lucia watched emotion chase across his face: pain, shame, defeat. She wanted to protest, but she knew Sam was right. The boy could not be allowed to simply lash out—no matter why he did so. *So much torment.* Which left her torn between the rage that lived ever-present in her heart and wanting to wrap him in her arms.

"You don't abandon someone who needs help," Sam continued in a hard voice. "If you sacrifice them to save yourself, you're already lost. Understood?"

Lucia expected another explosion, maybe even more violent than the first; Alexander did not respond well to touch. But the boy only shuddered and stood stiffly beneath Sam's hand. Finally, he nodded.

"Good," Sam said. He squeezed Alexander's shoulder and then released him. "You stay here with your brother. Don't touch anything; most of the electrical wires are probably live. Lucia and I will take a look for survivors." He slid off his pack and walked over to what remained of a small, grassy patch of ground, bare of glass and debris. He set down the pack and Ben's Snoopy bag and turned to look at them.

"Move," he ordered.

Definitely military. *Ay, yai, yai.* Because that was just what she needed. Because he couldn't possibly be something far more simple and easy to manage, like an accountant. Or a dentist.

Destiny is not for the weak. But Lucia was beginning to think that destiny could suck it.

She sighed and moved to set Ben down. He clutched at her, a soft whimper breaking from him.

"Easy, monkey," she told him softly. "You are going to stay with Alexander for a little while, okay?"

His brown gaze was huge, dark, awash in tears. He wouldn't let go. "But what if a dinosaur comes?"

"Monkey," Lucia said gently.

"Or aliens. Or the Stay Puff Marshmallow Man!"

"I'll protect you," Alexander said and tugged at him. "C'mon, Benny."

Ben went reluctantly, his tiny fingers clutching at her in protest. Lucia handed him his Snoopy bag and told Alexander, "You must change out of those wet clothes. And put your coats back on, it is getting cold. There are snacks, too. Please eat something."

"Chicken nuggets," Ben whispered.

"Maybe later, monkey," Lucia replied, although it was doubtful. She smoothed his hair and kissed his cheek and then stood to face Sam. "You have a plan?"

Because he seemed like the kind of man who would have a plan. *Unlike her.*

"You go left, I'll go right." He turned to survey the debris fields. "If you find someone, call out. Don't try to get them by yourself."

Which made her bristle, even as she understood it was good advice. In addition to intelligent and difficult, Sam was arrogant. *An alpha.* A man who gave orders and expected them to be obeyed.

Bad enough, but worse was what Lucia couldn't put her finger on, something about him that made all of the volatility she felt surge to the surface, a scalding geyser of fear and fury and pain, one that had the ability to obliterate everything else, including her common sense. *Reason.* Whatever this man stirred within her, it was dangerous, and she'd already made enough stupid mistakes; she didn't need to make any more.

The sooner they ditched him, the better.

Sam limped away, and Lucia looked at the boys. "Stay here."

"We should go now," Alexander said, watching Sam

retreat. He pulled Sam's pack to him and began to remove their things from it, separating them. "While he's busy."

It was not a bad idea, and for a moment, Lucia considered it. Sam would be distracted, and losing him within the debris fields would not be difficult. But she could not in good conscious walk away without at least a cursory search for survivors. There were simply some things she could not do, and abandoning someone she might be able to help was one of them. She would look, and she would do what she could, and it would have to be enough.

Then they would deal with Sam.

CHAPTER 7

"First, I'm sorry. I know you're fresh out of Baja, that it was a shitshow of epic proportions, and this was the last thing you needed. I owe you an explanation, and you'll get it. I promise. Second, thank you—because I need you to stash that package I asked you to retrieve until I figure out what the hell is going on. The feds are on me like flies on shit; no way can I get out of here to meet you. They found the car, so I hope you're on the move. I'll check in again soon. Don't call me; I'll call you."

Famous last words. Sam squeezed his phone and snarled softly.

As he continued to make his way through the shattered remains of Canyon Falls, Idaho, he wondered if he was cursed. First Baja and now this…whatever the hell this was. Because it wasn't clean, and it sure as hell wasn't simple. And now that Mother Nature had decided to throw her hat into the ring, it was an official natural fucking disaster.

So far, he'd found no signs of life. No moans or groans or cries for help. Nothing but the occasional body and complete, mass destruction. Dead birds dotted the landscape. Trees had been snapped in half, their trunks splintered like broken teeth, their tops shredded into green, pulpy mush. The concrete was scoured, as though someone had taken a giant Brillo pad to it, and electrical wires hummed and hissed as he gave them a wide berth. He hoped the boys listened and left them the hell alone; one touch would be enough to kill.

The day was growing colder, darker, and the storm to the west was almost upon them. The wind wasn't bad—yet. But it was only a matter of time, Sam thought grimly. And before that time came, he needed to have Lucia and the kids someplace warm, dry, and secure.

Yeah. Good luck with that.

"Fuck," he muttered and pinched the bridge of his nose. His shirt clung to the dried blood on his back; he felt like someone had taken a paring knife to him and peeled a layer off. It burned like hell. His head still hurt, he could have eaten a small horse, and his thigh was throbbing like an obnoxious dance song. In that moment, he would have given anything for a goddamn cigarette.

Just one.

But it was not meant to be. Half a block down, four gas pumps stuck out from their concrete moorings at odd angles, but any station that had once existed was nothing more than rubble. Nothing had been left whole. Most of the debris was almost unrecognizable, and finding a whole, pristine pack of smokes would be akin to finding the proverbial pot of gold.

A miracle.

Something he'd never before been granted, and it was

highly unlikely one would find him now. No, he was on his own. Which—had it been just him—would have been a pain in the ass, but easily doable. The fact that he was suddenly responsible for Lucia and two young kids made it a full-blown fiasco.

Not that Lucia would agree. Sam had a feeling she would tell him to shove his presumption of responsibility up his ass; in point of fact, he was pretty sure she was already planning her escape. It was inevitable, and only the search for survivors had circumvented it—at least, momentarily. Because the oldest boy—Alexander—wanted nothing more than to be *gone.*

We have to go now. We have to save ourselves.

The kid's horrified desperation left a bad taste in Sam's mouth. He'd seen that kind of raw terror before, but only in the worst of circumstances: on the battlefield, in an Afghan village dead from disease, at the end of his Glock. Never had he thought to see it in the eyes of a ten-year-old boy—especially a ten-year-old boy who, by all accounts, should have had a permanent residence on Easy Street. But there was no mistaking that panic. That level of fear.

It always smelled the same: sour sweat and bitter breath. Sam knew it well.

You said we wouldn't stop. You promised you wouldn't give up. You lied to me.

The kid had been pissed. Sam wasn't certain he would have belted Lucia, but he sure looked like he'd wanted to. And those words...they troubled Sam. Because nothing about them shouted "kidnapping victim!" In no way could they be construed as a stolen child pleading with his captor to return home. The boy wasn't afraid of Lucia...he was afraid for himself.

Afraid. A pale word for what Sam had witnessed. The kid was fucking terrified. Frightened of something so horrific, it made him blind, deaf and half dumb. That took some doing.

That took something worse than death.

Goddamnhellfuck.

Dread cloaked Sam like a dark shroud. Not just because he was currently an accessory to felony kidnapping, tromping through a decimated town in fruitless search of anyone still breathing—or because the storm headed toward them was both metaphorical and quite goddamn literal. No, the heavy, thick darkness that slid through his veins was due to the inescapable realization that nothing was what it seemed: not Lucia Sanchez, not this crazy kidnapping, and sure as hell not the story Tony had fed him.

Sam wanted the truth, no matter how unpalatable. He wanted to understand the fear he saw in Alexander Cruz, and he wanted to know why Lucia had been so desperate to get him away from his father that she'd used a death trap on wheels for her escape. Why her grand plan was nothing more than a tent, two sleeping bags, and a handful of Little Debbie snack cakes.

What the hell did she think she was doing?

Because she wasn't dumb. Sam didn't know her well, but he knew that. He could *see* that. He'd dealt with enough stupid people to know the difference. But the rage he saw in her could make smart people do dumb things; was that what happened? Had she reacted instead of acted? The fire in her eyes said she was more than capable of following her temper down the rabbit hole. And he knew she was strong; he'd seen that strength first hand in the aftermath of the storm. She'd been shaken and terrified, but she'd just gritted her teeth and gone matter-of-factly on, keeping the boys calm and moving forward. Even the carnage they'd found in Canyon Falls, which had damn sure shaken her, had been dealt with in a pragmatic fashion. *This is what I've trained to do, mijo. I must do it.*

Which meant what?

"Fuck," he said again.

Because he couldn't get past *What made her that desperate? Why had she done something so fucking stupid?* Because she wasn't stupid. Even if what she'd done was.

So much for my beer, he thought. His alpine meadow. His fly rod.

Some fucking peace and quiet.

Because he wasn't walking away until he had answers. Until he understood why. And beyond that requirement, not much else mattered. He was a man sworn to protect, and those boys damn sure needed protecting. From what—or whom—was the question, one he would answer, even if he had to squeeze Lucia Sanchez until she popped like a balloon. He didn't want this problem, but he couldn't bail, not anymore.

There were too many unanswered questions, too many inconsistencies, and too damned much at stake. His instincts were howling, and the sense of duty Magnus had drilled into him made them impossible to ignore. Whether or not he was up for the task was moot. That he was exhausted and numb from his existence only seemed to bring things into vivid clarity. He was here, and he was the man for the job.

He didn't have to like it.

But he wasn't following orders—not Tony's, not Donovan Cruz's, and not the Feds'. He might have drawn the short stick, but that didn't mean he was going to let anyone poke him with it. This was going to happen his way, and to hell with anyone who disagreed.

"*Fuck*." He stepped over an unhinged refrigerator door. There was no sign of the icebox it had come from, but rows of jelly, pickles and condiments sat tucked within the interior shelving, unbroken and pristine. He found it bitterly ironic, when the entire town lay in shambles around him.

Irony, the sole constant in life. In his life, anyway.

The wind lifted, cold, sharp, scented by rain. Far off, thunder rumbled. Around him, debris fluttered into the air, a whirl of despair and inexplicable loss. He'd walked down streets littered with the dead, into villages where nothing but ash remained, through killing fields stained red with blood, but nothing left him as hollow and hopeless as this aftermath. Searching for life seemed useless.

"Sam!"

The sound of Lucia abruptly calling his name made his heart slam into his ribs.

"Coming," he shouted and turned in the direction of her voice. He zigzagged around piles of rubble, dented appliances and fallen walls. When he glimpsed her behind what remained of someone's home, his pulse leapt. A response he neither wanted nor appreciated. On top of everything else, the woman had to go and be fucking alluring as hell.

Goddamn it.

"I found someone," she said as he approached, but her eyes were bleak and sober, and Sam knew immediately it wasn't someone they could help.

Someone they could save.

He stepped into what appeared to be the remnants of a bathroom. Piping stuck out from the floor, and a round hole indicated where the toilet had been. Lucia knelt beside a battered bathtub, where a bleeding and battered old man lay cradling a small dog. She held one of his gnarled hands in hers.

Sam approached and crouched beside them carefully; his leg protested with a twist of breath-stealing pain. He ignored it and focused on the man.

"Hey there," he said quietly. Blood-creased lids lifted to reveal faded brown eyes with huge, unfocused pupils. Black bruises mottled skin that was spotted and so thin it looked like little more than tissue paper. Deep cuts bled sluggishly on his forehead, his chin and his nose looked as though it had been smashed by a brutal, relentless fist. "How are you doing?"

The man's mouth opened, and a harsh gurgle broke the eerie silence of the destruction that surrounded them.

"Shhhh, *abuelo*," Lucia murmured softly. "Do not try to talk." She looked at Sam and shook her head and pointed into the tub. Sam looked down to see a metal pipe sticking from the man's stomach, nearly two inches wide. Blood pooled beneath him, thick, dark, and deep.

A dead man, Sam thought. And from the glint in the

old-timer's eye, he knew it. Sam met Lucia's gaze; she knew it, too.

The man's mouth opened, and the ugly bubbling of blood and oxygen sounded once more. His free hand lifted and caught in Sam's t-shirt, fingers like claws, shaking violently.

"Easy," Sam murmured, and clasped that hand, so cold and thin and fragile it was like holding delicate blown glass. "I've got you."

The man shook his head and tried again, another ragged, wheezing groan that made Lucia lean over him and put her hand on his papery cheek.

"Shhhh," she whispered again. "You must be still, *abuelo*. Please."

But the man jerked away. He tugged his hand from Sam's, and it landed heavily on the little dog's back. The animal flinched and lifted its head, revealing a bloodied, teddy-bear face. A pink tongue emerged and licked tentatively at the man's chin. Tears glazed the man's eyes; he struggled again to speak.

"*Sí, abuelo*," Lucia said, her voice thick. She touched the animal he held, a gentle stroke that made the dog quiver, golden hair shivering in the pale light. "*Sí*. We will take care of your pet. Do not worry. But you must be still now. Please be still."

The man's gaze sought Sam's.

"I promise," Sam told him, his heart like lead in his chest.

"All will be well," Lucia told the man, but her voice wavered and a tear slid down her cheek.

The man held Sam's gaze for a moment longer, the unwavering stare of a dying man looking for something only he could find. Sam had seen it before, from strangers, from enemies, from men he considered family. He only nodded again in silent affirmation of the promise he'd made; there was nothing else to be done. Death was inescapable, solace moot.

At least the old guy wasn't alone.

Sam felt Lucia's gaze, but she said nothing. Finally, the man nodded. He stroked the little dog he held with trembling fingers, and Lucia began to pray.

Her voice was low, barely audible; she whispered in Spanish, a prayer he didn't recognize, an invocation that spoke of circles and rebirth and hope. Sam stared at her, his throat thick and tight, his heart a heavy drumbeat in his chest. He'd seen enough death to last two lifetimes; it never got easier.

Not even when it was a stranger.

The man's eyes drifted shut; one by one, his limbs relaxed. The dog he held whined mournfully, and as thunder rumbled in the distance, his last breath escaped, a harsh, wheezing rattle that echoed between them before being taken by the wind.

Sam didn't move, frozen in place. Beside him, Lucia took a deep, gulping breath. Then another. And then a harsh, angry sob broke from her, and she leaned her forehead on the edge of the tub and cried with quiet, wrenching fury.

Sam's heart contracted, and his hand lifted of its own accord and hovered just above her, a hairsbreadth from touching her. *Just a small touch.* Just to comfort her—

No. His hand fisted; he forced it to lower.

She murmured as she wept, another prayer he didn't recognize, again in Spanish, and he said nothing, unwilling to let her know he understood, both her words and her pain. Watching her made his chest ache, and the nails of his clenched fist dug deeply into the flesh of his palm.

He wanted to walk away. Just turn and go. His lungs burned, and his blood roared in his head like a vicious animal. He felt hollow. Furious. *Alone.* Touching her was a bad idea, and yet the need gripped him like a vise, an instinct as much about taking as giving.

Dangerous and stupid; a war within himself he couldn't afford to lose.

Finally, she quieted and turned to look at him, her eyes dark and wet and desolate, and the need to touch her beat at him with razor-sharp wings. But then she looked away, turned her gaze to the little dog, and lifted a hand to stroke it gently.

"Ah, little one, you will miss him, no?" Her voice was hoarse, and the dog trembled beneath her touch. "But do not worry. We will take very good care of you." A deep sigh escaped her, and Sam knew she was thinking of the impossibility of keeping the promise she was making. "You are not alone, *nene*. I know a boy who will love you more than any boy has ever loved a dog."

She lifted the pup and curled it to her chest, pressing a soft kiss to its tiny head. Her gaze again sought Sam's, and for a moment they just looked at each other, shaken, raw, aching with loss. A life they would mourn together; a connection neither would forget. A bond forged of blood and pain and death.

"I'm sorry," Sam heard himself say roughly. Which was too much and not enough, but all he had.

"As am I." Lucia pushed to her feet. "I must check on the boys."

She didn't wait for a response; she only turned and left him.

Sam watched her go, painfully aware that any illusion of walking away had just died an abrupt and brutal death.

No, there was no walking away for him.

Not until it was over.

CHAPTER 8

The Cruz residence was located on the northern edge of the city, a tall structure of steel, rock and darkened glass that speared from the earth like a tower of smoky quartz. A lush sprawl of ridiculously green grass surrounded it, along with a wall built of stone, easily three feet thick and nearly twelve feet tall. Two giant palms flanked the home.

Home, Isabel Bjorn thought. *Hardly.*

Beside her, Detective Anthony Malone, swore softly. "What is this, fucking Jericho? What an asshat."

She almost smiled. Although she didn't know the Detective well, and she didn't trust him any further than she could throw him, she *was* tempted to like him. A mistake she wouldn't make, of course, but still…it had been a long time since a man had made her smile. Long enough, at any rate.

She supposed she was due.

Because he was also arrogant, difficult, nosy, and a liar. She could handle arrogance—she was, after all, a woman in a field dominated by men, so she was quite used to ego leading the charge—and difficult was nothing new. Nosy was just an annoyance, but the lying...well, that was unacceptable. On every level.

The good Detective knew Lucia Sanchez. Although he hadn't confirmed that fact, it was quite obvious. They had a history, Isabel was certain. But what kind of history? Had they been friends? Lovers? The Detective was a handsome man; it was certainly possible. With his bronzed skin, light hazel eyes and that well-drawn, wide mouth, he would have no trouble attracting women. Even she was susceptible to the charisma he wore like the finest fragrance, and she was rarely susceptible to anything.

Driven, intelligent, and—from all accounts—honorable, the Detective was formidable. His record—which she'd checked discretely as they'd driven into the city—spoke to two factors: his relentless pursuit of justice, and his tendency to take matters into his own hands. She wondered if it was his stint as an Army Ranger that made him behave like a force unto himself. Why he got results. If that was the reason his people followed him without question.

Even Detective Peabody, who'd shared his own reservations, had acquiesced. But Isabel didn't take those reservations personally. The reputation her badge carried cut both ways. For her, it was simply means to an end.

A tool in her arsenal.

"Are we cleared to go in?" Tony asked, turning his gleaming silver SUV into the entry, where the stone gave way to thick iron gates.

"Yes," Isabel said. Although Mr. Cruz was not happy about it. But how could the man argue when his children's lives were at stake?

Telling, that she'd had to make the point in order to gain access. Asshat, indeed.

Tony slid to a stop beside the intercom. He announced them, flashed his badge, and a moment later they were pulling through the gates and sliding to a stop before the arched entryway, a perfectly cut curve of thick granite that glittered in the dimming sunlight.

It was almost six p.m. The drive down from Yellowgrass had taken three hours, time Isabel had spent making notes, downloading files on the good Detective, Donovan Cruz, and Lucia Sanchez, and ignoring how good the man beside her smelled. He'd asked questions, and she'd deflected them. Eventually, he'd let it go, and simply concentrated on driving. He drove with skill and competence; Isabel had a feeling that was how Tony Malone did everything. Like her badge, he would cut both ways.

"I want a look at those kids' rooms," he said before they climbed out of the SUV.

"I want a look at everything," she replied and stepped out.

He didn't trust her, she thought as she headed up the entryway. Which was only fair, as she didn't trust him, either. But trust wasn't truly necessary, if they had the same goal.

A big if.

The large wooden entry door swung inward. It, too, was arched, and detailed by an intricate carving of a heavily-maned lion. Old growth wood, something dark and rich, maybe walnut. Beautifully done.

"Agent Bjorn," said the woman who appeared behind

the door, a tall, narrow woman with hard features and flat green eyes. Her voice was cold. "Detective Malone. My name is Agnes Livingstone. I am Mr. Cruz's head of household. If you'll follow me, I'll show you to Ms. Sanchez's quarters."

She stared at them, as warm and welcoming as a frozen fence post. Her black hair was threaded with gray, wound tight at the base of her skull. Clad in pressed black slacks, an equally pressed black blouse and freshly shined black flats, she was a testament to severity.

"Thank you," Tony said from behind her. "We appreciate your cooperation."

"I do as I'm told, Detective," Agnes replied and turned on her heel.

Charming.

Isabel followed as the woman led them deeper into the house. Walls of dark navy, slate-tiled floors dotted with sleek contemporary furniture. Abstract art filled the space, paintings harsh with bold color, misshapen and headless, free-form statues. Ugly, Isabel thought, but then art was subjective. Still, the environment contained a cultivated darkness that rubbed her the wrong way. There were no photographs, no knick-knacks, no toys, nothing that spoke of the children who occupied the home.

Home, she thought again. *Most definitely not.*

Agnes led them through a large great room with thick leather furniture, a massive stone fireplace and hand-knotted Persian rugs. The windows revealed a crystal blue, glittering swimming pool and the mandatory Las Vegas fountain, all surrounded by more stone.

A tall, wooden staircase swept up to the second floor, more walnut, the handrails carved into thorned vines and roses with large, ornate petals. Agnes said nothing as she turned toward it and began her ascent. Isabel was aware of Tony following closely, his scent trailing her as effectively as any bloodhound.

The second floor was much like the first: dark, ugly, with narrow hallways lined by macabre art. No plants, no flowers, nothing soft or warm. Nothing welcoming. They followed Agnes down a series of halls into the western end of the house, which was cut off from the rest of the residence by a set of thick wooden doors. Wolves snarled and circled on the doors; they looked ferocious and feral, as if fashioned from the ugliest of fairy tales. Isabel thought that if she was a five-year-old—as Benjamin Cruz was—they would scare the hell out of her.

"Jesus," Tony muttered.

"This is the children's wing." Agnes flung open the doors. "Ms. Sanchez's quarters are through the second door on the left. As her duties did not include overnight stays, she rarely made use of them. You are welcome to look, but I daresay you won't find much."

Isabel looked around, surprised by the sudden appearance of color and light. The walls were pale yellow; several benches lined the hallway, long planks of thick wood covered by bright red pillows. Glossy prints decorated the walls: *Alice in Wonderland, The Wizard of Oz, The Call of the Wild*. Wide windows let in the sun. It looked…normal.

"What did you think of Lucia?" Tony asked Agnes. "What's your take on all of this?"

Agnes halted. She turned slowly, her brows arched. "I am not paid to think anything, Detective."

"You have no opinion?" Isabel asked.

That flat green gaze glinted. "No, I do not."

"That's helpful," Tony told her. "Thanks."

"How long have you been with Mr. Cruz?" Isabel asked, undaunted.

"Mr. Cruz hired me immediately after the death of Mrs. Cruz, several years ago."

"A tragedy, that," Isabel said, watching Agnes closely. "A car accident, wasn't it?"

"You have ten minutes," Agnes said, as if she hadn't spoken. "Use them wisely."

She stood staring at them, clearly indicating they would not be left alone in their search. Isabel wasn't surprised, but Tony scowled openly.

"This is a federal investigation," he said, his tone hard. "You do understand what will happen if you impede that investigation?"

Agnes only blinked at him. "You're wasting time, Detective."

Isabel turned and walked into Lucia Sanchez's room. The walls were the same pale yellow as the hallway; the plush carpeting was deep, emerald green. A queen-sized bed sat in the center of one wall, flanked by two small bedside tables. A dresser, a wardrobe, a handful of tasteful flower prints. The closet sat open, empty of everything but a handful of wooden hangers. Looking around, anger flared through Isabel.

The room had obviously been cleared and cleaned. *Of everything.*

She checked the drawers of the bedside tables, the dresser, the wardrobe. Under the bed, under the mattress. The shelf of the closet, beneath each lamp.

Nothing.

A snarl in her throat, she turned to step through one of the two connecting doors that led off the room. Lucia's quarters were, apparently, connected to each of the boy's. The room she stepped into was much the same as Lucia's, except for a small twin bed in place of the queen. Colorful posters covered the walls: *The Muppets, Transformers, The Lion King.* An overflowing box of toys sat on one wall; Legos littered the carpet. A stuffed Winnie the Pooh sat in one corner, Snoopy in the other.

Benjamin Cruz's room.

Brightly colored clothes filled the wardrobe and dresser drawers. Several miniature suits hung in the closet, along with a mixture of shoes. A battered skateboard, a small pair of skis.

Nothing unusual. Nothing she was looking for.

Isabel strode back into Lucia's room to find Tony going through the drawers of the wardrobe. He'd closed the door, shutting Agnes out, and Isabel walked passed him without comment, moving to the other connecting door and stepping through it. Alexander Cruz's room was also pale yellow, with a larger double bed, a dresser, and a wardrobe. There was an additional desk and chair, and the posters were more age-appropriate: *X-Men, Avengers, The Flash.* There were no toys or stuffed animals, but above the bed sat a bookshelf which held a small collection of books: *Harry Potter, Lord of the Rings, Brothers Grimm.*

Like the posters, they were escapist work. Fantasy.

Not that Isabel could blame him.

The closet contained clothes, shoes, skis, a lacrosse stick and a bike helmet. The dresser and wardrobe were filled with expensive, logo-splattered clothing, most of which looked brand new and unworn. She could find no computer—no electronic devices of any kind—and the desk contained only a handful of pencils and a stack of copy paper. Isabel was about to give up when she spotted a set of sleek black drawing pens tucked into the back corner of the bottom drawer, their plastic casing cracked, cloudy and well-used. Her heart jerked to life.

Maybe, she thought.

She turned and looked at the bookshelf. A pair of cast iron owl bookends held the row of hardback books in neat order. Harry, Frodo, fairy tales…a few more, books she didn't know, and tucked just behind a dog-eared dictionary, a slender, black, leather-bound book.

A sketchbook.

Adrenaline surged through her, and Isabel told herself sternly to calm the hell down. It might be nothing. Plenty of kids liked to draw. Yes, the pens were clearly well-used. Yes, they were stuck far in the back of a bottom drawer, when the top drawers were almost empty. But they were not, in and of themselves, auspicious. They did not necessarily *mean* anything.

Yes, they do, experience whispered. Which she did not appreciate.

She pulled the book out and flipped it open. The image that greeted her made her sit down, hard, on the bed.

The drawing was done in black ink, no doubt with one of the pens in the cracked case. A boy lay curled into a fetal position in the center of the page, his expression so pained, *so terrified*, that Isabel felt a wave of emotion crash into her, unexpected and unwelcome. His arms were outstretched, as if to ward off something. *Someone.* His mouth was open, a silent, eternal scream that chilled her. Tears streamed from his eyes, and chains bound his feet.

Isabel made herself turn the page. A man lay, eviscerated. His intestines spilled out, his ribs thrust through his skin. His arms and legs were missing, and his decapitated head sat at his feet, his black eyes staring into hers. There was no mistaking his identity.

Donovan Cruz.

Drawn in exquisite detail and blood curdling; Isabel couldn't look away. She'd seen things like this before; she understood—better than anyone—what it meant. But understanding was different from feeling, and as she stared at the picture, the past whispered to her, dark, restless, ever-present. The hair at her nape stood to attention, and the contents of her stomach simmered like a pot set to boil.

"Five minutes," Agnes called, and Isabel started.

She closed the book, swept the room with another glance, and went back into Lucia's room. Tony stood next to the window, staring down at something in his hand. He didn't move as she approached, and when Isabel halted beside him, she realized it was a photograph.

An old, worn, creased photograph, faded with age and

curled at the corners. Three kids sat on a set of cracked concrete steps, two boys and a girl. The boy on the left was grinning; thirteen, maybe fourteen, a good looking kid with a wide smile and laughing eyes. The boy on the left stared soberly into the camera, no smile in evidence, his features drawn. A girl sat between them, a year or two younger, a shy smile curving her mouth. Isabel's gaze returned to the grinning boy. There was *something* about him—

"That's you," she whispered, and Tony jumped, as though she'd screamed "Boo!"

He turned away.

"Where did you find that?" she demanded. "I looked everywhere."

"It was on the floor behind the bedside table." He stared down at the picture, so tense Isabel could've bounced a quarter off of him. "I'm surprised she even had it. We didn't...part well."

"Is she family?" Isabel asked, moving around him to look at the photo again.

"No," he said. Lines bracketed his mouth; his eyes were dark. "But she was close to it. Once. A long time ago."

Not lovers, Isabel thought, looking at the girl in the picture with new eyes. Childhood friends. Something she would not have expected, although she couldn't have said why.

Foolish of her, she thought.

"What's that?" Tony asked, looking at the book she held. Isabel opened it wordlessly to the picture of the headless man and showed it to him.

"Jesus fuck," he said, staring at it in horror.

"Yes," she agreed quietly.

His gaze met hers. "That's Cruz."

"Yes," Isabel said again.

"Does that mean what I think it does?"

She shook her head. She wasn't willing to define anything. But—"Abused children often utilize...certain outlets to exorcise their abuse." And punish their abusers. "Some kids cut, some hurt others, some keep journals, and some...draw."

Tony's brows rose. "Was that a yes?"

Annoyed, Isabel closed the book and tucked it into the waistband of her pants, pulling her suit coat down over it. Tony watched, a faint smile tugging at his mouth, and she turned away.

"Statistics estimate that four out of five girls will be the victim of an attempted sexual assault in their lifetime," she told him. "Three out of every five boys. Those numbers are based on victims who come forward; you can image where the true figures lie. It isn't guns and drugs that turn the global marketplace—above ground, or below. It's human beings."

He stared at her. "What makes you an expert?"

Isabel held his gaze. The book was cold against her back. It had shaken her, but it had also firmed her resolve. *This was what she did.* No matter how hard it was. She might not trust Tony Malone, but they were in this together, now. And there was no reason to lie.

"I'm part of the Bureau's Violent Crimes Against Children unit," she said after a moment. "That's why they sent me."

A dark look crossed his face. "They think she's guilty."

"No stone unturned," Isabel replied diplomatically. She could've told him that she was one of the Bureau's best, that it wasn't just professional expertise that drove her. That she understood in a way few could. That it was *always* personal, something that made her very effective at her job.

But she didn't.

The door opened abruptly, and Agnes stuck her head in. Tony turned away, sliding the photo into his pocket. Isabel looked at her, aware of the book digging into her hip.

"Time's up," Agnes said, her gaze sweeping the room, as though she expected to see upended furniture and slashed curtains. "Did you find everything you need?"

"From a cleared and cleaned room?" Isabel asked coolly. "Doubtful."

Agnes didn't so much as blink. "I'll escort you out."

Isabel's hand itched, which was both aggravating and amusing. It had been a long time since she'd been tempted to smack anyone around. But Agnes had managed it.

They followed her out, along the narrow hallways, down the wide, sweeping staircase. As they came to the bottom of the stairs, a cell tone sounded, and Agnes pulled a sleek black phone from her pocket.

"Agnes speaking," she announced into the phone. She halted abruptly; a look of irritation swept over her features. "No. Don't do *anything*. I'll be right there."

She poked the touchscreen angrily and turned to them. "I have to attend to something. I trust you can find your way out?"

Beside Isabel, Tony tensed.

"Of course," he said. "Thanks for your help."

Agnes grunted and walked away, leaving through one of the sliding glass doors that led out to the swimming pool.

"Thanks for *nothing*," he added, watching her go.

Isabel had to agree. They turned toward the front entry, but as they walked down the wide hallway, Tony moved to the side and began to open doors, peeking his head into each one as they passed. Isabel glanced behind them, to where Agnes had disappeared, her heart pumping hard.

"What are you doing?" she demanded.

"Looking for an office," Tony replied, opening another door. "Bingo!"

"You can't—" Isabel began, but he was already gone. She stuck her head in the door he'd disappeared through. "Ten to one, there are cameras covering every square inch of this place."

"I hope so," he muttered, looking around. The room was dark, thick wooden blinds drawn tight against the harsh desert sun. A huge wooden desk, two plush leather chairs. A barrister, a small bar, and a stylish wooden filing cabinet. A zebra head was mounted above the desk, its glassy eyes staring blankly down at her.

"Ick," she said.

"Like I said: asshat." Tony scowled. "No computer. No PC, no monitor, no printer. What kind of corporate kingpin doesn't have a computer?"

"He probably has it with him," Isabel pointed out, glancing back over her shoulder to make sure Agnes wasn't headed toward them. "Let's go, Detective. Getting thrown into jail for criminal trespass isn't going to help your friend Lucia."

Tony shook his head, still looking around. "There has to be one he doesn't travel with."

"Why?" Isabel asked, exasperated. "Tech has come a long way. Plenty of people have downsized to tablets and phones."

"Not him."

"Come *on*," she hissed.

The sound of the glass door sliding open made Isabel's heart lunge against her ribs.

Tony's gaze narrowed, but he stepped out, pulling the door shut behind him. Footsteps sounded, and they booked it toward the front entry. Tony opened the large door; Isabel walked through, her blood a loud roar in her ears.

Agnes approached from the rear, frowning, suspicion written clearly in the harsh lines of her face.

"Just checking out the art," Tony told her. "That's some sick shit."

Then he closed the door in her face.

CHAPTER 9

"Did you find anyone?"

Lucia glanced up from the dog she carried to see Alexander waiting for her, his eyes shimmering in the pale light.

"Not anyone we could save," she replied, her chest tight. The beat of her heart was painful; even in the blood-drenched hours of her worst day she'd not felt so hollow. So hopeless and helpless and angry with fate.

"Can we go now?"

"*Sí*," she said wearily. "We can go."

Sam had not followed her; instead, he'd gone the opposite direction, further into the twisted mass of wreckage that had once been a town. They would have no better opportunity to leave him behind, and even if that thought suddenly sent an unexpected pang of regret through her, it must be done.

The dog squirmed against her, and Alexander focused on it with laser beam intensity.

"What's that?" he demanded.

"What does it look like?" Lucia walked past him to kneel beside Ben, who sat balancing himself on one of the sleeping bags, his thumb in his mouth, his eyes dark and wide and scared.

"Here," she said and carefully placed the little dog in his lap. The pup was a sweet, tiny little thing, more fur than dog, trembling and cold. In shock, Lucia thought. Like all of them. "She is all alone now, so you will have to take good care of her, Benjamin. Can you do that?"

"No," Alexander said behind her, his voice cold.

Lucia ignored him. Ben immediately wrapped his arms around the animal and looked up at her as though she'd handed him a living rainbow. "Holy cow, holy cow, holy cow, it's a puppy! A real live puppy! Can I keep her, Lu? For really?"

"*Sí*," Lucia said, because what she needed on top of everything else was a dog. But she couldn't abandon the animal any more than she could its owner, and she and Sam had promised. "But do not put her down until we can find something to use as a leash. She might run away, and that would be very, very bad in this place."

"*No*," Alexander said again, more forcefully.

Ben only nodded solemnly. "I won't. Promise and hope to die."

"That's not how you say it," Alexander growled.

"Her name is Daisy," Lucia continued. And according to the tags on her flowered collar, she was both vaccinated and microchipped. "She is very scared and very cold. You must keep her warm, and pet her gently."

"No," Alexander repeated.

"I'm a good petter," Ben said earnestly and carefully ran his hand along Daisy's back. The little dog shivered and burrowed closer. "I think she likes me."

"You can't keep her," Alexander snarled. "She'll just slow us down. Let her go, Ben."

Lucia rounded on him. "Stop it."

"What are you going to feed her?" Mockery, as biting and sharp as the wind. "An oatmeal pie?"

Sometimes she really, really wanted to swat him. A good, stinging smack on the butt, the kind her grandmother had delivered. But he'd suffered enough blows in his young life; they would gain her nothing.

"Are you jealous?" she asked instead, her brows arched. "Is that the problem?"

Color rushed into his cheeks. "No. I don't want a stupid dog."

"No?"

"No!"

"Then zip it."

"This isn't smart," he said coldly.

Lucia met his pale gaze. "Nothing about this is smart."

The boy looked away, and a dark scowl settled across his face. Lucia followed his gaze to see Sam walking back toward them, and the sight of him both calmed and annoyed her, because she didn't want to feel anything when she looked at him.

But she couldn't forget. Not about the storm he'd sheltered them from, nor the dying man whose hand he'd taken in effort to offer comfort. Not the promise he'd made to that man—one Lucia knew he would keep—nor the calm, cool acceptance he'd displayed at the man's death. Sam had clearly seen more death than anyone ever should, a realization which had shaken her. Death was nothing new to him, and although it was not new to Lucia either, she was not able to treat it as graciously. Death took from everyone and gave back nothing; she despised everything about it: the grief, the mourning, the intractable amount of time it took to make one's peace with it. As a healer, she fought death with every weapon in her arsenal, and when it won, she was the sorest of losers.

No, death was her enemy. That Sam could look it in the eye without flinching was something she both admired and feared. Because if death didn't make a man flinch, what did?

He was still limping as he walked toward them. Lucia was tempted to make him sit down so she could look at his leg, but he was hardheaded, and he would argue, and that would annoy her. Beyond that, they needed to get out of this town before the police and emergency personnel showed up. They had to get away from *him,* which meant they needed a convincing distraction, a method of travel, and a route of escape.

Sí. No problemo.

"I'm going to get rid of Sam," Alexander told her, as if echoing her thoughts. "And then we're leaving."

He strode away before she could stop him and headed toward Sam, his hands clenched into fists. Lucia watched, nerves twisting in her belly. The boy was incredibly smart, but so was Sam. He wouldn't be put off easily, and he wouldn't go away simply because Alexander told him to.

But Alexander was pointing off to the left, talking rapidly, his face ripe with expression; he looked, for once, like a normal boy, earnest and concerned, which was both disconcerting and disappointing. *Lying.* He was lying, something he was quite proficient at, much to Lucia's dismay. Although he couldn't put much past her, he didn't have the same trouble with others, and he had absolutely no qualms about telling a tale so tall it dwarfed Everest.

Sam's gaze lifted, flickered to hers, and Lucia did her best to give him a poker face. She knew she wasn't good at it, but she also knew it was necessary. Because they *did* have to separate. Nothing good would come of allowing this…whatever it was to continue.

Alexander was right. Even if she didn't like his methods. Even if some tiny part of her had arbitrarily decided that—*perhaps*—it wasn't right to leave Sam behind.

It must be done.

Sam said something she couldn't make out and turned to limp in the direction Alexander had pointed. The boy waited until he'd disappeared behind the rubble to hurry back toward them.

"What did you tell him?" Lucia asked, uneasy.

"I told him we heard cries for help."

Her stomach dropped. "Did you?"

Alexander shot her a narrow look. "Of course not."

Yes, just one good swat.

He picked up his pack and slid it on. Lucia reached down reluctantly to take hers. The sleeping bags and the tent protruded from the top, and it was awkward to slide on. Ben's Snoopy bag was last, and when she lifted it, she almost dropped it again due to its unexpected weight. She opened it and looked inside.

Food. Beef jerky, nuts, granola bars. Apples, a package of bagels, a wedge of cheese. Hot dogs. Pretzels. And more Little Debbies. Enough food to feed them for several days, if they were careful.

She looked at Alexander, who only stared back at her, his silent equivalent of *duh*.

"Good job, *mijo*," she told him quietly.

"I know," he replied in a tone of frost.

She sighed. Ben watched them, holding Daisy close. "Are we gonna leave now?"

"*Sí*," Lucia replied. "Are you ready?"

Ben's gaze slid to where Sam had disappeared. "But what about Sam?"

"We don't need him," Alexander said. "He's trouble. Get up, Ben. We have to go."

Go where? Lucia wondered. But he was right. They had to go. The next storm was almost upon them, and the wind was getting stronger. There was nothing here for them: no shelter, no protection.

Nothing but Sam. And if she felt a flicker of guilt over leaving him, she didn't allow it to catch flame. The man was law unto himself; he would survive their defection. No matter their shared experiences, he was still a stranger—a snarly stranger—and one to whom they posed a grave threat, whether he knew it or not.

An odd, inexplicable sorrow filled her at the thought. Another thing there was nothing to be done for.

"But Sam's our *friend*," Ben protested, clearly confused. "We can't leave him behind. What if he needs us?"

Lucia could not imagine Sam needing anyone. "We must," she said simply and held out her hand.

Ben sighed, took her hand, and stood up, Daisy firmly anchored to his chest. "I didn't get to say goodbye."

Me either, monkey.

"Forget him," Alexander ordered. "And follow me."

He turned and marched away, leaving them little choice but to follow. They made their way carefully through the debris fields, around what remained of the buildings, past overturned cars and demolished homes. They headed north—or at least Lucia thought it was north—until Alexander suddenly halted and turned to look at them, something that looked suspiciously like pride stamped across his features.

"I found our ride," he said, and Lucia blinked, because he was almost...*smiling.*

"*Sí?*" she said, confused.

"Yes," he said, and stepped to the side. Behind him was a camouflage four-wheeler, completely enclosed, with a thick black roll bar, sturdy plastic windshield and two round headlights.

Lucia stared at it. The vehicle was untouched. *Whole.* And uniquely capable of getting them out of the mess they were in.

Thank you, Destiny. I am sorry I told you to suck it.

"It will get us approximately 120 miles per tank of fuel," Alexander said, and there was no doubt that it was pride she saw gleaming in his eyes—something so rare, she wasn't sure she'd ever witnessed it before.

"Only if it starts, *mijo,*" she pointed out.

"It does. They key was in it, so I checked. And the gas gauge is on 'F.'"

"It's like Fred Flintstone's car," Ben told her. "'Cept we don't gotta run."

"My clever boys," she murmured.

"We can take trails," Alexander said. "I found a map in the glove compartment. There's trails through the National Forest all the way up, into Canada."

Canada. Her goal had been Alaska, but Canada would do—if they could get across the border undetected. *If they could stay undetected.* A worry for then, not now.

Now was enough.

Lucia shook her head. "You are quite brilliant when you want to be, aren't you?"

Alexander said nothing, but the gleam in his eye sharpened.

"Okay, get in," she said. "Time to go."

"Lucia!"

The sound of Sam's voice made Lucia freeze. For a moment, she couldn't move. Alexander tossed his pack in and ushered Ben and Daisy into the backseat. He climbed into the passenger front seat and stared at her.

"C'mon, Lu," he said. "We have to go. Before he sees us."

She knew that; she did. But…

"Lucia. *Now.*"

Yes. No choice. No matter her suddenly churning insides, the remorse that speared through her. The odd, heavy melancholy that gripped her at the thought of abandoning the man who—in spite of his abrasive manner—had done nothing but help them. *Who'd saved them.* First the old man had died; now, she was leaving him, too.

But he is better off without us.

And that was no lie.

She climbed into the ATV and started it. A couple of rough starts later, they were winding through the rubble that remained of Canyon Falls, headed north toward the sloping hills of pine trees in the distance. If she heard Sam call her name again, she didn't react.

And she definitely didn't look into the small rearview mirror to see him watching them disappear.

CHAPTER 10

Sam—

You asked for an explanation. This is it.

I met Lucia when I was fourteen. Her family came from Belize, and Father Domingo roped my mother into making me be her brother Elian's friend. I wasn't interested, but you know my mother.

Elian and I hung out every day. Played ball, chased skirts. Stood on the Alter during mass at Our Lady of the Sacred Heart. He was my friend, probably the first friend I had who really meant something to me. Elian wasn't like everyone else. He'd seen some shit. I don't know what went down in Belize that made them leave, he didn't talk about that, but whatever it was, it left a mark. Lucia was two years younger, and she was smarter than the two of us put together. When she got mad, she went off like dynamite. We made her mad a lot, just for fun.

Elian was my first real friend, and I fucking betrayed him, Sam.

We spent the summer at a camp run by the Church. Nothing fancy, just games and Bible verses. Girls. But Elian, he stopped looking at the girls. He stopped playing ball. He stopped everything. I didn't know why. I had other friends; I didn't worry about it. But when we got home, he showed up at my house one night and said he had to tell me something. It took him a long time to say the words. I couldn't figure out what his problem was. I wish I could say I was worried, but I was fourteen, and when I wasn't thinking with my dick, I was being a dick.

Elian told me that the Deacon from Our Lady, the one who'd gone with us to camp, had messed with him. Raped him. Right there at camp, in the maintenance room. Elian said it wasn't the first time. He came to me because I was his friend, and he asked me for help.

You know what I told him? That I didn't fucking believe him. That he was a liar, and even if he wasn't, that maybe he'd asked for it. Yeah, like I said, a dick. My only defense is that what he told me scared the shit out of me. I didn't want to believe him, so I didn't. But part of me knew it was true. Part of me heard him. And I ignored it, because I was just a dumb kid; I didn't know how to handle what he was saying. I didn't know what to do.

At least, that's what I tell myself. I didn't know what would happen. If I did, maybe I would have done different. But you know as well as I do, that doesn't make a damn bit of difference now.

I stopped being his friend. I told both him and Lucia to get lost. I didn't tell anyone, not even my mother, who was mad as hell at me. I just pretended I'd never met them. That it'd never happened.

Three weeks later, Elian put a gun in his mouth. Lucia found him.

I told myself it wasn't my fault, but I knew it was. Not entirely, but enough. Like a fucking bomb going off—shrapnel I still carry. Two weeks later, my mother came home from Church, cornered me, and demanded to know if Deacon Dean had ever tried to hurt me. Several boys had come forward, and their parents had gone to Father Domingo to lodge a formal complaint. When the police arrested the fucker, Dean had a hard drive full of kiddie porn and a NAMBLA membership. Seventeen boys, Sam. That they knew of.

Fuck.

My mother made me go to the funeral. I'll never forget the look Lucia gave me. Her words. Not ever. She wanted to kill me. But I didn't blame her. I knew I was responsible, and I thought about following Elian, more than once. I think that's what finally drove me into the service. Why I became a cop. For him. To try and right the wrong I'd done.

Yeah, good luck with that. But that's why Lucia came to me. She thought I would listen. When you've lived through that, you can't deny its existence. We both know there are monsters, and she put herself out there and trusted that I would hear her. That I would help her. And I failed in a thousand ways.

Lucia isn't a criminal, Sam. She's trying to save those kids because she couldn't save Elian.

She wouldn't lie. Not about this. If she believes Donovan Cruz is abusing his children, then he is. And I'm going to find the evidence to prove it. I'm going to burn him at the fucking stake.

I'm sorry I can't tell you this in person, but I can't reach you, and I hope to God you're all okay.

I've attached a drawing we found in Alexander Cruz's room. The kid had a sketchbook filled with things that would make your goddamn hair stand on end. I really need you to understand this, Sam. I need your help. So here I am, asking a friend for the same help I once denied. Life is so fucked.

I just hope you're a better friend than I was.

T.

"Shit," Sam said, staring down at his phone. When it'd beeped, he'd been surprised there was even service. He certainly hadn't expected what he found.

Tony had been his friend for over a decade; they'd served together, survived together, killed together. Mourned their lost brothers-in-arms, drank themselves stupid, hell, they'd even vacationed together. But history...that wasn't something they spoke of. They'd bonded over blood and death, an experience shared in real time. They watched each other's backs and kept each other sane when the violence threatened to erase them. But this...

This was new.

"Shit," Sam said again, staring down at Tony's words. *Words.* A goddamn essay: The History of Tony Malone. *Fuck.*

While Sam appreciated the explanation, he wasn't at all happy with its revelations. Because this meant it was *personal.* That Lucia was family. That this situation wasn't just happening—it was happening *again.*

And that changed everything.

A growl welled in his throat. Which didn't make much

sense, considering he'd abandoned the idea of walking away several hours ago, but *this*...now he was all fucking in. Now she was his responsibility.

Now he had to save her.

"Goddamn it," he snarled, and stabbed at the touchscreen of his phone, opening the document Tony had attached to the email. A moment later a drawing appeared, and Sam stared down at it in horror: a decapitated man with missing limbs and his guts spilling out around him.

A man no one could deny was Donovan Cruz.

Jesus.

"Shitgoddamnhellfuck," he said.

He hit the reply button but hesitated, unsure what to say. What was there to say? That he believed? Hell, he wasn't sure what he believed. But he knew he would help. That it was his job to help those in need—and Lucia and those boy were sure as hell in need. Sam didn't want to be the guy, but he'd already resigned himself to the fact that he *was* the guy, if only by default. Unfortunately, default had just flown out the window. Now it was a decision to be made with his eyes wide open, fully cognizant of the repercussions, which were considerable. No longer circumstance, but choice.

Donovan Cruz was a powerful man. He wielded both financial and political influence worldwide. No one would want to believe he was an abuser, even if it was the truth. Choosing the lie was easy, and folks were good at excusing all manner of sin if the sinner was shiny enough. If they benefitted. And plenty of people benefitted from a man like Cruz. He would be protected. Defended. He would be afforded every doubt, while Lucia would be crucified.

And his children would pay.

But ultimately, it was not a hard decision. Sam had chosen his current path long ago, and turning from it now would only betray every sacrifice it had taken to get here. He protected; that's what he did. This was no different. Donovan had power, but he was just a man.

And Sam had killed plenty of men.

Killing wasn't fun, and it wasn't easy, but sometimes it was necessary. He was okay with that.

He scowled down at the tiny letters on his touchscreen. *Words.* Not something he was friendly with. In the end, he kept it simple.

On it.

Whoosh!

"Now you're fucked," he told himself.

He thought about Alexander Cruz and his tall tale of cries for help, about Lucia and the boys taking their things and hightailing it in a four-wheeler. Sam was certain Lucia had seen him as she drove away, but she hadn't hesitated. *Goddamn her.* And even if part of him felt a begrudging, reluctant respect for what they'd managed to pull off, the rest of him was furious.

He'd discovered where the ATV had come from after they'd gone; the remains of a dealership sat only a block away from where they'd left the boys. There were demolished jet skis, twisted snowmobiles, upended ATVs and several large RVs on their sides. Luckily, there was also a three-wheeler that had survived the storm. Even luckier, Canyon Falls had, apparently, been a town filled with trust, because the key was still in it. Sam assumed the same was true of the four-wheeler Lucia had taken, because it was highly unlikely she knew to hot-wire an all terrain vehicle.

Unlikely, but not impossible. Nothing was impossible.

She was smarter than both of us put together.

Sam had seen that intelligence. Her fire, her compassion and her grief, and now he wanted to know more. He wanted to understand what the hell was going on.

Really going on.

He had Tony's words, now he wanted hers.

Goddamn answers. And he was going to get them.

CHAPTER 11

On it.

Tony stared at Sam's reply to his email, acutely aware that he'd never be able to repay the risk his friend was taking. If Sam's role in this fiasco was discovered, his entire career would be nothing but a memory. Accessory to felony kidnapping was not something the Marshal's Service would overlook; no, Sam would go to prison. Hell, they'd probably strip him of every military award he'd ever been given.

Something Sam would have taken into account, because Sam took everything into account. When they'd been Rangers, he'd been the one on the team to assess the dangers—the best route, the easiest in and out, all of the knowns versus the unknowns—and plan accordingly. He was damned good at it; the fact that Tony was still breathing was living proof.

So his involvement was a boon Tony hadn't dared hope for…but it was also a highly calculated risk. Because Tony didn't want Sam to pay for his mistakes, his stupidity. He didn't want anyone but Donovan Cruz to pay. But there were no guarantees, no matter the truth. *No matter the evidence.* Something else Sam would have considered. And yet, he was on board anyway.

Sink or swim; Tony didn't deserve him. But he would take him, all the same.

"Everything alright?" Isabel asked, her dark gaze flickering over him. She sat across from his desk, a barely-touched carton of sweet and sour shrimp abandoned beside her as she poured over the information they'd gathered on Donavon Cruz.

She had some serious contacts, Tony would give her that. She'd laid hands on dirt it would have taken him weeks—if ever—to uncover. When he'd made the observation that federal resources were damned handy to have, she'd only shrugged, leaving him to wonder what other resources she had at her disposal. Because looking through the documents...whoever those resources where, they were expert. There was paperwork on all of Cruz's dummy corporations and their assets, assessments of his worth—which far outstripped any of the numbers Tony had previously seen—and an approximation of what he held in various international and offshore accounts. There was a bio for every one of his employees, a detailed overview of the Cruz International company hierarchy, complete with criminal and civil records. Reports on his dealings with the Saudi royal family, the sitting Russian Premiere, the British PM. He traveled often, and those records were there, too, every flight, every country, every stamp of his illustrious passport.

Impressive. And more than a little disconcerting.

"Everything's peachy," Tony replied finally, watching her.

In spite of the revelation of his history with Lucia, Isabel hadn't asked any more questions. She hadn't probed or speculated. She hadn't lectured him on the conflict of interest he was engaged in or even urged perspective. She'd simply accepted it and moved on.

It isn't guns and drugs that turn the global marketplace—above ground, or below. It's human beings.

And wasn't that a sickening state of affairs. One which—as a Detective with the LVMPD—Tony had always been aware of, but not something he'd come face to face with, something he'd had to look in the eye. Isabel Bjorn, it seemed, stared it in the face every day.

Why? Was it a chosen field or something she'd fallen into? Who the hell would choose to deal in human trafficking? Ugly, evil, and overwhelming; one might as well try to stop the tide. Had she lost someone she loved? What made a woman like her devote her time and skills to such an impossible task?

But then, maybe the enormity of it was moot. Maybe she counted her victories in single souls; one less lost. One more saved. Sometimes that was all life gave you.

And that, Tony could relate to. Still, in spite of his determination to stand at arm's length, he was curious about her. Too curious; he wanted answers. He wanted to peel her like the ripest fruit and sample the flesh within.

Not gonna happen. But a guy could dream.

His gaze moved over her: the severe suit, the tightly-wound hair, the icy, unimpressed expression. It was a slow perusal, one which she ignored. Or, at least, *tried* to ignore. Because he was very good at persistent.

Who was Isabel Bjorn? The cool, austere fed he'd met this morning? Or the woman who'd growled at Agnes Livingstone and stuffed a sketchbook down her britches?

Tony knew which he preferred. Not that his preference made a damn bit of difference. Trusting her was simply not an option, no matter who she proved to be. No, this shitstorm was his, and his alone. Giving into the growing temptation she presented would only make matters worse, and he'd already fucked up enough for two lifetimes. Lucia needed him. And Sam was counting on him. He couldn't fail in this.

Not again.

Which meant that Isabel was simply a means to an end. Even if he was growing to like her. Even if she *did* smell like heaven. Even if he wanted to—

"Yes?" she asked coolly, her brows arched.

"Anything interesting?" he asked innocently.

She narrowed her gaze, and Tony again got the distinct impression she saw right through his bullshit. It was both intriguing and alarming.

"Both of Cruz's children are homeschooled," she observed. "Neither one has ever stepped foot into a public, charter, or private school."

"Plenty of people homeschool," Tony pointed out. "Doesn't make them sexual predators."

"No," she conceded. "But it does create an atmosphere of total control, something Mr. Cruz appears to cultivate in every area of his life."

"Maybe he's just type A."

"No maybe about it," she replied, her tone grim. "Nothing happens without his stamp of approval. He makes the word 'anal' seem insipid."

"Narcissistic, neurotic, cunning; he's probably a goddamn sociopath," Tony said. "His security is top-rate. Former special ops and hired mercs. Men who kill for profit and aren't easily bought. Between his personal security and his political connections, he's got a wall around him three feet thick."

"Jericho," Isabel murmured.

"Take a look at this guy." Tony slid one of the dossiers toward her. "Cruz's head of personal security. Ivan Dragovitch. Looks like fucking Quasimodo."

Isabel picked up the file and looked at it. Tony knew what she was seeing. Filled with police reports and prison records, the dossier was a succinct testament to a life spent doing unto others. The stark, black and white photo that christened the pile portrayed a big man, all blunt edges and raw bones. Pale skin pitted by acne scars, a bulbous nose and narrow, hard mouth. Dark hair hung unkempt around his face, and his eyes…his eyes were black as night. Not unlike Isabel's. But Ivan Dragovitch's eyes were flat, shimmering like stones, and Tony saw death in them.

"Ah, but Quasimodo was a good and kind soul," she murmured, studying the file. "Mr. Dragovitch, not so much."

"Attempted rape, aggravated assault, battery." Tony sat forward. "He's the guy."

"What guy?"

"The one Cruz will send to hunt her."

Isabel arched a brow. "You don't believe Mr. Cruz will afford the federal authorities the twenty-four hours he promised them?"

Tony only snorted. "You don't believe it, either."

"No." Isabel stared down at the dossier. "If he's guilty, he'll want her dead."

Tony ignored the falling sensation in his belly. This was not news. "We need to find Dragovitch."

Isabel gave him a look. "Good luck with that."

"We can't just fucking *sit here*," he snarled.

"No, we can't just chase rainbows," she retorted calmly. "What we can do is look for evidence."

"We found evidence," he said, staring at her, daring her to argue.

"We found something that could be construed as evidence," she corrected. "Something which was obtained *illegally* and which could be interpreted a thousand different ways, depending on the translator."

"We both know what the fuck it is," he growled. "That SOB *is* guilty."

Isabel only shook her head.

"You know it," Tony countered and reached out, wrapping his hand around hers, trapping her in his hold. She stilled. "I know it. How the hell do we prove it?"

Isabel blinked at him, motionless, the pulse in the hollow of her throat fluttering like wings. "We find definitive evidence."

He squeezed her hand, painfully aware of her heat, her scent, the delicacy of her bones. Her skin was like silk against his rough palm, and the feel of it awoke every nerve ending in his body. Awareness flared between them, and for a moment he allowed it, awash in temptation, his attention wrenched from the matter at hand to the desire and need that only continued to grow with every moment spent in her presence. Dangerous and seductive; far too distracting. And she was not immune. He could see her response: the color that touched her cheeks, the faint dilation of her pupils, that delicate beat pulsing wildly in the slender column of her throat. In his hold, her hand trembled.

"Let me go," she said, very quietly.

But he didn't, every part of him rebelling.

"Help me," he murmured and stroked his thumb along the soft skin of her wrist, unable to resist.

She jerked from his hold, and in her dark gaze he saw her own conflict. She wanted him right back. But it was not something she would pursue; like him, she would fight. And for the first time, Tony felt the bite of regret. Because neither of them had the luxury of indulging themselves; too many lives depended on them doing their jobs.

Nothing else could exist.

"I think we should start here," she said and glowered at him, a hint of the spark he'd seen earlier. She thrust a different file at him. "Cruz owns a residence two hours south of the city. It's been very well hidden, titled in an LLC that is a subsidiary of a subsidiary of a subsidiary, and so on. Looking at the map, it's in the middle of nowhere. If there's any evidence of Mr. Cruz's…activities, I think it might be there."

Tony looked in the file, his heart suddenly thumping;

adrenaline surged like a rocket firing. He stood. "Let's go."

Isabel shook her head. "It's nine-thirty at night, Detective. What do you expect to find in the dark?"

"I don't need a lecture," he told her, disappointed. He slid on his suit coat. "Come or don't. But don't lecture me."

"Tony," she said, and he halted, because it was the first time she'd said his name. "We need to be smart about this. We need to have a plan. Do you really think Cruz's top rate security won't extend to this property—one so extensively hidden, its very existence makes it suspect? Do you really think barging in is a good idea, when it will only tip our hand and alert Cruz to our suspicions?"

He stared at her, hating that she was right. "I can't do nothing."

"That's not what I'm saying," she said, clearly exasperated. "I'm saying we don't act rashly. That we use our brains—not our hearts. And we work together, not against each other."

"I can't go home and go to bed," he muttered. "So don't tell me to. I can't stop with this. Not until it's over."

For a long moment, she just watched him, her eyes dark and glinting and impossible to read. Then she gathered the pile of files into the sleek leather bag beside her and stood.

"Fine," she said. "Lead the way. But we are *not* going inside. We are doing reconnaissance only."

Tony almost smiled. Her reluctance and consternation were written all over her gorgeous face, but she was coming anyway. In spite of herself. And while he couldn't let himself forget that she carried a federal badge, and that she couldn't be trusted, he was glad.

"No B and E," he said. "Scout's honor."

"I'm holding you to that," she told him seriously. "And if you break your word, I'm going to handcuff you to your steering wheel."

Tony was pretty sure she meant that as a threat. Too bad his libido thought of it as foreplay.

"Done," he said.

CHAPTER 12

"What are you doing? Sending smoke signals?"

A growl welled in Lucia's throat, but she ignored Alexander's derisive and unhelpful observation. The rain had finally stopped, and she was attempting to start a fire—which they desperately needed—but in spite of the fact that she'd managed to gather what she thought was dry wood, her small stack of kindling refused to catch flame. So far, all she had was a whole lot of stinky smoke. Thick, white, billowing smoke; Alexander was not off point.

"You might as well draw a map," he added, scowling down at her.

"Your concern is noted," she snarled.

"The wood's too wet."

Thank you, Captain Obvious.

"Everything is soaked," he continued. "Including us."

Yes, and that was dangerous. Ben seemed okay, all bundled up with Daisy, but Alexander was shaking, whether or not he would admit it, and Lucia's hands were so cold they hurt. They'd headed north for almost two hours utilizing the winding Forest Service trails that led into the Sawtooth National Forest. When the slow, steady drizzle had ended, Lucia had stopped, and they'd found a nice spot next to a winding stream to set up their camp, protected on one side by a ridge of pine trees. Across the stream, a wall of hard gray granite stretched toward the sky.

The wilderness. Not a place she'd envisioned them utilizing in their escape, and not a place she knew at all. These mountains were nothing like the jungles of her childhood, nor the desert she'd spent the last decade in. She felt unprepared and ignorant, and the lead weight in her chest only grew heavier with every moment that passed.

Putting up the tent had been simple—it was not a very big tent—and collecting water in the water bottles she'd brought was easy enough. But building a fire with wet wood was proving problematic. *Almost impossible.*

And that could not be. They had to have a fire. Fire was survival.

She thought of Sam—who would have undoubtedly had no trouble starting a fire—and then gave herself a brisk mental smack. It was far better that they'd left him behind, no matter the dangers they now faced. The cold, the rain; bears and wolves. Lightning. She'd assumed that Ivan the Terrible would be the biggest threat they encountered.

She'd been wrong. *So very much stupid.*

"Mierda." She blew fervently on the tiny coal she'd managed to ignite, and it glowed brighter, but flame was elusive. Smoke continued to waft into the air around her, as thick and opaque as the clouds hitting the mountains around them.

Water suddenly cascaded down from above. Alexander stood over her, emptying one of the water bottles onto the fire, which only made the smoke worse, and Lucia fell back and landed on her butt in the wet grass, her eyes burning.

"We have to put it out," he announced decisively. "That's too much smoke."

She pushed herself to her feet, ready to strangle him, but before she could act a voice came from the darkness and said, "He's right. I could see you for miles."

Sam.

Her heart stopped, and a wave of butterflies took flight in her belly. Ben jumped to his feet with a delighted cry and ran to the man who was striding into their camp, his face dark, a bundle of wood in one hand, his backpack in the other.

"Son of a bitch," Alexander said.

"Sam!" Ben cried and threw himself against Sam's legs. "I missed you so much! Did you know I got a dog? Her name's Daisy. You wanna pet her?"

The sight of Ben's small hands wound in the denim of Sam's jeans made Lucia's head start to hurt. When had that happened?

"He's not your friend, Ben," Alexander said in a hard voice. "Come here."

Ben only held up a hand to Sam, indicating his desire to be held, and Lucia took a step toward them, anxiety suddenly surging through her. "*Benjamin.*"

But Sam set aside the wood, bent down and lifted both boy and dog, and carried them over to where she stood, shivering, her eyes watering from the smoke that continued to flood the camp. Sam stared down at her, his face cold, his gaze glinting with anger, and a tremor moved through her, because she was tired and hungry and freezing her butt off, and the last thing she wanted to deal with was that look.

Blasted, willful man.

"You need to leave," Alexander growled at him.

Sam only ignored that and stared at Lucia, the line of his jaw like stone. "You didn't have to run."

Guilt flickered, followed by consternation. "You didn't have to follow."

"I should just watch you disappear into the wilderness?" His tone made the fine hair at her nape bristle in sudden, prickling awareness. "And do nothing?"

He wasn't just mad; he was furious.

"Yes," she told him honestly.

"Because you have it all so well in hand." He swept their smoky camp with a narrow, derisive gaze; a muscle ticked in his cheek.

"You need to go," Alexander said, louder. *"Now."*

"No," Ben argued and clutched at Sam's coat. Lucia watched him settle his head on Sam's broad shoulder and felt what little remained in her control fall entirely out of reach.

"Haven't I proven myself?" Sam's voice was low, and in his eyes Lucia saw a churning darkness she couldn't read. Her heart squeezed hard in her chest. "What the fuck does it take?"

A stranger, nothing more. You owe him no explanations.

And yet...he'd helped them. *Saved them.* Didn't he

deserve something for that?

Yes. But the point was moot, because she had nothing to give. Shared experiences did not bind them, no matter how extreme. They were not connected. And leaving him behind had been necessary; there was no choice in that. It protected him.

Even if he didn't realize it.

Why had he followed them?

"We are not your responsibility," she told him.

He took another step closer. "You are."

She shook her head, baffled by his presumption. "Why would you believe such a thing?"

"It's fact."

Lucia stared at him. *Was he insane?* Was that the problem? "We do not need your help."

"Yes, you do."

He sounded so certain, panic bloomed, thorned and ugly.

"Without my help," he continued, his voice hard, "you'd be dead."

An arguable point, even if he was likely correct. And one which underscored every mistake she'd made. *Damn him.*

"Why do you care?" she wanted to know, because his sudden presence, the depth of his anger—it made no sense to her. *Why had he followed them? What did he want?* And then—*did he know? How could he know?*—and her blood turned to ice.

"You need me," he said shortly. "Whether you like it or not."

"We need no one," she told him, angry that he might—*possibly*—be correct.

"Pride's expensive. You want to pay, that's fine. But what about them?"

Lucia stared at him, her heart beating so hard she nearly vibrated. "What do you want?"

"I'm here to help. You need to let me."

"Just leave us alone," Alexander interceded and moved to stand beside Lucia. He glared up at Sam. "We don't need you."

"The hell you don't," Sam told him. "You have no idea what the fuck you're doing. You built your fire next to your tent, which is a bad idea unless you want to start it on fire. It's also too close to the water, which is rising. Those water bottles next to the creek indicate you filled them with runoff, which means by morning, you'll be sick as dogs. That food over there needs to be hung from a tree; that's called bear bait. And unless you get a flame started soon, you're all going to get hypothermic. A nice, slow, painful death in otherwise fair conditions. Why not just jump off a cliff? It would be quicker."

His mockery was a hot blade that sliced Lucia's tenuous control to ribbons, and her fear faded beneath the overwhelming swell of her temper. "I was going to boil the water," she bit out. "I am not an *idiot*."

"Good luck without fire." Sam watched her, his eyes glittering and hard. "You're going to get them killed."

A direct blow, one she felt. Anger simmered across her skin, and she was painfully aware of the heat climbing into her throat, her rising blood pressure, the infuriating mixture of guilt and relief she felt at his sudden appearance.

"No one asked for your opinion," she told him and reached for Ben. "Come here, monkey."

Ben shook his head stubbornly against Sam's shoulder.

"Benjamin," she said sternly.

"I've got him," Sam said. "He's fine."

But Lucia didn't think anything was fine. "Give him to me."

"You're in over your head," Sam said flatly, ignoring her. "It's time to admit that."

When pigs fly. Even if he was right. "You have no place here," she snarled, trying not to yell. "You need to leave."

"I'm not going anywhere, sweetheart."

She growled at him. "We do not want you here."

"I do," Ben protested.

Sam's brows arched—*See?*—and Lucia counted to ten because strangling him while he held Ben would be bad for everyone involved. "You must go, Sam. Now. *Please.*"

"No."

"*Yes.* You must."

He only stared at her, unmoving, as obstinate as any mule, and Lucia glared at him for a long moment, her pulse a violent throb in her skull. She didn't understand. Not any of it. Why had he come? Why did he believe they were his responsibility? *Why was Ben clinging to him?* And she fought the desire to scream at him, because she couldn't let her temper get the best of her. She couldn't rant and rave and curse everything: the past, the present, herself.

Stupid destiny.

She couldn't vent until she felt hollow and spent, until there was nothing left but silence.

No. Not an option. Because Sam knew nothing of them, and that's how she must keep it, no matter how tempting a target he made. Silence was *safe*. Regardless of the words damming in her chest, and the vein throbbing in her neck. No matter the cold, inflexible look on his face. That pigheaded look she was coming to despise—*no. Silence.* She could do it. She was not an *animal*—

"*You stupid, stubborn son of a goat!*" she cried in Spanish. *"Get out of our camp!"*

"You move the tent," Sam said, ignoring the outburst. "I'll start the fire."

"You cannot stay with us," she enunciated sharply. "You are not welcome here."

"Yes, he is," Ben said in a small voice. "He's my friend, Lu."

A sudden, unexpected glint of humor shimmered across Sam's gaze, and Lucia found herself contemplating violence. There was nothing humorous in this; there was only eminent disaster. For them all.

"It is not *safe*," she cried. "You must *listen* to me."

"Safe for whom?" Sam took another step toward her, until he was close enough she could feel the immense heat he emanated. "Because the only danger here is *you*."

She was trying to *save* this *stupid, intractable, arrogant* man. From being arrested—at best. *At best.*

Why would he not *listen?*

"You," he added softly, "and your ignorance."

And that was it. Lucia blew.

Spanish expletives burst from her like a spray of bullets: every colorful obscenity her grandmother had taught her, every ugly profanity, every curse word and vulgar invective she'd ever learned, all spat at him like automatic gunfire. When he only blinked beneath the onslaught, Lucia gripped the slippery material of his coat in her fists and shook him angrily. "You will leave right now, *cabrón*," she hissed. "Or you will regret it."

"Will I?"

Something in his tone made a bolt of powerful, visceral awareness arrow through her. He was unmoving in her hold, and the intensity of him slapped against her, a physical force that only made her angrier. "*Sí*, you will!"

"Fine," he said, and she blinked. His gaze traveled over her face, lingered on her mouth, and she felt something disarming and inappropriate slam into her. "I'll just call the Forest Service on my way out to let them know you're here."

Panic and terror sheared through her anger. She stared at him, her heartbeat almost deafening. Her fingers flexed around the material of his coat; his chest was hard and warm and unyielding beneath her fists. The butterflies in her belly circled furiously.

"No," she said.

"No?" he repeated. His eyes caressed her; something flickered there, and nerves crawled up her throat, and they weren't solely because of his threat. "Why's that?"

"*Because we are being hunted, you fool!*" she snarled in Spanish and shook him again. "*Will you make me shoot you?"*

The sudden slash of his smile, and the flash of white, even teeth that gave life to a crease in his left cheek made her go still. Dread speared through her. Surely he didn't—

"You could try," he replied in perfectly accented Spanish. "But I wouldn't recommend it."

Mierda! He'd understood her, and he'd said *nothing*. "You—"

"Temper, temper," he tsked softly. "Be careful, sweetheart. I'll only take so much."

Lucia blinked up at him, a frisson moving through her at the warning she heard, a serious admonition, no matter the humor glinting in his gaze. *Muy estupido! What did you tell him? What did you do?*

But the words were lost, gone, and it was too late to retrieve them. She stood far too close to him, her fingers tangled in his coat, the warm, tensile heat of him solid and real beneath her palms. His scent curled around her like an embrace, and part of her was insanely tempted to step closer, which was stupid and scared the hell out of her, a fear that had nothing to do with Ivan the Terrible or Donavon Cruz. Nothing to do with her thoughtless, foolish words. This man…he was *dangerous.* For many different reasons.

"It is not safe for you to be here," she told him, and pain, sharp and unexpected, pierced her. "Please, Sam, you must leave."

"Worried about me?" His gaze was far too astute.

"*Sí*," Lucia said bluntly. "You do not understand. You must go. For your own well-being."

He said nothing, simply stared down at her with that

luminescent, blue-green eyes, so close she could see a ring of dark green around his iris. The faint golden beard lining his hard jaw was getting thicker, darker, and the ugly, jagged scar that split his left eyebrow in two appeared to have nearly taken his eye, leading her to wonder what happened. He was so warm, she couldn't bring herself to step away. At least, that was what she told herself, because her reluctance to move could have nothing to do with the tension slowly invading her veins, or the almost primitive awareness prickling across her flesh. *Nothing.*

"I'll take my chances," he said.

"*No!*" She shook him again—no matter that he hardly moved—and stamped her foot, infuriated by his unwillingness to listen. "You will not! You will leave *now.*"

But he only reached up and gently dislodged her hands from his coat. "Get the tent moved, sweetheart. I'll get a fire started." He squeezed her cold fingers in his much warmer ones, and her stomach clenched. Fear, she told herself, knowing it was more. *More.* Something she didn't want to examine; something she could not afford to feel. "We'll finish this later."

Lucia watched him turn and walk away, emotion churning in her belly. Fury, fear, anxiety. But worse—*relief.*

Because she knew she could not allow this. She could not tell him the *truth;* she could not *trust* him.

And she was afraid part of her already did.

CHAPTER 13

You stupid, stubborn son of a goat!

Sam had been called many things, but being labeled the offspring of a farm animal was new. Not that he could really argue; his pop had been a braying, abusive, worthless drunk. If anything, "goat" was a kindness. At least goats produced milk and cheese; Leland Steele had never produced anything but hate.

Sam supposed the insult shouldn't have surprised him; Lucia Sanchez was a firecracker. But in spite of her simmering fury—a goddamn siren song to his own—he hadn't expected the ferocity of her response, especially that lambast of profanity in Spanish that she hadn't realized he would understand. Hell, he'd hadn't even recognized some of those words, and he'd been fluent in Spanish since he was sixteen. The experience had been…enlightening.

You fucking enjoyed it.

He had. He'd smiled, something he hadn't done in…too long to remember. Not that she'd appreciated it, but damned if it didn't feel good—even if his head was still throbbing, he was starving, and his leg hurt like an SOB. The look on her face when Ben had chosen Team Sam was priceless.

And more than a little dangerous. Because Lucia's fire appealed to Sam; the desire to test that flame was growing, and part of him didn't care if he got burned. He was starting to fucking *like* her. And that attraction had no place in this mess. It was a distraction, one he couldn't afford. One none of them could afford.

Even if she felt it, too. And she did; Sam had no doubt. Awareness hummed between them whenever they got within fifty feet of each other, and it was only growing stronger. *Fucking sparks.* Visceral and alluring and impossible.

Something he had no choice but to ignore, because they had much bigger fish to fry.

Donavon Cruz, for one.

And remembering the look on Lucia's face as she'd tried to convince Sam to leave—for his own good, no less—told Sam that, as far as she was concerned, she was on her own. Because who would help her against a man like Donavon Cruz? Everyone she'd gone to for help had turned her away, including Tony. The fact that she felt alone was not a surprise. No, the surprise was her determination to stay that way. Her concern that Sam would pay a price he was unaware of had been something he didn't expect, and it'd gone a long way in soothing his anger at having been ditched like a bad date. He was used to people laying their responsibilities at his feet with full expectation he would carry them—and he did. Carrying them was his job. But Lucia refused to draw him into the mess in which she'd gotten herself.

Part of it was fear. But mostly, it was just decency.

Lucia is not a criminal, Sam.

A conclusion Sam had come to all on his own—in spite of her threat to shoot him. That she'd made the threat made him wonder what she was armed with, a question he would have to answer sooner rather than later.

Because he was done pretending. They were going to have it out: all cards on the table. She wasn't fucking alone anymore.

"You can't stay with us," Alexander said, suddenly materializing next to Sam, his face cast in hard lines, his pale eyes cold. "You need to leave."

Sam only shook his head and continued to rake dirt from the small fire pit he was digging. He was using his knife, scraping down past the grass and roots, to where it was dry. Ben sat beside him with Daisy in his lap; both watched avidly.

"Did you hear me?"

The challenge in the boy was open and hostile, and Sam wasn't sure how to deal with him. He didn't know jack about kids, especially a kid like this one. Damaged and filled with enough rage to kill. Ironic, because Sam knew the feeling, but for far different reasons.

And therein lay the crux.

"I'm staying," Sam told him shortly. "Hand me that pile of moss."

Alexander only blinked, unmoving. "No."

"Ben?"

Ben hopped up, retrieved the small pile of dry moss and pine needles Sam had gathered from deep beneath a dogwood bush, and brought it to him. "Here you go, pardner."

"Thanks, little man." Sam accepted the bundle.

"Stop it," Alexander said sharply.

Sam arched a brow, stuffing the moss into the small teepee of narrow kindling he was building. "Stop what?"

"Stop pretending."

Fair enough, Sam thought. "I will if you will."

Across the campsite, Lucia wrestled with the tent—which Alexander was supposed to be helping her with—and eyed them in concern. Sam shook his head at her, and she scowled, but didn't move to interfere.

"We don't need you," Alexander grated. The kid was tense as a board, his small hands clenched into fists—something Sam noticed he did often—his thin form humming with suppressed energy.

Suppressed violence. Like a powder keg, already lit. Just a matter of time before he blew.

"Do you want to get where you're going?" Sam asked conversationally and continued to build the fire. Thicker sticks, just a few, before he lit the moss.

Alexander only stared at him, silent.

"Well?" Sam prodded.

"Of course," Alexander bit out.

"Then I'll make you a deal," Sam said. "I'll promise to get you where you're going if you promise to stop squawking at me like a hungry hen every five minutes. I'm not going anywhere, and it's getting old."

"*Cock-a-doodle-doo!*" Ben crowed.

Lucia glanced up, and again, Sam just shook his head. She muttered something—probably another barnyard comparison—and went back to pounding a tent stake into the ground.

"That's a rooster," Alexander told his brother with a scowl.

"Close enough," Sam said easily. He lit the moss with his zippo lighter and leaned down to blow on it gently.

The boys watched him. Daisy wagged her tail, apparently familiar with fire and the warmth it would bring. The moss caught and burned reluctantly. Several of the small twigs caught too, and soon the slender kindling was being licked by bright orange flame. Sam added more, careful not to smother the tiny fire.

"Fire on the mountain!" Ben cried and clapped.

"You don't even know where we're going," Alexander said, but with less hostility.

"Doesn't matter," Sam said.

For a long moment, Alexander just stared at him. "Why? What do you want?"

"I want you to get where you're going, safe and sound," Sam replied grimly. "Do you think that's going to happen without me?"

They both looked at Lucia, who was pounding in tent stakes with a large round rock.

"No," Alexander admitted in a low voice, surprising Sam.

"She needs help," Sam said. "I can help."

Alexander watched him, suspicion and uncertainty warring across his features. "What do you want—really?"

Because nothing came free. Sam didn't like it, that the

boy already knew that, but he couldn't argue. At Alexander's age, he'd known it, too.

"A long time ago, I made a promise," Sam said, which was true enough. "And I aim to keep it."

"A promise to who?"

"That's another story for another time." He continued to add wood to the fire, and soon it was blazing toward the sky, crackling and throwing chunks of pine sap around them. Steam from the few wet pieces he'd added curled into the air. "We got a deal?"

Alexander said nothing, but his stare wavered, and Sam saw him understand. That trusting Sam might be a mistake, but that not trusting him might be a disaster. Sam felt for him; damned if he did and damned if he didn't.

Sam could relate.

"You want something," Alexander said. "You have to want something. Everyone wants something."

"You think?" Sam nodded toward Lucia. "What do you suppose she wants?"

Alexander watched her straighten and move to the next tent stake. She was filthy and damp, her hair escaping her braid to curl down her back. She looked exhausted.

"She's different," Alexander muttered.

"Why's that?" Sam asked softly. "Because she's trying to save you?"

The boy shot him a panicked look. "Why would you think that?"

"It's pretty obvious," Sam told him. "Question is, what's she trying to save you from?"

Alexander said nothing, his pale eyes glinting. His pulse pounded hard in his throat.

"It's okay, Zander," Ben said suddenly, and Sam started, because he'd forgotten the boy sat beside them, listening. "Sam's our friend. He's on our side." Ben looked at Sam, utter trust in his sunny smile. "Right?"

Alexander went stiff. His hands, which had finally relaxed, fisted again. But Sam only smiled back at Ben, because hell, it was impossible not to.

"You bet," he told Ben, and it was true. Sam had made his peace with that; he didn't have to like it. He looked at Alexander and offered his hand. "That's the deal. You in?"

Alexander stared at him, pulse pounding, fear and doubt and animosity simmering in him like a pot set to stew. Sam waited patiently, unwavering. Finally, the boy nodded, and he shook Sam's hand once, quickly, before dropping it and stepping away.

"Good," Sam said.

"You'd better mean it," Alexander warned, his voice hard. His eyes shimmered in the firelight, and for a moment Sam felt an echo of what he saw: terror and chaos and rage, pain so deep it could pull a body down and never let him surface. "Because if you don't—if you're lying—I'll kill you."

The boy turned and stalked back toward Lucia. Sam watched him go, rage flickering to life deep inside, in that place he rarely visited, where his own bleak and violent childhood lived in dark, silent stillness. A place of chaos and pain and fury, not unlike what he saw in Alexander.

It was the same path, he thought. He'd just been lucky

enough to find his way. He'd had Magnus to show him. To protect him, to shelter him. *Love him.* And now it was time to pay that gift forward.

Personal.

For Lucia, for Tony.

For them all.

CHAPTER 14

"You are *not* going in there, Detective."

"Settle. I'm just looking."

Isabel shook her shoe, which was filled with sand, and scowled at the broad shadow in front of her. The moon painted Detective Tony Malone in wash of soft silver, but it did nothing to diminish the blunt power of his presence. He had too many edges, too much untapped energy. Even in stillness, he vibrated, which was beginning to annoy the hell out of her.

"Reconnaissance *only*," she reiterated to his back, for all the good it would do. The blasted man *was* a force unto himself.

"Yeah, yeah, I hear you," he muttered, staring through a pair of night vision binoculars.

Considering his military background, she shouldn't have been surprised by either his attitude or the equipment he kept on hand. Never mind the fact that—as far as he was concerned—"reconnaissance" meant standing on the edge of the property line with a spyglass and a scowl.

"No bodies," he said. "But there's something kicking

off serious heat in there."

Isabel peered past him, through the tall lodge pole pine trees to the small, rustic cabin they were scouting. It was an unremarkable building, small and stout and square, built of logs and narrow strips of pale chinking. A small woodstove pipe stuck from the metal roof; across from the pipe, a large patch of solar panels covered the south-face. A narrow wooden porch bordered the north side. The drive leading to the cabin was rutted and unpaved, a seven mile long stretch of hard-packed dirt and sand; there was no mailbox, no satellite dish, and no welcome mat.

It looked like nothing more than an old hunting cabin, and one rarely used. But the trees stood out, an anomaly among the barren rock and scrub brush. Someone had planted them, and since a steady supply of water would be required to keep them alive in the harsh desert environment, someone was continuing to care for them.

"Security," Isabel supposed. "I wonder how far it extends."

Tony leaned down, swept up a handful of sand and dirt, and blew it onto the property. A faint red grid shimmered for an instant and then was gone. The cabin sat in a cluster of trees on a five-acre lot; the grid covered every square inch.

"Lasers in the middle of the fucking desert," Tony growled. "You tell me he doesn't have something to hide."

Isabel couldn't tell him that, so she said nothing. Her internal alarms had been going off ever since she'd discovered the deed for the property amongst the huge cache of information Aequitas had supplied. Considering the hundreds of properties Cruz and his endless list of entities owned, it was like finding the proverbial needle in the haystack, but Donavon Cruz preferred the desert, and Las Vegas in particular. He spent more time in his desert dwelling than he did anywhere else, so when Isabel had stumbled across the deed for a small piece of property in the Dead Mountains Wilderness Area only a few hours southeast of the city, it had nearly slapped her in the face. Close but remote.

A cabin surrounded by wilderness; nowhere to run, and nowhere to hide. Private, isolated, and insulated from society. It was the perfect place for a monster at play.

What they would discover inside, however, was anyone's guess. Because in spite of Tony's certainty—or the sketchbook she'd located—Isabel was not willing to put all of her eggs into Donavon Cruz's basket. She'd been fooled before; it would not happen again.

No assumptions and no conjecture.

Only facts. Hard evidence she could see and touch and despise.

"We need to get in there," Tony murmured, scanning the property left to right, then, slowly, back again.

"Good luck getting that search warrant," Isabel told him.

She should never have accompanied him on this ludicrous excursion; Alexander and Benjamin Cruz were still missing, and that was her job. Not chasing maybes. Still, she'd started it, poking Tony as she had, prodding him to investigate Cruz, so she supposed she was only where she'd put herself.

Smack in the middle of nowhere.

"Fuck a search warrant," Tony replied.

The man was succinct, Isabel thought. And far more dangerous than she'd realized. When he'd touched her in his office—just a hand on hers, something that shouldn't have mattered, something that shouldn't have affected her in the least—her heart had threatened to pound its way out of her chest. Sudden, inexplicable, and underlined by heat, shimmering, painful warmth that streamed through her veins like the most illicit drug.

How long had it been since she'd responded to a man? Years, she thought. If—truly—ever. Her past negated the typical male-female dynamic; it was a dance she didn't understand and had never desired to learn.

Tony, on the other hand, was probably a master. No doubt he'd been doing the two-step since puberty.

"We need to assess the security system," he said. "And then we need to find a way through it."

Yes. Isabel had thought about that. Considered it, weighed it, chewed on it until it was tasteless and gritty. To move forward in that vein went against her eggs in one basket determination, against the laws drafted to protect against illegal search and seizure. Against the task assigned her only this morning by Special Agent in Charge, Lawrence Gill, head of the Bureau's Violent Crimes Against Children unit and her boss.

It was foolish and rash; it threatened any ability to build a credible case. To not only find the truth, but to expose it.

Still, she was considering it. Partially because logic and reason were overrated—sometimes crazy needed crazy—but mostly because no matter her decision to be levelheaded, her instincts were screaming that Donavon Cruz was a predator. And she trusted her instincts.

"Isabel."

Tony was looking at her, his eyes glittering in the moonlight. *Handsome bastard.* Charismatic, smart, funny. And loyal. It was an intoxicating mix, but one Isabel didn't trust, and one in which she would not be indulging. Even if the curious mixture he stirred within her was unusual, and the idea of seeking its conclusion was far more tempting than she would have imagined. Even if he made her feel...*alive* in a way that made her wonder how long she'd been dead.

"Detective," she replied calmly and ignored the small smile that curved his mouth.

"What are the odds your source can identify the security system in this joint?"

Ah, yes. Her source. The one Tony assumed was on the federal dime, when in reality, Aequitas was on the federal list. The Most Wanted list. And while utilizing the contact was dangerous—the Bureau would not take kindly to her making use of their most wanted—it was necessary, because there simply was no one better. The faceless, genderless Aequitas was an endless font of information—any and all information, regardless of source—and had turned into an invaluable ally in the war Isabel waged.

The informant/hacker/cyber criminal had contacted her three years ago during her work on a case involving child trafficking out of Thailand. One morning she'd turned on her computer and discovered a message from AequitasOne, and when she'd opened it, bios on every member of the trafficking ring she was investigating—and every document even minutely pertinent to them—had opened on her screen. Photographs, correspondence, phone records, medical records, business records, links to websites they utilized to advertise and sell the human beings they collected like errant cattle. There had been family trees and social connections, Instagrams and Facebook posts. But best of all, there'd been a detailed, lengthy list of their clientele.

An avalanche of evidence, one Isabel had utilized to put down every single one of them—including the men and women to whom they'd sold those human beings. The few who'd been protected—those sheltered by their governments and their wealth—had all mysteriously disappeared, something Isabel chose not to dwell upon. After all, there was a reason Aequitas was on the List. Still, she couldn't find it within herself to give a damn.

Someone had to police the monsters, and she would take all the help she could get. She'd never understood how or why Aequitas had chosen her, but truth be told, she didn't care.

"Fifty-fifty," she replied finally, although she had no doubt Aequitas could easily provide whatever she needed. Still, that wasn't something she was comfortable sharing, especially with a man who would utilize anything—and anyone—in search of his goal.

Because even though she'd accompanied him on this wild goose chase, Isabel was not certain she and the Detective had the same goal. She wasn't particularly interested in saving Lucia Sanchez—regardless of Tony's connection to the woman, Isabel had made no determinations of Lucia's guilt or lack thereof, and in the end, the truth would either free the woman or damn her—no, it was the Cruz boys Isabel cared about. Their well-being, their future. Tony was only concerned with exonerating his friend; to him, the boys were secondary. But to Isabel, they were everything.

A chasm which could not be bridged. Still, he was her sole ally at the moment, and he could make whatever foolish assumptions he chose. She knew and understood her task.

"Find out," Tony ordered, his impatience a tangible force. "Sooner is better than later."

Isabel arched a brow at him. "Are you asking or telling?"

He leaned toward her; heat and the scent of sandalwood surrounded her. She almost stepped back, unnerved by ripple of awareness that licked across her skin. The bizarre urge to test him, to test herself.

No doubt about it, her hormonal response to the man was unusual. And distracting.

But it would not be a problem.

"Pretty please with sugar on top?" He ducked his head down toward her. She sensed his deep inhalation, and her heart stuttered in her chest when she realized he was breathing in her scent. She froze.

"Inappropriate," she muttered.

He grinned, a slash of white in the darkness, and inhaled again. "You shouldn't smell so good."

"No, I shouldn't have to forgo a shower in order to be treated like your equal," she told him, her tone cutting.

But Tony's smile faded, and although he didn't step

back, the look he gave her was grave.

"Never doubt that I consider you my equal," he said seriously, and damn it, her heart jumped again. "No matter our differences or disagreements."

Isabel stared at him, her pulse a furious drumbeat, her blood a sudden, ludicrous rush in her veins. His scent swirled around her, and the desire to step back morphed into the desire to step toward.

Foolish and destructive. And far more intoxicating than she'd realized. Not something to be ignored; something to be actively fought.

Something which could derail everything.

Tony stared down at her, waiting for a response, so close she could feel his breath touch her skin. Isabel did the only thing she could: she stepped away and pulled out her phone.

She tapped in a brief message to Aequitas and hit send.

"Now what?" Tony asked, and Isabel got the uneasy feeling he was asking about far more than her contact, but she chose to ignore that feeling and take his words at face value.

"Now," she said. "We wait."

CHAPTER 15

"We need to talk."

Lucia looked up to find Sam walking toward her, and the chaotic mixture of fury and fear that had been welling within her for the last several hours threatened to burst like an ugly boil.

The boys were tucked into their sleeping bags in the tent, along with Daisy, for whom Sam had somehow secured a short length of rope to use as a leash, and, amazingly, food. It was as good a time as any for them to speak, but Lucia no desire to do so. She was *furious*. With him, for following them, for his stubborn refusal to leave, for being such a veritable encyclopedia of outdoor knowledge and skill that she wanted to punch him in the face. But mostly she was furious with herself, for allowing this ridiculous situation to ever come into being.

Her fault. Entirely. Even if he was difficult, arrogant and autocratic. This was *not* his fault, no matter how irritated he made her, and she could not blame him for anything that was happening.

No matter how much she wanted to.

"I have nothing to say," she informed him, standing before the blazing fire he'd built. He'd made it look easy—no surge of thick white smoke, no stinging eyes and burning lungs—just flame, pure and hot and lifesaving.

The jerk.

"I do," he replied, his tone hard. He circled the fire toward her, and she began to circle it as well, walking in the opposite direction, away from him. She glared across the flames, her heart beating hard.

Ready to rumble. Which was foolish and stupid; they had no time for such things. But this man...*he made her crazy.* He was too strong. Too presumptuous. He believed she would simply lie down and allow him to take control. He would decide. *He* would lead.

But Lucia wasn't a follower. She never had been, never would be, and although her current path was dark and twisted and strewn with mortars, it was *hers.* She would not let him take it from her.

"Stop it," he growled, circling toward her.

"You stop it," she retorted, pacing him.

"This is childish," he snarled.

"Chasing me is childish," she replied.

He halted, staring at her, and something ominous bled across his face. Lucia stilled, and her skin prickled, and fear fluttered suddenly in her chest, because she did not know this man, and she could see the darkness washing over him, the tension that slid through his veins and turned him to stone. It scared the hell out of her.

She watched him carefully and told herself that running was not an option. *There is nowhere to go.* And he would only catch her, a thought that sent a powerful, unexpected bolt of heat through her.

Something she did not appreciate. *Yet one more thing to work against me.* Because she needed her hormones added to the list.

"What?" she demanded finally, uneasy with his stare—so hard and cold and angry.

"Tony sent me," he said flatly.

For a long moment, she only stared at him. *Tony?*

The police detective, the man who'd become of the boy she'd once known. A man she'd forced herself to reach out to, to trust in effort to help Alexander, only to have him betray her—*again*. Tony, who was as spineless and selfish as everyone else, the same as he'd always been. A man whose badge and gun were nothing more than accessories.

Badge and gun.

Terror surged through her, followed by blinding fury, and she turned to head straight for the tent. She got all of two steps before Sam lifted her from her feet.

"Goddamn it," he snapped, his arms wrapping her waist, plucking her from her path as though she were a child. "Just fucking stop and listen."

"Liar!" she hissed, twisting in his hold, cursing his strength and her own stupidity. *Chivalry—bah.* "Deceptive bastard! Asshole! Son of a—"

"I warned you to be careful," he grated in a tone that made another rush of that primal awareness suddenly wash over her, and then he was swinging her away from the tent, back toward the fire.

Lucia fought, kicking at him with her heels, pounding with her fists, snarling threats in a disjointed mixture of English and Spanish. She wanted to *scream* at him, but the knowledge that the children were only a handful of feet away stayed her. She didn't want them waking to her cries of fury, no matter how justified they were. The need to utilize every defensive and offensive skill she'd been taught burned in her blood, but Sam was too damn strong, and she didn't even have her *feet*—

She elbowed him, and he swore, and she felt an intense, brief moment of satisfaction until he pushed her against one of the trees that ringed their campfire, captured her hands behind her back in one of his and held her in place with the immense weight of his body. The tree bark bit into her cheek; the scent of pine sap filled her nostrils, and the strong, corded forearm wrapped around her middle was like a steel band.

"You about done?" His breath was warm and moist in her ear. Lucia shivered and bucked against him, but it was no use. The man had no give. She might as well fight gravity.

A thought which only infuriated her more.

"Now?" he wanted to know, and she trembled against him, so furious she could barely speak.

"I should have shot you," she growled.

"Settle," he said, and his beard rasped against her cheek. Her skin rippled in response, and the primal awareness he'd sparked morphed into something darker, more visceral, a flash of white heat and clenching need.

Unexpected and unwanted.

"Let me go," she said, her voice low, trembling.

"Not until you hear me."

"This is why you stopped to help us." Not because he was a decent human being. No. That was her own idiotic assumption. She should have known better, should have seen through his ruse and—

"Liar," she said again, part of her heartbroken at the realization.

"No. I never lied to you."

"A lie by omission is still a *lie*."

"Takes one to know one," he told her grimly.

Color rushed into her cheeks. She bucked again. "Get off me."

"I've got all night, sweetheart." Another brush of that prickly beard, like the rasp of a rough tongue against her neck. His voice was deep. "However long it takes."

Lucia shivered. He'd completely immobilized her, and the hard length of him pressed against her back like a second skin. Too big and too strong for her to ever win a confrontation.

She forced a deep breath, then another. "Will you arrest me?"

His mouth touched her ear. "No."

She shivered. Her heartbeat hard at the back of her throat. "Then why have you come?"

"I'm here to help." That prickly beard stroked her jaw. "And you sure aren't making it easy."

She fought another shiver. He was astoundingly warm against her, and his hold seemed too intimate: her hands clasped in his, his mouth at her ear, that damn beard rubbing over her like an affectionate cat. His weight pressed against her, his size and strength utilized as a weapon to intimidate her.

Bend her to his will.

"You are law enforcement," she said, certain.

"Sam Steele, Deputy U.S. Marshal."

She froze. *A Deputy Marshal.* A fugitive hunter. No wonder Tony had sent him.

"Damn you," she whispered, torn between terror and fury, a growing awareness of him she didn't want. His scent, his voice, the press of his body against hers.

She wanted to run. To grab the children and the dog and hightail it into the wilderness as fast as she could, but he wouldn't let her go, and if she fought him—*really* fought him—she would lose. She knew that.

So you must be calm. You must be smart, no matter the betrayal.

"Tony believes you," Sam continued softly, his tone gentle, as if she was a bird poised for flight. Or a woman on a ledge.

"*Now* he believes me?" A bitter laugh escaped her. Who cared what Tony Malone believed? She'd given him a second chance, and he'd crushed it into dust. So what if he suddenly had a change of heart?

Fat lot of good it did her *now*.

"He can go to the devil," she hissed. "And you can go with him."

"Maybe someday." Sam rubbed his jaw against her

cheek. "But not today."

She tugged against his grip on her hands, but he refused to release her.

"If you have not come to arrest me, then why are you here?" she demanded, deeply disturbed by the response he was drawing from her, as if enticing awake a part of her that had long slumbered. But she didn't want to awaken—not now, and not with him.

"To help you," he repeated.

"This is you helping me?"

"You want a fight, sweetheart, I'll give you one."

The bark was abrasive against her skin, the trunk of the tree unyielding. *A position of weakness.* Which wasn't doing her any good at all. That Tony had sent a Deputy U.S. Marshal after her was not a surprise; his treachery had been predictable. But *Sam*...who'd appeared almost...chivalrous—when no one was chivalrous, not anymore—and who she'd begun—*moronically*—to trust. Who she'd felt guilt over abandoning. A man who had—for the first time in her life—made her question what it might be like to feel *safe*.

But she wasn't safe. No one was ever safe.

"Tell me about Alexander," he said.

Lucia was silent, painfully aware that the small, fragile trust growing between them had been nothing more than her own wishful thinking. *Tony's foot soldier.* Nothing more. And she realized too late how foolish she'd been, to be tempted to believe in anyone.

"You have to talk to me, sweetheart," Sam murmured. "So I can do my job."

"Your job," she repeated, her voice tight with the wedge of anger and pain lodged in her throat. "To deceive me."

He bit her, nipping her earlobe with sharp teeth, and Lucia started violently. "*My job.* To keep you safe until Tony can nail Cruz's ass to the wall."

"Forever is a long time," she retorted and yanked at her hands, desperate to free them. Her ear stung, and the intimacy of the act crossed any lines she might have thought in place.

Dangerous. For any number of reasons.

His hold on her tightened. "You have to trust one of us."

But he was wrong. She didn't have to trust anyone.

Why would he voluntarily involve himself in this mess if not to apprehend them? *Why would he help them?*

And then the memory of him gathering them to him in the storm drain suddenly flashed through her; the strength and warmth and sheer determination that had held them secure even as the wind raged and the flesh was stripped from his back. His comfort, given freely to a dying old man. His words to Alexander.

You don't abandon someone who needs help. If you sacrifice them to save yourself, you're already lost.

Did he believe that? Was that the man he was, or simply a convenient façade, easily donned when necessary?

"Lucia."

Her name on his lips made a strange sensation flutter deep within her. Something anxious and painful. Something she didn't trust. *Anger*, she told herself, *or fear*. But she didn't really believe it.

"I can help you," he said. "But only if you trust me."

A stalemate. Because Lucia had no doubt he could—and would—lean on her until she broke. But that did not mean she had to trust him.

He could have the truth, but nothing more.

She'd given countless people the truth, for all the good it had done. The truth, which should have been the most powerful weapon in her arsenal, but did little good when no one was brave enough to engage. And he would be no different. *No one was any different.* She would tell him, and he would run—as they all had—and that would be the final, crushing blow.

But this was not about her, or her fury, or her angry heartbreak. This was about Alexander and Benjamin, and they needed someone like this man on their side, because there was no guarantee she would be around to fight for them. Donavan Cruz would not stop until he had her head on a pike, and Ivan was coming. He would have to be dealt with. If she turned Sam aside—for any reason—she stole from Alexander and Benjamin the potential for a powerful ally.

It didn't matter what she felt, only what she did.

"Let go of me," she said quietly. "And I will tell you what it is you wish to know."

Sam's breath filled her ear. "Promise?"

Her teeth ground together. "*Sí.*"

The grip on her hands released. The arm around her waist dropped, and he stepped back.

She turned to face him and forced herself to meet that intent, waiting gaze. He was far too close; he'd barely moved at all. And when she took a step back and smacked into the tree again, he followed and erased her gain. The fire outlined him where he stood before her, and he seemed even bigger painted in shadow. Her superstitious grandmother would have seen significance in the golden aura the flames cast around him, but Lucia was not a believer in such things.

"You will protect them," she said, and it was not a question. "You must promise me."

"I'll protect all of you."

"I do not need you to protect me." She shook her head decisively. "I need you to protect *them*."

Sam only stared at her, his eyes glittering.

"You must promise," she told him. "Or I am done talking."

"That's bullshit." He scowled and leaned down so close their noses almost touched. "And you know it."

"Why?" she demanded. "Because I want your promise?"

"Because I've been protecting you since the minute I laid eyes on you."

Lucia flushed. "I meant no insult."

"Of course I'll fucking protect them. And you, too, whether you like it or not."

"No." Again, she shook her head. "I need to know you will choose."

Sam's eyes narrowed. His big hands settled against the tree on either side of her, a tall, broad, heated human cage. "Come again?"

"You must promise that you will protect them, even if

that means leaving me behind," she said.

"Fuck that," he retorted.

"Yes," she insisted. "You will, if you have to. That is what I am asking."

"You for them?"

She ignored the growl in his words. "Yes. Will you promise?"

He stared at her, unmoving; he was close enough she could see the furious thud of his pulse in his throat, the ring of green in his eyes, and he was so warm she almost shivered. But that ominous look was again bleeding across his features. "No fucking way."

"Then I have nothing else to say," she said, her own pulse a violent drumbeat.

"I won't make that promise, Lucia. No."

She glared at him. "They are all that matters. You must know that."

"No," he repeated.

Desperation gripped her. "*Please.* I need to know you will put them first."

He said nothing, watching her with that singular, relentless focus, so close she could almost feel his heartbeat and the steady rhythm of his breath. Lucia stared at him, painfully aware of the baffling, intense pull she felt toward him, even though she was furious with him, *even though she didn't trust him*.

So much stupid. There wasn't a trophy big enough.

"I'll do whatever is necessary," he said after a moment, but his eyes glinted, and she knew it was only lip service.

He would do what *he* believed necessary, which was not at all what she was asking of him.

And arguing the point was fruitless. *Until the cows come home.* She wouldn't win, for all her effort. She was just going to have to make sure that, when the time came, she made the decision easy for him.

"Tell me about Alexander," he said again.

Everything within her rebelled. But there was no choice; if Sam was to help the children, he had to know.

And maybe this time, telling someone the truth would make a difference.

CHAPTER 16

Lucia crossed her arms tightly beneath her breasts, and her delicate jaw clenched, her reluctance clear.

"I began to work for Donavon Cruz last fall," she said grudgingly. "I was hired to replace a woman named Rosa Sanchez, who was the boys' nanny. Rosa had been diagnosed with breast cancer and had to go to Phoenix for treatment. She was an old friend of my mother's, and she recommended me for the position. Her recommendation was the primary reason Mr. Cruz hired me. That, and my education."

"Education," Sam repeated, watching her. Her mouth was tight, her body language both defensive and defiant.

"I have a BA in Medical Sciences and a BS in Biochemistry," she continued. "I am—*was*—in my final year of medical school. Mr. Cruz thought my education and medical training would be an asset. I did not—"

"Medical sciences and biochemistry," Sam interrupted.

"Yes. Are you going to repeat everything I say?"

His gaze narrowed on her. "Maybe."

"The boys have a tutor, Mrs. Mills. She is very strict. Most of the time, they are with her, studying. But at night, and in the morning, they are with me. I see to their schedules, and monitor their activities."

"What kind of activities?"

"Benjamin likes to ride his bike."

"And Alexander?"

"He...draws."

The hideous sketch of a headless Donavon Cruz flickered through Sam's head. "What else do you do?"

"I make sure they eat, brush their teeth, put away their clothes, things of that nature." She shrugged. "I read Benjamin stories and kiss his bumps and bruises better. We play games. Last month, we began to learn the constellations."

"And Alexander? What do you do for him?"

Her mouth flattened. She said nothing.

"I think it's time you told me about that," Sam said. For a long moment, she held her silence, and Sam wondered what the hell it was going to take to get the truth. And then, in a voice vibrant with quiet fury, she said, "I tried to tell many people."

Sam moved closer, just a little, far too tempted to touch her. Her anger sang to him, and he felt the pulse of it echo in his blood. He wanted to sink against her and swim in her rage.

His hunger, his pain, his exhaustion, none of it mattered. There was only this.

Fucking stupid and goddamn dangerous. But he didn't

move.

"Tony," she continued softly. "A woman at Child Protective Services. A man at the Department of Family Services. I spoke to people at Victim's Advocate, and the woman who answered the phone at Children Now. I reached out to over a dozen people and organizations, and as soon as I said the name Donavon Cruz, they all stopped listening."

Sam wasn't surprised. "I'm sorry."

Lucia met his gaze, her eyes a blaze of brilliant, glittering gold. "People fear the truth, because then they might have to *act*. Because abdication is a way of life. What does it matter, so long as it is not them? Until it is."

"Yes," he acknowledged softly.

Her pulse was a wild flutter in the hollow of her throat. "I did not want *this*."

"No," he said.

She shook her head. A sharp laugh escaped. "And now I am the criminal."

Sam only waited.

"Alexander…" She faltered. "He is damaged."

"Yes," Sam repeated. "Why?"

Her jaw clenched. "I did not understand at first. His coldness, his rage, his dislike of human contact…I thought perhaps it was genetic. Autism or Asperger's, or some kind of dissociative state. A disease, not a defense. I should have known better. *I should have known.*"

"Why?" Sam asked. "Why should you have known?"

But she only shook her head. "Reaching past his isolation seemed impossible. I could not ask Rosa for help, and everyone around him acted like he was perfectly normal. But that was a lie."

"What did you do?"

Her eyes were dark, glinting amber that burned. "I did *nothing.*"

Something for which she clearly didn't forgive herself.

She took a deep breath, then another, so tense she was ready to snap, and Sam reminded himself that he had no comfort to give. *Shouldn't have bitten her.* Even if he'd been frustrated and angry. He shouldn't have touched her. *Not like that.* Because now the sensory memory of her—the press of her body into his, the silk of her skin against his rough beard, the soft catch of her breath when he put his mouth to her ear—was branded into his brain, and he knew he wouldn't forget.

Goddamn it.

"It happened when I was supposed to be away," she continued. "A friend had invited me to Joshua Tree for Easter weekend, and I took time off. I planned to go. But when he called and cancelled, I—"

"He?" Sam interrupted.

"*Sí.* We—"

"A boyfriend?" he demanded, his voice low; he ignored the voice inside him that mocked his determination to observe the lines he'd drawn between them.

"No. A classmate. But he cancelled, and we did not go. So I decided to surprise the boys with an Easter egg hunt. They are rarely allowed such things, but sometimes I would sneak around the rules and do it anyway. They are just *children.* They need happiness."

No apology, her eyes flashing.

"When I arrived," she said, "I discovered Benjamin had gone to attend Mass with his father. I thought the house was empty but for Ivan, who was walking the grounds."

Fear. Just a flicker spearing through her rage. "Ivan?"

"Ivan the Terrible. He is Mr. Cruz's head of security. He is...a very bad man. A very *dangerous* man." Lucia's gaze met Sam's. "He will be the one who comes for me. You must not try to stop him; he will kill you."

Sam stared at her for a long, silent moment. *Ivan the Terrible.* Words that wavered, her fear a cold echo that chilled him. But Sam wasn't afraid of anyone, and her certainty that Ivan the Asshole would be the victor in any battle between them was a fucking insult. "Are you suggesting I let him have you?"

"I will deal with Ivan."

Sam fought the urge to lift her up and shake her. "What the fuck does that mean?"

"Saving the boys is your priority. I am not."

Fury bled into his veins; *did she really think he would let her take on one of Cruz's personal assholes by herself?* But the answer was clear. She stared up at him, determined, unflinching, and Sam understood then she'd already made the decision.

Accepted what she believed to be inevitable.

Not on my goddamn watch.

"When Ivan comes," she said softly. "You will understand."

Sam's rage pulsed in his blood, and he fought the need

to unleash the darkness he held in such careful check. Did she think he was spineless? A coward? Someone who would rather run than *fight? Someone who would trade her life for his own?*

"Benjamin was with his father that night," she went on, her voice tight, her eyes flitting from his, and Sam drew a deep breath and made himself listen. They could go back to her decision to martyr herself. *Later.* "But Alexander was home. I found him upstairs, in the bath." She paused and swallowed, and Sam could see her gathering herself, and his own spine went taut with tension. "He did not hear me come in. He lay in the tub, curled into a ball. Normally, I would have left him alone. He is ten; he needs his privacy. But there was something about the way he held himself...and then I saw the bruises. Dark, angry purple spots on his hip and buttocks, as if someone had held him in place. I did not understand. Not until I saw the water and realized it was pink. Pink from blood."

Sam stilled. His brain thrust forward, filling her silence with any number of horrified conclusions, and he ground his teeth and clenched his fists and locked himself into place. *Just wait. Just fucking listen.*

Even though he knew what was coming.

"I could see no open wounds," she whispered. "No cuts or scratches, nothing that would bleed so much that it would turn the water pink. And he was weeping. I had worked for Donavon Cruz for eight months, and I had never seen Alexander cry. Not even when he broke his arm while playing on Benjamin's skateboard." Her gaze again met his, angry and ashamed. "I did not want to understand, Sam. In that, I am no different than Tony, and I have even less excuse. I had forgotten, and I did not want to remember." A tear streaked her cheek, and she wiped it away impatiently. "But when I went to Alexander, the look in his eyes… I have seen that look before, too many times. Once you have seen it, it is always recognizable, always the same. Even in a stranger. Fractured and hopeless and…rage is too pale a word. To see that in him…to see the blood, his injuries, what his father had done to him… Donavon Cruz had brutally sodomized his child, and it was not the first time."

Sam stared down at her, his guts churning, his lungs tight. Her rage was palpable, stirring his own, and he remembered the boy's terror, his feral defensiveness, his desperation. *You promised you wouldn't give up.* And he wanted to tear Donavon Cruz into tiny, bite-sized pieces.

In the silence, the fire crackled and popped; thunder rumbled. Somewhere far off, an owl hooted.

"Did Alexander tell you that?" Sam asked then, because he had to.

"I know rape when I see it," she replied coldly.

"And you're sure it was his father?" he pressed, the lawman in him forcing the issue.

"Yes," she snarled.

"Why?"

"*Because Alexander told me,*" she hissed. "He did not mean to, and once he realized he had admitted it, he was horrified. He begged me not to tell." An ugly smile twisted her mouth. "He is ashamed. He believes he has done something to invite his father's twisted perversions. He believes it is *his* fault."

"Fucking Christ," Sam muttered.

"Yes. I have told him otherwise. I have shared with him the stories of others…but none of it makes any difference. He has accepted responsibility, and nothing will sway him."

"So you asked for help."

"Yes. *In vain.*" Her gaze met his, sharp enough to cut. "I wanted to kill them all."

Again, her fury resonated. Sam set his jaw. "So you decided to run?"

"No. I wanted to, but Alexander would not agree to leave, and I would not take them against his will."

But here they were, so something had changed. *Something had happened.*

"What?" Sam demanded softly. "What happened to make him change his mind?"

Her eyes closed, and another tear escaped. She gulped in a breath, like she had when the old man died, then another. A fine tremor shook her, and Sam found himself tucking a strand of her hair behind her ear; a small act, meaningless, comfort he shouldn't have sought to give. An act that escaped the bounds of his control, and he didn't care.

"Lucia," he murmured when she didn't speak.

Her thick lashes lifted; her eyes met his, dark, churning, and he almost touched her again.

"Last night," she replied, her voice uneven, "I found Alexander hiding in his bedroom closet. He was naked, and he was bleeding. There was a knife from the kitchen in his hand, and he was trying to cut his wrist. I only happened upon him by accident. I had forgotten one of my textbooks in his room." She paused. "I almost put them both in the car and drove away right then. But I made myself wait. Ivan was walking the house, and I knew he would stop me."

Ivan the Terrible. Her fear resonated between them.

"He's flesh and blood," Sam told her flatly. "A man. He will bleed when I cut him."

Her gaze met his, and Sam could see her doubt. It fucking infuriated him. *Not the time.* But it would come.

"I snuck them out through the servant's quarters when Ivan was in the garden," she said, her voice hushed. "I should not have. I should have waited and done it *right*. I know this. But I just…snapped."

"And Alexander agreed?"

"*Sí*. Because of Ben."

Sam's rage throbbed. "He's afraid for his brother."

"Yes."

"That's why you didn't have a plan," he surmised darkly. "The piece of shit car, the lack of preparedness. Little fucking Debbie for dinner."

"Yes. I panicked."

He shook his head. "What a shitshow."

"Yes," Lucia said again, shooting him an annoyed glance. "I freely admit it was thoughtless and stupid. I was running on fear. On rage. I was rash and foolish; believe me, I regret running without a plan." Her chin lifted. "But I would do it again. No matter the consequences."

"You let me handle the consequences," Sam told her.

"You do not understand. Ivan will come for me, and I am prepared for that. You must be prepared, as well."

"Oh, I'll be prepared."

Her gaze narrowed. "I told you: I will deal with Ivan. You will take the boys to safety."

Anger slid through him. "That's a fucking insult, sweetheart."

"I do not mean for it to be."

He leaned closer, until he was just a heartbeat away, and he could see the shards of brilliant green spearing her iris. Her heat beckoned, and her scent flooded his pores, and the need to touch her was a drumbeat in his blood. *Foolish and impossible.* But he wasn't listening to that voice anymore. He was too damned mad. Her mouth trembled as she stared at him, but she held his furious gaze. *Decided.* She had decided everything, *accepted it*, and she would not allow him to help her. To give her hope. The realization infuriated him.

"No one is going to *touch* you," he promised, his tone raw. "No one but me."

Her gaze widened; the pulse in her throat beat like wings. She swallowed.

"You have a plan?" she asked unsteadily, her doubt plain. *Painful.*

But she would learn. *Him.* She would learn him, and she would accept his fucking hope, and *she would not die on the altar she'd built.*

He would make certain.

"Sam?" she whispered.

And he smiled, a beautiful, terrible thing. "Sweetheart, I always have a plan."

CHAPTER 17

"Your twenty-fours hours were up seventeen minutes ago. Where are my children?"

Donavon Cruz was tall and well-built, with a sweep of golden hair threaded by streaks of platinum, and gleaming, pale green eyes. Good looking, but not too good looking, a tiny imperfection negated by the vibrant charisma that shrouded him. He wore a custom-tailored, twenty-thousand dollar western suit, a bolo crowned by a piece of rich jade, and a pair of M.L. Leddy hand-made alligator skin cowboy boots. An aura of genteel wealth cloaked him, accentuated by the faint, deeply southern accent which shaped his words.

He didn't look like a pedophile, Tony thought. But then, few of them did. Shiny did not equal virtue.

"We have a report on the car—it's in Idaho, along USI84—but we haven't been able to confirm its exact location, not yet, but we're working on it." Agent Kent's words were strung together like a kid trying to get out of trouble. "Getting to the site has proven problematical due to the storm that tore through the area—this storm, it's a once in a lifetime event, something we couldn't possibly have accounted for—and getting boots on the ground is our first priority, but right now FEMA—"

"You're babbling, Agent Kent," Cruz said. "Get to the point."

Kent twisted his hands together behind his back. "We have people on stand-by, but many of the roads are completely impassible. The FAA has closed the airspace in the immediate area to everything but emergency transports. Bridges are down, and even with four-wheel drive, we're forced to wait it out until the Guard can get there and set up something temporary. The storm isn't over—currently it covers almost seven western states—and the forecasters predict at least three more days of hurricane force winds, torrential downpour and widespread lightning—that, in addition to the FEMA evacuation order, makes it difficult to—"

"I have no interest in your excuses. I want my sons. Where are they?"

"We aren't...certain. We believe they're close to the location where the car was spotted, but until we can get to the car to ascertain if it *is* the vehicle Miss Sanchez used—"

"You have nothing."

Color turned Kent's cheeks bright, rosy red. "We have a sighting of the car," he said stiffly.

Cruz's brows rose. "A sighting of the car? Really?"

"Yes, sir. Really."

A moment of silence punctuated that statement. The clock on the wall ticked loudly; beside Tony, Isabel stood motionless, staring at Donavon Cruz. She watched him with unblinking focus, as though she considered him both predator and prey. Clearly, she did not share Agent Kent's anxious need to placate Mr. Cruz. But that wasn't really a surprise. Tony had a feeling Isabel never gave anyone a free pass.

Standing against the opposite wall, Bob Peabody took in the scene with his typical bland countenance, jelly donut in hand. Rain spat against the window beside him. Neither Tony's lieutenant nor Isabel's boss, Special Agent in Charge, Lawrence Gill, were in attendance at this impromptu meeting. But then, no one had anticipated Donavon Cruz suddenly appearing and demanding an update. That he was there at all was an oddity Tony was still trying to understand. All Cruz had to do was make a phone call. Why come in person?

"And what of an accomplice?" Cruz drawled.

Kent looked startled. "We believe Miss Sanchez is alone. We have no knowledge of an accomplice or—"

"You have no knowledge of anything," Cruz said coldly. "You're not even certain it's her vehicle you've found."

"Well...not for certain, no."

"Then tell me, Agent Kent, what use are you?"

Something sharp flitted across the young agent's face, then was gone. "I can assure you, Mr. Cruz, we are working diligently—"

"You are wasting my time. Every moment spent making an excuse is another moment Lucia Sanchez spends assaulting my children."

"Assaulting your children," Isabel repeated, stirring. "Can you be more specific?"

Cruz's gaze slid to her and chilled. "That is a family

matter, Agent Bjorn."

"Child abuse is a criminal matter," she told him quietly. "An accusation we have a legal duty to investigate."

"You cannot even locate my children. Do you really believe I would trust you to investigate something as delicate as an abuse allegation?"

Cruz's tone was cutting. He turned away and dismissed her entirely. Ironic, Tony thought, considering she was his biggest possible ally in this mess.

"Neither your trust nor your permission is required for an investigation, Mr. Cruz." Isabel's tone was colder than Tony had ever heard it. "And I will personally see to it that any and all allegations of abuse are investigated to the fullest extent of the law."

Donavon Cruz turned back to her, his features hard and lined, his eyes flat. Any semblance of the southern gentleman was gone, the shine stripped away to reveal the ugly, abrasive surface beneath.

"Be careful, Agent Bjorn," he said softly. "I am not a man to threaten."

Isabel took a step toward him, and Tony barely caught her, hooking a finger through one of her belt loops to halt her.

"Settle," he murmured.

She ignored him and stared at Donavon Cruz with unflinching challenge. "Have you received a ransom demand, Mr. Cruz?"

Cruz blinked; his gaze narrowed. He stared at Isabel for a minute, as if trying to work out her train of thought. "Not unless you discovered one in Miss Sanchez's room—which I kindly allowed you to search."

"Ah yes, our search. Of Miss Sanchez's obviously cleaned and cleared room. So helpful of you."

Snark. Tony hadn't known she had it in her.

"Did you find anything interesting?" Cruz asked, equally as snide.

"Nothing we are at liberty to discuss," Isabel replied coolly and smiled.

Cruz's gaze narrowed on her.

"Do you anticipate a ransom?" Kent jumped in

"Yes," Cruz replied. "Of course."

"You believe this is about money?" Isabel clarified, pulling against Tony's hold.

A flicker in Cruz's eyes, and then nothing. "Obviously."

"And the abuse you've asserted…is it physical?" Isabel leaned toward him, her head tilted. "Is it sexual?"

Faint color flushed Cruz's face. He took a step toward Isabel, and Tony took a step as well, fully recognizing the threat Cruz made no effort to hide. Adrenaline shot through him like a geyser.

"The children are our only priority at the moment," Kent put in hurriedly, as if he scented blood, "and we're doing everything in our power to locate them and bring them home safely. Unfortunately, right now, all we can do is wait."

Cruz said nothing, staring at Isabel. She stared back. Trapped in Tony's hold, a fine tremor shook her, but he didn't think it was fear. He had the feeling she wanted to go for Donavon Cruz's throat.

He approved, but his hold tightened anyway. Now was

not the time. They didn't have what they needed.

"Either you find them," Cruz bit out softly, "or I will."

Kent blinked. "You should really leave Miss Sanchez's apprehension to the professionals," he said.

An ugly smile turned Cruz's mouth. "Professionals?" he repeated. "Is that what you call yourselves?"

Another blink.

"If you do not find my children and deliver them to me," Cruz continued matter-of-factly, "I will have you stripped of your badges. I will personally blacklist each and every one of you and see to it that no law enforcement or security agency in the world will hire you. Any career you might have had will be nothing more than a bitter memory. Make no mistake, I will *erase* you."

Kent's features went taut. Bob only arched his brows above another bite of donut. But Isabel...Isabel smiled.

Tony tightened his hold, his heart suddenly beating like a drum.

"I'll be waiting," Cruz said coldly. He turned and walked out, slamming the door behind him.

A harsh breath broke from Kent. "He just threatened us."

"Welcome to the big leagues, kid." Bob took another bite of his breakfast.

"Jesus Christ," Kent said. He looked at Isabel. "We need to get to Idaho."

She shook her head and tugged once more against Tony's hold. He didn't release her.

"Knock it off," she growled over her shoulder.

"Settle," he said again, but grinned. He couldn't help it. "Tiger."

Her gaze narrowed, but before she could respond, Kent was talking.

"Get your stuff," he told her. "We're leaving."

She stiffened. "No."

"Yes," he snapped. "We need to find that fucking car."

Tony's hackles rose at his tone, but Isabel beat him to it.

"I am not your subordinate, Agent Kent." Her tone sliced through the room like a blade; her eyes glinted, polished obsidian. "I was sent here to investigate, not chase a fugitive who has not yet been located. There is no reason for me to run all over Idaho in search of Lucia Sanchez. My time is far better spent trying to discover the motive behind this crime, and Miss Sanchez's intended destination. If I discover either of those things, you will be the first to know. Until then, I will use my time as I see fit, not as you—or Donavan Cruz—dictate."

Kent blinked again. Tony's grin widened. Isabel tore from his hold and grabbed her bag.

"Let's go," she barked at Tony.

He reached for his suit coat. "Where to, boss?"

She glowered at him. "We have an appointment."

"We do?"

"Yes."

Tony followed her and winked at Kent. "Good luck with the car, Boy Wonder."

"Sorry," he added to Bob, who only shrugged.

Isabel was already walking out the door, her stride

aggressive, her mouth set in hard lines. Around the handle of her bag, her knuckles were white.

She was furious.

"He knows," she hissed.

Tony reached out to grab her elbow. "Who knows?"

She jerked from his hold. "Cruz. He fucking knows."

The word "fucking" threw Tony, and he almost stopped. "Knows what?"

She strode out the front door of the station and swung around, unmindful of the light, misting rain that fell.

"He knows where they are," she said, her teeth clenched, her eyes shooting sparks, and Tony's blood went cold. "He knows *exactly*."

"What do you mean?"

"I should have realized it," she muttered. "What an idiot."

Tony gripped her arms and halted her when she would have turned away. "Realized what, goddamn it?"

Isabel's black gaze met his. "He's tracking them."

"What?" Dread sliced through Tony. "How?"

"Microchips."

Tony was lost. "What?"

"I've been around hundreds of parents whose children are missing, Tony. *Hundreds.* Do you know what the common denominator always is? *Fear.* No matter who they are, they are always scared shitless for their kids. *Always.* But Donavon Cruz was far more interested in threatening us—in finding out what *we* knew—than he was in the immediate welfare of those boys. He isn't worried, because he knows—regardless of the claims he's made—that Lucia won't hurt them. And because he knows where they are. Because he's going after them himself."

Tony froze. "How do you know that?"

"GenTek."

"What?"

"GenTek. They developed GPS capable chips several years ago. Cruz is a major shareholder." She shook her head. "I should have made the connection sooner."

"You're sure?"

The look she gave him was cold. "Believe what you will, Detective, but I do this for a living."

"Fuck," Tony said. "Dragovitch."

"Yes."

Tony stared down at her, his blood a vicious roar. He thought of Lucia, of Sam and those boys. Of Ivan Dragovitch. The hellacious storm bearing down upon them all. The contents of his stomach churned.

"Fuck," he said again.

Isabel pulled from his hold and slid her phone from the breast pocket of the steel-gray pantsuit she wore.

"What are you doing?" he demanded, tension like steel along his spine.

"Contacting my CI. Maybe we can lay hands on the chips' ID numbers."

"And track them."

"Yes." Isabel turned away, phone in hand, and Tony pulled his own cell out and dialed Sam.

No answer; par for the goddamn course. Sam's voicemail sounded a moment later: *Speak*.

"Those kids are chipped," Tony said brusquely, adrenaline like electric current in his veins. "You'd better get the hell off the grid. Someone is coming. I'll send you a file."

He turned back around to find Isabel staring at him, her arms crossed, her eyes as cold as the outermost reaches of space.

"Who was that?" she asked quietly.

The rain continued, rolling down her cheeks, soaking the artful twist of her hair. People walked around them; a few feet away traffic roared past. Tony stood trapped in her dark gaze and knew the gig was up.

Time to roll the dice or fold. No more in between. And everything hinged on whether or not Isabel Bjorn was a good bet. But instinct told him that without her, he was going to get nowhere fast.

"We need to talk," he said.

CHAPTER 18

Those kids are chipped. You'd better get the hell off the grid. Someone is coming. I'll send you a file.

Sam was going to stop checking his goddamn phone. Because the weather report for the foreseeable future wasn't bad enough—gale force winds, torrential rainfall, hail the size of golf balls—no, there just had to be another message from Tony warning of a falling sky.

When Sam opened the file and scanned its contents, the unease that had dogged him since yesterday—when he understood that walking away was no longer an option—turned to cold lead in his belly. *Ivan The Terrible.* A brutal, ruthless man, with a trail of death behind him, and whose dark, opaque eyes hinted at hell. His history was bloody and violent, and his gaze promised more.

When Ivan comes, you will understand.

He would chase her to the ends of the earth, and then, when he found her, he would punish her.

And he would glory in her pain.

Sam could look at him and know it.

Ivan will come for me, and I am prepared for that. You must be prepared, as well.

Jesus Christ, she thought Sam would let that fucking *be*?

"Goddamn it," he snarled.

The calm acceptance in her enraged him. She fully expected Sam to allow her to take on Ivan the Asshole by herself. While he *ran away* with the boys. While he *fled*.

Sam could hardly wrap his brain around it. That she would put herself in front of all of them was insanity—not really a surprise, not now that he was starting to know her—but that she expected him to *allow* it...that was another matter entirely.

Not fucking happening, sweetheart.

No way was he letting Lucia go kamikaze, with Ivan or without. That she didn't seem to think he was capable of keeping her safe—that she believed he would agree to let her simply take on the son of a bitch—was the worst of insults.

I do not mean for it to be.

No, she hadn't. She didn't expect anyone to fall on a sword for her—him least of all. But those boys...that was a different matter. She'd wanted a promise from him to put them first; they were her priority. Sam understood, but he didn't agree. He wasn't going to fucking trade her for them. He wasn't going to forfeit anyone, and she was going to have to understand that.

Understand him. Like he was beginning to understand her.

He got it now. Her rage, her rebellion, her desperation. The crime that had been done to Alexander was one of the worst; a transgression no amount of justice could rectify.

There was no equitable retribution for such an act, nothing that could rebuild all that had been destroyed. Alexander would do battle with what had been done to him every moment of every day for the rest of his life. It would affect every aspect of his existence; there would be no escape. A hellish punishment for a crime he didn't commit.

Sam had seen his share of abused children. One could not travel the world and go into the places he had been and not see them: chattel, property, goods to be bartered and sold. Sickening and infuriating; he wondered at the soul of the world, that such a thing could be so commonplace everywhere he went. But what was the difference? Perhaps Cruz's crime was worse: a violation of his own child, a sin so great it was incomprehensible. An offense so vile even death was too easy a price.

Sam's pop had used him as a punching bag on a regular basis; he'd broken bones, teeth, Sam's nose, and nearly blinded him with an old army knife. He'd touched him with violence, but never with *that* kind of intent. It was a jarring realization, Sam thought, to understand that for all the blood and pain and tears he'd suffered, there was worse out there. That he'd been fucking *lucky*.

Lucky. A word seven-year-old him would have spat upon.

Life was fucked up.

The dangerous, simmering fury he saw in Alexander made sense now. The boy's aversion to touch, his mistrust, his desperation, so thick and rank it could choke a man. Ten goddamn years old, trying to save himself.

Sam was a grown man. He knew the savage cost of

physical abuse; he knew the horrors of war; he knew the scent and taste of death. But he couldn't wrap his head around the terror Alexander Cruz was experiencing. Such a heavy burden; that the weight hadn't crushed him was a fucking miracle.

But no more. No. Magnus had been right: Sam *was* strong on the inside. And no matter how shitty he felt about a whole hell of a lot of other things, on this he was crystal clear: he was needed. *The guy.* And when he thought about the walking atrocity that was Donavon Cruz, he was glad.

Hang him from his fucking guts and strip him with a dull blade, inch by inch. It would make the picture Alexander had drawn look like goddamn Walt Disney.

"Are we leaving?"

As if conjured by Sam's thoughts, Alexander stood next to him suddenly, the cool sheen in his gaze underscored by anxiety. Fear. He was damned good at hiding it; the kid had more self-control than many of the men Sam had known. But his terror was ever-present, a living, hungry thing that only continued to grow, and the more Sam learned the kid, the clearer it became.

"Yes," Sam told him. "The water's rising. We need to get to higher ground. Wake Ben and Lucia, and walk Daisy. We need to head out soon."

No argument, no derision, not even a question. Alexander simply turned and headed toward the tent.

Well. At least something about today would be easier.

Sam took down the pack of food they'd hung the night before and stored it in the four-wheeler, along with the extra water he'd brought, and a five gallon container of fuel, both of which he'd retrieved just after dawn from the three-wheeler he'd driven in on the night before. His sleeping bag was back in his pack, which he also found a home for in the small black box on the back of the ATV. They'd lucked out, it was a hell of a nice little rig, plenty of room for both them and their gear, fairly fuel efficient and able to handle the terrain—so long as it didn't turn into a swamp.

As if in answer to that observation, thunder rumbled overhead, and Sam felt the throbbing begin in his skull. He'd patched up his leg, and it would do, but it hurt. His belly was empty again, the hotdogs and nutty bar he'd eaten next to the fire last night long gone. But there would be no fire this morning, no breakfast to linger over.

They needed to move. Not only was the water rising—on the heels of another round of storms—his phone still had service, and they needed to get out of range, fast. As soon as he lost a signal, he would feel better, and even then they would keep going. Sam knew men like Ivan. Neither the weather nor the terrain would stop him. They were hunted now.

It was time to start acting like it.

Ben crawled from the tent. Daisy bounded past him, yipping excitedly. Alexander scooped her up and tied the short length of rope Sam had managed to find around her neck; she licked him, and Sam swore the kid almost smiled. Lucia followed, blinking, her hair a thick, curling mass around her shoulders, her skin flushed from sleep. She halted in the open screen of the tent and yawned hugely.

Sam watched her stretch and remembered how lush she'd felt pressed against him, the scent she carried in the curve of her neck. How she'd shivered when he touched her.

So fucking close. But not close enough.

Christ.

He made himself turn away and continued to break camp, burying the hole he'd dug for their fire, tossing the stumps they'd used as seats back into the undergrowth. By the time he approached Lucia, all that was left was the tent.

"We need to go," he told her shortly. "Get packed up."

"Good morning to you, too," she replied in a disgruntled tone.

"Do it quick."

She froze. "Why? Has something happened?"

"Just do it," he said and walked away. He would tell her about Tony's message, but not until they were out of satellite range.

He moved the three-wheeler back behind a large bolder and covered it with pine boughs. By the time he returned from that, Lucia had the tent down and stowed away, along with their packs. She eyed him with a dark look, but said nothing.

Sam went through and kicked at the grass where the tent had been, disturbing it. He covered the hole where the fire had been with dead logs and leaves. He did his best to mask the few foot and ATV trails they'd made, but he knew it wouldn't be enough. He would have spotted it a mile away.

"It looks like we were never here," Alexander said, looking around.

"Not to a professional," Sam said. "Let's go."

The boys climbed into the ATV, Daisy in tow. Lucia followed, settling into the seat next to Sam. She waited until he'd started the four-wheeler to ask, "Why are we in a hurry?"

"Why aren't we?" Tension rode him hard; his gaze flickered to the small rearview mirror. Alexander stared at him, and Sam could see his trepidation. The kid knew something was up, but for once, he held his tongue.

"What's happened?" Lucia demanded and looked over her shoulder. "Did you see someone?"

"No." Sam hit the gas, and they lurched forward. The trails were heavily rocked, which was good, because the ground was so wet, the path was little more than mud. They would leave one hell of a trail, at least until the rain came.

He maneuvered up and over the swell of the land, dotted by huge granite boulders, lined by rows of tall, old growth pine. The foothills shimmered in the distance, and he wondered how long they would be able to stick to the trails before they had to go off-road. Because they were going to have to abandon the groomed track they followed now; eventually, they were going to have to just drive into the wilderness and go as far as they could.

"He goes a lot faster than you did," Alexander observed from the backseat.

Lucia lifted her chin. "I am a *safe* driver."

"Like a herd of turtles," Alexander replied, and Ben giggled.

"Hardy-har-har," she told them. She dug into her pack, pulled out two apples and two oatmeal pies and handed them to Alexander. "Here. Eat your breakfast."

"I'm not hungry," he said with another glance at Sam in the mirror.

"You should eat," Sam told him.

The boy sighed and reluctantly accepted the food.

Lucia scowled at Sam. "What did you do?"

Sam looked at her. "What are you talking about?"

Her gaze narrowed, shimmering amber in the pale morning light. "With what did you bribe him?"

"Safety," Alexander said.

Sam glanced at him in the mirror, and Alexander stared back. Balls. The kid had them by the truckload.

"Safety," Lucia echoed and turned in her seat to stare at the boy.

"You aren't enough," Alexander told her, and Sam watched a flurry of emotion cross her features: pain, anger, resignation. "He can keep us safe."

"So you traded up?" she asked.

The boy only took a bite of his pie and stared at her.

Ben watched the byplay, nibbling at his own pie. He reached out and patted Lucia's arm. "Don't worry, Lu. I'm going to keep you."

She tried to smile. "Thank you, monkey."

Annoyance crept over Sam. He understood why Alexander was the way he was, but that was an explanation—not an excuse.

"Not enough," he repeated and pinned Alexander with his gaze. "And just where do you suppose you'd be without her?"

Sam felt Lucia eye him, but he didn't look at her. He only watched Alexander and waited. Christ, he felt like Magnus, pushing the same buttons his uncle had always had a finger on.

Full fucking circle. That was life.

Alexander said nothing. To his credit, he didn't look away, but he certainly didn't have an answer.

"That's what I thought," Sam continued. "She got you out. She got you *here.* You owe her. And if you can't be man enough to say thank you, at least be enough of one to keep your mouth shut."

Alexander blinked. Sam turned his gaze ahead and concentrated on the trail, which was beginning to narrow as they climbed higher into the mountains. The rig handled well, considering the number of passengers and gear they carried, but then it should. Damned thing cost as much as a car.

"I didn't mean I wasn't grateful," Alexander said stiffly after a moment.

Lucia turned again and looked at him. "I know, *mijo.*"

Sam knew the boy was looking at him, but he just kept driving. The kid needed to stew in his own crap for a while and think about someone other than himself. Lucia hadn't just broken the law with this insane getaway—she'd marked herself for death. She deserved some goddamn credit for that.

Silence fell. They made their way deeper into the wilderness, and above them, the skies once again grew dark. Thunder boomed in the distance; lightning speared across the churning, thick roll of blue-black clouds in delicate, white-hot veins. The trees around them swayed, and pine cones fell like confetti.

Sam kept one eye on the clouds, the other on the trail.

He watched for any sign of someone following them, and checked the sky for aircraft. He tried to ignore the warmth and scent of Lucia beside him and the closed expression on her face. He didn't like that expression; all of her fire shuttered behind a wall of impassive control. It made him want to shake her.

To push, until that fire burst into flame and burned them both.

He should have never laid hands on her. *So fucking stupid.* Weak. So today he wouldn't touch. Today he would do what he'd promised: he would protect them. No matter the temptation that beckoned or the awareness that pulsed between them, immune to the realities they faced: Donavon Cruz, the coming storm, the small army of men who were undoubtedly chasing them.

Because he wanted her, and that want lit a fire in his belly and whispered in his ears and prickled his skin with awareness and heat.

Hunger. Vibrant and powerful, something he hadn't felt…ever. And something he had no choice but to ignore.

Damned if you do, and damned if you don't.

The fucking story of his life.

CHAPTER 19

Hail fell, so thick and dense it looked like fresh snowfall.

Lucia stole a glance at Sam, whose jaw seemed carved from stone. He'd been terse all day, his tension rising until it was a force that pressed against her skin with suffocating presence. He was hyper-vigilant, his gaze never halting in any one place too long. Before them, behind them; in the sky, through the trees.

He'd grown quiet and curt; he was watching for someone.

His vigilance was cold and relentless and foreboding, and it scared the hell out of her. A part of him she'd not seen, one which hinted at a darkness that both reassured and frightened her. She was seeing the truth of him, the core of the man who'd wrapped himself around them in the center of the storm and held them together. He was not just law enforcement, she was certain. He was...*more.*

Tony's friend. Tony, who she knew had once been an Army Ranger. Was that how they knew one another? Were they fellow soldiers?

Warriors. An apt description for the man who sat next

to her, grim and determined, who hadn't batted an eye at deliberately putting himself in front of them. Who issued orders like a drill sergeant and expected them to be followed. And who'd managed to convince Alexander—the most untrusting person she'd ever known—to believe in him, if only temporarily.

For safety's sake.

It hurt, but Lucia understood. Because in spite of how volatile Sam made her feel, she believed he would do everything in his power to keep the boys safe. She could hardly blame Alexander for recognizing and utilizing that fact, because if it had been possible for her to barter for that guarantee, she would have done so as well. But for her, safety was relative, and fleeting at best. Because Ivan was coming.

Ivan.

She'd pushed him into the furthermost corners of her consciousness; she hadn't wanted to think about him, so she didn't. Even though she knew he would be the one to come for her—for the children—and even though she understood only one of them would come out of any confrontation alive.

Because Donavon Cruz's right hand man was a cruel, giant brute of a man who'd spent the last nine months watching her with a hungry, dissolute expression that made her skin crawl. *A monster.* One her primal brain recognized at the deepest level, an apex predator who saw her as nothing but prey. Only her position in the Cruz household had prevented him from hunting.

Now there was nothing to stay him. He would come. *And he would enjoy it.*

Part of her had been waiting since the moment they'd fled. Preparing, planning, steeling herself, because there was no choice in what must be done. From the moment she'd taken the boys, Lucia had understood she would have to deal with Ivan—even if she hadn't let herself think about it. No matter how far they made it, she knew he would continue to hunt them until they were found, so if they truly wanted to be free, Ivan had to go.

Her responsibility—even if Sam disagreed. Because Lucia wouldn't allow him to interfere in this; as she'd told him, she would deal with Ivan. So long as Sam had enough time to flee with the children, that was all that mattered. She hadn't wanted Sam involved, but if he was determined to help, then that would be his mission. And Lucia knew he would refuse to leave her—she was going to have to make that happen, somehow, because he was not a man to abandon a fight, too stubborn by half—but he'd promised he would protect the children, and she was going to hold him to that vow. Ben and Alexander were her only concern; what became of her no longer mattered. She'd given up that control the moment she'd taken them. There was no do-over now.

What a shitshow.

A sentiment with which she could only agree. Lucia knew she'd messed up. *A mountain of stupid.* Because if she'd done things properly, they wouldn't be stuck in the middle of the wilderness, wholly reliant on the man beside her. She could have laid a false trail—or two—and had an actual plan instead of simply taking off down crazy lane. It was *stupid*, what she'd done, and the boys would pay a far greater price than she. If she were honest, she might admit she was grateful to Tony for sending Sam. His presence was a gift she'd not expected.

But she did not want to reflect on what that meant. She'd become very used to hating Tony, and while her animosity had been born at a time when chaos was the only constant and was not, she knew, entirely reasonable, that hate had become her companion over the years, one she had no wish to abandon.

It was so much easier to blame *him* instead of herself.

"Can you use that little pea-shooter you're carrying?" Sam asked abruptly, his voice low.

Lucia stiffened, wondering how he knew she was armed. But then, she *had* threatened to shoot him... "*Sí.*"

"Good."

She turned to look at him, aware of Alexander listening. Ben was asleep, his head hanging low, Daisy snoring in his lap. When they'd stopped to pee a few hours ago, it had been Sam's hand Ben reached for, something she was still grappling with.

You're not enough.

Something Ben obviously knew, too. And in spite of Sam's defense—which had surprised her—Alexander was right. She *wasn't* enough. She wasn't sure an army would be enough. *You owe her,* Sam had said, but they didn't; they never would. And she wasn't sure how she felt about Sam coming to her defense. Because while she would rely on him to take care of the boys, she did not want him trying to take care of *her*.

She could take care of herself.

"Why is that good?" she asked.

But Sam only shook his head, his gaze shifting to the rearview mirror. Annoyed, Lucia reached over and poked him in the arm. Her finger met with muscle as taut as steel. When he glanced at her, she repeated, "Why?"

"Later," he said shortly with a meaningful look at Ben.

Secrets.

A thought that made her angry. Bad enough he was tense as a strung bow, not even softening for the boys. Worse was what he knew that he hadn't shared. Lucia did not appreciate secrets; she still hadn't forgiven him for lying to her. Regardless of how protective he was being, she would not stand for any more surprises. And he was the kind of man who would shield her from anything he thought she didn't need to know, something he would have to learn different. Because she was not putting up with lies.

Tony, she thought. No doubt they were in touch. What had Sam learned?

The ATV slid a little along the wet trail, and Sam swore softly. His tension ratcheted up a notch, and the fine hair at Lucia's nape bristled in reaction. It was like sitting next to a snake poised to strike, body coiled in wait, tail rattling. Her nerves were screaming in protest. Her butt hurt, she ached all over from the jostling ride, and she was hungry enough to eat a small farm animal. She wanted to suggest they stop, but she knew Sam would only growl at her, and if he began to growl, she was going to snarl back.

Because last night she'd given him the truth. And perhaps she shouldn't have expected anything from him in return, but *she did.* Understanding, if nothing else. Instead, he'd built a wall between them. It was yet another betrayal—no matter that he was little more than a stranger—and she felt the blow acutely. Added to her physical discomfort, her worry for the boys, and the continual rise of tension within the small vehicle, it was more than enough to spark her temper.

Which would get her nowhere. She *knew* that. Trouble was the only thing that would come of losing her head. *Always.*

"Look. A house." Alexander's slender arm suddenly speared through the space between them. "There, in the trees."

The ATV rocked to a halt. Sam stared up at the small wooden structure—far more a shack than a house—his gaze narrowing. Thunder chose that moment to boom overhead, and Ben woke with a sharp cry.

"Easy, monkey," Lucia murmured, leaning around her seat to smooth his hair. "It is only thunder, nothing to scare you."

"Thunder sucks," Ben said and began to cry.

Lucia clucked softly. Poor little peanut. He was exhausted, hungry and terrified. She knew the feeling.

"We should stop," she told Sam. "They need a break."

"It's not safe," he replied shortly.

"It will never be safe."

His gaze met hers, hard, glittering, no hint of warmth. It only made her angrier. He'd extended his hand, and she had—reluctantly—taken it. And now he was pushing her away with that same hand. Pushing her, which was not a good idea. Because although she was—normally—a calm, level-headed and logical woman, when her ire was raised, she became the hot-headed Latina her grandmother had celebrated and her mother lamented.

Had he not already learned this?

"Fine," he muttered. "Weather's shit, anyway."

Lucia's hands curled into fists.

"Just one night," he continued and shot her a dark look. "You'd better hope we don't regret it."

She ground her teeth, aware of Ben crying softly, and Alexander murmuring to him.

They followed the trail until they came to two worn tracks, overgrown and rutted, which led up to the cabin. Sam turned onto the make-shift drive and pulled up behind the gray, weathered building. Another small shed and an outhouse sat behind the cabin, but there were no vehicles, and it was apparent from the thick overgrowth that no one had been there in a long, long time.

Some of the tension in Lucia's spine eased. And then Sam said, "Get the boys inside, and be quick about it. We need to stay quiet and out of sight. Make sure they know."

She only blinked at him.

"Go," he said sharply. "Now."

Uno. Dos. Tres. Cuatro—

"Move," he ordered.

Lucia was not a violent person. When she lost her temper, she put on a grand display, but she was not given to physical assault. She could fight because there'd been no choice but to learn. But damned if she didn't *really* want to punch the man beside her in the face. Just one good hit, dead on. It was easy to picture: his head snapping back, the look of incredulity, blood leaking down his chin from his broken nose.

Some people imagined mountain meadows and the graceful sweep of the ocean to sooth the beast. She imagined blood.

"I gotta poop," Ben announced with a hiccup.

Lucia sighed. Beside her, Sam scowled, and Alexander muttered, "Thanks for the update."

She climbed from the ATV, her limbs stiff, her joints aching. The hail had turned to a soft, cold, misting rain that seemed to be ebbing. Thunder rolled away. She pulled open the back door and helped Ben climb out.

"Take him," she told Alexander and shoved the roll of toilet paper—*another* gift from Sam—into his hands. "Stay close. And take the shovel to bury it."

Pale green eyes shimmered at her. "You take him."

But Lucia had no patience left for his rebellion. It was gone, bled away by the intractable nature of the man who was now unloading their supplies. A man she had a few words for.

"Go," she ordered, her voice hard. "Stay close."

Alexander blinked. Scowled. And swiped the toilet paper from her hand with an unhappy glare. She waited until they were walking away, toward the outhouse, which they inspected and then abandoned. When they'd disappeared, she turned to Sam, who was unpacking their gear, his face cast in stone.

"If you used that tone more often," he said, "the kid might actually listen."

Fire licked at her veins. She stepped next to him, her heart a violent drumbeat in her chest, blood a faint roar in her ears.

"You," she told him, struggling for calm, "are worse than a menstruating woman."

He stopped what he was doing and turned, very slowly, to look at her. "What did you just say?"

"You heard me," she hissed softly. "You snarl and snap and order us around as if we are a herd of *cattle*. You lie, you keep secrets, and you demand trust when you give *none* back. I have had it with your moodiness and your militant attitude, and if you do not have it in you to be a decent and respectful human being to me, you *will* be a decent and respectful human being to them, or so help me, I will make you regret ever laying eyes on us." He only stared at her, unmoved, his face that cold mask she was beginning to hate, and, unable to help herself, Lucia reached out, gripped his t-shirt and gave him a good shake. *For all the good it would do.* "Do we understand each other, *cabrón*?"

He was utterly still in her hold, watching her. Rain coursed his lean cheeks. "Goddamn you."

"What does that even mean?" she demanded.

Hard, strong hands suddenly captured her hips. Squeezed. Her knees went weak, and her breath went tight. Sam was looking at her mouth, his eyes glinting in the pale light, and alarm shot through her. The hands holding her yanked her toward him, even as she pushed at the hard wall of his chest.

"Sam..."

"You did this," he growled softly. "You remember that."

And then his mouth was on hers. Hot, wild, angry. Her heart shuddered; her blood burned in her veins. He pushed his tongue into her mouth, a carnal stroke that she felt in the hollow between her thighs, and rubbed it against hers. Electricity arced through her; a fork to her breasts, her belly, a spasm in her womb. He nipped her, licked her, sucked her tongue into his mouth and devoured her as though she were the most succulent of treats. His beard rasped against her skin, and Lucia moaned beneath the onslaught. She slid her hands into his silky golden hair, and unable to resist, kissed him back.

Everything else winked out, gone, *nothing,* and the intensity of him slapped against her like a wave breaking. One in which she wanted to drown.

He made a deep, rough sound, and the rumble of it made her nipples peak against the hard wall of his chest, and Lucia clenched her hands in his hair and rubbed against him—*so hard and hot, no matter how grumpy, he* was *magnificent*—

"Bear!" Alexander's scream tore between them like a bomb blast.

In a heartbeat, Sam was thrusting her aside and running around her, headed toward the sound. Lucia followed, stumbling a little, the heat that had flooded her only a moment before turning instantly to ice. Sam ran into the thick stand of trees where the boys had disappeared and halted so suddenly Lucia slid atop the wet grass and crashed into him and almost went down. He caught her with a hard arm around her waist and hauled her against him, looking around. A small hill sloped down from the outhouse; at its base Alexander stood in front of Ben and a growling Daisy. Less than ten feet away, a black bear stood motionless in the softly falling rain, surveying them.

Lucia's heart nearly burst through her chest. She took a step only to have Sam wrench her back with a growling, "*No.*"

It was instinctive to fight, but he tightened his hold, his arm clamping her to him in an unbending hold, and Lucia realized for the first time how strong he truly was.

"Don't run," he said in a low voice, loud enough to carry, but not loud enough to startle the bear.

"Why not?" Alexander demanded.

"Because then it will chase you. Stay there. I'm coming." Sam pressed his mouth to Lucia's ear, his voice deep and rough. "Work your way toward them, and get them safe. I'll distract our furry friend."

Somehow her fingers had wrapped themselves around the thick cord of his forearm, and with his words, they dug deep. Because he might be tough and smart and brave but that was a *bear*. "Can't we just shoot at it? Scare it away?"

"And announce our presence?" His breath washed over

her, and goose bumps pebbled her skin. "No."

Her grip on him tightened unwillingly. "But—"

A sharp nip on her earlobe, making her start. "Trust me, sweetheart."

And then he walked away, whistling loudly. He threaded through the trees, turned, and disappeared from sight.

Lucia stared after him, her earlobe stinging, her pulse a dull throb in her head. She turned and went in the opposite direction, circling slowly around to where the boys were crouched. Her knees were weak, and her hands were shaking, and terror sat in her throat, ready to erupt in a blood curdling scream. The rain was thickening, and the boys were pale, trembling, locked in stillness. Daisy growled and yipped and fought to escape Ben's hold.

"Hey, Yogi!" Sam's voice suddenly broke the silence. "Over here, fur-face!"

A small, quivering smile turned Ben's mouth. Alexander only watched, so still he looked like a statue. The bear's large black head swung toward the sound of Sam's voice.

"I'm talking to you, Yogi," Sam yelled. "Come and get me. I dare you!"

Stupid, courageous, idiot man. Lucia watched the bear turn and lumber in the direction of Sam's taunts, both relieved and terrified. Then she scrambled to reach the boys, sweeping Ben and Daisy into her arms, and urging Alexander back up the incline. But the boy fought to move around her, his gaze following the disappearing bruin.

"We can't leave Sam," he protested, which Lucia found

painfully ironic. "He needs help!"

Yes. And as soon as she got the boys into the cabin, she would grab her peashooter—no matter what Sam had said—and go after him. Even if the thought of it made her knees knock together like chattering teeth. She would not abandon Sam; she could not. But the boys came first.

"Move!" she ordered and realized she sounded just like him.

"But..." Alexander tried again to get around her, and Lucia tripped him. He sprawled into the wet grass and glared up at her through the rain, which had turned into a steady downpour.

"That was mean," he muttered.

"Get up," she said, ignoring the guilt that brushed her. Better bruised and safe than bear brunch. "I will go after Sam."

"You promise to save him?" Ben asked, his eyes huge and dark. Tears clung to his thick lashes and he was sucking his thumb. That he wasn't screaming hysterically astounded her and helped to calm her own panic.

She tugged his thumb from his mouth and pressed a kiss to his forehead. "*Sí*, monkey. I promise."

She hurried around the front of the cabin, Alexander on her heels. The door was shut, but not locked, and as they stepped into the dim, gray interior, the musky scent of mildew assaulted her senses. It was a sparse, one room cabin, with a small woodstove in the center. A stained mattress atop a sagging metal frame sat in one corner; a makeshift kitchen with a scratched metal sink and row of pine cupboards along the opposite wall. An old wooden table, two chairs, and a single, cracked window made of leaded glass.

Lucia set Ben and Daisy down on the bed.

"Watch them," she told Alexander.

"Take your gun," he replied, fear shimmering in his pale gaze.

"Please save Sam," Ben pleaded, and a fresh wave of tears slid down his cheeks. "He's my best friend!"

"I will, monkey, do not worry," Lucia said grimly. "That bear will not know what hit him."

But when she turned to leave the cabin, she found Sam standing in the open doorway, watching her. Soaking wet, unharmed, his brilliant gaze glittering with a look she couldn't read.

"Sam!" Ben cried and wiggled from the bed to race across the cabin. He threw himself against Sam's legs. "Are you okay?"

Lucia had been baffled by Ben's immediate, inexplicable trust of Sam ever since she'd first witnessed it, but watching Sam lift Ben into his arms, she suddenly understood. Ben saw with crystal clarity who Sam was. He had none of her fear or prejudices or burden of experience; he had only his gut. And he went with it.

"Right as rain, monkey." Sam ran a hand over Ben's head, a tender, protective motion Lucia didn't expect. "How about you?"

"I'm glad you're okay. Lucia was coming to get you." Ben laid his head against Sam's chest, his small hands curled tightly into Sam's wet shirt. "She was gonna shoot that bear!"

Sam's gaze moved to her; his brows arched. "I told you no."

Which made her want to punch him in the face again. Heat crawled into her cheeks, and his eyes fell to her lips, and suddenly she could feel the rasp of his tongue stroking hers, his fingers pressing into her hips, the hard wall of his chest against her breasts. The vibration of the sound he'd made echoed through her. And she grew damp as she stared at him, *ready,* even though he was three feet away, even though he held Ben, and Alexander stood, watching silently.

As if he was still touching her. Dios mío.

This was so not good.

"I was going to do what was necessary," she replied finally, unwilling to back down.

She was not a *dog.* She did not take commands.

"To save me?"

She saw a flash of humor in his bright gaze and his mouth curved, which she didn't appreciate, but acknowledged was just as alluring as the quiet, competent charisma woven into his skin. Her belly tightened, because he was not a man who smiled often. She did not need to know him well to know that. And it was a beautiful smile, at her expense or not.

"Of course," she told him brazenly. "We will need a fire."

He laughed softly, and need flushed her skin, and *damn the man*, she smiled back.

CHAPTER 20

"Mr. Cruz, he is a *good* man."

Isabel watched Tony struggle to reign himself in. She shouldn't have sensed his anger as strongly as she did—not after only forty-eight hours in the man's presence—but she could almost feel it, like the rasp of a rough tongue against her flesh.

We need to talk, he'd said. And Isabel supposed she should be angry with what he'd disclosed: his history with Lucia and her brother, Elian; the complicated and problematical addition of a U.S. Marshal to the equation (something Isabel was secretly rather glad for, because the idea of Lucia Sanchez and those boys at Ivan Dragovitch's mercy was the stuff of nightmares); and last, though never least, Tony's determination to "*burn Cruz at the fucking stake.*"

The man was furious. He'd alternated between apology and defiance while making his confession, and if nothing else, he'd been sincere. He'd also been very blunt.

"*I'm fucking trusting you, Isabel. Don't make me regret it.*"

Isabel had not yet decided what she would do with the information he'd disclosed. Because, although she *was* a federal agent, and it was her duty to report everything he'd told her, Isabel was also unorthodox in her approach to both information and its disclosure to her superiors. The rule book was all fine and good—there were plenty of agents who needed it—but oftentimes it was simply superfluous. She was perfectly capable of determining what was pertinent and what wasn't; there was no need to muddy the waters with inconsequential data.

Right now, the presence of Sam Steele was not pertinent to her investigation. Nor was Tony's relationship with Lucia or her brother. If she'd believed Lucia had orchestrated the allegations of abuse due to her brother's history, Isabel would have immediately shared the information with her peers. But she did not. The drawing she'd discovered in Alexander Cruz's room, the excessive security at Cruz's remote cabin, his open and derisive manipulation of federal law enforcement—those were all perfectly legitimate, material indicators that necessitated further investigation. Indicators she would utilize to pursue the truth, regardless that she already knew who and what he was.

Monster. She could see it. She could *always* see it.

Still, she needed evidence. Proof beyond a shadow of a doubt. That put her and Tony on the same page.

For now.

"A *very* good man," the woman who sat before them added. "Like a saint!"

Tony's hands fisted, and a rough breath blew from him like a whale surfacing. He was doing everything he could not to shatter the frail old woman he faced. Rosa Sanchez, who'd just returned from Arizona and nearly nine months of breast cancer treatment, who was Donavon Cruz's former nanny and the woman Lucia Sanchez had replaced. Her age was only fifty-three, but she looked a decade older, her illness—or its cure—turning her haggard and faintly yellow. Lines of pain and exhaustion carved her into rawboned hollows, and her dark eyes were sunken and joyless.

She wore a shapeless caftan in pale blue, which matched the scarf wrapped around her head, and her feet were covered in thick black socks. They sat in her son's living room, a small, square room with a love seat, two recliners and a set of TV trays. Her son was at work; her daughter-in-law had gone to pick up the kids from school.

"You never saw any hint of abuse?" Tony asked—growled—and Rosa shook her head. Again.

"No," she insisted. "Never."

But her pulse beat furiously, and the hands in her lap were fisted and white-knuckled around her wooden-beaded rosary.

Isabel looked around the modest, two bedroom home, and said, "Who is paying for your treatment, Mrs. Sanchez?"

Rosa's eyelids flickered. Isabel felt Tony's gaze touch her, but she only waited.

"I have...insurance," Rosa replied.

"That Mr. Cruz pays for?" Isabel asked.

Color flushed the woman's cheeks, spots of bright pink that only served to highlight the yellow-gray tint of her skin.

"Yes."

Tony leaned forward, his gaze narrowing, but before he could speak, Isabel continued, "Generous of him, to insure a former employee, especially one so critically ill."

Rosa only blinked, lines drawing her mouth tight. "I told you: he is a *good* man. When I got sick, he said he would take care of me."

"Why?" Isabel wanted to know.

"I was with the family for many years, some of them not so good." Rosa shrugged. "Mr. Cruz said he was grateful."

"Not so good?" Tony repeated.

The lines around Rosa's mouth deepened. "The death of Mrs. Cruz was very…difficult. He loved her very much."

Isabel swallowed the urge to snort. Based on the research she'd done, the death of Mrs. Cruz had amounted to little more than a brief article in the society pages and an abbreviated obituary. There'd been no investigation into the car accident that killed her—a single car roll over—and no autopsy. With no other living relatives, there'd been no one to protest. Thus, Eleanor Cruz had passed with barely the blink of an eye.

According to an interview in *Las Vegas Today,* Eleanor had met Donavon Cruz at GenTek. She was the executive assistant to the head researcher; Cruz its biggest shareholder. *A Cinderella Story!* the magazine had proclaimed, *Love At First Sight!* After marrying Cruz, Eleanor quit her job and gave birth to their first son: Alexander Matthew Cruz. Soon after Alexander was born, Eleanor stepped from the public spotlight. She no longer accompanied her husband to events; the boards, non-profits and various organizations she'd volunteered for were given notice of her resignation. Five years later, Benjamin Alan Cruz was born—not in a hospital, but deep within the confines of the Cruz estate—and from that moment forward, Eleanor Cruz became a shut-in. She never left her home, was never photographed, and did not communicate with anyone outside of her children and her staff.

That she'd suddenly decided to climb into her car—after staying hidden within her home for *years*—and go for a drive into the desert, where she then died in a single car accident no one witnessed, was worse than suspect. It was laughable. *Obvious.* And yet no one had investigated. No one argued.

No wonder Lucia had met such resistance; no one was willing to cross Donavon Cruz.

No one, Isabel thought, *but me.* Tony. And Lucia Sanchez.

"And what of Lucia Sanchez's allegations?" Isabel asked. "What do you think of those?"

Rosa shook her head. It was not lost on Isabel, that the woman was clinging to her rosary like it was a lifeline. *As if holding it afforded her absolution, no matter the lies she told.* "Lucia...she is a good girl, but there is ugliness in her past. I believe she is just...confused."

"Confused how?" Tony demanded, and Isabel nearly put a hand on his arm. He was almost vibrating.

"Many years ago, there was...an incident with Lucia's brother, Elian," Rosa said slowly. "Lucia's mother, Selena, was my friend. We were both widows with young children, and we went to the same church—"

"Our Lady of the Sacred Heart," Tony interrupted—snarled—and Isabel did lean toward him then, and let her arm settle lightly against his. He went still, that glittering hazel gaze touching her profile.

"Yes," Rosa said, obviously surprised. "How did you know?"

"It was in Lucia's file," Isabel murmured.

"Oh. Well, her mother—Selena—was very...devout. The rituals, they comforted her. She never missed Mass, and every day she would light a candle for her husband who had passed." Rosa caressed her rosary. "He was murdered."

"Murdered?" Tony echoed.

"It was not something Selena spoke of. I know only because Father Domingo mentioned it in passing."

"And the incident?" Tony pressed impatiently.

Rosa took a deep breath. "Yes. Of course. It was summer, and Selena decided to send her son Elian—Lucia's older brother—to a camp run by the church."

Tony went as tense as coiled wire, and Isabel pressed slightly closer. She knew this part of the story; he'd already told her. And in spite of the even tone he'd used, she'd heard his guilt. Felt the sting of his sorrow and regret, the power it had even today, a wound that still bled. But they needed to hear it from Rosa. No matter how painful.

Part of Isabel knew she was bending too far. The Detective's simmering anguish was not her concern. But she didn't move, because they could not afford to have his rage tip their hand, and they needed Rosa Sanchez to trust them, which wouldn't happen if Tony jumped the cheap coffee table and went for the woman's throat.

For the greater good, Isabel told herself, as the hard heat of him seeped into her skin. And knew she was a liar.

"It was a very good camp," Rosa said seriously. "There were sports programs and Bible classes and arts and crafts. A wonderful experience for the children. But when Elian returned, he told his mother that the Deacon who had gone with them to camp had been...inappropriate."

"Inappropriate?" Tony repeated, and his tone sent a sudden, icy chill through Isabel. She'd seen him angry, annoyed, amused. He'd been charming, belligerent, manipulative. But not...*dangerous*.

Her heart jerked in response. Rosa blinked and lifted her rosary to her lips.

"There were accusations of...molestation."

"Molestation," Tony repeated darkly, and Isabel thought about what a benign word it was, so pale in comparison to the terror and evil it wrought. Man's attempt to deflect the horror he was capable of. "You mean *rape*."

Rosa froze. Her gaze shot to Isabel. "That was in the file, too?"

"Elian blew his brains out in his bedroom," Tony replied, so cold Isabel clenched her hands into fists. "Lucia found him. Of course it's in the file."

Rosa scooted back in the chair she occupied, as if just realizing how volatile the man before her was. "Yes, of course."

"How did Selena react when he told her?" Isabel asked calmly.

"She did not believe him. She could not. The Church...that belief...it was all she had left."

"And once her son was dead?" Tony asked in that same brutally cold voice. "Did she believe then?"

"I don't know." Rosa worked the rosary through her hands. "She withdrew into herself afterward. We did not speak of it. Then the police came and arrested the Deacon..." She shook her head. "He was such a nice young man."

"He was a fucking monster," Tony said.

Isabel leaned harder into him. "What happened then?"

Rosa stared at Tony, fear flickering across her features. "Many people abandoned the church. Selena was one of them. I tried to stay in touch, but she just...went away. Then one day, I heard she had died. It was very tragic."

Isabel had read Selena Sanchez's death certificate. Under cause of death it had stated organ failure due to dehydration and starvation.

The woman had starved herself to death. Part of Isabel wasn't surprised. She'd seen parents lose their children; it was not something a person ever recovered from. To outlive your child went against the paradigm, the natural order. Parents were prepared to go before their children, but not after.

Never after.

Add to that the relentless, unforgiving guilt Selena must have experienced.... A self-imposed death sentence had probably seemed a relief.

But not to Lucia.

Anger flared in Isabel. "How did Lucia end up working for Mr. Cruz?"

"I saw her at the clinic where my doctor worked. She volunteered there sometimes. When I was diagnosed, she came to me and told me not to give up. To have hope." A shaken smile turned Rosa's mouth. "She is a good girl. She is. This...what is happening...she is just confusing *then* with *now*."

Beside Isabel, Tony growled.

"You helped her get the job working for Mr. Cruz?" Isabel clarified.

"Yes. I recommended her, and with her schooling, Mr. Cruz hired her. I thought...I thought it would be okay." Another shake of her head. "She is a *good* girl."

"You never saw anything?" Tony asked, very quietly, and far too calm.

Something moved through Rosa's veiled gaze, brief, fleeting, but Isabel caught it.

"Please," she urged. "Off the record, just between us. He will never know. There will be no report, no witness statement. Nothing. You have my word."

Silence fell, broken only by the sound of traffic moving past outside.

"He's going to kill her," Tony said bluntly. "You know that, right?"

Rosa paled, which left her looking like the walking dead. "He would not—"

"He will. You know he will. He will make her disappear."

"Like he did with Mrs. Cruz," Isabel added, her heart beating hard. She could see Rosa's internal struggle.

Frightened for herself, for Lucia. The woman's mouth worked, and her throat bobbed. Her battle was obvious: her life or the truth.

"There is nothing," she said finally, but would not meet their gazes.

"Goddamn it," Tony snarled and stood up. "This is on *you*." He pointed at her with a shaking hand. "Whatever happens to her—to those boys—it's on your fucking head."

Rosa flinched. In Isabel's pocket, her phone beeped. She stood.

"Thank you for seeing us," she told Rosa quietly.

Tony turned and stormed from the house, slamming the door behind him. Isabel followed, more subdued, and checked her phone.

An email from Aequitas, one they'd been waiting for.

She climbed into the SUV and put a firm hand on Tony's arm when he went to start the car, halting him.

"Settle," she said softly, and when his angry gaze met hers, she squeezed his arm. "It wouldn't have been admissible anyway."

"She fucking *knows*."

His fury was hot and ripe, like a furnace blast against her skin. Isabel only nodded. "Yes. But we are asking her to barter her life for something she has probably talked herself out of believing. No one ever wants to believe, Tony. No one. Only those who've suffered believe. They know how easily it happens, everywhere, all the time. But to those it has never touched, it is almost sacrilege to speak of. That's simply fact."

He wanted to argue; Isabel could see it. But he couldn't. He hadn't believed, either. So to be angry at Rosa Sanchez was to be angry at himself, and perhaps that's why he was so enraged. Not at her, but at himself.

"Fuck," he said.

"I have the information on Cruz's security system at Dead Mountains," Isabel told him, and deliberately dragged him into the present. With her. "We need to go somewhere I can print it off. Where do you suggest?"

CHAPTER 21

"Take off your pants and sit down."

Sam tried hard not to take that command personally, but his body had other ideas. It rose to the occasion as if the woman making the order was naked and smiling instead of holding a first aid kit and scowling at him.

Because he knew what she tasted like now. And no matter how much he wanted to blame Lucia for that, he knew it was his own goddamn fault.

"Sam," Lucia said.

He turned away and stripped off his sodden shirt, taking his time, willing the sudden, relentless hunger that beat at him to subside.

He shouldn't have kissed her. *What the fuck was his problem?* Soft, plump lips, putting him in his goddamn place, that was his fucking problem. Spicy and sweet and *fierce*, and he wanted to drown in her. *All of that fire licking over him, pulling him into the inferno.*

He wanted to burn.

Totally fucking fucked.

"Sam," Lucia said again, sternly. "*Sit down.* I am going to look at your leg. You are bleeding again."

That was because he'd spent the last hour hiking a mile-wide perimeter around the cabin, making certain it was—for now, at least—secure. The rain helped, heavy, cold, unrelenting. The smoke from the woodstove was barely visible, dispersed by the water and the wind, and the small amount of light cast by the two kerosene lamps they'd found was almost invisible from the outside. He'd hidden the ATV, and the tracks they'd left on their way in had all but disappeared.

They were finally out of signal range, but that wasn't enough—Sam wanted them so far into the interior not even Smoky the fucking Bear could find them. Idaho had a hell of a lot of wilderness; they could hide very effectively. But not by camping out next to a well-used trail. Not by staying confined to the areas heavily utilized by people. Tomorrow they were going to have to break their own trail with the ATV, and then, when the rig could go no further, they were going to have to walk.

So having Lucia patch up his leg was a good idea. Too bad the last thing Sam wanted was her hands on him. And not because he didn't want them on him. No, because he wanted them *all over* him.

And that was a big fucking problem. A distraction that could get them all dead.

That's why he'd deliberately put some space between them today. He'd taken the same role he always took with the people he protected: he became the watcher. Hyperaware, vigilant, every sense attuned for any sign of trouble. He didn't involve himself with *them*; instead, he worked the perimeter, watching and waiting and working the trenches. He protected from the outside in.

And he'd gotten a strip torn off his hide for his trouble.

You are worse than a menstruating woman.

Goddamn her, he'd almost *laughed.*

Instead, he'd kissed her. And he wanted to do it again.

"Sam," Lucia repeated, and he could hear her annoyance. "Are you listening to me?"

God help him. That accent, that temper, that *mouth.* She tempted him in ways he hadn't even known it was possible to be tempted. And that could not be. Because he didn't have the luxury of thinking about anything other than keeping them safe. Because if he gave into the insane, pervasive, growing need she stirred, Dragovitch would get the drop on them, and someone would end up dead. There were no good choices here, only varying degrees of disaster, and it was up to him to mitigate those degrees.

That was his job. His only fucking job. And he couldn't forget that just because she made his dick hard and his mouth water and tempted him into thinking about a future.

Who the fuck do you think you're kidding?

"*Sam,*" she said a fourth time. Snarled, really, so Sam turned and walked toward the scarred wooden table. He halted and stared down at her where she sat in one of the ancient chairs.

The fire crackled; it was cozy warm in the cabin, and rain pounded against the old tin roof like miniature hammers. Ben and Daisy were in bed; Sam could hear Ben murmuring softly to her. Alexander lay beside them, drawing in a worn three-ring notebook Lucia had found along with the lamps. She stared up at him, holding his gaze stubbornly, color flushing her cheeks as she said, "I want to see that leg."

Sam didn't move. It was better that he dealt with it himself. He was no medic, but he had plenty of experience in the field. He could do the job. And then she wouldn't be touching him. He wouldn't be sitting there in his underwear with her breath washing across his skin while the memory of that kiss hovered between them, giving life to any number of erotic fantasies that could never come true.

"Do not be obstinate," she told him. "I will tie you down if necessary."

Speaking of fantasies...

"I'll help," Alexander added, his pale gaze sliding to meet Sam's.

The kid had done well today. He'd kept his head with that bear—luckily a young black bear and not a mama grizzly—and he'd listened. Followed orders. Considering how difficult he'd been up to this point, Sam figured it was a miracle he hadn't gotten himself—or Ben—mauled.

"You're bullies," Sam told them, unmoving.

"Please, Sam," Lucia replied quietly. "Let me help you."

If she'd argued, Sam could have resisted. But the husky sound of his name on her lips, the plea in her gaze, that stubborn, persistent will, and the goddamn knowledge that she would touch him—when he'd just spent the last three minutes explaining to himself why that was a *bad* idea—won out over his common sense.

He unzipped his jeans and let them fall. Lucia held his

gaze, her chin lifting just a bit, and turned as rosy pink as a fresh Georgia peach. He pulled up the only remaining chair and sat down across from her, his back to the boys, aware that he was growing hard as hell beneath his jockeys.

She was just going to have to deal.

"Thank you," she said. Her gaze flickered to his erection and away; she turned red as a beet. Then she focused on the make-shift patch job on his thigh and frowned. Blood and pus had turned the gauze sodden and black, and the tape he'd used was frayed and curling at the edges. Blood trails swept down the outside of his leg, down his knee, into the vee of his thighs.

He was a mess.

"Ay, yai, yai," she muttered, leaning over the wound to take a better look. She shook her head. "What have you done to yourself?"

Her hair was loose, a lush mass of curling, chocolate brown tresses with streaks of deep red and pale gold; it swept his thighs, and he stiffened.

"Relax," she admonished. "I am not going to hurt you."

Fuck. Sweetest goddamn torture ever.

She pulled away the bandage with gentle, efficient hands. When the jagged, ugly wound beneath was revealed she looked up at him with narrow eyes. "This is a bullet wound."

Sam only shrugged.

"You were shot," she whispered in outrage. "Who shot you?"

"He's dead."

Her mouth opened, then closed. She shook her head and began to clean him up with peroxide-soaked cotton balls that were soft as butter and cold as ice. Sam watched her work. He'd been worked on a lot—by field medics, paramedics, doctors, nurses, hell, even a dentist once, in Columbia—and Lucia was good. Her touch was firm but light, her manner professional, her skill natural. Doctoring was a skill just like any other—you either had it or you didn't.

Lucia had it.

"You need stitches," she told him. "The internal sutures are torn, but they will do. You are healing. However, the outer stitches should be resewn." She looked up at him. "I have a kit. Will you let me help you?"

No force on earth could have made him say no. *So fucking pathetic.* But this was all he could let himself have: her hands on him while she fixed him. It wasn't enough; he had a bad feeling nothing would be enough. Not after that kiss. But it was legitimate, and he needed the work. Bleeding like a stuck pig wasn't going to do him any favors. He needed to heal; he needed to be one hundred percent.

Because Ivan the Terrible sure as hell wasn't going to give him a handicap.

"Be my guest," he said.

Lucia nodded and dug into the box beside her. It was an old tackle box she'd pulled from her pack, filled to overflowing with all manner of medical supplies. Gloves, syringes, needles, ointments, bandages, iodine, peroxide. A snake bite kit, a tourniquet, even a small splint. Sam was impressed. At least she was prepared for *something.*

A needle was removed, followed by a narrow spool of

clear thread. A small pair of scissors, a clamp, another clean bandage. Lucia scooted closer and positioned his leg between hers, holding him still with the supple muscle that lined her thighs. When she squeezed his leg lightly between her own, lightning shot down his spine and his cock jerked. Heat flooded him, and his hands fisted against the compulsion to reach for her. Just pull her into his lap and—

"What happened?" Alexander asked, suddenly right next to them. Sam swore internally, with vicious precision, and luckily, the boy's appearance helped deflate the blood flow to his nether regions until he appeared almost normal.

Almost. Except for the dull, aching throb that gripped him. And the knowledge that, should the boy turn and walk away again, he would be hard as stone in an instant.

Double fuck.

"Did that happen in the storm?" the kid continued, watching as Lucia threaded her needle.

"*Sí*," Lucia replied, lying without compunction. But her eyes sought Sam's, and her cheeks burned bright, and her gaze asked him not to argue.

He didn't. That was not a conversation he wanted to have with either of them. He was doing his best to forget what had happened in Baja; he still hadn't heard jack shit about Fieldstone. He didn't want to talk about it, relive it, *remember.* What was before him was enough.

Here and now.

Alexander shot Lucia a look; he knew she was lying, too, but he didn't argue. Instead, he studied Sam's wound and said, "You still came after us."

"Yep."

"Didn't it hurt?"

"Like hell," Sam told him.

Alexander turned that pale green gaze on him, silent for a long moment. He examined Sam with piercing directness, and Sam could see the wheels turning in the kid's head, even if he didn't know their direction. But he had no problem with being assessed. He was who he was, and he'd make no apology for it, so he let the kid look, his own stare unwavering.

"What happened to your eye?" the boy asked finally, the tense set of his shoulders easing a bit. "Where did you get that scar from?"

"Alexander," Lucia chastised, tying a knot in her thread. "That is not your business."

But it was a good distraction, so Sam answered. "My old man did it."

Lucia stilled, hovering over his torn up leg, needle poised in the air. Alexander stared at him.

"This…" Lucia cleared her throat. "This will hurt."

"I know," Sam replied grimly. "Just do it quickly."

"I will go as fast as I can."

Her eyes were dark, worried for him. Sam couldn't help but touch her. Just a brief graze of that silky hair, a light touch, another indulgence he shouldn't have made, but she responded to the reassurance of it with a brisk nod, and he didn't regret it.

"Was it an accident?" Alexander asked.

The kid was motionless, his eyes locked on the scar that split Sam's brow in two, one of the many souvenirs his pop had left him. Lucia's gaze met Sam's as she moved to make her first stitch, her fingers pulling his torn skin together just above the small clamp she'd put in place. Sam only nodded for her to continue and answered the boy's question. "Nope."

"He did it on purpose?"

"Yep."

The needle slid through his skin smoothly, but Lucia had that look again, her mouth pinched, line between her brows. *Temper, temper.* Mad on his behalf, which shouldn't have pleased him, but did. She said nothing, concentrating on her task. Another stitch, and the needle burned; Sam looked away, hardening himself against the pain. It was only a little pinch, nothing compared to the bullet that had ripped into him. Just one more thing to endure.

"Why?" Alexander demanded, and Sam noticed the kid's fists were clenched again, white knuckled at his sides.

"Because he was a mean son of a bitch when he was sober. When he was drunk, he was a monster." Sam met the boy's gaze, held it. "I'd taken off. I was eleven, and I was done being his punching bag. So I hightailed it to the highway, figured I'd hitchhike into town, catch a ride out of state. Didn't work out that way. He caught me before I even made it to the road. Beat me down, sat on me, pulled his knife out and told me I couldn't run if I couldn't see."

Lucia inhaled sharply, and her gaze lifted to his. Sam felt a bead of sweat trickle down his temple, but he only nodded again. Her jaw hardened, and she bent over to make another smooth stitch.

"He tried to *blind* you?" Alexander asked incredulously.

"He tried," Sam said, gritting his teeth. *Goddamn needle.* "He failed. He was three sheets to the wind, could barely hold his damn blade. When he started carving into me, I hit him in the face with a rock, knocked him cold."

The rain grew thunderous around them then, almost deafening against the metal roof. Lucia continued the line of tight, neat stitches, her hands steady and efficient and so gentle, Sam felt a piercing moment of regret on her behalf. She was more than good at what she was doing; she was *meant* to do it. That she'd given it up for the boy standing next to him made rage spark somewhere deep inside Sam, the unfairness of it scraping him raw. *Choices.* Life was all about choices. One trade for another. This was something he knew intimately, a fact for every living being, but that Lucia had felt there was no other option infuriated Sam. Tony should have helped her. He should have fucking *stopped* her. Because this was going destroy her life, and she deserved better.

"And then...what did you do?" Alexander asked, his voice so quiet, so hesitant, Sam looked up at him.

"I went home. I knew no one would pick me up bleeding like I was, and even if they did, they'd call the cops, and I'd end up in foster care again. So I went home, cleaned myself up, and tried to keep my head low."

The boy scowled. "You let him get away with it."

"I thought it was normal. I figured every kid knew the taste of his own blood."

Lucia made a low, harsh sound, but didn't falter. Alexander looked away, color touching his cheeks.

"What about your mom?" the boy asked.

"Alexander!" Lucia blew out a breath. "Enough."

"It's okay, sweetheart." And it was. A distraction from the stitches and maybe an understanding. Maybe this would help the kid trust him, because Sam needed Alexander to trust him. "I never knew my mom. She took off after having me. I think that's why my pop hated me so much, but hell, who could blame her? If he was as loving a husband as he was a father, she probably ran for her life."

"Selfish," Lucia muttered in a hard tone, her indignation clear. Sam touched her hair again, because he couldn't help himself.

"Maybe," he conceded. His feelings toward the woman who'd had him and then left him were complex and volatile, but he'd made his peace with her decision long ago. Still, he appreciated Lucia's anger on his behalf. Lucia, he thought, was not a woman who would abandon her child.

Ever.

"She just left you?" Alexander whispered, staring at Sam.

Sam shrugged. "She did what she had to do, I guess."

Silence fell. The rain had eased to a steady patter, and Ben's soft snores floated toward them. Sam glanced down at the line of stitches; almost halfway. He blew out a breath.

"Do you forgive her?" Alexander asked.

Sam looked at the kid. "I should. I understand why she went. But in my heart? Hell, no."

The boy nodded. "My mom died."

Lucia moved the clamp further down the wound, her mouth a tight line.

"I'm sorry," Sam said.

Alexander shrugged. "I didn't know her. She was…sick."

Lucia met Sam's gaze, dark, churning, *angry*. So damn mad. For him, for the boy. The same rage that simmered in Sam's gut, and for a moment, they occupied the same place in time, another shared instant of grief and pain and fury. A connection neither of them could afford, one that happened outside of control or will or choice. A tie woven of understanding and experience, compulsory and strong, no matter the circumstance.

Something else to bind them. And he knew all of his excuses were just words, and if he got the chance to put his mouth on her again, he was fucking going to.

"Did you…did you ever get away from him?" Alexander asked, moving closer.

"When I was thirteen, my uncle Magnus came to visit," Sam replied. "I'd never met him. He was my pop's older brother, my only other living family. I hadn't even known he existed until he showed up on the front porch one day. Magnus was the only person I ever met who scared my pop." Sam shook his head. "I didn't expect that. *That* was a revelation."

"Did he save you?"

"Magnus would say I saved myself, that I made a choice. But it was him."

"What happened?"

Sam met the boy's gaze, darker now, glittering, free of the cold, remote shell he donned so easily. "Magnus stayed for a week. I tried like hell to avoid him, because I knew my pop wouldn't like me talking to him." Even though he'd wanted desperately to know the man who made his father flinch. "But Magnus knew. Knew his brother well, I guess, and one day when I escaped out to my fishing hole, he followed. Brought his own line and his tackle and set up beside me without saying a word. When he offered to let me use some of his stuff, I agreed, and he hooked me up with a sweet little spinner—which I lost on my first cast." Sam smiled wryly. "I totally panicked. I figured he was going to beat my ass, because that's what my pop would have done. I pulled off my shirt and leaned over the closest log, ready to take his belt. Hell, I figured I deserved it."

Alexander's lashes flickered, and Sam knew he understood. The memory of Lucia telling him the boy believed his abuse to be his own fault had gnawed at Sam ever since she'd said it, because Sam knew that road, was familiar with every hole and bump and bend, and it had taken him far too long to understand that none of what had happened to him was his fault. To accept the truth that all of that pain and blood and terror had been incidental, circumstance, *impersonal*. Just the bad fucking luck of being born to an asshole.

"What did he do?" Lucia asked softly.

Sam stared at her bent head, and something painful moved in his chest. Something that stole his breath and made his heart pound hard; something he had no desire to feel. Something far more powerful than the lust she stirred.

So incredibly fucked.

The needle slid through again, and he focused on the pain like a drowning man grabbing driftwood.

"He got mad." Sam remembered the fury on Magnus's face as he'd stared down at Sam's back, scarred and pitted from the thick metal buckle of his pop's favorite belt. "He hauled me up off that log and marched me back to the house. Told me to pack my stuff, that we were leaving. I just stood there. I didn't understand why he didn't punish me. I didn't even know who he was mad at. None of it made sense to me."

"Because no one had ever helped you." Alexander's gaze flickered to Lucia, then back to Sam. "He took you with him?"

"Well, *first he had a talk with my pop. With his fists.*"

"*Bueno,*" Lucia said, her voice cold.

"He wiped the floor with my old man, and he made it look easy. Then he put me in his truck, and we drove away."

"Forever?" Alexander asked, and something—maybe hope—flared in his eyes.

"Forever," Sam said. "Took me home to Oklahoma and raised me on his cattle ranch. He was a damn fine man. I miss him."

Lucia looked up from her stitches. "He is gone?"

"Yes. A long time ago." An ache bloomed in Sam's chest, as piercing as the needle breaking his skin. He would always miss his uncle, hard, taciturn, intractable and kind. He *had* saved Sam, even if he'd never taken credit for the act. He'd changed the trajectory of Sam's entire life, which in turn had changed countless other lives through Sam's own choices. *Paying it forward.* The world worked in circles, strange, connected, inexplicable rings that enclosed them all.

"I am sorry," Lucia murmured, her eyes shimmering

deep, golden amber in the light.

"Me, too," Sam told her.

"What—" Alexander began, only to be cut off by a sudden, shrill cry from Ben. The little boy sat up in the bed, tears streaking his cheeks, and Daisy yipped and crawled into his lap.

Lucia began to rise, but Alexander stopped her.

"It's okay," he said. "I'll go. Finish Sam."

And he turned and went to the bed, climbing in beside his brother and speaking to him softly. Lucia watched them, her gaze softening, and Sam knew that no matter the anger he felt on her behalf, she didn't regret what she'd done. That she would do it again, no matter how it ended, no matter what it meant.

Any sacrifice.

It was a concept Sam understood, one he'd undertaken himself when he'd joined the service. Something he respected. Added to everything else he was beginning to feel for the woman who sat before him, it was a damned powerful aphrodisiac.

Like you even need one.

Lucia met his gaze, and her cheeks flushed, and Sam knew the hunger he felt was written on his face. He was tired of hiding it.

"My father," she said quietly and bent over to make another stitch, "was murdered in his bed."

CHAPTER 22

Sam's gaze had weight.

Lucia always felt it, even if he only skimmed her with it. A corporeal sensation, as effective as touch. Sometimes heavy with darkness, but other times, like now, piercing and charged, a whisper of electricity splintering through her veins.

"When I was a child, my family owned a citrus farm in Belize," she said, uncertain why she felt compelled to share one of her worst memories. It was not something she had ever spoken of, not even with her brother or her mother. The pain had been too great—for them all. "The farm was in my family for generations; he was very proud of it. My brother and I grew up working in the orchards, surrounded by their bittersweet scent. It was a place I loved very much." She watched her hands stitch Sam's flesh together as if they had a mind of their own. "My mother did not like it. She was American, from California. Her father had been a vinter from Spain, and she preferred the warm desert to the tropical rainforest. But my father, he was the head of the household, and we did as he said. Even her."

"How did they meet?"

Sam's voice was low and rough, and Lucia deliberately kept her gaze from traveling any further up his thigh than his wound. There was no missing the hard line of flesh beneath the soft black cotton boxers he wore. Wholly unashamed of his desire, watching her with unflinching heat.

The memory of his kiss flashed through her, and her skin prickled as he stared down at her. Her cheeks flushed; her heart beat hard in her throat. A revelation, that's what that kiss had been. A reminder that she was a woman, and alive; a bittersweet lesson. One she held tightly guarded, secreted away, buried in that place that held her few treasured moments. Because that was all it could be. She wasn't sorry it had happened, but it could not be repeated.

No matter the seed he'd planted when he'd put his mouth on hers.

"It was an arranged marriage," she went on, not wanting to think about that. "My grandfather wanted a stake in the citrus trade, and my father wanted an American wife."

"Did they love each other?" Sam asked, frowning.

"I like to think so, but truthfully, I do not know. My father, he worked in the orchards from dawn until dusk, and my mother was often at Church, so my brother and I spent most of our childhood with my *abuela*—my father's mother."

"What was she like?"

Lucia shot Sam a look, surprised at his interest. But he only gazed back at her steadily, waiting for her response.

"Wild," she said after a moment. "Fierce."

"The apple hasn't fallen far," Sam said, smiling a little at her, his eyes glinting.

Lucia knew that wasn't true; her grandmother had been the smartest, strongest, bravest woman she'd ever known. Matching her was an impossibility, but that wouldn't stop Lucia from trying. "She was descended from the ancient Mayan. She would tell me, 'You have the blood of kings in your veins, *nieta*. We have been here since time began, and we will see it end.'"

"Mayan," Sam echoed. "That's some family tree."

Lucia shrugged. "It was a good life, until I was eight. Then everything changed." She smoothed her hand over the hard, warm flesh of Sam's thigh, part of her thrilled to be able to touch him so freely. He was a beautiful specimen of man, his body cut in clean, muscular lines, his skin as golden as his hair. The scars that marked him were profuse: knife wounds, bullet wounds, burn scars. She'd seen the marks left by his father's belt, and while she did not consider herself a bloodthirsty person, she would have very much liked to introduce that man to her scalpel. "The land dried up, and the orchards began to die. My father could not afford to pay his men; he could not afford to replace his trees. He could barely feed us. Such a proud man brought so low, so quickly. My mother wanted to leave. Her father had gone back to Spain, and she wanted us to go there and start over. But my father would not have it. He could not let go of his family's legacy. So he went to the *traficantes* and made them a deal."

"Aw, fuck," Sam muttered.

"Yes. He told them they could cross our lands to move their goods in return for enough money to keep the farm going. My grandmother warned him it was not a good idea;

she told him there would be a price. But for a while, it was okay. We had food, my father bought new trees, my mother stopped talking about Spain. But then one night, there was a knock on the door. One of the *traficantes* had been shot, and they wanted my father to help them. He refused. He did not want them beneath his roof, with his family, and so he turned them away. It was a fatal mistake."

Sam's palm rasped against her hair, a tender, soothing motion that disarmed her each time he did it. Lucia kept stitching, focusing on her task instead of the unspoken words that welled forth, eager to be given sound. Her oldest nightmare, no less horrifying for all the years that had passed, a screaming echo that never faded.

"They came two nights later," she said. "They killed my father, raped my mother, and almost beat my brother to death." Lucia could feel Sam's gaze, but she didn't look at him. The words wanted *out*, and she was afraid if she stopped, they would get trapped forever, poison she would never purge. "My grandmother died the next morning," she continued and moved the clamp along Sam's wound. *Almost done.* "The doctor said it was a stroke, but he was wrong. It was her heart; it was broken."

Another stroke of her hair. "And then?"

"We fled, smuggled out by the priest from the Holy Trinity, my mother's church. We went to Las Vegas and moved into a small apartment provided by Trinity's sister branch, Our Lady of the Sacred Heart." Lucia shook her head. "I hoped we would go to California, but I think my mother was too ashamed of what had happened. Instead, she found work as a seamstress, and my brother Elian took care of me."

"Elian," Sam repeated, one word filled with a hundred questions.

Lucia met his gaze and suddenly understood that Tony had told him about Elian. She could see it in Sam's gaze, and she grew chilled, because it was not Sam's business. Nor was it Tony's. It belonged only to Elian, and it had no place here.

She said nothing.

"Lucia."

She glanced up and met that brilliant, waiting gaze. "No."

"Please."

Damn the man. Looking at her like he cared, like he wanted the words from her. More words, the illumination of yet another nightmare.

But he had no right. He was taking too much already.

"No," she said again. Her heart was a heavy, leaden thud against her ribs. She was almost done sewing him up; just a few more stitches. Stitches he'd sat through with a stillness and self-control that made her aware, once more, of his familiarity with violence and pain. A man so outside the scope of her experience he might as well be an alien.

"I know you found him," Sam said.

Memory washed over her like a tide, unexpected and unwelcome, sweeping her into the undertow of an event she had tried for years to forget: coming home after school, worried because Elian hadn't been himself in months, because what he'd told her—what had happened to him— was *horrific,* because she only partially understood it, and because, for the first time ever, he hadn't been there to walk her home.

Because she knew something was very, very wrong.

The house, empty, her mother at Church. A strange smell in the hall, Elian's closed door. The hair-raising, despondent cry of Panther, their mother's tabby cat. And then opening Elian's door: his body on the floor, his face gone, the walls red with blood and bone and brains... The screams that had torn from her throat, nearly shredding her vocal cords, screams that brought the neighbors running and made Panther yowl and which still escaped her in the dark of night, when the dreams would come.

"Yes," Lucia said, hoarse, as if still screaming.

"I'm sorry," Sam told her softly.

A tear she hadn't been aware of slid down her cheek, and she wiped it away impatiently. *Why did he want to know this?* None of it mattered, not anymore. Elian was gone, and had been for a long time. And even if what had happened to him had been the catalyst for where she now found herself, that was not Sam's concern. That truth belonged to her, and he had no right to demand it from her.

A gentle tug on her hair. "Talk to me, sweetheart."

"Do not call me that," she told him. Because part of her was becoming accustomed to it. Part of her was beginning to *enjoy* it; so much stupid, to wish for something that could not be. So many things that could never be. It made her angry. With him, for pretending, and with herself, for wanting to.

So much anger. At him, herself. Her past, her present, her lost, impossible future.

She secured the final stitch and cut the thread and stood,

but before she could move away, Sam caught her arm, a gentle but unyielding hold she knew she wouldn't escape until he was ready.

"Tell me," he ordered quietly.

"Tell you *what?*" she snarled in a low voice, aware of Alexander and Benjamin, of her own tenuous control. A violent tremor moved through her. "That when Elian told me what happened to him I could not even *comprehend* it? That I did not understand what it meant, or how it would destroy him? That my mother would not listen, would not *act,* would not even look at him? That his friends called him a liar—and worse!—and turned him into a pariah? *That I fell at his feet and bathed in his blood?* Is that what you would like to know?"

Sam made a rough sound. The hand that held her arm jerked her toward him, and he pulled her down onto the thigh she'd just sewn shut.

"You will tear your stitches," she growled.

"Then be still," he said and slid his arms around her.

Suddenly she was surrounded by the powerful flex of corded muscle rippling beneath naked golden skin, immersed in his immense heat and drunk on that fresh, minty scent. A fine pelt of golden hair covered his chest, which was scarred and stamped with several intricate, triangular tattoos. Both of his nipples were pierced by delicate silver rings. Lucia sat stiffly in his hold, her heart beating with painful intensity, almost shockingly aware of the hard thigh beneath her and the even harder ridge of flesh pressed into her hip. But it was not a sexual hold. It was...

Do not think about it.

But it had been a long time since anyone held her…and never like this.

He stared at her, so close the ring of green in his eyes glinted like cut emerald. "What happened then?"

Grief pulsed in her chest, and her breath grew tight. Lucia didn't want to tell him. It was not his right to demand anything, to hold her against her will, but once again the words were filling her throat, as if someone had pulled the plug, and everything that had floated around in her for the last thirteen years was ready to pour out.

"I told Tony it should have been him." She looked down at her clenched hands, where the needle she held stabbed into her palm. "And I told my mother I would never forgive her. By the time I understood, it was *too late*." She lifted her gaze to meet Sam's, but then looked away again, because the compassion—the understanding—she saw was more than she could bear. "Always too late. Elian was dead. I could change nothing, and it ate at me, every moment of every day. My mother would not even say his name. She died that day, too. She stopped eating. Drinking. Being my mother. She locked herself in her room with her rosary and her altar and her guilt, and she gave up. I hate her for that."

The words were stark, shamed, something of which Lucia was not proud. But they were true.

"She left you," Sam murmured and tucked a strand of hair behind her ear, his fingers grazing her neck.

Lucia shivered. "She had lost a child."

"She lost one; the other, she abandoned."

Lucia wanted to protest. She loved her mother, still, to this day. And she hated her. As an adult, she understood what had happened, why. The violence in Belize, her father's murder, Elian's death, the guilt that had ravaged them both...but the eleven-year-old who still lurked within her felt nothing but rage, pure, undiluted, and she wanted someone to *pay*.

"What happened to you after she died?" Sam asked softly. He nudged aside the neckline of her t-shirt and traced the naked curve where her neck and shoulder met with a rough thumb. Goosebumps washed over her, prickling her skin.

"Foster care," she said, her heart beating hollowly, her mouth dry. "Like you."

Like him. It seemed impossible. This hardened lawman with sharp eyes and a sharper tongue, who touched her with tenderness and watched her with lust. So foreign and inexplicable.

"Fuck," Sam said, low, and although he'd not spoken of his own experience in the foster care system, the word said it all.

"No," Lucia told him, trying desperately to ignore the hand that was slowly stroking up her throat—*learning her*—a proprietary touch, his callused skin rasping sensually against her own, thrilling her, terrifying her. "I was lucky. The woman I was sent to was very good to me. She was not...affectionate. Not loving. But she was strong and supportive. She helped me, made me understand I could become anyone I wanted, so long as I was willing to work for it. I do not know who I would have become if not for her."

Sam's gaze met hers. "I'm glad."

His kindness seared through her. She didn't want him to be kind. It only added to the volatile mix he stirred within her, the yearning for something she didn't truly comprehend, something she knew could never exist. Not for her.

No matter how good he feels. How warm, how strong, how safe.

The ache in her chest turned white-hot, as if it had caught flame and threatened to burn her through. Sobs crowded in her throat; violent, angry, an old pain reawakened by the unrelenting present. And it did not matter, what she wanted. Only what was.

"Lucia." Sam's thumb whispered along her cheekbone. "It's going to be okay, sweetheart."

But it wasn't, and part of her hated him for speaking the lie.

She moved to stand, and his grip tightened, became something to break.

"Let go," she demanded. Another tear slid down her cheek.

"No," he said.

She glared at him, all harsh angles and planes, eyes so beautiful it hurt to look into them. "I do not want your comfort, Sam."

His lashes flickered, and Lucia knew she'd hurt him. Which only made her feel worse.

"This cannot *be*," she whispered helplessly, at a total loss in how to deal with him. *Herself.* "Please. Let me go."

He didn't want to. He fought himself, and her, and for a moment he didn't move, his eyes bright and hard and unyielding. Then, abruptly, he released her.

Lucia scrambled from his lap, her heart thundering in her ears, part of her—the stupid part—yearning to return.

"This isn't over," he warned softly.

But Lucia only turned away, piercingly aware of the truth neither of them could deny, a chasm so far and wide, it would never be bridged. "Everything is over."

CHAPTER 23

"You've gone Cat Woman." Tony smiled at the quelling look Isabel shot him. "I like it."

She wore a long-sleeved, mock-neck shirt in flat black, hip-hugging, butt-loving pants in the same material and a pair of narrow black boots. A black fitted cap covered her pale hair. All she needed was ears and a tail.

"Meow," he added and wiggled his eyebrows.

She only snorted and ignored him, but that was okay. He had Isabel's number now, and no matter how cool and diffident and reserved she was, he knew a warm-blooded, generous heart beat within. Because today, she'd comforted him. She'd leaned into him and centered him; when he was ready to rip Rosa Sanchez's head off her body, Isabel had pressed her warmth against him and brought him back to himself. And maybe that had been partially self-serving—after all, Rosa needed her head in order to answer Isabel's questions—but it wasn't solely Isabel's end goal that had led her to share the solace of her presence. She might tell herself that, but Tony knew better.

After all, the woman was about to commit B&E with

him. They were in it to win it now. He'd spilled his guts about Elian and Lucia and Sam—who he couldn't reach even though he'd tried a hundred goddamn times, but which was probably his own fault for telling Sam to get off the grid—and Isabel had only stared at him with her dark gray gaze, silent for the entirety of the tale. Then—when he'd feared she would reach for her phone and report his ass to her boss—she'd merely said, "Thank you for telling me. Rosa Sanchez lives on Arroyo and Rochester."

Not that he thought that would be the sum total of her reaction to what he'd told her. He figured it would surface at some point, but Isabel was very good at compartmentalizing. The woman had the singular focus of a bird of prey, and right now she was focused on Donavon Cruz. Tony almost envied the man; the thought of being Isabel's sole focus held infinite appeal. And for all that he'd told himself it was impossible, that now was not the time, Isabel was a growing presence within him, a flicker of moonlight in the periphery of his vision that grew brighter with every moment they spent together.

"Better Cat Woman than GI Joe," she mocked and slid his black camo pants a snarky look.

They sat parked just behind Donavon Cruz's Dead's Wilderness property, waiting for Isabel's contact, Aequitas, to hack into Cruz's security system. They would have four precious minutes within which to find the evidence they sought—which wasn't enough, not by half—but it was all they were going to get before the internal override kicked in and reset the system. They could disable the override, but that would alert the security company instantly, and neither one of them wanted Cruz wise to the fact that someone was sneaking around this property. So four minutes was it.

They were going to have to work fast.

"We need a plan," Isabel continued, her fingers flying over her tablet. "I'll search out the digital equipment—computer, laptop, hard drives. You should—"

"Why do you get to do that?" Tony protested, just to mess with her.

"Because I'm the one with decryption software."

"Nice. A gift from your contact?"

"You should concentrate on physical evidence," she said, ignoring his question. "But you need to be careful. Wear your gloves, and put everything back exactly where you found it. If you don't—"

"Sugar, this isn't my first rodeo."

"Glad to hear it, baby." So much sarcasm delivered in such cool, austere tones. Tony wouldn't have thought it possible, but the woman had it down to an art.

"I have zero problems with you calling me baby," he informed her seriously.

She only shook her head, but he saw the small smile she tried to hide. He wished they sat in sunlight instead of darkness; he bet her cheeks were flush with color. And if they weren't, he could always—

Down boy. Adrenaline was flowing through him like cheap scotch; his nerves were buzzing, alight with anticipation. The time limit didn't worry him; it excited him. And to have her joining him—hell, she'd arranged it—only added to the thrill.

"How much time?" he asked, checking his watch.

Almost one-thirty in the morning; there was nothing around them but high desert wilderness, and no movement beyond the nocturnal creatures that inhabited that wilderness. No cars, no people, no lights from other residences. Just a harsh, arid landscape washed silver by the narrow crescent of moon above them, which cast just enough light to see.

"Two minutes," Isabel replied. "You miss it, don't you?"

"Miss what?"

"The rush. Civilian life can't be an easy adjustment for a former Army Ranger."

Tony turned in his seat to study her. "Checking up on me?"

"I check up on everyone," was her chilly reply, which made him grin.

"I'm flattered. And yeah, I miss it. Every day was a shit show, but the high was addictive. Hard to let it go."

"Then why did you?"

She was curious. This woman, who rarely strayed into personal territory, was asking him very personal questions. Heat splintered through him, pleasure that had nothing to do with the want she stirred. "It was time. I was sick of killing."

She looked at him, her eyes the color of slate in the darkness, but she said nothing. *Waiting.*

Tony obliged. If they were ever going to tangle, there were things she needed to know about him. "I killed more men than I can count. Most of them were evil fucks who needed to be put down. But a fair number of them were just kids—young, dumb, armed and aimed by men who had no problem sacrificing them in order to spill American blood. I'm not proud of that, but a bullet is a bullet. They might have been kids, but they weren't pulling any punches. Sometimes, there's no good choice."

"No," she agreed softly.

"Sam and I buried a lot of brothers. We came back from Afghanistan, and they started making noises about sending us into Syria, and we knew it was time. I've paid my dues; it's someone else's turn. So we got out."

"And both became law enforcement."

Tony shot her a smile. "Once a soldier, always a soldier."

She nodded. "One minute."

They slid quietly out of the SUV and halted at the perimeter of the property. Isabel held her tablet in one hand; with the other, she reached down and grabbed a handful of sand and dirt. A soft chime sounded, and she tossed the dirt into the air.

Nothing. No red grid; no lasers. The system was down.

"Go," she said.

They sprinted toward the cabin. There was nothing to be done about their footprints; time was too precious to spend erasing their tracks. But they stuck to the stubble of greenery that wove across the property until they reached the back door, a narrow exit with a worn wooden step and hardware befitting a castle. The door was slightly ajar.

Tony cast Isabel a questioning look.

"It's tied into the security system," she answered shortly.

And then they were moving slowly through the

doorway, halting just inside to click their headlamps on and take stock. Isabel had set her tablet to count down their four minutes audibly: *tick-tick-tick.* The sound scraped across Tony's nerves, but it was necessary. In addition, they would have two warning chimes before the security system went back up. The first at two minutes, the second at sixty seconds. By the time the third chime sounded, they had to be outside the grid and safely on the other side. Tony had synchronized his watch with the tablet.

"You go left," Isabel said in a hushed voice. "I'll go right."

Tick-tick-tick.

Tony watched her turn and disappear into the shadows. The cabin was one large room; the inside bore no resemblance to the outside. Outside, the wood was grey and aged, weathered and beat to hell. The roof was aged metal, the windows small and narrow. But inside, the floors were laid in thick, gleaming wood, the walls painted some pale color and textured like suede. The furniture was dark, hand-carved: a wooden chair, a bed, a series of nesting tables. A large desk—which Isabel went straight for—and a thick leather sectional sofa. A large, built-in cabinet sat recessed into the northern wall, and thick rugs covered the floor. A small bathroom sat off to one side. Tony checked the bathroom first: nothing but a sink, toilet, and narrow shower stall. Then he went to the recessed cabinet and tried the doors, surprised when they opened.

What was in the cabinet surprised him even more.

Slender leather whips, thin golden chains, and several black crops hung in a neat line. Below them was a coiled cat o' nine tails, its ends frayed. Beside the cat, a row of aged, steel instruments were displayed: a primitive mask with wide eyes and a slit for a mouth, whose interior was lined with wicked, narrow spikes; a pear-shaped device with four metal leaves curled around a long internal screw thread; a triangular piece of steel with two u-shaped hooks on the long end, turned inward like claws; a long, strange pitchfork with thick tines that were flattened halfway down. Among the oddities, hand saws of all shapes and sizes were mounted in various positions, large, small, curved and straight. It took Tony a minute, staring at the collection. And then—

"Jesus Christ," he breathed.

Torture devices. An entire collection: antique, rusted, *used.*

Below them, a line of cubbies contained other unrecognizable items, but he didn't lean down to get a closer look. No. He couldn't move, his eyes locked on the objects whose sole purpose was pain, some of which still bore the rusty orange bloodstains of their victims.

Not just a pedophile. A motherfucking sadist.

He stepped back, pulled out his phone, and took a picture. The flash caught the glare of something that sat high up to the left, built into the cabinet: *a camera.*

"I've got eyes," he said to Isabel, his throat raw, his stomach suddenly churning. He looked right—another camera, a different angle—and then turned around to sweep the cabin with his headlamp in search of more. He found none.

"Copy." Isabel said from behind the desk.

Tony forced himself to close the cabinet, to *move*—he could throw up later—and strode toward her, hyperaware of the tablet continuing to count time. *Tick-tick-tick.* There was nothing else obvious to capture his attention, no pictures, none of that fucked up artwork, nothing but furniture. Nothing under the bed, under the couch cushions, nothing in the narrow, galley kitchen cabinets or the sink.

Isabel was crouched behind the desk; Tony kneeled down behind her and said, "Two and a half minutes."

She didn't respond. She was picking the lock of the bottom right-hand drawer, so Tony looked through the other drawers, all of which were unlocked and empty, but for a handful of pens and thick parchment stationary.

"Need some help?" he asked, moving behind her, far closer than she would have liked had she been paying attention.

"I've got it," she muttered.

"Never would have pegged you for a thief," he continued, focusing on her heat and scent, trying to erase the images in his head. Moving closer, until they were almost touching.

"I have many skills," she replied coolly, and he almost smiled.

"I bet you do," he murmured.

Tick-tick-tick.

A soft snick sounded above the countdown of the tablet, and Isabel pulled the drawer open. Tony's heart beat hard, and adrenaline fountained through him like a geyser, but the drawer was nearly empty, containing nothing but a small collection of paperclips and two red rubber bands.

"Fuck," he growled.

"No one locks an empty drawer," Isabel retorted, and stuck her hand in to check the bottom of the drawer above the one she'd opened. She hissed softly, and Tony tensed, and when she pulled her arm free, she held a small, square external hard drive.

"Many, many skills," Tony said.

Isabel ignored him and hooked the hard drive to her tablet. A few deft touches later, and the screen filled with a security prompt: user name and password. She launched the decryption software and held the tablet tensely, her eyes glued to the screen.

Tony's heart was a thunderous gallop in his chest. The tablet continued to track the march of time: *tick-tick-tick*, even while running the software. His nerves tightened; memory of what lay in the cabinet across from them filled his throat with bile.

He didn't want to think about that. Not yet.

"So, this contact of yours," he whispered and leaned closer to Isabel, until the scent of cinnamon filled his head. "Is it a man or a woman?"

"I don't know," she said.

"You've never met?"

"No."

Annoyed, Tony thought. Capable of asking personal questions, but not so keen to answer them.

"*Is* there a man?" he added, suddenly struck by the thought, because it was not something he'd considered.

Silence, but she stiffened, as if just realizing how close he was. So close his chest nearly touched her back, close enough he could press his mouth to her bare nape. He settled for nestling his mouth to her ear, where her hair tickled his nose and her cap pressed into his cheek.

"You don't wear a ring," he said softly.

"Do you really want to have this conversation *now*?" she snarled.

Tick-tick-tick.

"Now's as good a time as any," he replied. On the heels of that statement, the first chime sounded.

"Two minutes," she muttered.

"Well?" he asked.

"Well what?"

"I'll take that as a no," Tony said, satisfied in spite of his churning belly and his nerves, which were shrieking that they were almost out of time. "You sure that software's going to work?"

He watched the tablet's screen. It had gone black; the only thing on it was a blinking cursor at the top left hand corner. It didn't appear to be doing anything, and—

"It will work," Isabel said, her confidence absolute. A heartbeat later, the screen on the tablet flickered; a wash of blue appeared, followed by the opening of a screen that held countless .wmv files.

"Fuck yes," Tony said, scanning them. They were all similar in size, arranged by nothing more than date, and none of them were labeled in any significant way. There were easily a hundred files—

"Here." Isabel chose the one at the top and clicked on it. "This is dated two nights ago, the same night she took them."

Tick-tick-tick.

Time seemed to bleed away as the player opened to reveal the cabin they stood within, brightly lit with the curtains closed. The angle of the view made it clear it had been recorded by one of the cameras in the cabinet.

Alexander Cruz sat on a tall, narrow wooden chair in the center of the room. He was nude—which made Tony flinch—his form pale and slight, his hands curled into fists in his lap in effort to cover himself. The look on the boy's face was one of desperation and fear and *knowing*. Frozen, as if carved from stone in a moment of infinite horror; a statue cast in terror.

The kid understood what was coming, that there was no escape. *Resignation, survival the only goal, so he would take it.* Tony saw it plainly, like accident footage playing out in slow motion, and such hot, pure fury burned through him, he had to close his eyes and take a deep breath. Stop himself from throwing that wooden chair through the fucking window.

If the kid can take it, so can you.

He grit his teeth and forced himself to watch as Donavon Cruz approached the boy, who fought to be stoic in the face of his fate. But the kid was shaking and shuddering, and so sickeningly vulnerable, part of Tony was screaming. Cruz's steps were slow, deliberate, his smile a curve of gentle mockery. He was fully clothed in a hand-tailored three-piece suit; the contrast against Alexander's nudity only further illustrated the power Cruz wielded, a weapon as effective as any of those he collected. He circled the boy slowly, and

Alexander watched him with wide, waiting eyes, going so motionless it made the fine hair across Tony's frame bristle.

"We both know why you're here," Cruz said softly, and Isabel turned up the volume on her tablet until the words were crisp against the *tick-tick-tick.* "You, and not him."

Alexander said nothing.

"You confessed to a crime you didn't commit," his father continued. "Didn't you?"

The boy only stared at him, unblinking.

"You lied to me." Cruz's gaze swept his son's naked form; another smile flickered across his face, *pleasure and anticipation, drunk on his power,* and Tony wanted to reach through the screen and kill him. "But you did it out of loyalty, to protect him, and I can't fault you for that. Protecting him is your responsibility. So I'll allow you to take his punishment—this time. But only this time. Because no matter what you do, Alexander, nothing will stop me from claiming him. He is mine, as you are mine. *Mine.* You do understand that, don't you?"

Something flickered across the boy's features, something Tony knew instantly: *hate.* A furious, burning rage that turned the bile in his throat to acid.

"Your fealty pleases me, but we both know it is only a means to an end. Because for all your protests, you want this. You *need* this. Even if you won't admit it." Cruz slid off his suit coat and tossed it aside. He reached up and began to loosen his tie, still circling the boy, still smiling. "Perhaps it's time to take the next step. Is that what this is about? Are you asking me to test your limits? There are many different methods I can use to discover your thresholds. Many different tools. I waited, because I thought you weren't ready. Was I wrong, Alexander? Are you hungry for the full initiation into your bloodline? Have you grown eager to become blooded?"

A sound rumbled in Tony's chest; he couldn't stop it. Cruz discarded his tie and moved on to the buttons of his shirt, which he began to undo, one by one. The boy watched like snared prey, and every one of Tony's muscles went tense, as if he could leap through the tablet screen and save the kid. His breath tightened; his heartbeat echoed the countdown: *boom-boom-boom!*

Horror was seeping into his veins like ink bleeding through paper.

"Yes. I can see I'm right. You're beginning to understand that this is your heritage. *Your gift.*" Cruz removed his shirt and tossed it on top of the suit coat. His hands flexed, his eyes rapt on his son's small form. "Here is where your value and your power lies, Alexander. Do you feel it?"

Cruz halted in front of the boy. He reached down to the erection clearly visible beneath the fine fabric of his trousers and began to stroke himself, and Tony felt his skin grow tight, his nerves sparking like live wires. His stomach clenched hard; it was everything he could do not to throw up. The boy was still, waiting, his hands clenching and unclenching in his lap, his eyes unmoving from his father's face.

"You feel it, don't you?" Cruz's hands went to his zipper. "I want to feel it, too. *Submit.*"

The boy jerked, as if he'd been struck, and for one,

breathless moment, didn't move. In that instant, Tony saw everything: his terror, his hate, his rage, the blinding need to defend himself crashing into the knowledge that nothing he could do would be enough. *Acceptance.* And then he stood stiffly, turned, and knelt down before the chair. He reached out and gripped the seat, his knuckles white, a muscle ticking wildly in his jaw. He leaned forward, rested his chest on the seat of the chair, and stuck his buttocks into the air, and the purpose was so hideously clear, Tony had to physically contain himself.

"Sick sadistic fuck," he snarled, and his heart screamed at him to *move, to save him,* even as his brain recognized the futility of such an act.

There was nothing to stop; it was already done.

Cruz shed his pants. His entire body bore scars, whip marks, pockets, odd, curved marks. Long, ugly lines and raised, round burns. *A man who liked receiving pain as much as he enjoyed delivering it.*

He stroked himself again. Licked his lips and smiled. Then he reached out and grabbed his son's hips with both hands and pulled the boy toward him, and Tony broke. He looked away.

He'd seen men blown apart, decapitated, shot. Limbs disintegrated, heads explode; he'd been awash in blood and brains and bone, but he couldn't fucking handle watching what he knew was happening. He couldn't. He fucking *couldn't. Jesus H. Christ.*

Beside him, Isabel continued to stare at the screen, her only sign of distress the hard, tight, white line of her mouth.

Ding. The second chime sounded, and Isabel's hands

moved across the surface of her tablet.

"Sixty seconds," Tony said, his voice rough, squeezed past the gorge sitting in his chest.

"Downloading."

"Clock's ticking," he muttered and swallowed once, twice, his heart beating double-time, his guts churning. He wanted to kill Donavon Cruz.

He needs us, Tony. Like Elian needed us. We cannot fail him.

The memory of Lucia's plea sheared through him, and regret made the caustic mix in his chest surge into his throat. He realized it wasn't just Lucia he'd betrayed with his denial and deliberate inaction—it was a goddamn ten-year-old kid who had *no one*—and fury burned in his belly, fury at Donavon Cruz, but mostly at himself for being such a stupid, selfish, *scared* SOB.

"Let's go," Isabel said, disconnecting the hard drive, and shoving it back into the cubby beneath the drawer. Tony shoved the drawer they'd removed back into the desk, and then they were hauling ass out of the cabin, out the back door, and running full speed across the length of the Cruz property.

Tick-tick-tick—

They leapt over the perimeter just as the last chime sounded; Tony slammed into the side of the SUV and looked back to make sure no alarms were screeching. All was silent.

"Well, we got what we came for," Isabel said breathlessly, sagging against the car. "Now we just have to figure what to do with it."

Tony bent over and threw up.

CHAPTER 24

Sam was a big man.

When Alexander stood next to him, he felt like a narrow blade of grass in the shade of a giant Sequoia. At first, that had scared him. Not that he would ever admit to such a useless and futile emotion—fear—but that did not change the fact that he felt it. Every moment of every day, forever. Or that it caused him to do stupid things. *Selfish things.*

Something of which he was not proud.

But for some reason, he'd stopped being afraid of Sam. And it wasn't because Sam wasn't dangerous—Alexander fully recognized how far Sam would go if Sam believed in something. *All the way.* And he would leave a brutal, bloody trail in his wake. Sam didn't hide, as Alexander's father did, behind words. *Games.* Sam was just Sam. And the anger Sam carried was something Alexander shared, something he understood. He hadn't expected to ever have anything in common with someone.

And yet, he did.

The story of Sam's father—and seeing those scars, too many to count, and suddenly understanding that some scars were visible, but others, others weren't—had made Alexander contemplate their similarities, which was a new experience. He understood there were others out there like him, but they hadn't seemed real—like he didn't seem real—and he'd found no consolation in the statistics and stories he'd come across.

I figured every kid knew the taste of his own blood.

Sam made him think. And part of Alexander despised him for that; he didn't want to *think*. He simply wanted to survive. But his brain was always busy, always murmuring, painting pictures and telling stories and helping him to escape, if only for a moment, and Sam intrigued his brain, because while part of him was painfully aware of what Sam could *do* to him, the other part was—oddly—wholly trusting, as if recognizing Sam as someone who might actually have the ability to *help* him.

Which was wrong. Foolish, stupid—*grow the fuck up*—and hopeless. That he would even consider such a possibility enraged him, that boiling heat, so close to the surface. Something he utilized to keep people away, but something which—sometimes—overtook him. Never ebbing, never easing, just a steady, eternal combustible flame. Alexander accepted this; his rage was part of him, in every cell, every breath. There was no fighting it. But part of him…some tiny, stubborn, *certain* part of him actually believed in Sam. In hope. In miracles. *In spite of everything.* And despite the cold, hollow, infuriated place in which Alexander existed, so remote and removed from the world, he wanted to believe, too. When he looked at Sam, something raw swelled in his chest, a living, breathing thing that made his lungs tight and his heart beat too hard.

He'd tried to crush it, and it was Lucia's fault that he couldn't, because that sensation...*she* was responsible for its birth. Her fury and her fierceness and her love had broken through the icy, furious wall he'd spent so much time building as though it were nothing. *Nothing.* He couldn't forget the look on her face the first time she'd found him, and it wasn't something he wanted to remember—because forgetting was the only solace he had—but she had been so *enraged*...Alexander knew she wanted to kill. He could see it. Not like Rosa, who had no words, no tears, only silence—*acceptance*—her face locked, her eyes unwilling to meet his. Not like Mrs. Mills, who saw only what she wished to see, or Mrs. Livingston, who knew everything that went on in the Cruz household and watched him with disgust. *Scorn.*

Alexander had become accustomed to those around him simply floating past, as if he were a forgotten planet, spinning along his own cold, solitary trajectory, but Lucia...Lucia had crashed into him like a blazing meteor, and that had forced him to awaken. To feel. And he was not grateful, not one bit. *He didn't want to feel.* Hate was so much easier than hope. Because now he had to decide whether or not to step into the light, and that light exposed everything. It *burned.* So much so, he was afraid—sometimes—that he might turn to ash beneath it.

To take that step...the idea terrified him, *infuriated him,* far more than his father ever had. He could handle his father—*he could*—but he couldn't handle false hope. He could not reveal himself only to have that revelation dismissed. Ignored.

Judged.

Because Alexander knew Lucia had told…others. And that they'd all sent her away. Lucia didn't understand how powerful his father was, how he could twist and turn things until they were unrecognizable…especially the truth.

There is only one truth, mijo.

But that wasn't true. That was wishful thinking.

Alexander had allowed her to steal them away for only one reason: Ben. Ben was the sole person Alexander loved; Ben was the only person for whom Alexander would give everything, do anything. Ben was smart and funny, his heart pure and good, and Alexander would not watch their father destroy him.

He would not.

The next time, it will be him in that chair. You can't stop that, Alexander. He's a Cruz. He will be initiated.

Over Alexander's dead body…and not because he would again take a paring knife and spilt open his veins. No, that had been wrong. *Weak.* And that he'd sought such an escape—while leaving Ben to fend for himself—shamed Alexander deeply. That was why he'd allowed Lucia to usher them through the dark house and into that decrepit death trap on wheels, why he'd kept Ben quiet and strapped them both in as she'd backed from the driveway and raced away.

For Ben. Because in his heart of hearts, Alexander knew he would never be saved. He was already ruined. But Ben…Ben still had a chance. Even if that meant hiding. No matter what it meant, if he was *free*... Then it didn't matter what happened to Alexander. It would all be worth it. Because if he could save Ben, that would mean he'd *won.*

And that his father had lost.

Not that Alexander didn't dream of escape. Of freedom. Of his father's blood marking the walls; of his hoarse screams echoing across the vast, endless desert. And he knew that, if the opportunity ever presented itself, he would make that happen. No matter the price.

Fantasies, his busy brain distracting him with hope. Something to live for. He knew better than to believe.

But now there was Sam. Sam...who bore his own father's marks. Who'd saved them. And who'd promised to get them where they were going.

Wherever that is. Lucia had talked about Alaska, somewhere in the far north where she knew someone, but so far they hadn't even made it any further than Idaho.

Alexander had strained to listen to the conversation that had taken place between Sam and Lucia the night before, as he lay beside Ben, but he hadn't heard much over the hiss and crackle of the fire, the drum of the rain and faint howl of the wind. He'd seen Sam touch her—the tension between them made Alexander uncomfortable—and he'd seen Lucia walk away. He remembered the sad look on her face, and the determined one on Sam's, and he worried about what it all meant.

He didn't understand the dynamic of human relationships. He never had; he didn't particularly *want* to. He was alone, but for Ben, and he always would be. Still, he knew the value in understanding that dynamic, that there was knowledge and power there, something he could benefit from. That he should work to comprehend the complexity of inter-personal relationships, because even though he felt nothing but isolation and cold rage when it came to the world around him, others did, and it was important to his survival that he understood them.

So this morning, when he'd seen Sam leave the cabin, he'd snuck out behind him and followed, and now he stood watching as Sam dug through an old pile of junk in the small lean-to behind the cabin. There had been heavy silence this morning; the rain came down in a torrent, and Ben had woken with a runny nose and a fever. Sam decided they would stay put, at least for a few hours, and Lucia hadn't argued. They'd eaten a silent breakfast of oranges and granola, while Sam watched Lucia like a cat watched a mouse, and Lucia pretended not to notice.

"You need something?" Sam suddenly asked, and Alexander started and realized he hadn't been nearly as stealthy as he thought.

"No." He took a step closer. "What are you doing?"

"There's an old fishing pole here. Thought I might find some tackle, maybe try and catch a fish or two. We could use the protein."

Alexander stared at the broad expanse of Sam's back. He wore a flat black coat that the rain rolled right off of, and Alexander knew there was a gun beneath that coat, because this morning, he'd seen it. Gleaming, black and big—way bigger than the tiny little one Lucia had in her purse—and Alexander wanted to know why he had it.

He wanted to know who Sam was. *Really* was.

"Can I come with?" he asked, even though he had no interest in fishing.

Sam looked at him over his shoulder. "You prepared to

be wet and cold and get skunked?"

"Skunked?" Alexander echoed.

"It means we probably won't catch anything but a cold."

"Then why try?"

Sam arched his brows. "Aren't you hungry for something besides an oatmeal pie?"

"Yes."

Sam nodded. "Then go tell Lucia, and put something warmer on."

Alexander turned, then halted. "You'll wait for me?"

Sam met his gaze, nodded.

Alexander hurried into the cabin. Lucia was on the old, worn out bed, reading to Ben—*Cloudy with a Chance of Meatballs,* his favorite—and the warmth of the fire made Alexander shiver. He dug through his bag and pulled on another shirt, then his fleece. When he reached for his coat, Lucia narrowed her gaze and said, "What are you doing?"

"I'm going fishing," he replied, words he'd never before said, which seemed heartening somehow. "With Sam."

"Does Sam know this?" she asked.

"He invited me," Alexander said, which was kind of true. "He found an old pole out back."

"I wanna go fishing with Sam, too," Ben said and sat up. Lucia pushed him gently back down.

"No, monkey," she said. "You are already not feeling well. No fishing for you today."

"I'll catch one for you," Alexander told him, even though he had no idea how to catch a fish.

"Okay," Ben said, disappointed.

"Are you sure it is alright with Sam?" Lucia wanted to know, watching him with suspicion.

"Yes," Alexander said, ignoring that suspicion. "He's waiting for me."

She looked like she wanted to launch an investigation, so Alexander hurried back out of the cabin. Sam stood waiting out front, a fishing pole in one hand, a battered, five-gallon bucket in the other.

"No tackle," he said. "But I found a few hooks. You're on worm detail."

"Worm detail?"

"We need bait." Sam turned and headed toward the stream they'd followed for most of the day yesterday. Instead of heading back the way they'd come, he headed further up the stream, which was narrow and frothy and *cold*. Alexander knew, because he'd been the one to fill the water bottles last night, and he didn't think he'd ever felt such cold water.

"Bait," he echoed.

Sam shot him a look. "How much fishing have you done?"

Alexander felt his cheeks flush. "None."

"Every man should know how to fish." Sam shook his head. "Guess you'll get your first lesson."

"Why should every man know how to fish?"

Sam halted and looked down at him. "Because every man should know how to take care of himself—and those around him. If you can fish, you can feed yourself. Maybe that's something someone like you takes for granted, but you shouldn't."

"Someone like me?" Alexander asked, and unease rippled through him.

Sam started walking again. "Someone whose never had to worry about being hungry."

Alexander hurried to keep up. His stomach began to churn. "How do you know I've never had to worry about being hungry?"

"Son, I know exactly who you are. And damn sure you've never stared into an empty fridge with your belly aching so hard you feel sick."

Alexander halted. He said nothing, his heart beating too hard, that odd, inexplicable welling in his chest growing tight. He watched Sam get further upstream, and his hands clenched into painful fists at his sides.

He knows. How does he know? Had Lucia told him? Why would she—

"You coming?" Sam wanted to know.

But Alexander didn't move. He'd wanted...he didn't know what he'd wanted. *To not be who he was.* If only for a little while. A stupid wish, impossible, like everything else. He should've known better. Nothing was ever—

"I know everything," Sam said, suddenly right in front of him, staring down at him. "And it's okay."

Alexander looked away. His fingernails bit into his palms, and he wanted to throw up. He didn't want Sam to know. He didn't want Sam to look at him like—

"Alexander," Sam said and reached out to settle his big

hand on Alexander's narrow shoulder. "Look at me."

Alexander trembled and fought the urge to pull away. He didn't like being touched, not by anyone. But Sam wouldn't let him go; he already knew that, and he couldn't win, not against Sam. *Asshole.* And he hated the feeling washing over him, like he was nothing, *shit,* worthless and useless, a waste of skin and space. He stood still, trying not to move. *To fucking cry.* He should just go back and—

"Look at me," Sam said again, his fingers squeezing gently.

Alexander's jaw clenched so tight it hurt. He held himself tensely and made himself meet Sam's eyes.

"What I know doesn't change anything," Sam said.

But he was wrong. It changed everything.

"Not for me, it doesn't." Sam shook his head. He stepped closer. "You think you're the only one? Hell, if only. My pop might not have hurt me like yours hurt you, but he sure as fuck hurt me, and there are days I'm sorry I didn't kill him with my own two hands." A muscle ticked in Sam's jaw; his scar was white, and for a moment Alexander glimpsed something dark and roiling in Sam's eyes, something he recognized. "He's been dead for almost twenty years, and sometimes I can still feel his breath on my neck. It never goes away, son. Not ever. That's why you've gotta deal with it—or it will haunt you every second of every day for the rest of your life. And that bastard's already taken enough. Don't let him have that, too. Don't let what he did define you—because that was about *him*, not about you. That was all him. And you mark my words, Alexander, he *will* pay for what the fuck he did to you. I'll make certain."

Alexander stared at Sam. Tears stung his eyes, burned his throat; the swelling in his chest felt like a bubble ready to burst. His lungs hurt, and his nails dug so deep into his palms, he knew he was bleeding.

"Fuck him," Sam said bluntly. "Let's go fishing."

And then he turned and began to walk upstream again. Alexander watched him, uncertain, his knees strangely weak, something he didn't understand loosening within him.

"You coming or what?"

Sam didn't stop and wait. He kept going.

After a moment, Alexander kept going, too.

CHAPTER 25

"You feel it, don't you? I want to feel it, too. Submit."

Isabel studied the faces of the men around her.

Bob Peabody stood at the back of the room, next to the door, his hands shoved into the pockets of his polyester pants. He watched the video she and Tony had procured—*stolen*—from Donavon Cruz's external hard drive with a killing look on his face. A mark in his favor.

Beside him, Special Agent Kent stared at the screen, his face drawn, his eyes dark.

Seated before the screen was Tony's Lieutenant, a man named Lester Forks. He was short, round and solid, and when he'd shaken her hand, he'd met her gaze and said, "I've heard about you. The pleasure's mine." And while she was rarely swayed by flattery, Isabel was affected by his sincerity. So few appreciated what she did. The Lieutenant watched the scene with a flat expression, but a muscle ticked in his jaw like the flutter of rapid wings.

Tony stood at the window, staring out at the rain. The video disturbed him deeply; his revulsion and rage were obvious. He'd been shaken violently by what he'd seen in

Donavon Cruz's cabin, and he'd been so angry on the drive back into the city that he hadn't even managed words, just growls and insensible mutterings of rage.

If Tony had his way, Donavon Cruz was a dead man.

However, it was the look on Special Agent in Charge, Lawrence Gill's face—*her* boss—that concerned her. He stared at the rape of Alexander Cruz as though it was a painful infomercial he was being forced to sit through.

She'd worked under Gill for only six months and didn't know him well. He'd come to the Violent Crimes Against Children unit from Domestic Terrorism, and so far, he'd left her mostly alone. He was a man more concerned with the politics of the Bureau than the actual policing it did, which was not uncommon, and so long as she was left to her own devices and allowed to work freely, Isabel hadn't paid much attention to him. She saw now that had been a mistake.

Politics. A word dirtier than any expletive.

"Fuck," Agent Kent said when the video ended and the screen went blank.

Bob Peabody met her gaze and nodded, just once. Tony stood motionless, the line of his body so tense he appeared carved from stone. Lieutenant Forks leaned back in his chair, silent, and Gill turned to her and said, "That's all you've got?"

Isabel straightened, clasped her hands before her, and said coolly, "You need more?"

"A video from an anonymous source is inadmissible. You know it, I know it. It doesn't prove shit."

She arched a brow, aware of Tony slowly turning around, of Bob Peabody stiffening, of Lieutenant Forks stilling in his chair. Even Agent Kent shot Gill a sharp look of disbelief.

"I agree it's inadmissible; that point is moot," Isabel responded calmly. "The bigger picture here is the fact that Donavon Cruz is a sadist, a pedophile and a rapist—a fact now known by law enforcement, if not proven by a court of law—and he is—at minimum—unequivocally guilty of raping his son. I daresay it isn't the first time. I also doubt his son is his first and only victim; men like Donavon Cruz spend their entire lives stalking and victimizing their prey. When you take into consideration Mr. Cruz's wealth and reach, that pool becomes an ocean. He is a predator. I have no doubt that if we can secure a search warrant—"

"Forget it," Gill said and pushed to his feet. "We have no evidence the thing is even legit. Anything can be Photoshopped nowadays."

"According to our techs, it's unedited," Lieutenant Forks put in, his tone sharp enough to cut. "And that sure as hell looks like Donavon Cruz to me."

Thank you, Lieutenant Forks.

"I don't care," Gill said shortly. "We're not acting on it. We don't let anonymous sources dictate our investigations."

Isabel stared at her boss, and he looked away. He smoothed his faintly wrinkled, expensive suit and straightened his tie. He was not an unattractive man: tall, lean, his dark hair threaded by silver. Well-dressed and cloaked in professionalism. But color flushed his cheeks, and a fine sheen of sweat covered his brow.

You know it's real, you son of a bitch. And he was going to bury it.

"You're going to protect that fucker?" Tony asked softly, staring at him.

"There's no evidence that film is legitimate," Gill repeated. "And even if it is, it's a family matter."

"No," Isabel said then, rage suddenly blossoming within her like an ugly, thorned bloom. "It's a criminal matter."

Gill turned away, dismissing her. He focused on Agent Kent. "Where are we in the hunt?"

Tony took a step, but his Lieutenant stood and cut off him with a dark look.

"We believe we've narrowed down their general location," Kent muttered. "FEMA has given us permission to enter the area tomorrow, and they've agreed to let us use the airspace. We've confirmed that the vehicle that was spotted was Miss Sanchez's, at least what's left of it, but we have no idea what direction they headed after abandoning the vehicle. They would have been on foot, and most of the surrounding area is high desert and foothills, so their options for shelter would have been limited to surrounding towns. At least two of those towns were destroyed by the tornado that touched down. Quite frankly, sir, we don't even know if they survived the storms, and we won't know until we get people on the ground. Even then, we're looking for a needle in a haystack."

For a long, silent moment, only the patter of the rain was heard. Special Agent Gill stared at Kent, and Isabel wondered if Kent realized both of his hands were clenched into tight fists.

"Cruz is not a patient man," Gill said softly. "I'd suggest you people start doing your jobs or there's going to be hell to pay."

"For us or for you?" Tony asked, watching Gill with a grim, predatory stillness that made Isabel aware, for the first time, of the man who'd spent so much time killing.

Gill stilled, as if catching a hint of that man. "For everyone involved. Cruz isn't Joe-Blow off the street, he's the fucking one percent, and no one in this room can afford to make an enemy of him."

I can, Isabel thought. She met Tony's enraged hazel gaze and saw the same answer reflected there. Even the Lieutenant arched a brow.

"So we let him get away with raping his child?" Isabel asked, but she already knew the answer, and the fury that always existed, far down in the cold storage of her memories, flared high and bright within her.

Gill turned and met her gaze, and she saw resignation. *Acceptance.* His sense of decency had been surpassed by whatever motive drove him. Greed, perhaps—because going up against Donavon Cruz would break any ladder that had once existed to be climbed—or maybe simple fear, because Cruz *did* have power, an unspeakable amount. The man could, in fact, *erase* every single one of them. And even though that threat was not enough to stop Isabel, she knew she was not the norm. For her, it was personal. But for others, it was just a job, no matter the atrocities witnessed on a daily basis, and for them, Cruz was simply too big a fish to fry.

Too much personal risk.

But for Isabel…*fuck personal risk.*

"Any allegation of abuse is not our immediate concern,"

Gill told her sharply. "We need to find those boys. So let's just start there, shall we?"

She only arched a brow. This was not a battle she would win; Gill was as dirty as the window behind him. He was going to force her to take matters into her own hands.

"Good luck with that," Tony said. "Let us know how it turns out."

Gill looked at Lieutenant Forks. "I have the full authority to utilize any and all resources of this department. I trust that won't be a problem?"

Tony smiled, and Isabel's gaze narrowed on him. It was not a smile she'd seen before; no humor, just the promise of pain and death. *Chilling.* And not something she should have responded to, but she did.

Damaged soul that she was, she *liked* that smile.

"I've got a city to run," the Lieutenant responded with a shrug.

Gill turned fully to face him. "Which means?"

"You want to be Cruz's personal little FBI force, go for it. But my people are real cops, and I've got kids who go missing every day. There's murder and mayhem twenty-four seven in Sin City, and I've got an ass-deep pile of case files on my desk as it is. Your crime scene is here, fine. We'll give you any support you need to deal with that. But I won't send my men on a seven-hundred-mile goose chase. It's not happening, not even for Donavon Fucking Cruz. So don't ask."

No wonder Tony was smiling. Kent looked between the two men: the Lieutenant, who spoke matter-of-factly, his gaze hard, shoulders back, clearly willing and able to deal with the Special Agent in Charge, and Gill, who watched him, his features a mask of cold, unbending arrogance.

"Don't force me to call your Commissioner," Gill said softly. "You may not understand who Cruz is, but I can assure you *he* will. I'll make certain of it."

"Commissioner's in Tahiti," Bob Peabody said.

When they all turned to look at him, he shrugged. "It's yellow fin season."

Tony's smile widened.

"I'm sure he has a cell phone," Gill bit out, the color that painted his cheeks growing deeper.

"Save your threats," the Lieutenant advised him. "You might be responsible to Cruz, but we're responsible to the people of this city, and despite what you might think, those people matter. Make your call. Be my guest. Maybe when the Commissioner tells you the same thing, you'll listen."

A cool smile suddenly turned Gill's mouth. "We'll see." He turned to Isabel. "I want you with Agent Kent. You'll leave immediately for Canyon Falls, Idaho."

No, she would not, but she didn't argue. She felt Tony's gaze, but didn't look at him.

"And I want that video destroyed."

A low growl rumbled through the room, one Isabel wanted to echo. Not because she was worried about the video; it was safe enough. Isabel knew how to cover her bases. No, it was the incensed fury she felt toward anyone who traded on another's life, and that's precisely what Special Agent in Charge—Head of the Violent Crimes Against *Children* unit—was doing. Trading Alexander Cruz's life for the ease of his own. *Safety.* For Cruz and from him...procurement by blood. As if the boy was nothing more than chum.

Kent had gone motionless. "Destroyed?" he repeated carefully, and Isabel heard an unexpected hint of steel. His eyes were narrow, his jaw hard. His hands were still clenched into fists.

"Every single copy," Gill said, "is going to disappear forever."

Kent stared at him, and Isabel could see him working it through, his realization that this moment would affect every one that came after. For him. For Alexander Cruz. The immensity of that one heartbeat of time. He seemed so young to her in that instant, she almost felt for him.

Almost. Because this is where he would decide who he would be.

She didn't expect him to raise his gaze to hers, or to see what she saw, something that hadn't been there before they'd watched the video, something she wouldn't dare name, but that she recognized. *Knew.* Something that connected them in the most brutal of ways.

"Every copy?" Kent clarified, his tone a breath of frost, the look on his face distinctly unfriendly.

"Every last one," Gill said, watching the young agent with hawkish eyes. "That will be your job, Special Agent Kent. To make sure that video is nothing more than a bad memory."

"Except for Alexander Cruz," Tony muttered darkly.

For a long moment, Kent only stared at his superior, and Isabel watched in idle curiosity. In spite of what she'd seen in the young man's eyes—something that was unmistakable, something she'd seen countless times in countless others—she wasn't particularly hopeful. It was so clearly a test; surely Kent would do all he could in order to pass. He was young and ambitious and just beginning his career with the Bureau. To openly challenge the man who held his future in hand would be professional suicide.

Isabel didn't think he had it in him. But then Kent smiled, a cold, empty curve that made the hair at her nape stand on end. *Such an old smile.* One she would have never expected from him.

More fool you.

"You have my word, Agent Gill," Kent said, flat words that in no way reflected the icy fury Isabel could see. "Nothing but a bad memory."

Gill's gaze slid to her, his brows arched. "I trust that won't be a problem for you, Agent Bjorn?"

Pushing her. But he wouldn't like the results.

"Canyon Falls, Idaho," she replied coolly, and Tony's gaze flew to her, but again, she didn't look at him.

"Excellent." Gill turned on his heel and strode toward the door. He shot the Lieutenant a look, for which he received only a hard, cold stare. "I'll just go make that call to the Commissioner."

As threats went, it wasn't particularly impressive or ominous, and the Lieutenant didn't look worried. The door closed behind Gill with a sharp click, and silence fell. The rain pounded against the window so hard, the glass rattled.

"Fuck," Kent said softly, viciously.

Isabel looked at him. "Are you going to destroy the video?"

She wouldn't let him, of course. Nonetheless, she wanted to know.

He stared at her. Tony and the Lieutenant watched, silent. Bob waited.

"You have a choice to make, Agent Kent," she told him. "Right here and right now: who will you be?"

"Not him," Kent said instantly.

"Good," she said.

"No federal judge will touch a search warrant with the name Cruz on it," Lieutenant Forks interjected. "But I know a couple of local folks. Cruz is a resident of the city; we have jurisdiction."

Isabel transferred her gaze to him. "Can you get them to watch the video even though it was illegally obtained?"

"It's worth a try." He looked at Kent. "You gonna have a problem with that, Agent Kent?"

A harsh breath of air escaped the young agent. "Fuck no."

Forks nodded. Tony eyed Kent with a narrow, reassessing gaze.

"You need to go to Idaho," Isabel told Kent. "Someone needs to find those kids before Cruz does."

"You're not coming?"

"No."

"You go AWOL, you're done," he told her, his voice flat. "You know that, right?"

"He made this necessary," she replied softly. "Not me."

"I'm not happy you were right," Kent added, and she heard the fury he hid so effectively.

Isabel met his gaze. "Me either."

Kent nodded, and she turned toward the door.

"Where are you going?" Tony asked sharply, and Isabel knew he'd started walking toward her, but if she let him catch up, she would have to deal with him and his questions, so she only met his gaze over her shoulder and said, "I'll be back."

But he didn't stop coming, he only repeated, "Where are you going?"

"I have something to take care of," she said coolly.

Those glittering hazel eyes narrowed, and Isabel ignored the sensation that went through her. *He knew.* Exactly what she was going to do, and how. Something he should not have been able to ascertain given what little he knew of her. But then, he probably knew more than she realized. He was sneaky that way, all flash and cheek on the outside, keen and dangerously perceptive on the inside. A bait and switch, one she kept falling for.

Idiot.

"Isabel," he growled, closing in.

"Later," she told him and shut the door in his face.

CHAPTER 26

This isn't over.

Lucia stared into the rain, Sam's words echoing through her, and did something she rarely allowed herself to do: she made a wish.

That Sam was right. That possibilities still existed, that everything she'd worked so hard for remained within reach. That by some miracle Tony would not fail her again. That Donavon Cruz would pay for his horrendous crimes, and his sons would be *free,* to live and love and laugh as children should.

That everything would be okay.

"A Milky Way of stupid," she told herself in disgust. And she damned Sam to eternal hell for making her think different. For tempting her. "*Ay, yai, yai, chica.* You know better."

Because she did. Even if they were not caught, she would spend the rest of her life running. There was no happily ever after here, and that was *okay.* She'd accepted that. And now Sam...Sam had made her want *more.*

A future. When there was no future beyond today.

Damn him.

Behind her, Ben slept fitfully, sweaty and congested, and she kept a close eye on him. Too much stress, too little decent food. Too much rain and cold and uncertainty.

For them all.

She'd gotten an apple into him, and some water. Perhaps Sam and Alexander would bring back a fish, and she could make a stew of some sort. They could all use a good, hot meal. *And some hope.*

Another useless wish.

"Bah," she muttered.

The rain was lessening; she needed to take Daisy out and get more firewood. Sam would not be happy if she let the fire die. The man would never let her forget it. Obstinate, arrogant man.

And yet…she would not change him. What he'd shared while she'd sewn him up had helped to make her understand why he'd accepted responsibility for them—even if that was not his place. The tale he'd told of his father, of his negligent, absent mother, of his abuse…so matter-of-fact, the truth, spoken in simple words with quiet acceptance. It had touched Lucia, far more than it should. Worse, it had drawn forth her own bloody history, one she hadn't planned on sharing. But it was the look on Alexander's face that made her realize how important the telling had been. Sam's revelation had forged a connection with the boy, a common ground where Alexander might be comfortable. *Where he knew he wasn't alone.* And for that, Sam had earned an indelible piece of her loyalty. She'd seen violence, murder, death, but she didn't know what it was to walk in

Alexander's shoes. Sam, at least, had some idea, a fact which would bind them, and Sam wouldn't shy from that tie; he would encourage and strengthen it. He was a good man.

Better than many she'd known.

No one will touch you. No one but me.

The memory of that vow made her shiver. There were moments when she saw with crystal clarity who Sam was. Beyond his anger, his orders, his intransigence. The man at the core, who was honest and hard and loyal—because if he wasn't there in an official capacity, that meant he was there because Tony had asked him to be there. Because Tony was his friend. And Lucia could respect that. She could only hope it wasn't a lie, that Sam wasn't there in any official capacity. Because *a lie by omission was still a lie.*

And he would bend that rule as far as he could. *Whatever was necessary.* A part of him that was not unlike herself, but also something she couldn't trust. Because what she thought was best, and what he thought was best, were two very different things.

Polar opposites. And he was strong and tenacious and inflexible. An immoveable object she could not shove easily aside.

The bullet wound in his thigh had been an unpleasant surprise, one she continued to brood over. That he'd gone as far as he had while wounded in such a manner—without uttering a word—told Lucia he was far stronger than she'd realized, and even more stubborn. The injury was less than a week old; as an intern at one of the inner-city's emergency clinics, she'd treated enough gunshot wounds to know. When had it happened? How? Who had shot him?

He's dead.

Yes, sometimes she saw Sam with vivid clarity. And while she saw the darkness—which was not something she shied from, because she understood that darkness, had plenty of her own corners steeped in shadow—she also saw something that drew her with visceral force. A strength—a *belief*—that Sam carried, one which he followed and trusted with his life; an unquestioned certainty that his path was right and true and just. Lucia envied that. Because although she believed her own path to be just, her belief wavered. Not in herself, but in everyone else.

Because the world was a cold, unkind place, and it did not welcome those who shook its communal foundation. Outrage was easily donned, but unless it was intimate, *personal,* people didn't act. Too painful or too hard; Lucia didn't know. And she struggled to forgive them. Sam simply didn't seem to care. He was going to act; that would be enough.

Her grandmother would have liked him. A realization which wasn't helping matters. Because unlike her rigid, pious and fragile mother, her grandmother had been untamed, uninhibited, tempestuous and *strong.* She'd recognized her connection to the world that surrounded her, both its people and its creatures, and she'd drawn Lucia into that connection with every opportunity, until Lucia understood her place and her responsibility.

Like Sam knew his place and responsibility.

She was beginning to know him. *Understand him.* And she didn't want to either know or understand him. But there he was. Not going away. And she couldn't push him away as she wanted to; no, the boys needed him. He was their only chance.

So he was a very necessary evil.

If the stupid man hadn't kissed her, she wouldn't even be contemplating the idiocy of uttering a wish.

No. If he hadn't put his mouth on hers...she might have imagined it, secretly. Silently. But once he'd given her a taste... *Ay, yai, yai.* She'd never been kissed like that—just a kiss, so simple, not something she'd imagined could seduce her so thoroughly—and now every time she looked at him, she found her gaze falling to his mouth. *Remembering.* Worse was the riot of sensation that went off inside of her, tiny explosions in places she'd spent most of her life ignoring. So unfair and inconvenient and intoxicating.

And misplaced. Because she was a *fugitive*; there was no place for the thoughts that materialized in her head. The impossible fantasies that tempted her to imagine a life beyond the immediacy of her predicament. And she cursed him soundly for letting her forget that.

You did this. You remember that.

Another shiver moved through her. She'd pushed him—knowingly, but too angry to stop—and perhaps part of her had understood why. What it was she'd wanted, beyond the release of temper. Where it was they were headed with every clash. Perhaps she'd known exactly what would happen, and that's why she'd pushed. Because she wanted him to kiss her.

A sobering realization for a woman who'd spent the last decade alone. One who'd long ago stopped looking to others for anything. She was no virgin, but the few experiences she'd had were ones she'd sought out to relieve the isolation, to feel connected—if only for one, brief, fleeting moment—to the world around her. But those encounters had left her empty and unsatisfied, and she'd not gone looking again.

But Sam...Sam tempted her. And she was wholly unprepared for—and dangerously susceptible to—the blunt hunger in his gaze, the open invitation. Watching her as if he were touching her.

As if she belonged to him.

This isn't over.

But it had never begun, and it never could. No matter how much she might wish differently.

Ben sneezed in his sleep, rolled over, and began to snore. The rain had turned to a light mist, so Lucia pulled on her boots, her coat, and grabbed the piece of burlap they were using to carry firewood. Daisy got up from her place tucked next to Ben and looked at her expectantly.

"Are you ready, sweet girl?" Lucia smiled in spite of her turbulent state. Daisy had proven to be a good little dog, one who was adapting surprisingly well to her new set of circumstance, something Lucia took heart from.

She put on Daisy's leash and they stepped out into the damp, cool afternoon. It was almost two; Sam and Alexander had been gone since just before noon. If she was still, she could hear the faint murmur of their voices in the distance, and she was glad they'd stayed close. *Within shouting distance.* But she was equally glad they'd gone. She needed to get her head on straight, and she couldn't do that with Sam's silent stare resting on her, as if he was waiting for some kind of capitulation.

Damn the man. Demanding the impossible. And

tempting her into considering it.

Lucia slid the loop at the end of Daisy's leash down the steel stake Sam had driven into the ground beneath a large pine tree and told her, "Go potty. I will be back."

The wind lifted, and the mist became rain as she made her way to the back shed, where Sam had parked the ATV, and an ancient pile of firewood sat. A crumbling chopping log sat next to the pile, a small, rusted ax buried in its center.

Lucia put down the burlap and began to load it with the split wood Sam had left in a neat stack next to the chopping log. Rain hit the metal roof in delicate, staccato waves. The building smelled faintly musky, old hay, moisture, wood and wildlife. And something else, something—

Smoky.

Lucia froze, and her heart surged into her throat, and she could smell it distinctly then: the rich, strong aroma of a Dunhill cigar. The contents of her stomach lurched, and her knees gelled.

Terror was like a sudden, vicious punch to her solar plexus, and she went utterly still. She had no weapon; the .22 was in the cabin, still in her purse. And Sam was too far to reach. She looked around, desperate, her heart pounding with painful intensity, and her gaze landed on the ax. Small but sturdy, its head still sharp enough to split wood. *It will do.* It had to.

The worn handle slid in her palm when she grabbed it, and she had to yank hard to free it from the log. She pulled it to her chest, and made herself breathe. *Just breathe.*

Daisy suddenly began to bark, and Lucia felt sick with fear. The little dog was tied up, couldn't run. *Couldn't defend herself.* Another waft of cigar smoke, stronger, *closer*. The rain grew harder, nails pounding the roof; the sound of her heartbeat was deafening.

Lucia forced herself to lower the ax to her side. Then—because she would not let death creep up behind her, unchallenged—made herself turn around.

Ivan the Terrible.

She'd known he would be there; that scent was unmistakable. Even though he shouldn't have been there—how had he found them?—and even though the sight of him standing behind her was surreal, his giant form clad in a black rain trench, dark hair slicking his cheeks, his hooded obsidian eyes locked on her like the jaws of a great white. Her hand clenched on the ax, and she took a deep breath, then another.

Do not react. Act.

But her heart was trying to beat its way out of her chest as her gaze went beyond him, in search of his constant companions—*the other two stooges*—Misha and Enrique, who were never far, and fear was filling her chest with lead. No one but Ivan stood before her, which meant Misha and Enrique were probably out there—*Sam*—

"He said I can have you." Ivan's gaze flickered to the ax she held. He only smiled, and when his black gaze lifted to meet hers, it gleamed like polished onyx. *Hungry*. For pain, for blood. Lucia knew; she'd seen that look before. The men who'd killed her father had worn the same bloodthirsty expression.

She said nothing, her pulse a violent hammer in her ears. Ivan took a step toward her, and she made herself hold her place, her grip on the ax tightening.

"He said I can do whatever I want to you." The Dunhill was tossed aside. "He unleashed me."

A second dark, aberrant smile, and Lucia's blood turned cold. Ivan took another step toward her and cast her in his monstrous shadow, and she knew she was going to have to act. *Offense, not defense.* He would not expect her to attack—no, he would expect her to beg—and that surprise was the only other weapon she would have. But that meant doing whatever it took, even if that was burying the ax she held in his big, ugly head. That meant crossing a line she could not return from.

A choice that—in this moment—seemed moot. Because she wanted to live.

"I have such exquisite plans for you, little mouse." Ivan tilted his head, his skin pale in the gray light, pitted by acne scars. His teeth were uneven stubs, his lips thin. *Like a snake.* A reflection of his heart. He leaned close, and his ugly, sour breath surrounded her. "I've imagined this moment a thousand times. I knew he would give you to me, eventually. And now my patience is rewarded. Now you're mine. Mine to fuck. Mine to kill. *All mine.*"

Lucia grabbed his coat with her free hand, yanked him to her, and head-butted him. The blow was violent, her forehead slamming into his nose like a hammer, and pain burst in her skull. Ivan barely moved, as big and unyielding in her hold as a firmly rooted tree, and even though blood streamed from his nostrils, he smiled again, a gruesome, terrifying grin that made her want to scream.

Scream.

But she couldn't scream, not even to warn Sam, because Ben would hear.

"You want to *play*," Ivan whispered. His eyes sparked, and he reached out—

Lucia kneed him in the balls, a merciless, solid connection that almost sent him to his knees. *Almost.* But not quite, and smile barely wavering, he grabbed her shirt, swung her around like a rag doll and threw her down to the ground with brutal force. She slammed into the hard-packed dirt, her skull bounced against the unbending earth, and the ax tumbled from her hand.

Then Ivan climbed on top of her.

"I *like* to play," he breathed as he lumbered up her ribcage and straddled her. She reared up and punched him again, hard in the solar plexus, and he wheezed out a laugh, one of his hands catching both of hers to crush them in his grip.

She bucked, and he laughed again and buried his face in her neck, where he bit her so hard she felt her skin tear.

"You taste good, little mouse," he whispered, and her stomach heaved. "I want to eat you in tiny bites."

When he lifted his head and looked down at her, his black eyes gleaming, her blood on his lips, she head-butted him again, a direct hit. His nose crunched, and blood flowed down his chin in a river of crimson.

"Bitch," he said with a bloody grin. Then he backhanded her, and she slammed back into the dirt. Her bottom lip burst open and flooded her mouth with blood. Stars whirled in her head; her ears rang, and the weight of him threatened to suffocate her.

"I *knew* you would play with me." Ivan leaned down, his sharp teeth closing on the side of her breast through her shirt, and he bit her again, tearing into her flesh. She cried out, unable to halt the sound. "There is fire in you, little mouse. I want to be the one to put it *out*."

She bucked again, trying desperately to free her arms from his brutal grip. Horror was shearing through her, terror a relentless scream in her head—*can't move*—and panic was almost choking her. The ax was there—she could see it—just beyond reach, and if she could—

"Stop. Stop. We're going too fast." Ivan sat up, shifting his weight atop her ribs, and Lucia fought to breathe. "There are things I want to do. *I have plans.* You're trying to hurry me, but it won't work."

He pulled a flashy, silver butterfly knife from his interior coat pocket and produced it to her with another grisly red smile. "You see, you have your scalpel, little mouse, and I have mine."

His unholy, gut-wrenching glee made her buck again, but he only laughed and rode it out, as if she were an unbroken horse. She was bleeding from his bites and the backhand she'd taken, and his weight was immense, his strength unbeatable. His blood dripped down his chin and slapped her face.

"Perverted, evil bastard," she snarled.

The narrow blade shimmered in the light as he held it over her. "Yes," he said, his smile fading. "Since I was a child."

He sliced across the top of her right breast, his blade penetrating her shirt to split open her flesh like ripe fruit, an agonizing path of searing, white-hot pain. Again, she couldn't stop the cry that tore from her, and Ivan said, "Yes, like that. Scream for me."

A swift, burning cut across her belly; blood spilling down her abdomen, and then the knife passed before her eyes, dripping red, flecking her with blood. A fiery slice tracing her left collarbone; the skin of her right arm splitting in two; her right shoulder—*too fast*—he was carving her like a turkey, and Lucia reared against him, another angry, pained cry escaping her, and he leaned down and licked the weeping wound on her breast.

"So good," he whispered. "Tiny bites."

Lucia lunged toward him, locked onto his ugly, hooked nose with her teeth, and bit down as hard as she could. Ivan screamed; blood filled her mouth. He sprang back, but she went with him, her teeth locked, her only thought that of survival.

Him or me.

Silver flashed, and she waited for that blade to stab into her. But instead the hold on her hands released, and Ivan grabbed desperately at her hair with both hands, trying to wrench her away, to break the grip she had on him. Lucia barely felt it. She bit down harder and punched any part of him she could reach—his head, his temple, his neck—again and again, uncaring that he was tearing her hair from her scalp, that her fingers were crunching beneath the blows.

Him or me.

Beneath her teeth, his flesh tore, and he shrieked wildly, an unholy, unearthly sound as sharp as the steel of his blade. Lucia let go and shoved him backward with all her might.

He swayed, reaching up to cradle the bloody cartilage of his nose, a hysterical cry escaping him when he felt the loose flap of his nostrils, which were no longer attached to his face.

Lucia turned and lunged for the ax. Her fingers brushed the wooden handle as Ivan's hands caught her hair and yanked her violently backward. Tears streamed from her eyes as she fought that grip. *So close.* Just a little farther—

"*Fucking cunt,*" Ivan screamed. "You fucking cunt! I'm going to—"

Wooden splinters dug into her palm as it slid down the slender handle of the ax; she closed her hand, gripped it tight, and when Ivan tugged again, she turned and swung the ax for all she was worth; *thunk!* The rusted blade slammed into his chest, deep, and the reverberation shuddered down her arm with violent force. He went still and looked down at the tool protruding from his torso with almost comical surprise.

"May you burn in hell," Lucia hissed and slammed her palm against the head of the ax, driving it deeper.

Blood fountained from him, drenching her. His hands unclenched from her hair and fell to his sides.

"Die," she told him.

And then he did.

CHAPTER 27

"Do you ever worry that you'll be like him?"

Sam went still. He turned to look at Alexander, who was staring with quiet patience at the battered red and white bobber Sam had affixed to the fishing line he'd found. The water rippled around the bobber, spinning it, but it remained upright, and so far they'd caught only one small trout, but Sam was hoping for another. The rain had almost stopped, but the wind was starting to lift, and the ache in his leg told him that the brunt of the storm was just beginning to roll in.

One more fish, then home. *Home.* Jesus.

"Like who?" Sam asked carefully, pretty certain he knew exactly who the boy was talking about. He'd been surprised when Alexander sought him out and asked to join the fishing foray; it was obvious the kid could have cared less about casting a line. Still, he'd paid attention, hadn't batted an eye at baiting the hook and even helped reel in the small, slender brook trout that had eaten their worm.

Those pale green eyes stabbed into his. "Your father."

Sam thought about that. "I used to," he replied honestly. "I thought being an asshole was in my blood."

"But you don't think that anymore?"

"Nope."

The boy stared at him, his intensity more than a little unnerving. Sam only stared back. *He's just a kid.* No matter how adult his gaze, or how cold he could appear. And Sam could relate; when Magnus had brought him home, it had taken months for Sam to trust. To believe what Magnus said—because unlike his pop, Magnus *meant* what he said—and to accept that his life had changed. For him to realize he had to change with that life if he wanted it to mean anything.

If he wanted it to last.

"Why not?" Alexander demanded. His hands were white-knuckled around the fishing pole, but he didn't seem to notice.

"Because being an asshole is a choice," Sam told him. "And I choose not to be one."

"It's not that easy," the boy said.

"Isn't it?"

Thunder rumbled, and around them the pine trees swayed, sending cold rain and small pinecones to the forest floor. The stream they fished from was fast and frothy and ice cold; earlier they'd spotted an osprey, and Sam wondered if they weren't close to a large river or lake. He'd contemplated the wisdom of walking further out and taking a look. In the end, he'd stayed put, because a jaunt like that could take hours, and the closer he stayed to Lucia and the kids, the better. He'd woken with the same darkness that had dogged him yesterday, only stronger, a steady, terrifying beat of certainty that pulsed in his chest. That's why they'd gone less than a quarter mile upstream, close enough to hear. *Close enough to run.*

"My father..." Alexander looked back at the bobber. "He calls it an initiation."

Every muscle in Sam's body went taut, and his jaw locked tight against the words that welled in his throat. Anger was too easy. The boy needed more than Sam's rage; he had enough of his own.

"He says...he says that every Cruz must be initiated," Alexander continued, watching the bobber. "He told me he would initiate Ben next."

"And you want to stop him," Sam said.

Alexander met his gaze. "Yes."

No matter what it took; that much was obvious. But Sam couldn't blame him. Hell, it made him respect the kid. Surviving was hard enough. Taking on someone else's survival was more than most were capable of.

You'd better fucking come through, Tony.

Or Sam was going to have to do more than just keep them off the radar and safe. He was going to have to take care of Donavon Cruz himself.

Alexander shot him a narrow glance.

"What?" Sam asked.

For a moment, the boy said nothing, watching the bobber, his narrow shoulders hunched against the rain. Then, "I'm going to kill him."

"No," Sam said immediately. "There're other ways."

Another look, filled with scorn.

"Killing isn't free," Sam told him seriously. "No matter

how justified, that blood stains you, and you never get clean."

"I don't care," Alexander said coldly.

Sam rubbed at the back of his neck and wondered why he was arguing. As a kid, he'd felt the same. No price was too high if it meant freedom. And rage was good at making murder seem feasible. Attainable. *Justified.* And it would be justified. Men like Cruz were predators; putting them down was a community service. Sam knew his badge would argue, but most of the time that badge served only as a means to an end. If he didn't make it work for him—or anyone else—there wasn't any damn reason to be wearing it.

"It would ruin your life," Sam said quietly.

"My life is already ruined."

No tears, no outrage, just simple, devastating truth. Sam wanted to snarl, but he understood too well. Arguing would get him nowhere. But it reminded him so much of Lucia—*everything is over*—that he said, "That's up to you."

The boy shook his head, his mouth twisting. "Not everything is a choice."

"Hell yes, it is," Sam said. "Every moment of every day, we choose. How to feel, how to behave, to believe or not to believe. What you choose is up to you. But be careful, because life will follow the path you set. If you decide your life's shit, it'll be shit. Fact. Ten puny years, and you've decided it's over, so you're going to piss away the next sixty? That's fucking sad, Alexander. But, hell, it's your life. Your call. Do what you gotta do."

The boy blinked, frowning, as if trying to figure out how to argue. *Always with the arguing.* Lucia had taught him well. *Lucia*. Who'd ignored Sam this morning as though he was nothing more than a fly buzzing around, stoic in the face of her perceived fate, and it annoyed the shit out of Sam, because she had a choice in that fate, just like Alexander did. That neither of them saw a light at the end of the tunnel wasn't surprising, but it was unacceptable. That he was the optimistic one in this scenario was just fucking insane.

But if he had hope, they were going to have some goddamn hope, too.

"It not that easy," Alexander said, but then the bobber disappeared, and Sam leapt toward him and yelled, "Hook him quick!"

The boy jerked up hard on the fishing pole, and Sam grabbed the slender pole to steady it, telling him, "Now reel, son. Slow and steady—feel that weight, you got a good one—that's it, just like that."

Alexander wrestled with the fish and the pole and the stubborn, aged reel. Sam let him, because he saw the kid's eyes spark and knew that look. Even if the boy didn't land the monster he was battling, he'd be hooked.

That alone made it a good day.

The reel creaked in protest; the line stretched until Sam thought it would snap. Alexander grunted, and finally a thick, long brookie appeared, wiggling desperately in effort to free itself.

"Holy shit," Alexander said, and Sam laughed. He leaned over, caught the slippery fish and freed it from the hook. He held it out, aware that the boy hadn't been comfortable with the killing and cleaning of the first one they'd caught, and said, "It's your catch."

Alexander looked at the fish, then at Sam.

"You want me to do it?" Sam asked him.

"That's weak, isn't it?" Alexander said instead of answering. "That I don't want to kill it."

"Nope, that's human." Sam shrugged and crouched next to the stream. He put the fish down quickly with a large, round river stone, and cut it open, tossing the guts into the stream. "Killing is part of eating, but that's something most folks don't like to think about."

"But it needs to be done."

"Unless you're gonna live on granola and garbanzo beans," Sam said, shooting the kid a smile. "Plenty of people do."

Alexander only watched him soberly. "I don't want to kill anything. *Except him.* Is that wrong?"

Sam's chest tightened. "Makes perfect sense to me." He tossed the fish into the bucket. "That's two. One more wouldn't hurt. You up for another go?"

The sudden, shrill sound of Daisy barking made Sam go still. The little dog rarely made any noise, but they were in the middle of the wilderness, and anything could have set her off. Still, he didn't like it. The dog's frantic yapping made the lead in his chest bleed into his veins and his stomach clench hard.

"We should go back," Alexander said abruptly. He looked in the direction of the cabin, took a step, and Sam caught him with a firm hand.

"Wait," Sam told him.

"But—"

The sound of a branch snapping not far away—*too close*—made Sam suddenly crouch down. He hauled Alexander to the ground with him, and when the boy went to speak, put a finger to his lips in warning. He waited until Alexander nodded in understanding before removing his hand.

Another branch; like a fucking herd of elephants. Someone unfamiliar with the woods, who was off trail and not particularly worried about being heard. Or who simply didn't realize how far the sound carried, even with the wind and rain and rush of the creek.

Not Lucia, who would've stuck to the trail, and who would've had Ben with her.

Fuck. Shouldn't have left them. Knew I shouldn't have left them. Quarter mile, too far, goddamn it—

There. Just downstream, left of the trail, a large, dark figure wove through the stand of pine. He appeared to be alone and was clearly unused to picking his way through the wilderness, his steps uneven and off balance, breaking sticks and crunching leaves, and making the birds shriek in alarm.

"Misha," Alexander said in a hushed tone, watching the man. The boy looked up at Sam; terror had shattered his cold façade like splintered glass. "He works for my father. With his brother, Ivan."

Ivan the Terrible. Lucia's fear was echoed in Alexander, and Sam deliberately turned away from the horror show his brain produced at the realization Lucia was probably dealing with Ivan at that very moment. Because that way lay insanity. He needed to *focus*. First, Misha.

Then Ivan.

"Stay here," Sam told Alexander. "Don't move until I say."

"But Lucia—"

"I know," Sam replied grimly. "One thing at a time, son. Misha and Ivan. Anyone else I should be looking for?"

If anything, the boy went even paler. He nodded. "Enrique. Misha and Enrique are always together."

"Good to know," Sam muttered.

He left Alexander and made his way toward the man who was tromping through the forest toward them. One swift glance behind him told Sam that Alexander was listening and staying put—for now—so he continued toward Misha, staying low, using the landscape and the willow bushes that hugged the stream bank to provide cover. His leg ached in protest, but it felt stronger since Lucia had sewn him up, and the pain wasn't going to stop him, so he only ignored it. Above him, thunder suddenly rumbled, and the rain picked up again as the wind grew stronger. The trees swayed, groaning. Daisy continued to bark, hysterical, agitated yips and howls that made Sam's heart beat painfully hard.

Lucia. Ben.

Fucking Ivan.

"Focus," he told himself. Because getting dead wasn't going to help anyone.

He moved closer to Misha, cutting an angle through the pine stand, and found a good ambush spot. Then he waited. Less that a minute later, the tall, broad form who was Ivan Dragovitch's brother walked past. Big and solid and thick with muscle; *this might hurt.*

Sam went at him sideways with two punches: one to the kidney, and one to the throat. Then he kicked the guy's feet out from under him. When Misha went to his knees, Sam stepped up behind him, wrapped his arms around that thick neck and pressed hard into the man's carotid artery. But the son of a bitch was huge and strong as a bull, and he threw himself sideways in effort to dislodge Sam's hold, his fingers gouging into Sam's arm, his head slamming back into Sam's ribs like an angry ram. Sam followed him down, swearing. Christ, he didn't want to have to *kill* this asshole. Leaving a trail of bodies in their wake was not—

A brutal fist to Sam's face; blood burst from his nostrils.

"Goddamn it," he growled and punched the man he held viciously, once, twice, three times in the temple. Misha sagged to the ground.

"Fucking stay there," Sam told him and stood, his leg throbbing, blood leaking down his chin. In a heartbeat, Misha was rolling over—*playing fucking possum*—and silver flashed, then he was aiming a large steel gun—

Sam caught the weapon and lifted it; the gun discharged, and the only reason it didn't deafen him was due to the narrow black silencer on the end. He slammed his head into Misha's nose and felt it crunch; Misha's hold on the gun faltered, and Sam ripped it away and brought it down violently against Misha's skull. One, twice, a third time, until blood flew, and again the man fell limp beneath him. Sam stayed put, breathing hard, watching with narrow eyes, and when he was certain Misha was truly down and out, he rolled to his feet, took a step and—

A knife stabbed into his calf. Sam turned and kicked Misha in the face with the business end of his steel-toed boots. More blood, but the stubborn bastard lurched to his knees, and reached for the blade that was still stuck in Sam's leg.

"You stupid fuck," Sam snarled, not sure if he was talking to himself or his opponent. He kicked Misha again, a swift, brutal blow to the guy's ribs, but Misha only grunted and began to climb to his feet.

Fuck it. Sam again swept the man's feet out from underneath him, caught that big head as he went down and twisted violently.

Snap. He dropped Misha's body to the ground.

So much for not leaving death behind them.

"You killed him," Alexander said, and Sam started violently. He looked over to see the boy standing only a handful of feet away, bucket and fishing pole in hand.

"He didn't give me much choice," Sam replied. He wiped the blood from his nose, tucked Misha's 9mm into his waistband and pulled the knife from his calf, wincing, glad it had only penetrated an inch or so. Still, he was going to bleed like a stuck pig. "You should have stayed put. You didn't need to see that. I'm sorry."

Alexander only shook his head, his face growing cold. "They know what he does. They don't do anything."

Sam wiped the bloody knife on his jeans, folded it back together and held it out to the boy. "Put this in your pocket."

Those pale eyes met his. Alexander took the knife and turned it over in his hand. It was a nice one, good grade steel, a smooth, abalone-shelled handle. After a moment, he slid it into his coat pocket, and Sam turned to peer through the trees.

He could see the long, narrow outbuilding that sat behind the cabin, a faint wash of aged gray through the trees. But there was another dickhead out there besides Ivan—*Enrique*—and—

A woman's cry sliced the air, fury and pain and terror given piercing sound.

"Lucia," Alexander said and dropped the bucket and poles. Sam had to grab him with both hands and lift him from the ground to prevent him from running to her.

"No, goddamn it," he growled, even though he felt sick and furious and wanted nothing more than to run like hell toward that scream. "Just fucking wait. There's one more. I'm not going to be able to help her if I *run into some asshole's bullet.*"

The boy's gaze snapped to his. For a long, breathless moment, they stared at one another.

"You have to trust me, son," Sam told him in a hard voice. "This is what I do."

Alexander nodded, but Sam's grip only tightened.

"Say it," Sam demanded. "Say it so I know you'll do what the fuck I tell you to do. I have to be able to trust you."

Those pale eyes were wet, terrified. "I promise. But you have to *save her.*"

"I will."

Another cry rent the air, followed by the loud *crack* of another branch breaking, and Sam went back to ground, pulling Alexander down with him.

"This time," he told the boy. "*Stay here.*"

He moved carefully out into a small break in the open

pine and halted low, behind a large chunk of granite. The sky was growing darker, casting the land in deep violet, and the rain continued to get heavier. Thunder was steady now, and above the spears of jagged pine, lightning tore through the sky in thick, deadly webs.

The robins gave a sudden cry of alarm. *Crack.* Close. Much closer than before.

Sam slowly, carefully peered around the stone. *Son of a bitch.* The guy was less than three feet away.

Sam reared back. He had only seconds before Enrique was there, right beside him. Surprise was his only element, and since a punch to the kidneys, and a punch to the throat had been so effective with Misha, Sam gave them another whirl. But Enrique was faster than Misha had been, and his fist caught Sam under the chin before Sam could slam his knuckles into Enrique's larynx. Sam shook his head, his mouth full of blood, and put his boot in Enrique's gut. Enrique bent double, and Sam didn't waste any time, tackling him to the ground, wrapping an arm around his throat, punching his knees into Enrique's vulnerable spine. This time he didn't bother to give the guy the benefit of the doubt. His head was pulsing, he was bleeding, and his fucking leg hurt. *No more talking.* Sam tightened his arm around Enrique's neck, and when Lucia screamed again and adrenaline surged through him like a runaway freight train, he snapped it like a toothpick.

A fucking trail of bodies. Perfect.

Sam climbed from Enrique's body and looked around carefully, his heart like a hollow drum, endorphins spearing through him like whiskey. He forced himself to stand still, to look and listen and wait.

Nothing.

He turned to look at Alexander. The boy hurried toward him from his hiding spot.

"Stay close," Sam told him and spat a mouthful of blood to the ground. "There might be more."

"Ivan."

"Yes," Sam said grimly.

Daisy began to howl, hair-raising, unholy sounds that made Alexander take a frantic step, but Sam stopped him.

"Behind me," he ordered. "We don't know that Ivan is the only one left."

"He is," the boy said with certainty.

Sam hoped like hell the kid was right, but no way was he counting on it. So he kept Alexander behind him as they hightailed it toward the cabin, his eyes sharp on the woods around them, listening to the birds, aware of the storm getting stronger. Closer. They were almost to the woodshed behind the cabin when a man's voice suddenly shredded the silence, shrill and crazed—*you fucking cunt!*—and Sam's heart threatened to stop. He began to run. Along the end of the shed, around the corner into the narrow space behind the cabin, past the parked ATV—

And found an ocean of blood. A dead man. And Lucia, who sat motionless in the middle of it all. Beside her a large man lay on his back, the small ax Sam had been using to split kindling protruding from his chest.

So much goddamn blood.

Lucia looked up at him, her eyes dark. Her nose was bleeding, and her bottom lip had been split open. *But she's okay. She's*—Sam's gaze slid down, and he saw the bloody bite on her neck. *A fucking bite.* And he felt sick again, with rage and guilt, and the need to kill a dead man. The shirt she wore was in shreds, and she was bleeding from knife wounds at her collarbone—*Jesus, her breast*—down her arm, across her stomach and—

He turned and blocked Alexander, who'd just come around the corner, from seeing her. "She's okay. Go check on Ben."

The boy tried to get around him, his face white, but Sam side-stepped into his path.

"Go," he said.

"But…"

"Now," Sam told him. A calculated risk, to send the boy into the cabin without him, but the kid didn't need to see Lucia like that—and fuck if that pool of blood was *hers*—and his father's goons wouldn't hurt him, and Ben *did* need someone to make sure he was okay. Not a good choice—and he fucking knew it—but Sam couldn't bring himself to leave Lucia sitting in that lake of blood.

"She's okay," he repeated to the boy when he hesitated. "Trust me."

Alexander didn't want to go, and Sam realized in that moment the kid loved Lucia, even if he would deny it, even if he didn't know he felt it.

Sam reached out and cupped his narrow shoulder. "Check on your brother. I'll take care of her."

A long, level stare full of unspoken warning, and then a reluctant nod. The boy turned and ran for the cabin.

Sam pivoted to look at Lucia. She was staring down at

her hands, which were covered in blood. Every inch of her was awash in red. *Jesus Christ. How much of it was hers?*

His heart slammed into his ribs, and he strode into that wet, crimson pool and knelt slowly before her. The coppery scent of the blood made his stomach turn; *so many fucking wounds.* He reached for her slowly, carefully. She flinched away.

"You're bleeding." He grit his teeth in effort not to grab her and haul her into his arms. *To be calm.* "Let me help you."

Nothing.

"Lucia," he whispered, his chest tight. "Look at me."

Still, she didn't move. Didn't blink. Barely breathed.

Sam reached out and gently cupped her unbruised cheek. *So fucking cold.* Too cold. "Sweetheart."

Lucia jerked away and blinked, as if suddenly coming awake. "I killed him." Her gaze went to Ivan; her voice rose. *"I killed him."*

"I know, baby." *Christ.* What a fucking day. "I'm sorry. But now he won't hurt anyone else."

She turned and looked at him then, her face bleeding and bruised and spattered with blood. "Yes. I had not thought of that. Thank you."

She stared at him with eerie calm, as if she wasn't soaked in blood and bleeding. *In shock.* Her hands shook violently.

Sam reached for her again, slower.

"Come on, Lu," he coaxed quietly. "Those wounds need treatment."

Her gaze flickered to the bloody slash on her breast, then back to him, and Sam said, "Yes. Let me help you. Like you helped me."

She seemed to consider it for a long moment and then nodded. Sam cupped her arms, and they were cold and clammy and slippery with blood. But as he moved to lift her to him, Alexander suddenly came back around the corner of the cabin toward them, and as soon as Lucia saw him, she began to fight Sam's hold.

"No, no, no, please, Sam, do not let him see me like this. *Please.* Look at me, oh dear God—"

"Calm down, sweetheart. I won't let him see." Sam turned and put himself in front of her as Alexander skidded to a halt. The boy's gaze jerked to Ivan. The ax.

"Ben?" Sam asked.

"He's okay," Alexander replied breathlessly. "Daisy woke him up. I told him she saw a skunk, and that you and Lucia were getting firewood. He doesn't know what happened."

"Good." Sam said. "Thank you. I need you to go back into the cabin and heat some water on the stove. Use that pot we found. And then get Lucia's first aid kit out and put it on the table. Keep Ben inside, and keep him calm. We'll be right behind you."

Alexander looked down at the pool of blood, then at Sam. "I want to see her."

"No," Sam told him.

The boy darted around him, just out of reach, and screeched to a halt at the sight of Lucia, who made a soft, mournful sound and tried to turn away.

"L-Lucia?" he whispered, going pale. His hands fisted at his sides, and his eyes went to Sam, then back to her. "Are you…are you okay?"

She took a deep, shuddering breath and turned her head to meet Alexander's worried gaze. "*Sí, mijo.* Please do as Sam asked. I will be right there."

But Alexander's eyes were tracking her wounds. "Did Ivan do that?"

"*Alexander*," Sam growled.

"*Sí*," Lucia said simply.

The boy looked at Ivan's body, then back to her. "I'm glad you killed him."

A soft, sharp sob broke from her, and Sam said, "She's going to need that hot water."

Alexander nodded. He took a step back, then another. His gaze touched Sam's.

"I'll take care of her," he told the boy again.

For a long moment, that pale green gaze searched his, but whatever the boy saw was apparently good enough, because he whirled back toward the cabin and took off.

Sam turned back to Lucia and found her trying to unbutton her blood-soaked shirt, but her hands were shaking so violently she couldn't get the buttons undone. Sam brushed her hands aside and simply tore it open, sending the buttons flying.

Her bra was pale yellow; blood had soaked into the thin fabric and turned it a gruesome orange. It was cut where Ivan had slashed her breast, and torn where he'd bitten her. Sam stared at that shredded hole, at her bruised and bloody flesh peeking through, and felt the darkness that slumbered within him awaken with a vengeance. His skin rippled; his blood turned hot, and his heartbeat became a vicious throb at the back of his throat.

Donavon Cruz was a dead man walking.

Sam was going to see to it himself. Fuck Tony, fuck proof.

He's a fucking corpse.

"I'm sorry," he said harshly, the words raw, painful.

"This is not your fault." Her voice wavered. "I knew he would come."

Sam bit back the words that burned on his tongue, and carefully stripped away her shirt. *Don't argue with her.* Not now. Even if this *was* his fucking fault, because he never should have left her at the cabin alone. Never should have assumed he was close enough. And now she'd lost something—*had it fucking taken*—and it wasn't something he could ever give back.

Way to protect her, you fuckwit.

Christ.

"Sam," she whispered, but he only shed his coat and stripped off the t-shirt he wore under his flannel. He had a bottle of water in one pocket of his coat, and he opened it and wet the shirt.

"Sam," she said again, a hint of annoyance in her, and he felt relief.

But he didn't respond. Instead he applied one corner of the damp cotton to her face and, as gently as he could with a faint tremor of rage shaking his hands, began to clean her up.

"Sam," she growled, and her hand caught his, still trembling, still too goddamn cold.

He met her gaze, a sheen of glittering gold speared by dark, earthy green.

"This is not your fault," she repeated.

He said nothing and went back to wiping the blood away.

"Difficult man," she muttered. "You will listen to me."

Sam only continued to wash her off as best he could. The cuts were all fairly shallow—which was some kind of goddamn miracle—but those bites... The site of them burned into his gut, all the way through to his spine, and he knew he'd never felt such incendiary fury, never hungered for blood as much as he did in that moment.

Beaten and bitten and fucking cut. The regret was like acid.

"I'm sorry," he repeated.

"*No*," she snarled. "I won. Not him. Do not be sorry."

"I didn't mean—"

"*Stop.*" Lucia gripped his flannel with both hands and tried to shake him, and Sam realized how weak she truly was. "I do not want your regret, Sam. Your sorrow. *This was inevitable.* But I am still breathing. Please let that be enough. *Please.* Because it has to be enough for me."

Christ.

Sam stared at her, his heart beating like a drum, the rush of his blood a dull roar. She stared back, her eyes dark, her mouth trembling, and he tossed down the shirt and slid his arms around her, careful of her wounds. She shuddered when he pulled her into his arms, and a low, mournful sound escaped her. Her arms wrapped his waist; her fingers clutched at his shirt. He felt her breath on his neck.

"It's going to be okay," he whispered in her ear.

"*Sí*," she said.

And then she began to cry.

CHAPTER 28

The fire was almost out.

Alexander stared at the small, blackened chunks of wood coal, where only the tiniest ember flickered, and felt panic surge through him. *Lucia needs hot water.* And then he realized there was a small pile of kindling and several cut up logs sitting behind the stove, and he made himself take a deep breath.

You're freaking out.

But he couldn't get the images out of his head. Sam, kicking Misha's ass. Snapping Enrique's neck. Lucia. The blood. *Ivan.*

Dead. *Ivan the Terrible was dead.*

The knowledge was so overwhelming that Alexander knew if he hadn't seen it, he wouldn't have believed it. And he wondered how Ivan had found them. How—

"When's Lu coming?" Ben demanded from his spot on the bed, where Daisy sat beside him, still trembling from excitement. "I want her to come *now*."

Alexander grabbed the firewood and opened the stove. He remembered what Sam had done, using the smaller pieces to build the fire up, and did the same, blowing on those tiny embers until flame ignited. He carefully added the larger logs, closed the stove and went over to where the beat up old tin pan they'd found behind the woodshed sat on the table. He poured water into it and put it on the top of the woodstove.

"Did you hear me?" Ben wanted to know. "Where's Lu at?"

Alexander glanced out the small, dirty windows but there was no sign of Lucia or Sam. He thought about Lucia—all that blood, all those cuts—and how she'd looked at him—*horrified and ashamed and scared*—and his stomach churned, and tears pressed hard against the backs of his eyes.

She's going to be okay. Sam will take care of her.

Part of him recognized the stupidity of believing that—*believing in anyone*—but the panic slowly eating away at him left no room for doubt. He *had* to believe in Sam, because there simply was no alternative. Lucia—

"Zander!" Ben yelled. "Are you listening to me?"

"They're coming," Alexander snarled, his heart beating furiously. He went to Lucia's pack and pulled out her large first aid kit. He took it to the table, aware of Ben watching.

"What's going on?" Ben asked, a small tremor in his voice. Because Ben might have been young, but he was no dummy. And Alexander knew there would be no way to hide what had happened from him, not in a tiny one-room cabin, not when there'd been so much blood.

Not when Lucia was hurt.

The pressure in his chest welled, and Alexander stilled in

effort to combat it. *He hadn't believed.* Not in Lucia, not in Sam. He'd expected his father to come. The police, who would arrest Lucia and take her away. Ivan, who would put them in the car and take them home. And then it would all begin again—

... you mark my words, Alexander, he will pay for what the fuck he did to you. I'll make certain.

Goosebumps washed down Alexander's arms. No matter how many times he told himself they were just words, part of him believed Sam would keep that promise. Even though he knew how foolish and futile it was to trust anyone. To believe. That's why he *hadn't*. Even while he'd gone along with every crazy thing Lucia had done, he hadn't truly believed anything good would come of it.

Nothing would change.

But Sam had killed Enrique and Misha with his bare hands. *And Ivan was dead.*

It was all happening. Really, truly, fucking happening.

"Dander?" Ben whispered, his eyes dark and huge, and Alexander went to him and hugged him hard and tight, because he didn't have any good words.

"I'm scared," Ben said, his face too hot against Alexander's neck.

"It's okay," Alexander told him and hoped it wasn't a lie.

The door swung open, and Sam carried in Lucia. She was still bloody, but not as bad as she'd been, and she was wearing Sam's flannel shirt, which covered most of her wounds. Except for her face, which was bruised and bleeding and—

"Lucia!" Ben cried and leapt from the bed. Alexander caught him, and his heart hurt when Ben fought his hold.

"Lemme go, Zander!" the boy cried, tears trickling down his cheeks. "I want Lu!"

"She's hurt," Alexander said. "Look at her, Ben."

His brother stopped fighting and focused on Lucia as Sam sat her down in one of the chairs beside the table. Her left eye was almost swollen shut, and her lip was bleeding, and the wound on her neck looked like…*a bite*. Alexander stared at her and felt his chest tighten painfully.

This was *his* fault. If she'd never found him that night—

"I am alright, monkey," she said, but Alexander could tell by the look on Sam's face that she *wasn't* alright.

Not at all.

"She fought Ivan," Alexander told his brother. "He's dead now."

"Dead?" Ben echoed.

"Ivan," Lucia repeated and suddenly tried to stand. "He will have Misha and Enrique with him. We have to—"

"I took care of it, sweetheart." Sam gently forced her back into the chair. "Now you just sit there for me, so I can get you cleaned up."

She shook her head, and Alexander recognized the look that crept across her face, and it made the tension riding him lessen, because she was going to *argue*, and if she felt like arguing then maybe she'd be okay.

"I do not need—" she began, but Sam cut her off, snarling, "You're a fucking mess. Don't you dare argue with me. *Don't you fucking dare*."

And she sat back and grew quiet, and Sam did something Alexander didn't expect: he leaned down and pressed a kiss against Lucia's mouth. She shuddered, and a tear slid down her cheek, and she kissed him back, and Alexander stared at them, his heart beating hollowly.

"You let me do this," Sam told her in a low voice. "You let me take care of you."

Lucia nodded, and Alexander saw her hand reach up to clench in Sam's coat.

Alexander stared at them, dumbfounded. Sam had *kissed* her.

When had *that* happened? What—

"I need the towel in my pack," Sam said and looked at Alexander. "And that hot water."

Alexander nodded. He sat Ben back down on the bed. "Stay here," he said. "We need to help her."

Ben sank down next to Daisy without protest. He stared at Lucia, his face stricken.

"It's okay," Alexander told him again. "She's going to be fine."

He hoped.

He went and grabbed the thick green towel from Sam's pack and checked the water, which was warm but not boiling. He carried both over to the table and put them down beside Lucia's first aid box. Sam unbuttoned the flannel she wore, revealing her bra—which was stained orange with blood and made Alexander blush—and pulled the first aid kit closer. He pulled out a bottle of something bright blue and a handful of cotton balls, and then he dampened the edge of the towel and pressed it against the wound on Lucia's neck, the one that looked like a bite. *A bite.* Had Ivan...bitten her?

Why would he bite her?

"That son of a bitch died too fast." Sam's voice was harsh. "He deserved to feel it."

"He did," Lucia murmured. "I severed his aorta."

"He bled out instantly." Sam snarled. "Too fucking quick."

"No. I am not a monster; better it was quick." She looked up at the ceiling as Sam bent over her and dabbed a cotton ball with that blue liquid all over it against the wound on her neck. Alexander saw her flinch. "When they killed my father, they went slow. Cut by cut. It was a horrible death."

Alexander froze. Next to him, Sam slowly straightened. His gaze met Alexander's.

"Dig out some butterfly bandages," he said in a low voice. "We're gonna need quite a few."

Glad to be tasked with something, Alexander nodded and went to the first aid kid. His heart beat painfully hard as he dug through the kit in search of the winged, narrow bandages Sam needed.

"They used a machete," Lucia continued softly. "Piece by piece, they just hacked him apart."

Sam swore under his breath. He swept another cotton ball across the cut that traced her collarbone, and she flinched again.

"Then they cut Elian," she said, and Alexander couldn't help himself, he reached out and touched her, just a brief, fleeting touch against her shoulder and said, "Lucia—"

But Sam shook his head. "Let her talk," he murmured. "Let her get it out."

"He had terrible scars," she went on, staring up at the cobwebs that littered the pine ceiling, her voice soft. "On his back, down his arms. There was so much blood. The floor was slippery, and I fell. My mother was screaming. My *Abuela*, she tried to hide me, but I got away. I had to help them. Elian was crying, and he never cried..."

Alexander felt his eyes burn, and the contents of the first aid kit blurred. He knew who Elian was—Lucia had shared her brother with him, and part of Alexander had hated her for that, because he knew *why* she'd told him—but now he understood there was more, much more than he'd ever known, and it was *worse*. When he couldn't have imagined that ever being true.

Worse.

"But I could do nothing. *Nothing.* It was too late. It is *always* too late." Lucia lowered her head to look at Sam, and the expression on her face made a tear slide down Alexander's cheek. "Why is it always too late, Sam? *Why?*"

"I don't know, baby." Sam's hand shook faintly as he cleaned another one of her wounds, an ugly, thick slash across the top of her chest. "Some things just aren't meant to be."

"It is not fair," she said and her voice shook, and another tear slid down Alexander's cheek. *Stupid tears.* Why was he crying? "So much pain. So much injustice. I am tired of it. I want it to *stop.*"

"You and me both, sweetheart." Sam turned to

Alexander, and his lashes flickered. "You ok?"

Alexander swiped at his damp cheek. "Yeah."

"Good. I need you to hand me those bandages, one at a time."

Alexander nodded. He unwrapped one of the butterfly bandages and handed it to Sam.

"Put them close together," Lucia whispered. "Almost touching."

Sam said nothing. He pulled the tabs from the adhesive on the ends of the bandage and placed the strip across the wound on Lucia's collarbone so that it pulled the laceration together. Again, she flinched. He added another, and another, and then another, slowly closing the wound. Then he moved on to the long, deeper cut across her chest.

"There is antibiotic salve—"

"We've got this, Lu," Sam said calmly. "Just relax, sweetheart. Let your body rest now."

She shuddered, and her eyes closed. She still had a hand wrapped in Sam's coat.

They worked silently, steadily, until she was washed clean, covered in antiseptic, and all of the cuts that marred her were bandaged. Alexander checked on Ben and found him watching quietly, Daisy curled in his lap. The fire popped, and outside the dirty windows, the rain fell in sheets.

Thunder rumbled overhead. Alexander looked at Sam.

"We're not safe here," he said.

"Not anymore," Sam agreed. He slid his flannel shirt carefully back onto Lucia and buttoned her up, ignoring her efforts to do the buttons herself. "But she needs to rest. So for the moment, we stay."

"I am fine," she said instantly. "If we need to go—"

"We stay," Sam repeated.

"But—"

"No more arguing with me," he growled. "For one goddamn day, *no more arguing.*"

She blinked. Opened her mouth—

And Sam kissed her. *Again.*

"No," he told her and stood. He turned and looked down at Alexander. "I don't suppose those fish are still in the bucket?"

Alexander straightened. "I think so."

Sam nodded. "Good. I'm going to grab them and take out the trash. I'll be back."

The door shut behind him with a thud. Ben crept from the bed and ran to Lucia.

"Ah, monkey, I am okay. You see? Nothing to worry about." She winced as she bent over, but she lifted Ben to her lap and hugged him tightly. Tears shimmered in her gaze, and Alexander felt his throat grow tight. She held out an arm to him.

For a moment, he didn't move.

"Mijo," she whispered.

And then he was there, too, her arm sliding around him, Ben gripping his hand. And when the tears came this time, he let them.

CHAPTER 29

Tony pounded his fist against room 354's nondescript brown door, a door which sat in an endless hallway of nondescript brown doors, and knew—if it was the *wrong* nondescript brown door—he was going to start breaking things.

I'll be back.

But Isabel hadn't been back. No, she hadn't returned after this morning's shitshow of a meeting with her boss, and she wasn't answering her damned phone. In point of fact, Tony had been unable to reach her for the majority of the day—which he was really quite pissed off about—and he was done waiting. So he pounded again.

I have something to take care of.

Goddamn her. They were in this *together*. There was no going lone gunman, and Tony had a feeling that was *exactly* what she'd done. Well, she was going to learn a thing or two about her new partner, the first of which was that they *were* partners, that they did things *together*, and—

"Isabel," he snarled loudly. "Open this fucking door, or I'll break it down."

He knew she could hear him. And he knew she was in her room, because the tiny blue economy car she'd been driving was parked in the lot. What he didn't know was why she'd run. He understood her fury; she wasn't alone in that. And he understood that she would act, with or without her boss's permission, even if that meant flushing her career down the crapper. What he didn't understand was why she seemed to think she had to do it *alone*.

Had the woman not been paying attention?

"Isabel," he roared and pounded again.

The door was wrenched open, and Tony blinked, because for a minute he was certain he had the wrong room. The woman at the door was barefoot, clad in faded jeans and a *Goonies* t-shirt. Her pale blond hair was braided, her face free of makeup. She wore a pair of wire-framed eyeglasses, and behind the clear lenses of those glasses, eyes like black coal glowered at him.

"Who are you and what have you done with Agent Bjorn?" he asked.

"Har," she said and stepped back to let him in.

Tony went. He looked around her room, unsurprised to find it neat as a pin. Beds made, luggage—just one tall, narrow bag—tucked into a corner. Her tablet and phone on the small round table next to the window. The TV was on 24 hour news, muted.

"I've tendered my resignation," she said. "I'm afraid you'll be working the remainder of the case with Agent Kent."

Tony only snorted. "When pigs fly, baby."

She slid him a look over her shoulder. "I can assure you, I am no longer a safe bet."

"What the fuck is that supposed to mean?"

She sat at the small table. "No doubt your Lieutenant would not approve of your involvement with a former FBI agent who's gone rogue."

"Rogue," Tony repeated. "Sexy. I like it."

Isabel shook her head, her mouth tightening. "You should distance yourself from me now."

No way in hell. Tony sauntered over to stand beside her, just a little too close, exactly how he liked it. "Are you trying to break up with me?"

"Don't be glib," she growled. "I'm serious. If you value your career—"

"I value *you*," he replied.

She looked up at him, color flushing her cheeks. "You stupid man. You aren't listening."

"What did you do?" he asked, because he knew she'd done something, it had been glittering in her eyes when she'd ditched him that morning, and was still there, a spark of rebellion within the darkness.

Isabel looked back at her tablet. "Better you don't know."

"Better for who?" he asked. "Not for me."

She said nothing, staring at her tablet, her mouth a stubborn line. Tony crouched next to her.

"Tell me," he said quietly.

She turned to look at him; she looked heartbreakingly young, but the old soul that stared at him from her dark eyes belied her fresh-faced appearance. "You should leave."

He only shook his head. "You know better."

"They'll make you pay for my crime," she said. "I don't

want that."

Protecting him. Something within him went tight at the realization, because he would protect her, too. "Too late," he said simply. "I'm all-in."

"No." The hands in her lap fisted. "You're not. You can still walk away with your badge intact. If you go now."

He didn't move.

"Goddamn you," she snarled softly, and Tony smiled.

"There she is," he replied. "The Amazon at heart."

She turned to look at him, her dark gaze searching his.

"What?" he asked.

"You see what no one else does," she told him. "And I wish you didn't."

"I know the feeling," he replied.

They stared at one another for a long, silent moment.

"I don't give a shit what they do to me," he said, because he wanted to be very clear. "Win or lose, we're in it together."

"You're a fool," she said, but her eyes gleamed, and color flushed her cheeks, and Tony saw pleasure.

"Tell me what you did," he said again.

Somewhere outside, a siren began to wail. Rain spat against the window, and her tablet hummed quietly atop the table.

"I sent the video to Aequitas and requested distribution to the news organizations," she said finally. "I didn't want to. Exploiting Alexander Cruz was never my goal. But…" Her gaze met his. "Sometimes there are no good choices."

"No," Tony agreed softly.

"Better exposed and free than hidden and chained."

Something dark and bitter wove through Isabel's words, and beside her, Tony stilled. He studied the pure line of her profile, saw her lashes flicker, her mouth tighten.

"That would be the voice of experience talking," he murmured. "When are you going to tell me what happened to you, Isabel?"

She shook her head and looked away. Tony watched her swallow, her pulse a delicate hammer in her throat.

"Not today," she said, her voice cold, but he only smiled again.

"Well, there's always tomorrow," he said optimistically. Then he stood. "How long do we have before the shit hits the fan?"

"I don't know. I've never asked for this kind of…favor before. Aequitas might not agree." Isabel looked up at him. "What about the search warrants?"

"Nothing yet."

"Hurry up and wait," she muttered.

"Such is life." Tony took the small chair opposite her, sprawled his legs beneath the tiny table and trapped hers between them. "You need to tell me your plan. Not that I don't respect your decision to tell the Bureau to go fuck itself, but it seems like a very impetuous decision for such a careful woman."

"Careful?" she repeated. "Is that how you see me?"

"Control is important to you," he replied with a shrug. "Nothing wrong with that. So long as you know when to let it go."

"The Bureau isn't—"

"I wasn't talking about the Bureau."

Isabel met his gaze, and Tony stared back, his hunger plain. Direct, unflinching, exposed. Because he was done lecturing himself, done prioritizing. He wanted her. And he knew she wanted him. Whether or not they would happen had yet to be determined, but he wasn't fighting it anymore. This woman...she'd become his partner in the last two days, trusted and respected and important. He hadn't been lying; he *did* value her. And everything else notwithstanding, he'd decided he wasn't going to lose her.

What the hell that meant was anyone's guess, but he'd *decided.* It was only fair to let her know.

"We're good together, Isabel," he continued, and color surged into her cheeks. Those ebony eyes glinted at him. "Do you know why?"

"I'm not having this conversation."

"Because sometimes—*sometimes*—I get a little impetuous myself, and you're good at reining me in. A gentle hand, but a firm one. Capable and brave, and so fucking smart I have to run to keep up. *I like running, Isabel.* And I like you. You keep me grounded and focused. Just like I keep you balanced."

She arched a brow.

Tony leaned across the table, until he was close enough to inhale her scent, so incredibly tempted to touch her. But he didn't. He didn't want either of them distracted. "Because you," he told her softly, "can get a little intense. You focus like a bird of prey, and you work out a plan, and you get your man. That's all good and well for the rest of the world, but for you…it's not enough, sugar. You need more. Something to balance out the ugliness, something that makes all the sacrifice worth it. Something that belongs only to you."

Her cheeks were bright, furious red. "And you're that something?"

"We both know the answer to that."

She blinked at him. "You are…"

"The one," he said, nodding.

A sharp laugh of disbelief escaped her. "Could you be any more arrogant?"

"I could," he told her. "But we don't have time to fuck around."

She only stared at him, her eyes glittering, her cheeks flush with color.

"I want you to think about it," he said seriously. "Because I can't stop thinking about it."

"Your timing—"

"Sucks. I know. But things are going to start happening fast now, and I don't want this to get lost in in the rush. I don't want *us* to get lost in the rush. Because there is an *us*, Isabel. You know it, I know it. And when all this is over, we're going to deal with that."

"Are we?" she asked coolly, but he could see the wild flutter of her pulse, the slight dilation of her pupils, and when he let his gaze roam over her gorgeous face and linger on her mouth, she inhaled. Sharply.

"We are," he promised.

She narrowed her gaze, and his heart beat hard in his throat. He wanted to pull off her eyeglasses and unwind her braid and taste her. *He'd hadn't even tasted her yet.* A crazy realization that changed nothing. Because he already knew she would taste good. That he'd grow addicted.

Going to want to keep her.

"You," she said softly, "are the most—"

Her tablet beeped loudly, and she cut herself off and picked it up. She said nothing, staring at the screen.

"You going to make me come over there?" he asked.

Her gaze jerked to his. "Aequitas."

"Yea or nay?"

"Yea." She swallowed. "But that's not all."

Tony laid his hand gently over hers, which was clenched into a cool, trembling fist atop the table. "What else?"

"The coordinates." Her gaze met his. "The Cruz boys' last known location."

He stood. "Let's go."

"We can't." Isabel shook her head. "I'm no longer part of the investigation."

"That's horseshit," Tony told her. "You're an expert in your field, and I can enlist any expert I want. The Bureau has no jurisdiction over me. Let's go."

Isabel stared at him for a long, silent heartbeat. "They'll know I was the leak."

"Can they prove it?"

"Of course not." A hint of ice that made him grin. "I know what I'm doing."

"Then you're worrying about me for nothing," he pointed out. He leaned down, close, and gave into the urge to dip his head into the hollow of her neck and sniff. "But I appreciate the concern, sugar. It's good to know you care."

She bristled. "Regardless of any lack of evidence, they will *know,* and if I accompany you anywhere, that stigma will stain you, may do significant damage to your career, and I won't allow—"

"*Together*, Isabel. Remember? You let me worry about riding shotgun with your rule-breaking ass. *We can win this fight.* But only if we don't quit. Only if we do it *together.* So are you in or out?"

Tony stared at her, his heart beating hard, part of him terrified she would turn him away, that whatever dynamic existed between them—the one that had allowed them to get this goddamn far—would be crushed within the fist of her intractable will.

"Those boys are out there," he added softly. "Lucia, Sam. We're all they've got, baby. Just us. We started this. It's time to finish it."

She didn't move, and disappointment bled through him. It was heavy and dark and fucking painful. He wanted—

Isabel suddenly got up. She grabbed her tablet and phone, stepped around him, and marched over to slide the electronics into the pocket of her luggage. Then she sat on the bed to pull on a pair of bright pink socks. Tony watched her closely, frozen, afraid to hope, but she only stuffed her feet into a pair of low-heeled boots and donned a hooded, dark blue coat. She stood and glared at him.

"This is on you," she told him, but while her words were

cool, there was fire in her eyes and color in her cheeks. "There will be no whining when you get fired."

Tony grinned. "I'll take my chances."

CHAPTER 30

He'd kissed her to shut her up. Again. *Damn him.*

Because Lucia was growing to like Sam's kisses. *Too much.* Bad enough she'd been seduced by the hot, wild taking of her mouth while she'd been trying to chastise him. Worse was the emotion that had fluttered in her chest when he'd pressed his mouth to hers as he'd patched her up, so gentle and sweet, a tantalizing offer of comfort she'd absorbed like a sponge. Something she wanted more of.

Which was disturbing.

Double damn him.

That he blamed himself for Ivan's transgressions was also disturbing. Sam wasn't responsible for anything that had happened—she was. From the first moment she'd contemplated taking the boys, Lucia had known the repercussions would find her. *Ivan would find her.* She'd accepted that, had been ready and willing to face the consequences—and she *had* faced them. At least, the biggest, ugliest one.

And she'd *won.*

While her heart was heavy with the knowledge she'd taken a soul—even one so dark and damaged and dangerous—Lucia knew she would do it again if she had to. *She wanted to live.* And she refused to be sorry for that.

Every animal on earth fought for survival; she was no different. As she'd tried to tell Sam, she hadn't expected him to save her. The boys, yes, but not *her*.

And yet rage simmered within him; his regret was piercing and bitter, and Lucia didn't know how to undo it. There was simply nothing to forgive. Words, it seemed, were useless. He wouldn't listen. He seemed determined to punish himself, and she had no clue how to turn him from that path. As if his defeat of Enrique and Misha was nothing; as if his tender care of her—and his protection of the boys—was wholly negated by what he viewed as his personal failure to shield her from Ivan.

But Ivan had been her cross to bear. *I knew he would let me have you.*

An inevitability, even if Sam didn't realize it.

She wanted to shake him, to *make* him listen. Make him hear her. Which was why she'd followed him from the cabin—in spite of the continuous rain and her aching body—that, and because they needed to talk. *Really* talk. Without little ears listening.

Ben was very sick. He was growing more feverish and congested, and he was complaining of pain in his joints; he needed medical care. They were going to have to head toward civilization. There was no choice, because Lucia wouldn't allow him to get worse—no matter what that meant. And now that they'd been found...it was only a matter of time before more armed, murderous men came.

Before Donavon Cruz came.

Yes, it was time to go. *Now.* No matter how badly she hurt. Lucia didn't care if every one of her wounds reopened, if every cell throbbed, if her head felt ready to explode, and her left eye was almost swollen completely shut. They had to go. Ben needed a doctor. And then…

Then… She halted, a sharp, painful wedge caught in her chest. Her hands shook violently. *Get a grip, chica. You have no time to shatter.* Which was true. No time to digest all that had happened in the last three days; no time to lick her wounds. To mourn the loss of the life she'd left, or the one Sam—*damn the man*—tempted her to imagine. No, there was only the road before them, no matter how unpredictable, how dangerous.

You must keep going.

So she took a deep, gulping breath, and then another. *Later. You can fall down later.* And then she made herself continue on, following the sound of Sam chopping wood. *Thunk! Thunk!*

Not unlike the sound of Ivan's chest splitting open.

Thunder rolled through the small valley as she made her way toward Sam. Lucia had grown oddly used to the rumbling sound. And the rain. Even the lightning that shattered the sky had become so commonplace in the last two days she found it unremarkable. As if the world had been overtaken by an endless storm, a manifestation of the chaos they now found themselves lost within.

Ivan's body was gone when she rounded the corner, and there was old hay strewn over the crimson pool where he'd bled out. A sleek black ATV was parked next to the one they'd ridden in on, and Sam was splitting wood with the same rusty ax that had ended Ivan's life, its handle stained pale pink.

He paused when she halted before him.

"You should be resting," he told her, that dark look sliding over his features.

"Ben is sick," she replied, unwilling to argue with him. "He needs a doctor."

Sam swore softly. "He's worse?"

"Yes. And I have no access to antibiotics—which would only work if he has a bacterial infection. If it is a virus…no, we are not prepared for that. He needs care I cannot give him." A tremor moved through her at the thought this crazy mess she'd made could harm Ben—*kill* him if he became ill enough—and regret pierced her. *Choices. You made all the wrong ones.* But the realization changed nothing, forgave nothing, and fear welled in her chest. "We have to go now."

Sam tossed the wood he'd split down onto the burlap, where the pile she'd started before Ivan had appeared still waited. "They're chipped."

She blinked. "What?"

"The boys. Cruz had microchips surgically embedded in their skin. As soon as we hit satellite range, he can track them."

Lucia stared at him. "How do you know that?"

"Tony texted me this morning."

Dread spread through her like a stain. "Why didn't you tell me?"

Sam stepped toward her. "And when should I have done that? At breakfast, in front of them? Or later, when I was cleaning up your blood?"

His anger whipped across her, and she swallowed,

nodding in acceptance. "That is how Ivan found us."

"Yes." His tone was grim. "And as soon as we're back in range, they can watch us in real time."

A dark, heavy sense of doom settled over her. "Then it is over. There is no escape."

"Bullshit." Sam tossed the ax down into the wood, where it struck deep. "Cruz is a man, not a god. First, we'll deal with Ben. We'll find a doctor, and get him treated. Then we'll deal with the trackers. One thing at a time, sweetheart."

Lucia watched him lean down to fill the burlap with the rest of the wood he'd cut and realized his leg was bleeding. Again. Stubborn, tough man; that he would pay for helping them haunted her. He deserved better, because he was a good man. He shouldn't be penalized for her crime.

"You took care of...Ivan?" she asked hesitantly, remembering what Alexander had told her. *Sam killed Misha and Enrique with his bare hands.* And perhaps she should have been horrified, but she wasn't.

She was grateful.

"I stashed him out of sight, but the critters will probably find him." Sam shrugged. "Not much we can do about that."

"Then he will provide value in death that he did not in life." She paused. "You are still angry."

Sam only shook his head.

"You must not blame yourself," she said evenly. "We are better for everything you have done, Sam. Everything."

"You're my responsibility," he said, his voice clipped.

"No, we are not. We are not your job. We never were."

"The hell you aren't."

"*No,*" she said again.

"I shouldn't have left you. I knew better."

"I wanted you to leave," Lucia told him bluntly.

He flinched. "Good to know."

"Sam," she said softly and waited until he looked at her, those brilliant eyes of his glittering like finely cut stones. "You are a distraction I cannot afford."

His gaze narrowed on her. "That works both ways, you know."

Something warm and dangerous bloomed low in her belly, but Lucia said nothing, painfully aware of the heat burning in her cheeks. His eyes traveled over her, and she turned away, embarrassed by her battered appearance. *So much stupid.* But she couldn't help it; she knew she looked a fright.

"Don't," she said, her throat suddenly aching.

"Don't what?" He stepped over the pile of wood to stride toward her, not letting her hide. He stopped before her, so close his heat pressed against her skin, and his scent flooded her nostrils. So close she had to crane her head back to look up at him. *Too close.* And yet, not close enough. He reached up and skimmed his fingers down the unbruised side of her face, the pads of his fingertips rough and hot and proprietary. "Don't look? Don't touch? Don't *want?* It's way too late for that, sweetheart."

He stepped closer, until their bodies touched, and Lucia couldn't bring herself to move, even though she knew she should. No, instead her hands lifted to tangle in the slick, damp material of his coat, where his heart beat strong and steady beneath her palm. Because he was too tempting. All tensile muscle against her, hard and strong and warm; she knew what it was to be surrounded by that strength and heat. How carefully he wielded the power he contained. That alone was seductive; how gentle he could be, how tender. His restraint was far more enticing than another man's show of brute strength. And as he stared down at her, his thumb rasping along the line of her jaw, Lucia felt drunk on him.

What was between them…she hadn't lied to him: *it could not be.* She was a wanted fugitive, and nothing was going to end well for her. She had no future; to want him was foolish and selfish and unfair, but part of her had stopped caring. When she'd turned and found Ivan there, waiting… regret had engulfed her. All of the things she'd not done, places she'd not seen, people she'd not known. But more than anything…*Sam.* And now part of her was determined to take whatever little bit of him she could have, for however long she could have it. Something to hold close, *hers*, when she lost all else. She'd almost died; now she wanted to live. And Sam was a fine man. They were…almost friends. Collaborators. Conspirators.

A team. And no matter how many times she told herself to turn away, she remained. Life was short, and hers would be even more so. Whatever brief, fleeting moments of freedom she had left she wanted to spend living.

"You scare me," she told him, her voice raw, an admission she'd not planned on making. *Ever.* "I did not expect you. This. *Us.*"

That dangerous smile curved his mouth, startling her.

"Then we're even. Because I sure as hell didn't expect us, either."

She searched that bright, glinting gaze. "But you are not afraid?"

"Only a fool doesn't feel fear."

She blinked. The hand at her jaw slid down to cup her throat, gentle, possessive, and the wound left by Ivan's bite made a flicker of something dark and deadly move through Sam's gaze. "And yet you persist," she whispered. "You believe it can be."

"Yes."

The seriousness in him made her breath lock in her throat. "Why?"

"Faith." He leaned down, and his breath washed over her parted lips, and her heart lurched against her ribs. He moved infinitesimally closer, until her breasts met the wall of his chest, and his thighs pressed into hers. His free hand slid around her waist, curved down over her bottom, and then he lifted her carefully against him, bringing her flush against the hard plane of his body. "I have faith."

But faith is a lie... Lucia didn't get the chance to say the words. Sam's mouth pressed against hers, careful of her split bottom lip, a tender caress that made heat splinter through her, a fierce, white-hot webbing she didn't expect. His beard rasped against her skin as he kissed her: her mouth, her cheek, her closed eyes. His mouth whispered over her, pressing with gentle reverence against her skin. A gasp escaped her when his tongue licked delicately at her upper lip.

"Sam," she whispered, shuddering as a pulse burst to life

low in her belly. Awareness lashed across her skin; against his chest, her nipples budded, and his tongue stroked into her mouth, rubbing hers in a carnal motion she felt at the juncture of her thighs.

Lucia moaned and slid her hands up into his hair, clenching her fingers around the silky strands. She arched against him, forgetting about the throb of her wounds and her aching bones, and stroked his tongue with her own. Another streak of electricity arrowed through her at the hungry sound he made into her mouth. The hand on her neck tilted her head, and he ate at her mouth like a man starving for the taste of her.

Ay, yai, yai! The man could kiss. So fierce but so tender, and so careful of her wounds; his hunger was raw, consuming, matched only by the sudden, burning need that arced through her like live current. She grew soft and wet, and the strong, steady pulse at her core made her press her thighs together in need. He was so—

"You have to have faith, too," he breathed roughly, breaking the kiss. He pulled back to stare at her. "I can't do it alone."

Lucia gripped his hair tight. "I do not believe in faith."

His brows lowered. He leaned so close their noses brushed. "Do you believe in me?"

Lucia stilled. He watched her, his eyes gleaming, his hands proprietary; she could feel the hard, hungry line of his erection pressing into her belly, just below the wound he'd bandaged only an hour earlier.

"Yes," she whispered, even though she knew it was an admission she shouldn't make, because that truth would only bind them tighter, and no matter how good he felt, or how much she wanted him—

"Do you have faith in me?"

Damn him. "Yes."

A wider, clearly pleased smile, one which made the throb at the hollow of her thighs spread to her blood. *A smile.* How was that even possible?

"Then no more arguing," he told her. "I know you were alone, Lu. But you're not alone now. I'm right here."

"You should not be," she told him, more than a little desperately. *Alone.* So alone she didn't know how not to be solitary. *How to believe.* "You should be a thousand miles from this place. Helping us will only do you harm. I do not want that. I never wanted that. Why do you think I tried to send you away?"

"I made my choice on the side of that freeway, sweetheart."

She was silent for a long moment, staring into that luminescent gaze, her heart beating with painful force. She'd tried so hard to push him away, and yet here he was. And she wasn't sure she had the energy—or the willpower—to keep pushing. Being alone had never been a choice; it simply *was*. But it didn't have to be. That was what he was telling her. *What he was fighting for.*

"I am sorry," she whispered.

"For what?"

"For everything."

"You didn't do anything wrong," he said roughly.

A sharp laugh escaped her. "I did everything wrong."

"Sometimes there are no good choices."

Lucia held his gaze, and such heavy, viscous sadness filled her, her breath caught. "No."

He frowned. Then he leaned down and kissed her, a gentle, lingering caress where he flicked his tongue against her and made her thighs clench again. "You aren't the only one who's made mistakes, you know."

Something in his tone made her skin prickle. "No?"

"No." He pressed his forehead against hers. "My mistakes killed a man."

The hollowness behind his words made her throat tight. "What happened?"

"I trusted the wrong person. I believed the man I was protecting was too stupid to turn on me; I figured he knew better. I was wrong. Fucking arrogant, and when the piece of shit rolled over, he died, and the other deputy working the case—hell, I don't even know. He was in surgery two days ago. He could be dead, too, for all I know. Either way, it's my fucking mess, now. I own it. So trust me when I tell you we all make mistakes. It's how you climb back out of the hole that matters."

For a moment, she said nothing. Then, softly, "You are a fine man, Sam."

He made a deep sound and took her mouth. His tongue twined with hers, and Lucia clenched her hands in his hair and rubbed herself against him. Such heat and strength and intoxicating *pleasure.* She wanted to sink into him and never surface. But Sam pulled away and snarled softly, his fingers clenching into her bottom, which made her inhale sharply. "We'll cook the fish we caught and eat, then we'll head out. The rain will provide good cover."

She shivered when he rubbed his beard against her cheek. "It will be dusk."

"Yes. There's a map in the glove compartment, and we have headlights and a compass. We'll just take our time."

He was calm and pragmatic, and Lucia tried hard to absorb it. Because he was right: they could only move forward. Even though the knowledge that the boys were chipped turned her blood to ice, and she finally understood how impossible a task it was she'd set for herself, how stacked the deck was, and even though she'd killed a man, and her entire body ached with the force of her wounds, she—*they*—must keep going.

"What will happen when we get back into satellite range?" she asked, trepidation worming its way through her. "They will find us instantly."

"I've got it covered."

"Covered how?"

He kissed her, hard, brief, possessive. "I told you," he said and smiled that dark, dangerous smile. He let her slide slowly down his body, until her unsteady legs hit the ground. Then he gave her butt a lusty smack. "I always have a plan."

CHAPTER 31

"It's the end of goddamn days out there."

Isabel looked at Tony in the reflection of the mirror she stood before. He was staring out the window of their dilapidated motel room, into the storm that had nearly washed them from the road and precipitated their stay at *The Honeycomb Motel,* a squat, disheveled row of seventies-era motel rooms with shag carpeting and diamond-patterned wallpaper. The room smelled of cigarettes and cheap disinfectant, and the towel she was using to dry off was as thin as cheesecloth.

Still, it was shelter from the storm. Even if the walls groaned from the force of the wind, and the rain soaked in beneath the warped door.

Even if they had to share it.

"I hope they're all okay," Tony added, shaking his head.

Isabel did, too. The storm had forced them to stop several hundred miles shy of their destination of the Sawtooth National Forest in central Idaho, which according to Aequitas, was the last known location of the Cruz boys' GPS trackers. So far neither the FBI nor local law enforcement had laid eyes on Lucia Sanchez or the Cruz boys, and hopefully that was because they were so well hidden, and not because they were lying dead in a field somewhere. The storms that had proven such a hindrance in the last forty-eight hours continued unabated, making it almost impossible to get out into the field and conduct an actual search, and in spite of the airspace FEMA had finally opened, no planes or helicopters were braving the hurricane-force winds. The entire investigation had yet to even get off the ground.

Small favors, Isabel thought. Provided Lucia and Sam and the Cruz boys had survived those storms.

"We're still at least four hours out," Tony continued. "With any luck, this will blow over by morning, and we can get up there by noon."

But the weather forecast was grim, and there was no telling what morning would bring. The meteorologists were making educated guesses, but that education was based on knowledge gleaned from patterns—and a stable global temperature—which no longer existed. All they could do was wait and see.

Hurry up and wait. With the weather…and the storm that hovered on the horizon in the form of what Isabel had requested of Aequitas. So far, there was nothing of the video she'd sent her CI on the news or the web, and Isabel wondered what Aequitas was waiting for. But she trusted her source, and if Aequitas said it would be done, it *would* be done. So…patience.

Something of which Isabel was currently in short supply. She'd not expected Tony to show up at her room and utter that ridiculous statement of solidarity that had flummoxed and *pleased* her. No one had ever stood beside her with such unwavering determination, and part of her despised him for it, because now she knew what she'd been missing. She didn't *need* him, but it was nice having someone fight alongside her. Someone who was angry and determined and steadfast.

Being beautiful doesn't hurt.

Which was an asinine thought, but as her eyes traced the broad width of his shoulders, Isabel was forced to recognize its truth. And its influence. She was very attracted to Tony Malone, and his statement that they would be dealing with that attraction—*because there is an us, Isabel*—was both thrilling and terrifying. Considering how rare such emotions were for her...well.

She was in trouble. Deep, dark waters in which she had no idea how to swim.

You need more. Something to balance out the ugliness, something that makes all the sacrifice worth it. Something that belongs only to you.

But Isabel had given up on that idea—that someone could own her and she them—as a child. And the thought of reassessing that decision was not pleasant. She'd spent her life alone; she felt no loss due to that choice.

Not until she'd met Tony, and she didn't particularly appreciate the awakening.

But she wasn't a coward, and the child who'd cut all ties saw something in him. Wanted something from him, and Isabel wasn't certain she wanted to deny that child. Tony was right: the ugliness required neutralization. Something to soften the sharp edges; a light to illuminate the darkness. Was that him?

Or just wishful thinking?

Isabel was afraid the child had decided to answer that

question.

"What are you thinking?" Tony asked, and when her gaze flickered to his, Isabel found him watching her.

"That I'm glad you're here," she admitted, shrugging. She ignored the heat that flooded her cheeks; it was only the truth. "I usually work alone."

The smile that curved his mouth made a pulse flutter suddenly, low in her belly. He abandoned the window and walked toward her.

"No one at the Bureau is a team player?" he asked.

Isabel eyed him, watching him get closer, aware of her heartbeat growing stronger, that harrowing ripple of awareness licking over her skin. "I'm not a team player."

"Except with me," he said, halting just behind her. Their eyes locked in the mirror.

Isabel only arched a brow at him.

"I'm honored," he told her, and color again rushed into her cheeks, because she could tell he meant it, and she didn't think she'd ever met so honest a man, something which continued to take her off guard. And something she liked. *Far too much.* "Are you upset at leaving the Bureau? All that time invested lost?"

"No," she replied. "The Bureau was only ever a means to an end. The badge facilitated the investigations I conducted, but it was never necessary. And today it became a hindrance. The experience was educational, and I made some very good contacts, but there would have always been an end date."

"Still. I don't imagine you saw it ending like this."

She only shrugged. "It is what it is."

"What will you do now?"

Tony watched her with a stillness that made another rush of awareness wash over her. He was warm behind her, so close she could smell him, and her nape prickled beneath the touch of his breath. The temptation to step back into the tensile comfort of him was strong, more so because she knew he would welcome her, but nothing was over, and neither of them could afford—

"Isabel," he murmured, his hands landing on either side of her against the countertop she stood before, his skin like sun-kissed gold against the dingy white tile. He leaned down and rested his chin on her shoulder, and his cheek brushed hers, scented by sandalwood and faintly bristled. "Talk to me."

For a long moment, she said nothing, silently enjoying the rasp of his skin against hers. His heat behind her, his arms almost enclosing her. And she was tempted, so very tempted by him. But he would not be satisfied with one moment, one night, one experience. No. He would want *all* of her, and while most women would be thrilled by that realization, it scared the bejesus out of Isabel.

Because she wasn't certain what she had to give him, if anything. Was she capable of baring herself? *Sharing herself?* And if what she revealed repulsed him? What then?

Would that risk be worth the reward?

"You asked earlier what happened to me," she said, the words welling forth from a place only he seemed to awaken. Her gaze lifted to meet his in the mirror.

"Are you ready to tell me?" he murmured, watching her closely, so intent his focus felt like a touch.

No. But there would be no "ready" when it came to him. He'd crashed into her much like a runaway truck, and short of leaping entirely out of range, there would be no escaping him. If she took this chance, he would not be an easy lover. He would be demanding. Stubborn. Uncontrollable. But he would also be honest. Strong. Loyal.

A man who stood beside her. And for a woman alone that was...enticing. And terrifying.

"Isabel," Tony whispered, stepping closer, and she shivered when his hard, broad, warm chest pressed against her back. "You don't owe me anything. I can wait."

And he would. Which is what forced her to lift her arm and turn it into the ugly florescent lighting so that the delicate grid of scars that marred her skin shimmered like fine silver mesh. Even after all these years, looking at them made her stomach turn.

Tony made a rough sound.

"My mother," Isabel told him softly. "Was a very troubled woman." She raised her other arm, revealing more scars, intricate circles the size of a quarter, their designs as complex as the most difficult maze. They traced their way along her forearm like raised stepping stones. "People always assume men are the worst offenders, but plenty of women are monsters within their own right. Men tend to lash out. Their violence is brutal and reactionary. But women...women plan their cruelty down to the last detail. They often use multiple weapons: physical, mental, sexual. The psychology is different, less visceral, more vicious. In my experience, women are far more malicious than their male counterparts."

She met Tony's gaze, and his steady, unwavering look made her chest tighten. "Like Donavon Cruz, my mother was a sadist. She considered herself an artist of the flesh, and I...I was her canvas."

Hard, strong hands settled on her hips, warm, heavy, but he didn't speak, he only waited, his cheek warm against hers. Isabel lowered her hands to the edge of her damp t-shirt and slowly lifted the hemline to reveal the whorls and circles and delicate lines that marred the skin of her stomach, her sole, gruesome inheritance. "She preferred x-acto blades; they allowed her significant control in how deep she cut. If you look closely, you can see many different things: birds, butterflies, insects. Flowers and grasses and tree leaves. She was incredibly talented."

Isabel could feel Tony's gaze taking in the horrendous opus, one which covered nearly her entire body. No part of her had been too sacred to defile.

"Jesus Christ," he whispered. "Where the fuck was your father?"

The rage Isabel heard made her take a deep, shuddering breath. That fury, she felt it, like a hammer cracking the cold, adamantine shell she lived within, and she pressed back into the heated, tensile hold of the man behind her, painfully aware of the violent tremors she couldn't seem to control.

"In his lab. He was a geneticist. Well-known, well-respected, more concerned with manipulating future life than protecting the one he'd already created." Isabel shook her head. "They lived separate lives; he had no idea what my mother was doing." She paused, the words jagged in her throat like sharp, delicate nails. "Not until I tried to kill her."

She felt Tony stiffen, and for a moment panic seared through her. *What would he think? What would he do?*

Would he still want her?

Scarred and carved into human sculpture; there was no escaping it. She'd grown used to the ridges and circles and fine, delicate lines. The painful stretch of scar tissue over her bones; the ache that throbbed through her when a storm came. But it was a lot to ask of a man, to see beyond it, to want her in spite of the horror she wore. That thought made her heart hurt, and she knew if he walked away, she would never share it again. He would be the only one. *The only chance she would ever take.* Which was not, she understood, healthy, but having survived this long had taken everything. Going beyond that was not something she cared to contemplate.

Except with him. *Why was that?*

"Tell me," he demanded softly, and his cheek rubbed hers, and tears filled her throat, a sudden, aching mass she had to swallow several times to speak past. *So much horror.* It was too much; Isabel knew it was too much. His gaze had grown dark, sharp, yet it didn't waver, steady, relentless, as firm as his hold.

"I don't remember making the decision," Isabel told him, her voice muted. "One day she left her blade within reach and I just...stabbed her." The memory was like a brutal, unexpected slap. "I took her left eye, and when she began to scream, I laughed. Because it was *her* screaming, instead of me. It felt so good." Isabel stared at Tony, searching for the horror she still felt. "I enjoyed it, and the only reason she survived was because my father had come home early and heard her screams. He saved her."

"Her, but not you."

Tony's tone was guttural, his hands around her hips like a vise. Isabel pressed back into him, and her hands curled over his and held tight.

"Yes," she said huskily. "He protected her. His work and his reputation were too important; the truth would have destroyed him."

"So he let you be destroyed instead," Tony said flatly, and Isabel shuddered, because she heard the man who would kill to protect those he cared for, the one hidden behind that charming smile and glib tongue. "Where is he now?"

"Dead, both of them. Long ago." A heavy sigh escaped her. "Thankfully, I was an only child."

The hands at her hips slid around her waist, and he held her tightly, the bristle that covered his jaw stabbing into her cheek. "I'm sorry."

"I survived," she replied simply, her fingers curling into the hard muscle of his forearms, but suddenly those arms unlocked and slid away, and Tony moved back, leaving only sudden, chilling cold in the space between them, and Isabel's breath tightened, and panic whipped through her, because he was stepping away, and what she'd feared might happen—

Rough hands cupped her shoulders and turned her around, and then he was hauling her against him, surrounding her with his strength and heat, his arms holding her so tightly, she could barely breath. A fine tremor shook him, and Isabel wrapped her arms around his waist and held on.

"Jesus Christ," he said again, and his forehead pressed hard into her neck. "You are fucking incredible."

Isabel froze. "No."

"Fuck yes, you are," he growled and rubbed his chin against the sensitive spot where her neck and shoulder joined, his bristle poking her through the t-shirt she wore. An arrow of sensation shot through her, straight to her core, and Isabel shivered. *Such an innocuous touch.* How could it—

"Will you show them to me?" he asked, but before she could respond, he lifted her onto the counter, his strength unexpected, and he pushed between her thighs to stand so close, her breasts were suddenly pressed against the hard plane of his chest, his hips cradled in the vee of her thighs. It was a stunningly intimate position, one she hadn't expected, one she wasn't prepared for, but he only held her still with one hand splayed around her upper thigh, his fingers digging into her, the other wrapping her braid to tilt her head up, and there was no escaping the glinting hazel gaze that captured hers. "I want to see them."

Isabel stared up at him, her heartbeat deafening, her nipples turning to hard, aching points against his chest, a low, steady pulse bursting to life where he pressed against the juncture of her thighs. Her body jerked, suddenly awakened and aware and *hungry.* In an instant, she grew hot, damp, her focus shearing until there was only him, her, and need. Her hands slid up the plane of his chest, her fingers tracing the thick pad of muscle that shaped him.

"No," she whispered, struggling desperately for control,

terrified of what he would do when he actually *saw* her. When he felt that rough, ugly tissue. "Not yet—I'm not—I can't—"

"Easy, honey," he murmured and kissed her, a tender brush of his mouth over hers, swallowing her protest, startling her. "I told you: I can wait." Another kiss, suckling her upper lip, and Isabel inhaled sharply. "Thank you for telling me." Sharp teeth nibbled at her. "I know it was hard."

Tears massed in her throat, but Isabel swallowed them down. *Stupid, wonderful man.* If he walked away from her—

"They're horrible," she heard herself say. "Hideous and repellent. You'll see." She shook her head. "And then…"

The grip on her braid tightened. Tony pulled away and stared down at her. "And then what, Isabel?"

She blinked up at him. "I can't bear to look at them. How will you?"

"Ah, baby." He leaned down and pressed his forehead against hers. The hand on her thigh tightened, and his thumb began to stroke her there, sending glints of heat to the place where she was soft and wet and embarrassingly ready. "I fucking dream about you." The hand that held her braid slid down to capture one of hers, and before she understood his intent, led it down to the hard line of his cock, where he wrapped her fingers firmly around him and held her there. "Feel how hard I am, Isabel. Like fucking steel. I'm *starving* for you. And if you think your scars are going to run me off, you need to think again, because when I see what you survived, what made you, I just get harder. I want every part of you, sugar. There's nothing I don't want to see, touch, taste. There's nothing I'll let you hide from me. So you need to understand this: I'll take everything you want to give. And then I'll push for more. I'll always want *more*. Because I'll never get enough of you. Not ever."

Isabel trembled in his hold, her heart too big in her chest, and her hand squeezed him, hard, and he shuddered against her, a small growl rumbling from him. "Are you sure?"

"You squeeze me again, and I'm going to show you how sure," he told her.

Temptation seared her. Her nipples ached, and she wanted him inside her. That she'd never had sex, never shown anyone the scars that marked her, wasn't enough deterrent, not with what he'd just said. Not with his open, uninhibited response to her touch. Not with the hunger that beat deep within her, a greedy, selfish thing she wanted to feed. But before she could succumb, he leaned down and took her mouth, his tongue pushing into her mouth to stroke against hers, carnal, aggressive, as hungry as she felt. And in spite of his warning, her hand tightened on him, and he groaned into her mouth. She sucked his tongue into her mouth and rose against him and rubbed her aching breasts against him. He felt *so good.* And she wondered how he would feel inside her, what it would be like to—

"Goddamn it," he swore softly, tearing his mouth from hers, his hand on her thigh tight, his fingers clenching into her. "No. Not in this shithole." He shuddered again and, as if he couldn't help himself, kissed her again, a deep, hungry plunder of her mouth that made her lips throb—along with the rest of her.

"I don't want to stop," she protested and went to squeeze

him again, but his hand tightened on hers, stilling the movement.

"Not here, not now," he insisted, more snarl than words. "No more playing. I don't have enough control."

"You don't need control," she argued, and part of her wondered if she'd lost her mind.

"Yeah, baby, I do." He leaned down and rubbed his cheek against hers, the hand on her thigh trembling, and for a long moment they just stayed that way, fighting for breath, for calm. "I'm not going to take you like a sailor on leave, and that's what I'm ready to do. I don't want that. So please, hear me. When we do this, it will matter, and I want more for you than this place and this moment."

"I like this place and this moment," she whispered, some unknown part of her aching, her body pulsing.

"No," he replied with soft finality. "When we happen, there will be no fear. We're not there yet. But we will be."

It wasn't fair, that he would understand what she was still piecing together for herself. That he would put her first. What had she done to deserve this man? Why had he crossed her path?

Who did she thank?

"Alright," she murmured. When he lifted his head, she pressed a shy, hesitant kiss to his lips. "We'll do it your way."

His hazel eyes gleamed. "I'll remember you said that."

CHAPTER 32

"You should get some sleep, *mijo*. It is going to be a long night."

Alexander looked over at Ben, who was snoring loudly, his chest rattling. Daisy lay curled between them, her paw on Ben's lap. Outside the ATV, the rain continued to beat down, and lightning flashed, illuminating the darkened forest and turning the tall pines into stark, moody silhouettes. Thunder rumbled around them, making the seat beneath Alexander vibrate.

Sam was driving; Lucia sat beside him. In the darkened interior of the ATV, her face looked even more battered, the faint lights of the dash highlighting her bruised and swollen eye. It hurt Alexander to look at her, because the beating she'd taken was *his* fault.

He'd started this wheel turning. If he'd just *lied* to her, *hidden* from her—

"*Mijo*," Lucia said again, and when Alexander looked up, he found her staring at him, half-turned in her seat, her golden eyes glinting in the darkness.

"I'm sorry," he said, his heart beating hard. *Stupid tears.* In his throat again, pressing hard against his lungs. He didn't understand why, or where they came from, or what had abruptly—*horribly*—made him feel. For so long, there'd been nothing…nothing but the rage. *Hate.* The need to protect Ben. But nothing like what he felt now: terror and hope and guilt. He hated it. He—

"For what?" Lucia asked softly, turning more fully to look at him. She reached out and smoothed his hair, and he let her. "You did nothing wrong."

Alexander shook his head. "He hurt you because of me."

"He hurt me because he enjoyed it," she replied seriously. "You were just the excuse he used."

"It's my fault," Alexander insisted. "If we hadn't left…"

"What Ivan did is not your fault," Lucia said. "Just like it is not Sam's fault. Ivan was an evil man. He wanted to hurt me long before I put you in the Nova."

Alexander's heart jerked, and Sam turned to look at her, but Lucia only shook her head. "I knew he would come. It was inevitable; the price to be paid. You must not blame yourself."

But he did, and nothing she could say would make any difference. "How did he find us?"

This time Lucia looked at Sam, and they exchanged a glance that made Alexander stiffen. "What?" he demanded. "Tell me."

Lucia reached out and tried to smooth his hair again, but Alexander pushed her away.

"No," he said, panic suddenly lashing at him. "Tell me."

"You're microchipped," Sam said, his voice hard.

"Microchipped?" Alexander echoed, confused.

Lucia opened her mouth, but Sam said, "There is a

microchip embedded somewhere in your skin that emits a signal that—when in satellite range—provides your exact location through GPS coordinates."

"Embedded?" Horror slapped Alexander like a brutal hand. "You mean...*inside me?*"

"In the top layer of your dermis," Sam said. "It was probably injected when you had a vaccination of some kind. Tiny, no bigger than a grain of rice. But without the right equipment, we have no idea where, so removing it isn't an option."

"He...*bugged* me?" Alexander said, aware of his voice getting louder, of Ben stirring beside him, but the revulsion and dread filling him had sound, like a million buzzing, angry bees, and he couldn't breathe and— "He made it so I can never, *ever get away from him? He can find me anywhere? He can—*"

Suddenly the ATV jerked to a stop, and the door beside him was being wrenched open, and then Sam was there beside him, his hands wrapping Alexander's shoulders. "Easy, bud. Just calm down. It's okay. We'll fix it. I promise."

"Fix it?" Alexander repeated, staring at Sam in horror, his stomach churning, his head spinning, and he felt *sick* with fear and rage and—

"I promise," Sam said again, holding Alexander's gaze. "I'll rig something up until we can get it out of both of you."

"Both of us?" Alexander tore his gaze from Sam and looked over at Ben, who was awake, watching silently, his eyes big and dark and scared.

"Both of you," Sam said. Rain rolled down his cheeks;

his hands were warm and strong but gentle, and Alexander was seized by the foreign, irrational urge to hurl himself into Sam's arms and beg him to never let go.

"It will be okay," Lucia whispered. Her hand cupped Alexander's cheek, and he realized the tears had escaped, hot trails that slid all the way down to drip from his chin. "You must trust us, *mijo*."

He looked at Sam, who squeezed Alexander's shoulders, and said, "It's the only way."

He wanted to argue, but the rain was cold, drenching Sam and misting into the vehicle, and beside him, Ben was shivering. So Alexander nodded, and Sam let go and shut the door, climbing back into the front. Ben's hand found his, trembling, too hot, and Alexander scooted closer to him and wrapped an arm around him. His heart beat so fiercely it hurt, and he wanted to throw up, and in that moment he knew what he'd told Sam wasn't a lie.

He *was* going to kill his father. No matter how long it took, no matter what he had to do.

"Are you okay, Zander?" Ben asked, his voice shaking, and Daisy butted against them with a soft whine.

"Yeah, Benny, I'm okay," he lied, swiping at his tears, hugging his brother tight.

Strong and brave, for Ben. No matter how sick he felt. How *angry*. Angry. A word that didn't come close to describing the furious blaze burning inside him.

Sam watched him in the mirror, and even in the darkness, Alexander knew Sam saw it. But for some reason, that didn't bother him, because Sam would understand.

"How will we stop it?" Alexander asked, panic

continuing to swell within him. "The satellites are everywhere."

And he knew they were headed toward civilization; they'd told him that much when they'd left the cabin. *Ben needs a doctor. We have to find one.* And Alexander hadn't argued, because Ben was far more important than he was. He wasn't about to trade Ben's life for his own freedom. No. Nothing could happen to Ben.

Ben was going to make it.

"I can build something that will jam the signal," Sam said.

"You can?" Lucia and Alexander asked simultaneously.

"It's not rocket science," Sam told them with a snort.

"It might as well be," Lucia replied seriously. "I would never be able to do such a thing."

"Me either," Alexander said, his anxiety easing a bit. Until he thought about the foreign object his father had implanted in him, which somehow seemed even worse than everything else he'd done, even though it wasn't, not by a long shot.

Ivan was an evil man.

Takes one to know one, Alexander thought. And deep inside, the fury that lived within him simmered and seethed and hungered for blood. He recognized that it was a dangerous thing, that fury, as alive as he was. As real. And that scared him. Because someday it would get free. *Someday he would set it free.* And there was a line there somewhere, one that, once crossed, could never be returned from. Part of him worried about the fury and that line.

But part of him didn't care.

"You will need supplies to do this?" Lucia asked, watching Sam.

"Yes. We'll have to find an electronics store." Sam turned to look at her. "According to the map, we'll exit the forest just outside of Blue Ridge. We'll get a room, and I'll take Ben to the emergency clinic. Then I'll get what I need."

"No," Ben said, startling Alexander.

"*Sí,* sweet pea," Lucia said sternly. "You must."

"Will I get a shot?"

"I don't know."

"I don't wanna go." Ben looked at Sam. "Will you hold my hand?"

"You bet," Sam said.

Ben sighed and laid his head on Alexander's shoulder. "Okay."

Which just told Alexander how bad Ben actually felt. Which scared him.

"We won't have a car," Alexander pointed out, his chest heavy, his stomach continuing to churn.

Sam looked at him in the mirror. "We will."

"How?"

But before Sam could answer, Lucia turned to Alexander and said, "Do not worry, *mijo.* Sam always has a plan."

Sam smiled and nodded, but it wasn't enough; Alexander wanted the impossible. Promises. *Guarantees.* But life didn't work that way, especially not his life.

"One step at a time," Sam said, his gaze steady. "Can you do that?"

Not that there was any choice. Alexander nodded. "Good. Then try and get some sleep."

CHAPTER 33

Quack. Quack.

Tony did his best to ignore the sound of his phone, because sprawled across his chest was the slight, cinnamon-scented weight of a woman he was quickly coming to consider his own. *Isabel.*

Quack. Quack.

He didn't want to let her go, didn't want to open his eyes and look into the face of the chaos that awaited them. *No.* He wanted another five minutes of Isabel curled trustingly against him in the cheap, sagging bed, the outside world shuttered by ugly plaid curtains, the only sound the wind and rain and deep, rumbling thunder. He wanted to roll her over, steal another kiss and inspect her scars so thoroughly, there were no doubts left in her.

Quack. Quack.

But it was not meant to be. Not today.

Quack—

"Shit." He swiped a hand at the bedside table and grabbed his phone. Beside him, Isabel stirred and sat up. He checked the number. *Peabody.* "Malone."

"You seen the news?" Bob asked without preamble.

Tony's heart lurched. "No. Why?"

"Take a look, and call me back."

Bob hung up, and Isabel blinked at him. They'd slept atop the gaudy, orange-flowered comforter, fully clothed, but somewhere along the line her braid had come loose, and that glinting, white-blond hair shimmered in the dim light, curling nearly to her waist. Tony reached out, captured a strand and ran it through his hand, unable to help himself.

"Morning," he murmured.

Color touched her cheeks. "Who was that?"

Her cool tone was belied by her sleep-warmed appearance and the crease on her cheek from the button of his shirt. Stubborn woman. But that was okay; he was more than up for the challenge.

"Peabody," Tony told her and grabbed the TV remote that also sat on the bedside table. He turned it on—a lumbering, old RCA—and Gordon Ramsey appeared, red-faced and appalled as he stared down at a chunk of over-cooked tuna. Tony flipped through the channels—*Jesus Christ, how many were there*—until he found NewsDay, where a slim brunette stood before a still shot of Donavon Cruz, her face somber, a red banner running beneath her that read *Donavon Cruz Revealed*. He hit the volume.

"...the videos were delivered to over twenty news outlets world-wide, including NewsDay, and were simultaneously released on both *You Tube* and *Me TV*." The brunette was unsmiling, her tone solemn. "They appear to show Las Vegas billionaire Donavon Cruz, CEO of Cruz Technologies, performing criminal sexual acts on several young minors, including his ten-year-old son, Alexander, who was reportedly kidnapped—along with his younger brother, Benjamin—four days ago by the boy's nanny, Lucia Sanchez. Anonymous sources have confirmed that Ms. Sanchez went to several different city and state agencies—including the Las Vegas Chapter of Child Protective Services—and attempted to report Mr. Cruz's abuse of his son before fleeing with the children. The FBI are currently searching for Ms. Sanchez and the Cruz children, and the Las Vegas Metropolitan Police Department has issued several search warrants for the Cruz properties, as well as an arrest warrant for Mr. Cruz, whose current whereabouts are unknown. The disclosure of the videos is being attributed to the hacker known only as Aequitas, whose stylized justice vector symbol accompanied delivery of the images—images our tech department have determined to be unedited. The news has sent Cruz Technologies stock plummeting, and many of Mr. Cruz's high profile associates, including the current sitting Senators of Nevada and California, have released statements condemning Cruz's actions and calling for an investigation by the Justice Department. Due to the licentious nature of the videos and their content—and out of respect for the children victimized in them—the NewsDay network will not be airing the videos. Please stay tuned with NewsDay as we continue our coverage of this breaking story."

Tony hit the mute button, and in the silence that followed, thunder boomed far off, in the distance. He turned to look at Isabel, who was staring at the TV.

"Several minors," he repeated. "But we only downloaded one file."

Isabel's ink-dark gaze lifted to meet his. "Yes."

"Then where did the other videos come from?"

Her cheeks flushed. "I emailed the video using the wireless connection at Cruz's cabin and forwarded it from there."

"You made a trail to follow."

Her chin lifted, her eyes daring him. "Yes."

"Out-fucking-standing," he said. Before she could move, he thrust his hand into her hair, leaned down and kissed her, hard.

When he moved to straighten, her hands curled into his shirt and held him to her. "I wasn't sure Aequitas would use it."

Tony only arched a brow. "Yes, you were."

"I hoped," she admitted, and her gaze flickered to his mouth, and that quickly he was hard as stone. "But I didn't know for sure."

"You are a brilliant, wonderful soul." Tony kissed her again, a thorough, lush kiss he wanted to fall headlong into. Isabel made a soft, hungry sound and tugged him closer.

He resisted. Barely. "We need to go."

"I know," she said against his mouth. "In a minute."

Then she licked his upper lip, and Tony groaned and let her have her way. The woman was going to fucking *end* him. What she'd disclosed the night before had incensed and horrified and infuriated him. But it hadn't repelled him. If anything, it only made him more determined to show her her worth. *To win her.* And part of him knew she'd never shared the gruesome truth of her childhood with anyone else. That she'd chosen him was shocking. *Humbling.* Because she'd taken a huge chance; she'd *trusted.* And he was going to cherish and protect and guard that trust with his life.

Quack. Quack.

Isabel pulled away, and, to Tony's surprise, gave a small laugh.

"What?" he demanded.

She only shook her head. "Quack, quack."

"It lightens a crime scene," he told her seriously.

"I'm sure." Her head tilted, and her gaze swept him, and the heat he saw made his skin tighten. "You're pretty wonderful, yourself."

He really wanted to respond to that, but—

Quack. Quack.

"Malone," he snarled into his phone.

"You get a look?" Bob Peabody asked.

"In technicolor. What's happening?"

"They're searching the house in the city, the place in Dead Mountains, and his office building downtown. Can't find him, though. No one's see him since yesterday, and his bird is gone. Took off last night. Flight plan said he was headed to Boise, but he never showed. With any luck, he crashed. But more likely, he ran."

"No," Tony said, remembering the video, the look on Cruz's face. *He is mine as you are mine.* "He won't go without those boys. Arrogant fuck doesn't think the law applies to him. Is Gill still covering for him?"

"Funny that. As soon as those videos hit the web, the Special Agent in Charge flew himself off to Virginia. Left Kent in charge. We're in Mountain Home, Idaho. Freeway east and west is demolished; we had to take farm roads to get this far. Figure we'll head north. No one's seen Sanchez or the kids, and with the roads out, it's the only direction left to go. Where are you?"

"Just south of Pocatello. The storm stopped us."

"'Us'?" Bob repeated. "How'd you talk her into that?"

"I'm charming."

"She's out, you know. Kent said she told Gill to go fuck himself."

"That's my girl."

"Forks is looking for you." Bob paused, and Tony realized he was chewing. "He's real curious how that hacker laid hands on that video."

"The world works in mysterious ways."

Bob snorted. "Doesn't it though. Thought you should know the spooks showed up right after the videos posted, squealing like stuck pigs. NSA bastards, might a well be a bunch of nosy, eavesdropping old women. They want the hacker."

"It's good to want things." Tony looked at Isabel, who was bent over her tablet.

"Yeah, they've got it bad. Don't think they're smart enough to catch him, though. I did some digging. That Aequitas, he's some kind of special. Smarter than most the rest of the world." Respect echoed in Bob's laconic tones. "We didn't have criminals like that in my day. Kind of wish we did."

"I didn't realize you were such a fan of vigilante justice, Peabody."

"Nah, Malone, I'm a fan of justice, period."

Bob hung up, and Tony turned to Isabel. "The NSA are

looking for your boy."

She only shook her head, her fingers moving over her tablet. "I told you, I don't know if Aequitas is male or female."

"But the fact that the NSA is looking doesn't worry you?"

She smiled, that cool, composed curve that made his fingers twitch. "Let them look. Aequitas was a force long before we made contact."

"And if they connect you?"

"They won't."

Tony's gaze narrowed on her. "You sound very sure. You wiped your phone and computer before you turned them in?"

She sent him a look. "I never used them. My personal devices are heavily encrypted, and any text or email I receive from Aequitas is self-deleting. My firewalls are nearly flawless and far more reliable than the Bureau's experimental toys."

"Nearly flawless?"

"Tech changes too quickly to ever be fool-proof." She shrugged. "But I have a very…capable IT person."

Tony smiled, aware that he shouldn't encourage her, but unable to help himself. That happened a lot with her. "Think you could hook me up?"

One sleek brow rose. "What's in it for me?"

Heat slammed into him, but it was the sudden, expected tightening in his chest that made him go still. *She was playing with him.* And he knew then, no matter what—her past, the present, the uncertain future—everything was going to be okay.

They were going to be okay. *More than okay.*

He opened his mouth to respond, but her tablet *dinged*, and she stared at it, and tension shot through him. "What?"

Her gaze met his. "The Cruz boys' GPS signals just went back online."

"You have them?"

She turned the tablet and showed him.

"Fuck," he said. "Let's go."

CHAPTER 34

Need wheels. ASAP.

Sam sent the text and glanced at Lucia, who slept fitfully, curled against the thin plastic window of the ATV. In the backseat, Alexander snored softly, and Ben's breathing grew more labored. The rain hadn't ebbed; in point of fact, it was so thick they were moving at a snail's pace, and the rising of the sun had only lightened the world around them by a fraction. Lightning split the sky in delicate veins, revealing the churning black mass above them; there was so much standing water, Sam was afraid the foothills behind them were going to give way and bury them in rock and earth.

His phone beeped, and relief shot through him. They'd returned to the land of constant surveillance half an hour earlier, and while that boded ill for them staying under the radar, it did have some significant advantages.

Blue Jeep Cherokee, Plate No. 1T34790.

A moment later a notification from the GPS app on his phone appeared. *Coordinates received.* Sam stared at the notice for a long moment before responding.

TY.

He sent the message and sighed. If the path to hell was paved with good intentions, he was halfway to the abyss.

But desperate times called for desperate measures, and he knew the young woman he'd reached out to would help.

Honor always did.

He told himself it would be the last time, but he knew better. Even if their connection wasn't simple, or safe, or smart, it existed, and neither of them would abandon what tied them together. She was his first—and only—professional mistake (excluding his current predicament), but he didn't regret her, even if the legendary status she'd built for herself both gratified and scared the hell out of him, even if—when they caught her, and they would, because no one got away with what she was doing forever—she'd never see the light of day again.

Honor had made her bed; nothing he could do about that. He'd accepted that when she'd first reached out to him three years ago, when he'd realized the kid he'd willingly let slip through his fingers on his first witness protection assignment—*the one he'd killed and then resurrected*— had become a force unto herself, one who hunted the world's worst, and who was equally hunted in return. She was the smartest person he'd ever met, then or since, even at fifteen, but he would've never predicted the role she would carve for herself, nor the odd pride he took in her, even knowing her way would eventually get her locked up in a place no one returned from. He'd tried to warn her, a waste, because she already knew and didn't give a damn.

This is my path, Sam.

Stubborn shit. And that was the problem: like Tony, Honor was part of the small collection of people Sam considered family. When she called, he would come. *Always.* No matter what that meant. As she would for him—and had, whenever he needed her, for the last three years.

She'd been his first and last lesson in the tenets of being a Deputy U.S. Marshal; he'd done everything wrong with her. Gotten involved—because she was just a kid, fucked up and too smart for her own good, traumatized by what she'd experienced, what she'd lost—broken the law—orchestrating his own witness protection program in the form of her staged death—and risked everything—his badge, his reputation, his *life*—to set her free. In the end, he hadn't regretted it, because he knew she was safer dead than alive, because he understood the limits of the system he worked within, because he knew they would get to her no matter what that system did to protect her, but she was the only one of his witnesses he'd ever put his professional ass on the line for.

No, Sam had learned that lesson. But like him, Honor had no one, and when she needed someone, he was the one she turned to. The one she trusted. And because he thought of her as the kid sister he'd never had—no matter her shenanigans or the price on her head—he would be there.

No matter how often he told himself different.

In his hand, his phone beeped again.

YW. Keep the faith. Help is on the way.

Sam stared down at the tiny letters, frowning.

Just needed the wheels, he texted. *Thx.*

Because he didn't need her involved in this mess, too. Christ. Enough was enough. That she monitored his phone was something he accepted—tech was her lifeline, the one thing she felt she could control, so he allowed it, and hell, she made him pretty much hack-proof, so he wasn't complaining—but he didn't want her meddling.

He had enough to worry about.

His belly growled, the handful of trout he'd eaten earlier long gone. His leg hurt; several of his stitches had torn open during his battle with Misha and Enrique, but he hadn't let Lucia get near him, even though she'd tried. She was in no condition to patch him up, no matter how stoically she dealt with her own pain. Just looking at her made him want to carve Donavon Cruz into tiny, bloody pieces. And no matter whether or not she held him responsible for her current condition, Sam sure as shit blamed himself.

He'd known better than to leave her. He'd done it anyway. Why he'd done it didn't mean a damn thing. He'd failed her—quite fucking spectacularly. And there was no erasing that, no pretending it hadn't happened. All he had to do was look at her, and he remembered.

Fucking asshole.

He wished she blamed him; he wanted her anger. That white-hot fury. Something other than the empathy and exasperation with which she faced him. *The passion she'd given so freely.* He could still feel her rising against him, licking at his tongue, her belly soft against the thrust of his cock. Her fingers clenched in his hair.

You are a distraction I cannot afford.

No shit. Because all Sam had begun to think about was getting inside her—and that was a long way off. He wasn't sure when he'd determined that giving her up was no longer an option, when he'd succumbed to the crazy idea of keeping her. When he'd decided there *would* be a future, even if he had to raise it from the ashes of the fire waiting to consume them.

I do not believe in faith. But he did.

Faith in himself. In her. In Tony. *Let someone try and stop it.* Lucia wasn't the only one with a mile-wide streak of stubborn.

His phone beeped again, and another message appeared.

Got your back, Super Sam. Always. ☺

He stared down at it. Goddamn kid.

Not ur business, he responded. *Stay out.*

A winking emoticon was the only response.

"Son of a bitch," he muttered.

"Is everything okay?" Alexander suddenly asked, and Sam looked into the mirror to find the boy awake, those pale green eyes staring at him.

"As good as it's going to get," Sam told him.

"We're not going to make it, are we?"

Sam only handed his phone back to the kid, along with the map. "Pull up those GPS coordinates and check the map. I can't do that and drive, too."

Alexander scowled, but he accepted the phone and the map and focused on them. "That's not an answer."

"Can't give you something I don't have," Sam replied. "There's a main trail ahead. Sign says Crystal Canyon. Which way?"

"Right." Alexander looked up, fear flickering in his gaze. "We're only a few miles from Blue Ridge. The coordinates are in town. Where are we going?"

"To get wheels." Sam turned right. The trail widened out, more rock than dirt, and led steadily downward, into the narrow valley where the town of Blue Ridge nestled, tucked tight against the eastern mountains, surrounded by forest.

"How are we going to do that?" Alexander demanded.

"Very carefully," Sam replied.

The boy glowered at him. "That's not an answer, either."

"Sure it is." They halted when Sam hit another fork in the trail. "Which way?"

"Left." Alexander folded the map. "It's another mile to the GPS coordinates. Where do they lead?"

"To a blue Jeep."

"How do you know that?"

The suspicion Sam heard made him look at the boy in the mirror. "Still don't trust me?"

Alexander held his gaze. "I don't trust anyone."

But he wanted to; Sam could see the hunger in the kid, the need to believe in someone. *Anyone.* The hope hidden beneath the cynicism, persistent and resilient. He remembered the feeling, being surrounded by strangers and looking around, wondering if any of them could be trusted. If anyone in the world was worth a damn. Praying they were, no matter the evidence to the contrary. Magnus had answered that question for him, and Sam realized then that part of him had hoped to be the one to answer it for Alexander. But trust took time, and the sands in the hourglass were running out.

Because Ben was sick and getting sicker, the kids were

being tracked by GPS, he and Lucia were both wounded, and they were headed into civilization.

Shit was going to start rolling downhill. *Fast.*

And the heavy, cold dread he'd felt yesterday hadn't dissipated with the deaths of Cruz's men; if anything, something within Sam was readying, a portent born of experience and inevitability that escalated with every mile they traveled until certainty beat at him like a vicious hammer. And Sam knew he should trust that certainty. That certainty had saved him time and again—even in Baja.

Which made him think of Fieldstone, and he wished he could call and check on his colleague. But that wasn't a good idea. No matter how guilty he felt. And he did feel guilty. He hadn't been lying when he told Lucia his mistakes had killed a man. Only one—and that man had made his own mistakes, plenty of which had contributed to his death—but Fieldstone was *Sam's* fault. For being cocky and making assumptions he knew better than to make.

For taking his eye off the ball.

He couldn't afford to do that again, here, now. Because Lucia, for all her fierceness, wasn't a soldier. And the kids were just *kids*. All they had was him.

And Donavon Cruz had an army.

"Maybe someday you will," Sam said finally and met Alexander's pale gaze in the mirror. "Trust takes time. Knowing you're safe. And deciding. Took me a long time to believe Magnus wasn't going to take me back. That he wasn't like my pop. I didn't know what love was until him. I wish I'd understood earlier; we lost a lot of time. I was too busy being defensive and scared, and by the time I realized what kind of man Magnus was, he was dying."

"Dying?"

"Prostate cancer. After he was gone, I realized I had to decide for myself what kind of man I was going to be." The trail they were following ended abruptly in a wide expanse of gravel. A narrow strip of heavily-patched, paved road curved past the parking area, and a faded green sign stabbed into the earth at a sharp angle on the right-hand side.

Blue Ridge, Population 2368.

Sam felt his skin tighten, and in his chest, his heart beat a little harder. That feeling of ominous portent again washed over him, but moving forward was their only choice. So he turned the ATV down the road, incredibly glad it was only six-thirty in the morning.

"It was an easy decision," he continued, and looked up to meet the kid's gaze. "You're going to have to decide, too."

The boy only stared at him.

"We all have to decide who we're going to be," Sam told him softly. "And being the oldest, it's up to you to set the example. Like it or not, Ben's going to follow your lead. You can't forget that, son. Not ever."

A shuddering breath escaped Alexander, and he looked down at Ben. Daisy was curled into a ball in Ben's lap, and Alexander reached out and stroked her. "I know. He's really sick, isn't he?"

"Sick enough. But we'll get him to a doctor."

They traveled in silence for several minutes, and the sky continued to lighten, revealing thick white clouds that blanketed the surrounding mountains in mist. They passed several ranches and as they entered town, a row of manufactured homes and a Quick Stop. Further down, Sam spotted the Jeep, parked in the side lot of a fat, squat metal building that bore a faded orange sign that said Blue Ridge Auto Body.

"There's our ride." Sam pulled into the shop's lot, grateful it was dark and still and set back from the road. He steered the ATV toward the sleek, dark blue four-wheel drive, license plate number *1T34790,* which sat tucked within a row of other SUVs, and parked. On the right-hand side of the Jeep's back window, a rental sticker glowed bright yellow.

Good. Because chances were, a rental wouldn't be missed quite so quickly, and at least they weren't stealing some poor, hardworking soul's only vehicle. Sam turned off the ATV, told Alexander to sit tight, and climbed out to inspect the Jeep. He really didn't want to bust a window; maybe Blue Ridge was as trusting as Canyon Falls, and by some miracle it would be unlocked with the key just sitting in the ignition—

He was right next to it when the vehicle suddenly started, and the door locks disengaged with a loud *clunk.* Sam halted, staring at it, his heart beating too hard in his chest.

His phone beeped, but he didn't have to look at it.

Goddamn kid. He could almost hear her laughing at him.

He went back to the ATV. Lucia was awake, blinking at him sleepily, and Ben was stirring as well. Alexander looked at the Jeep, then at Sam.

"How did you do that?" he asked, his voice hushed.

"I'm just that good," Sam told him seriously. "Everybody up and out. We need to go."

CHAPTER 35

Isabel stared out the window of the Eagle County Sheriff's Department where the wind gusted at nearly sixty miles an hour, threatening to shred the flags that hung from the pole in front of the building. Signs rattled violently, trees bent from the force, even the windows trembled. Rain flew sideways, so thick visibility was less than twenty feet, and the lights overhead flickered uncertainly. Cell service was down, so the tablet in her lap was silent, and Tony had disappeared to find a landline to call his Lieutenant.

Tony. *You are a brilliant, wonderful soul.*

Over the course of her career, Isabel had heard many accolades. Words that praised her tenacity, her courage, her fortitude. But never her spirit. Never that inexplicable force which had pulled her from the dark, bloody pit of her childhood and impelled her to survive. The one that drove her to be better, to be *more*. To save those she could, no matter the price.

But Tony saw that essence, *inside*, far deeper than the twisted flesh she'd been so scared to reveal. He looked into the core of her and *smiled*. He shared his need and his adoration openly, *fearlessly,* something she could only admire. And his concern—

When we happen, there will be no fear. We're not there

yet. But we will be.

No one had ever put her first. Ever. She didn't know how to respond. No one took care of her; she took care of them. To be on the receiving end...scared the hell out of her. Because she *liked* it. Because that alone had shattered the foundation of the wall she'd spent years building, and without that foundation, the wall fell, crumbled ruins around her feet. And she didn't give a damn.

She wanted him, and to hell with the consequences. It was a shocking realization.

But those consequences... They had the potential to be devastating. *Would it be worth the risk?* In her life, she'd risked many things. Her badge, her reputation, her freedom. Her life. But somehow this was different...and she knew, no matter how many hours she spent debating it, tallying the pros and cons, that she would only discover the answer when she succumbed to the question.

Jump, demanded the child. *Hide,* advised the scarred and battered survivor. But she didn't want to hide. She'd spent too many years hiding the truth of who she was, the remnants of the fire which had forged her. She was tired of existing only within the darkness. She wanted to step into the light.

Ultimately, she had to trust—not just Tony, but herself. *To let go.* And let it be.

"What are you thinking about?"

Isabel started and looked up to find Tony standing in the doorway, watching her.

"Nothing important," she said. "What did Lieutenant Forks have to say?"

Tony frowned, and she knew he would press her later, but only replied, "Plenty. There was much swearing and many threats. He's pissed about the videos. He thinks we leaked them."

"He said that?"

"He didn't have to." Tony shrugged. "He'll get over it. It was a necessary evil, and he knows it."

Yes. Isabel wondered if Lucia Sanchez was yet aware of the videos and the chaos they'd generated. Of the arrest warrant that had been issued for Donavon Cruz and his currently unknown whereabouts.

The GPS signals of the Cruz boys that had gone quite abruptly online that morning just outside of Blue Ridge, Idaho while she and Tony were still a hundred miles south of the Sawtooth National Forest had disappeared just as abruptly less than twenty minutes later, and had yet to reappear. Isabel wondered if Aequitas was responsible for that, or if it was simply the weather. Wireless service had been spotty all day, and added to the terrain they'd traversed, wholly unreliable. They'd followed the directions of Bob Peabody, west through the Magic Valley, utilizing the same farm roads he and Kent had taken north and had arrived in the Blue Ridge valley just before noon. The valley was small—only thirty miles long before the mountains again closed in—and a mere fifteen miles wide. The small town of Blue Ridge contained a handful of motels, four restaurants, two gas stations, three bars, and two churches. Blue Ridge Ski Resort was the town's sole source of income in winter, and in the summer months tourists fished the narrow ribbon of the Salmon River and hiked the surrounding wilderness. A small, close-knit mountain community, one Lucia and

Sam and the Cruz children would not be able to hide in for long.

Provided they were here at all.

Because the GPS locators were no doubt embedded in the skin of the Cruz children, it was unlikely they'd been removed, which meant that either something—or someone—had interfered in the signal, or Sam and Lucia had figured a way to jam it. Either way, it left everyone in stasis—her, Tony, Special Agent Kent, and Bob Peabody. Never mind the Eagle County Sheriff, Nate Thomas, who was less than thrilled by the invasion of the federal government into his town.

"Signal still quiet?" Tony asked, walking toward her, and Isabel looked away, down at her tablet, painfully aware that the beast he'd awakened the night before was stirring. That she was so distracted by him—by this inexplicable *thing* between them—was ludicrous. *Laughable.* And had anyone ever suggested that such a thing could happen, she would have shut them down with vicious proficiency.

Unarguable evidence of your humanity. And surely a double-edged sword.

"Yes," she confirmed when she realized how closely he was watching her, seeing things with that warm hazel gaze he shouldn't.

"Damn." He halted next to her, put his hand on the back of her chair, and leaned down to nuzzle her ear. "You look hungry."

Heat curled into her cheeks, and Isabel glared at him, but he only laughed, a low, husky sound that made her skin prickle in awareness. Before she could respond, Sheriff

Thomas walked into the small room he'd reluctantly provided them, followed by Special Agent Kent and Bob Peabody.

Thomas appeared annoyed, Kent looked stressed out, and Bob Peabody, unsurprisingly, held a large glazed donut in his left hand.

"We have four agents stuck in Salmon due to the landslide north of Clayton," Kent said wearily, his face tight with strain. "For them to go around will take an entire day. If we could just utilize a few of your people for the search—"

"My 'people'," Thomas repeated, clearly exasperated. A short, stout, gray-haired man with a thick, bushy handlebar mustache, the Sheriff wore his badge next to the large PBR belt buckle that held his Wranglers in place and leaned heavily on a slender cane made of walnut. The Ruger tucked into his holster gleamed in the pale light. "Look around, *Special* Agent. How many 'people' do you think I've got? This department has three full-time officers—of which I am one—and two part-timers. My dispatch also handles fire, search and rescue and runaway livestock. I have no 'people' to give you."

"Sheriff—"

"You don't even know that your girl is here, and there's a thousand square miles of wilderness out there. Like looking for a needle in a haystack. Good luck with that."

"USI84 is in ruins—east and west, and there's nothing but desert to the south." Kent halted, his hands on his hips, a muscle ticking in the hard line of his jaw. Behind him, Peabody took a bite of his donut. "We're certain she headed north—into the National Forest—and she's going to need food and supplies. Blue Ridge is one of the few places she can get those supplies."

"The valley isn't that big." Tony turned to look at Kent. "You go north, we'll go south. Shouldn't take too long to cover most of it. Then we'll worry about heading into the backcountry."

Kent scowled. He was pale and exhausted, and for a moment Isabel considered whether or not they should share their current intelligence with him. Because Kent had no idea the Cruz boys had been tagged by GPS trackers, that he was far closer than he realized, and that as soon as the GPS signal again appeared—*if* it did so—they would have the exact location of Lucia Sanchez and the children she'd stolen.

But what would happen to Lucia when they arrived at that location was a question that had yet to be answered, because regardless of the warrant issued for Cruz—or what he was guilty of—Lucia was equally guilty of felony kidnapping. And probably child endangerment, as well. So the fewer armed agents around when she was apprehended, the better. And while Isabel didn't think Peabody would shoot first, she wasn't sure about Agent Kent. He was young, and an unknown. And if Tony's friend Sam was anything like Tony, he would deliberately put himself between Lucia Sanchez and the agents hunting her.

Clearly, this situation would require careful management.

"Great," Kent muttered. "Four people isn't shit. We're a lot more likely to miss something."

"Sheriff?" A narrow, young, pimple-faced deputy suddenly stuck his head into the room. He glanced at Kent and Tony, then Isabel. Color flooded his cheeks when she met his gaze.

Thomas turned to him with a sigh. "What is it, Joshua?"

"A call came in, sir."

"And?"

"It was Miss Mable."

Another sigh. "And?"

The deputy glanced at Kent and Tony again, clearly hesitant.

"Just spit it out, boy," Thomas ordered. "We're all on the same side here."

"Yes, sir. Miss Mabel said some folks checked in this morning from out of town." Joshua's cheeks grew deeper red as everyone in the room turned to focus on him. "A man, a woman, and two boys. She thinks it's them, the ones everyone's looking for. And she said someone else had just showed up, and that she thought..." His voice trailed off.

"Thought what?" the Sheriff demanded.

"That shit was about to get real, sir."

Beside Isabel, Tony suddenly shrugged into his raincoat. Her pulse fluttered when he took her elbow and gently tugged her to her feet. Kent was already moving.

"What kind of shit?" Thomas demanded.

Joshua only shrugged. "She just said we'd best get over there."

"Over where?" Kent wanted to know, his tone hard.

"Mabel's Mountain View Inn," Thomas muttered. "It's

over on—"

"I drove past it," Kent said and strode out the door.

"Get the rig," Thomas told Joshua.

"Yes, sir."

The deputy disappeared. Isabel grabbed her tablet, and Tony ushered her toward the door Kent had disappeared through. Behind them, Bob Peabody swallowed his last bite of donut and hurried to keep up.

"Finally," he said. "Some action."

CHAPTER 36

He didn't even touch the Jeep, and it started.

Sam Steele, Deputy U.S. Marshal, fire-starter, ass-kicker, and, apparently, wizard.

Lucia shook her head. She didn't know what Sam had done or not done—she'd been asleep—but Alexander was convinced Sam had "hacked" the vehicle they'd stolen, something Lucia hadn't even realized was possible. And something that scared the hell out of her.

A car could be remotely controlled? Who thought that was a good idea?

It sounded like an invitation to disaster—and she would know.

Of course, Sam, being Sam, continued to insist he was *"just that good"* when Alexander demanded the truth, which made Lucia want to laugh, something she hadn't done in…*forever.*

He could be charming when he chose, which disarmed her; charm was something she was unprepared to defend against. That wicked smile, that intense and captivating focus. He'd tempted her when he hadn't even been trying. Now that he was…

Ay, yai, yai. You are so screwed, chica.

"Are you almost done?" Alexander yelled through the bathroom door. "I'm hungry."

Yes, yes. They'd checked into the Mountain View Inn earlier and rented one of the small cabins. Then Sam had grabbed Daisy and Ben and left to take Ben to the Emerge-A-Care clinic in town and to find parts for the device he was going to build to jam the signal from the GPS trackers. *Trackers.* The idea of it both horrified and infuriated Lucia, and her desire to lop Donavon Cruz's head from his body only grew.

We never had a chance. The deck had been stacked from the beginning, and if it were not for Sam...

"We would be dead," she muttered grimly. And she knew it was not only Sam who'd saved them; it was Tony as well.

The jerk.

"Lucia!" Alexander rattled the locked door handle. "Come *on.*"

"In a minute, *mijo,*" she retorted. "I am changing my bandages."

Silence fell. Lucia looked into the mirror, at the ugly wounds Ivan had left. *So many marks.* Many of which would scar. And his bites—

"Breathe," she ordered softly. "Just breathe."

Because there was nothing to be done for them except to survive. To heal and go on. And Sam had done a surprisingly good job patching her up; she only had to redo two. She'd wanted a shower desperately, but nothing good would come of trying to stand under a cascade of hot water with half a dozen open wounds. No, a sponge bath was the best she could get, at least until her skin mended further. *Maybe tomorrow.* But she wasn't holding her breath.

She was just grateful to be alive. To have the boys safe, and for Sam. Even though she hadn't wanted him—had tried to save him from this—and even though she knew she couldn't keep him…she was glad he was with them. *Hers.* If only for one brief, fleeting moment.

Lucia would take what she could get.

She sighed, applying the last of the butterflies to the long, ugly gash on her belly. She tossed the wrappers and pulled Sam's flannel back on, comforted by the scent of him surrounding her.

I know you were alone, Lu. But you're not alone now. I'm right here.

A truth he'd proven again and again: on the side of that freeway, during the storm that had destroyed Canyon Falls. Over the course of every mile they'd traveled. He'd made sure they were warm and safe and fed. He'd killed to protect them.

How could she doubt him?

She couldn't. And that had forced her to recognize that in all of the years since Elian and her mother's deaths, she'd *chosen* to be alone. That the bleak reality of being on her own had been something she'd donned willingly, an albatross she'd worn in effort to combat the grief that choked her still. Because it simply hurt too much to care. But that determination flew in the face of her very calling—to heal, to care more than anyone else, to have the most personal stake in another's survival—and those two certitudes were wholly paradoxical and could not co-exist. No, she was going to have to choose.

To give all that she was. Or not.

That had always been true. Sam...Sam had simply pointed it out. Unknowingly, perhaps, but that didn't make the realization any less profound. And what was happening around her couldn't matter. This was an understanding beyond circumstance; a reality she must address in order to be true to herself. So that she could then be true to everyone else.

And if she were to reach out and take Sam's hand...*to believe*...she would have to give up the fury that burned within her, a silent homage to the loss she'd suffered. Her friend. Her fuel. Because it was far easier to be angry than to mourn. To rage against the evil that was so prevalent in the world; to hate. Healing felt like a betrayal.

But that rage had done nothing but hurt her—and by extension, Alexander and Benjamin—and it was no example to leave them with. Because Alexander already had enough rage within him. Enough hate to fill an entire ocean. He would have to witness her trusting another so that he might do the same. He had to believe, too.

What had happened to her father, her mother, her beloved *abuela*...to Elian...none of it could be forgotten. But those events had cast a long shadow, one she'd allowed to define her for far too long. It was time to move past them, to step into the future...no matter what that future entailed.

"You can do it," she told herself, taking a deep, shuddering breath. "You can do anything."

You have the blood of kings in your veins, nieta.

Perhaps it was time to start acting like it.

"Alright," she said as she opened the bathroom door and stepped into the main room of the cabin. "I am ready. We can go to the vending machine now."

But Alexander didn't respond. He stood before the television, his attention so rapt and still a ripple of unease moved through her. She moved to stand next to him and focused on the pale blond news anchor he was listening to.

"...Mr. Cruz's whereabouts are still unknown, however the FBI appears to have narrowed the location of the Cruz children and their nanny-kidnapper, Lucia Sanchez, to a small town in central Idaho. We're told that local police are working with federal law enforcement to apprehend Ms. Sanchez and recover the children safely, although Ms. Sanchez has garnered unprecedented public support on social media in the wake of the release of the videos. The videos show Donavon Cruz committing multiple sex crimes on a number of young minors, including his son, Alexander." They cut away from the blond to a scene that froze Lucia in place: a brightly lit room she didn't recognize where a pale, slender boy—*Alexander*, easily recognizable, no matter his blurred features—sat nude on a narrow, wooden chair. Donavon Cruz appeared a moment later, his expression faintly mocking but also underscored by something that made Lucia's stomach turn: *lust*. He was speaking as he reached up to slowly remove his tie, and he began to circle Alexander like a shark, and—

Alexander made a harsh, strangled sound and slammed his hands against the flat screen. The TV rocked backward, and the violence of the act broke Lucia's paralysis. She moved to grab him as he lifted his hands to hit the screen a second time.

"*Mijo—*"

"No!" he screamed, the sound shrill, heartbreaking, and he jerked from her hold with a force that nearly pulled her from her feet. He smashed his fists into the screen, and the glass fractured, and the TV slid sideways, almost off of the long, narrow dresser it sat upon. *"No!"*

He raised his hands again, and Lucia lifted him from his feet and swung him away from the TV, toward one of the queen beds, her heart beating with fearful intensity. His scream echoed in her head—*such pain*—and he fought her like an animal, growling and scratching and kicking, drawing blood and reopening her wounds, so strong in his furious hysteria she could barely hold him.

"Alexander," she said into his ear, struggling for calm, fear for him flooding her veins. "Calm yourself. *Alexander.* Stop. You must *stop—"*

He screamed again, so loud it was like a blade piercing her eardrums. His head slammed into her chest, and pain tore through her; his heels slammed into her shins, and she stumbled, dropping him to the bed. He rolled off it a heartbeat later, and before she could stop him, ran out the door.

The rain was thick and thunderous and drenching as Lucia rushed out after him, the wooden boards of the porch slick beneath her feet. She nearly took a header as she leapt down the handful of steps to the ground. The rain was almost blinding, but she could see Alexander's bright yellow fleece only a handful of feet away, and just beyond him—

She jerked to a stop. A large, black SUV was parked in front of the cabin. Alexander had halted in front of that

SUV, his hands fisted, and as Lucia's heart plunged to her toes and her blood roared in her head, the driver's side door swung open.

"Alexander!" She grabbed the boy's narrow shoulders and thrust him behind her. "Go back to the cabin. *Now.*"

She didn't look to see if he obeyed, her eyes glued on the man who was climbing from the SUV, a huge, hulking man she recognized instantly: *Marlow.* Donavon Cruz's constant companion, the silent, menacing bodyguard he took everywhere he went. A man even more frightening than Ivan the Terrible.

He stalked toward her through the slanting rain as thunder burst violently overhead, and she tensed, brutally aware she had nothing with which to defend herself. Her gun was still in her purse—in the cabin behind her—and the only thing in her pocket was a handful of spare change. She was battered and bleeding and being held together by butterfly bandages; she was in no condition to go up against a man like Marlow. But there was nowhere to go, and the cabin was far back off the road—nearly in the forest—and there were no other guests around, no one to hear her cry for help. And Sam and Ben...

Were safe.

Lucia closed her hands into fists.

You have the blood of kings in your veins, nieta.

She turned her gaze to the darkened windows of the SUV, and spoke to the man she knew was watching. "You hide behind your men like a frightened child." She could feel the cold weight of his stare. "Come out, *cabrón.*" She lifted her hands in mock surrender. "Surely you have no need of your bodyguard against me. Surely you are *man enough* to face one small woman. Surely you are not...*afraid*."

Marlow smiled grimly. He was almost to her, but Lucia didn't move.

The passenger side door of the SUV swung open.

CHAPTER 37

The .22 was cold in his bloody hand.

Alexander's heart beat like a jackhammer as he stared down at the gleaming silver weapon he'd dug from Lucia's bag. He could see his reflection shimmer against its surface, wavy and warped, even through the thin film of his blood; he didn't remember cutting himself. The TV, he thought, but that realization fell away as he weighed the gun, his hold so tight the metal cut into his palm.

There're other ways.

Sam's words echoed in his head, but Alexander wasn't going to listen. Not after what he'd seen. Not after that video of him—

No. Don't think about that.

But—

He recorded me.

And the whole world had seen it.

The horror inside him was crushing, every part of him breaking, crumbling, *ruined.* He would never be the same. Nothing would ever be the same. *Destroyed.* Something he would never, ever escape.

Something Ben might see.

Tears slid from his eyes, hot, salty; Alexander blinked

them away and tightened his grip on the gun, the rush of his blood like the roar of some great, infuriated beast. The contents of his stomach surged, but he shook his head and swallowed against it, unwilling to allow anything to stop him. No, it was time.

Finally time.

Adrenaline speared through his veins, making him jerk, his hand closing convulsively on the .22. He could hear Lucia's voice but not her words, and he knew he had to hurry, because his father was going to kill her.

He felt strange as he pushed himself to his feet and left the cabin, the gun foreign and heavy in his hand. Almost as if the storm that surrounded him on the outside—the raging wind and crackling lightning and terrible explosions of thunder—had burrowed through his skin to press against his bones, making them tremble and quake, turning his chest into a churning mass of chaos and pain and *hate.*

It was the hate that steadied him. The hate was familiar, the calm in the center of that frenzied storm, a place he knew intimately. *A place he knew how to exist within.* And so he focused on that: the emptiness, that hollow chill of darkness absent sound and scent, where nothing existed but the deep, steady rhythm of his own breath. Beyond the calm, the storm howled like an enraged animal, and he knew it would overtake him. *Swallow him.* But first—

"...surely you are not...*afraid.*"

Lucia's words rang through the air as Alexander stepped out of the cabin; the rain slapped his skin like tiny, stinging needles. Marlow was storming toward Lucia, and the passenger side door of the SUV was opening, and

Alexander's father stepped out into the downpour.

Alexander's hand tightened around the gun, his feet suddenly locked into place where he stood, atop the small wooden porch on the front of the cabin. He lifted the gun, his hand flexing around it, trying to remember what he'd seen of weapons in the movies. He'd made sure it was loaded—two 10-round clips—and found and disengaged the safety.

"Get in the car, Alexander," his father said, his gaze on the .22 Alexander held. He began to walk toward Alexander, and he didn't look afraid.

Alexander wanted him afraid.

Lucia turned and saw the gun and moved immediately to intercept him. But in that moment, Marlow caught up to her. He grabbed her by the hair and yanked her back, and she rammed into him, her skull smashing into his chin before she whirled around and punched him in the throat. Then she kicked him, hard, in the knee, and he stumbled. But she couldn't avoid his fist when it shot toward her, and it crashed into her face like a hammer. She slammed into the ground. Marlow lifted his big, booted foot and stepped on her, and held her there with his weight on her spine. He leaned on her when she struggled, and she cried out, and Alexander aimed the .22 at the SUV and fired.

The sound was deafening; he almost dropped the weapon when it jerked in his hand. The SUV's windshield shattered, and Marlow flinched. But Donavon Cruz halted, and a sudden, intense power surged through Alexander, the intoxicating realization that *he* was the one in control. *For once.* And he turned the .22 on his father and took aim at those pale green eyes, so like his that sometimes he hated his own stare. But in that moment those eyes...they weren't glittering, sharp. *Hungry.* No. They were flat, uncertain. *They wavered.* And heat made Alexander's joints weak, a molten wave that burned like white fire in his chest, and something deep inside him lifted its head. Howled.

Another burst of adrenaline washed through him. The calm cracked; the storm hissed in his ears. But it felt...*good.* Welcome. As if he was finally...free.

"Put that fucking thing down," his father growled at him and began to stride toward the porch, slicing through the thick downpour like a sharp blade. A look Alexander recognized slid over his father's features, one that made the boy's heart hammer painfully hard in his throat.

Shoot him.

The gun was warm from being fired. He could do it. He just had to pull the trigger again—

Getting closer, angrier, his big hands curled, ready to yank Alexander from his feet—

Another vehicle pulled up; for a moment the headlights were blinding. In that moment, Alexander's father tore the gun from his hand. His other arm was captured in a grip so tight, he felt his bones ache.

Terror sheared through him, and he stared at his father, unable to move.

Why hadn't he pulled the trigger? What was wrong with him?

Weak. He was weak.

"You do not touch him," Lucia snarled, and lunged up from beneath Marlow's foot. He kicked her, a vicious jab to her bleeding wounds, and Alexander flinched, and his

stomach turned. But when she hit the grass, Lucia rolled over and hooked her leg behind Marlow's. She jerked him from his feet, and he looked surprised as he body slammed the ground.

"Bitch," Donavon Cruz growled, his voice so soft only Alexander heard him. And suddenly he was yanking Alexander from the porch with that brutal, bruising grip on Alexander's arm and dragging him toward Lucia.

The heavy, frantic beat of Alexander's heart made him dizzy. His father held the .22 in his hand, his knuckles pressing white against his skin. *Like he meant to use it.*

Alexander stopped and twisted violently, and suddenly, he was free.

"No," he said. And then he yelled it. *"No!"*

When his father reached for him again, Alexander leapt back. He remembered the knife—*Misha's knife*—that Sam had given him, and he pulled it from his pocket. He had it open a heartbeat later, the fine, well-honed tip aimed at the man he faced.

"Try it," his father invited, his fingers flexing around the .22, his pale eyes glinting.

Alexander's hand tightened around the knife.

"Do it," his father murmured and smiled. "Cut me."

A violent tremor shook Alexander; again his hand squeezed the knife. His father didn't think he would do it.

Didn't think he *could* do it.

Just a fucking game to get him off.

Like everything else.

"No? Perhaps this will help." Alexander's father turned

and pointed the .22 at Lucia, who froze, her gaze flitting between the gun and the large form of Marlow slowly pushing to his feet over her, his face ugly with retribution. "Perhaps you need more incentive."

Alexander took an involuntary step toward her. "No."

Donavon Cruz cocked the .22. His pale eyes gleamed as they traced Lucia's bloody and battered form. "It's a shame there's no time to play. Look at how brightly she bleeds."

"*No*," Alexander repeated, and terror nearly choked him. "Please. I'll go with you. I won't fight. We can go right now. Just don't hurt her. Please. *Don't*."

But Donavon Cruz only laughed softly. Alexander's hand flexed around the knife, and he suddenly understood that it was up to him. That he had to act, or his father *would* kill Lucia. There was no doubt, and, Alexander realized, no bargaining. His father would not let her live.

Not for any reason.

He gripped the knife tightly and lunged in front of Lucia, ignoring her protest and smashing himself against her until the end of the .22 was pointed at his thin chest. He stared defiantly at his father, knife in hand, waiting. *Ready*.

"There's your spine." A sharp smile. "I've been waiting for you to find it."

Alexander leaned over and spat—very precisely—at his father's feet.

"*You will be punished*," his father hissed, the same chilling voice he used when Alexander was in the chair, the one filled with a thousand unspoken nightmares. "*Move*."

Alexander squeezed the knife. Inside him, a fire was spreading, licking at his bones. "No."

Eyes glittering, his father pressed the .22 into Alexander's sternum, and Alexander's heart pounded like a drum in his skull, but he didn't move. Couldn't. He was making his stand. If his father shot him, at least it would be *over*—

"*Hands on your head, Cruz.*"

That abrupt, barked command broke between them, as sharp as the crack of thunder. A man materialized from the torrent beside them, and in his hands was a gleaming steel handgun twice the size of the .22. It was aimed at Donavon Cruz's head.

Marlow froze, but Alexander's father didn't so much as flinch. "Stand down, Agent Kent. I have this under control."

"Put that fucking gun on the ground," the man demanded. "*Now.*"

"Turn around and walk away, Agent. This doesn't concern you."

The man took another step toward them, and for one brief moment, his gaze clashed with Alexander's, and Alexander saw the same black, churning turmoil that roiled within him. His heart squeezed with sudden, painful intensity.

"On the ground, you piece of shit," the Agent said flatly. "Right now. Or I will shoot you."

He wasn't kidding. The realization made Alexander go very, very still. The hair across his frame rose, bristling.

Marlow reached into the interior of his coat, and the Agent snarled, "Don't."

Alexander's father stilled; his eyes narrowed on the man.

He raked the young agent with his gaze, and the look that crawled across his features made Alexander wish he was brave enough to plunge the blade he held so deep into his father's belly that it came out the other side.

"It takes one to know one, I suppose," his father murmured, and the man took another step closer, and Alexander's hand tightened around the knife until his knuckles ached.

"On the fucking ground," Agent Kent whispered. His eyes were dark, his gaze focused absolutely on Donavon Cruz. His gun didn't waver; his hands didn't shake.

He wanted to kill him.

The thought jolted through Alexander, but before he could react, his father turned to him and—

Boom!

CHAPTER 38

Sam smiled as he turned off the main drag through Blue Ridge and onto the narrow side street that would lead to their rental cabin. The smell of McDonalds surrounded him in a grease-scented cloud, and in the backseat, Ben continued to chatter away, somehow managing to simultaneously hold a conversation and consume his Happy Meal. He was feeling much better, and according to the doctor at the emergency clinic, was on his way to a full recovery, something for which Sam was eternally grateful. Next to Ben sat a bag from Ernie's Electronics, filled with the parts Sam would need to create a wireless signal jammer. It was still raining to beat hell, but things were looking up.

Finally.

"I'm glad you feel better," Sam said. "Maybe we can—"

The words snagged in his throat at the sight that greeted him in front of the cabin they'd rented. Two vehicles—one of which was a red Ford Bronco with an *Eagle County Sheriff Department* logo emblazed on its side—were screeching to a halt in front of the cabin, their headlights shining brightly in the steady downpour, illuminating the people who stood in front of the cabin— *Alexander and Donavon Cruz and Lucia, who was on the ground, under some asshole's foot;* and that goddamn .22 was in Donavon Cruz's hand.

Sam slammed on the brakes, and the Jeep shimmied to a stop.

"Whoa!" Ben exclaimed, and Daisy yipped loudly. "I dropped my nugget! Daisy—*no!*"

"You stay here," Sam told him in a hard voice as he climbed out of the Jeep. "I'll be right back."

Then he ran through the rain, toward the unfolding scene.

Alexander was on the porch; Donavon Cruz stood on the ground beside him, one hand wrapping the boy's arm, one holding Lucia's .22. Lucia was only a handful of feet from them—*on the fucking ground*—and she was pushing herself up, but the big brute who stood over her—on *fucking top of her*—another goddamn Ivan?—gave her a hard kick, and Sam felt his skin tighten and his focus narrow, and he knew which bones he would break first. But then Lucia rolled over, caught the guy's legs with one of hers and swept them out from underneath him. He slammed into the ground and bounced.

When she turned unerringly to meet Sam's gaze through the dense rainfall as though she could feel his sudden presence, his heart jerked hard. Her nose and her lip were bleeding again, and her shirt was one big, bloody smear, and hot, incendiary rage made him run faster.

Cruz hauled Alexander from the porch, toward Lucia. Half way to her, the boy twisted away. Cruz halted and pointed the .22 at Lucia, and Sam's blood fired. A heartbeat later, Alexander was darting in front of Lucia, putting himself in the line of fire. Sam saw the glint in his hand and realized the boy was holding a knife.

Misha's knife.

"Hands on your head, Cruz."

That abrupt, unseen command made Sam suddenly slow. A man moved into view—young, suited, *a Fed?*—and he stood on the other side of the giant Lucia had felled. The sleek black .9mm he held was aimed at Donavon Cruz.

"Stand down, Agent Kent," Cruz said. "I have this under control."

"Put that fucking gun on the ground," the suit ordered. *"Now."*

Sam halted a handful of feet away, his gaze narrow, adrenaline chugging through him like a train.

"Turn around and walk away, Agent." Cruz's laconic drawl was cold. "This doesn't concern you."

But the suit—shit, more like *kid*—only took another fluid step toward Donavon Cruz, his weapon steady, and Sam realized not only was the kid serious, the way he was moving was pure predator; he wasn't just a suit, or a Fed. He was former military.

"On the ground, you piece of shit," Agent Kent said flatly. "Right now. Or I will shoot you."

He wasn't kidding.

Sam reached for his Glock. *Goddamn it.*

The giant Lucia had felled suddenly stirred, reaching into the interior of his coat, and the kid snarled, "Don't."

Cruz's gaze lifted to the agent's face. Whatever he saw made a smile turn his mouth, an ugly smile—*wrong*—and he said something too low for Sam to hear.

The kid only blinked. "On the fucking ground." *Last chance.*

Sam saw him ready his grip.

Shit. He took another step, but it was too late.

Boom!

*****

"The fuck is this!" Tony growled. He slid the SUV to a halt next to Sheriff Thompkin's Bronco. Beside him, Isabel threw off her seatbelt and pulled up her hood. "How the hell did Kent get here so fast?"

Isabel slid him a look. "Maybe he's afraid you'll shoot one of his perps."

Tony bared his teeth at her. "Only one of them."

They climbed from the car and were instantly soaked. Thunder rolled over, and the trees shuddered from the wind. The rain was a thick veil Tony strode through, past the Sheriff and Joshua and Bob Peabody, aware of Isabel beside him, and suddenly the scene came into view:

Donavon Cruz stood outlined by the vehicle lights. He held a handgun pointed at his son Alexander, who clutched something Tony thought might have been a knife, but he wasn't certain; the rain was too dense. The boy stood in front of Lucia, who was on her knees on the ground, battered and bleeding, and the sight of that blood struck Tony like a cold, hard fist.

Jesus Christ.

Beside her a big brute of a man was stirring. *Marlow.* Tony recognized him from Isabel's files. Donavon Cruz's bodyguard.

To Marlow's right, Special Agent Kent held his weapon aimed at Donavon Cruz in an aggressive stance Tony immediately recognized.

"*Put that fucking gun on the ground*," Kent ordered, and Tony recognized that, too, the intensity of his tone, that distinct warning.

Fuck.

Tony halted. He reached out and grabbed Isabel's arm, forcing her to stop as well. She glowered at him, but didn't fight his hold.

"Turn around and walk away, Agent," Cruz replied, as if swatting away a fly. "This doesn't concern you."

Isabel tugged against his grip, but Tony only pulled her closer, and Sam suddenly materialized through the rain on the other side of Lucia, Glock in hand—*that's my man*—and he approached the scene cautiously, his gaze intent.

"On the ground, you piece of shit." Kent's words flat, and Tony's nape prickled with unease. He held firm when Isabel tugged against his hold, and ignored the growl she emitted. "Right now. Or I will shoot you."

There was no bluff in those words.

Donavon Cruz seemed to realize it. He turned to look at the young man whose gun was pointed at him, but whatever he saw only made him smile, a taunting, dark smirk Tony wanted to beat from his face. He said something Tony couldn't hear. *Something malicious.* Cruelty painted his face.

"On the fucking ground," Kent snarled, and Tony knew it was game over.

On the other side of Lucia, Sam started walking. But Donavon Cruz lifted the .22 and—

Boom!

CHAPTER 39

Alexander jerked violently with the sound of the shot, but there was no pain, and when he looked down, there was no blood. *But—*

He looked at his father, not understanding. And then he saw the ugly red hole in his father's forehead, his cold features oddly blank. *Erased.*

Donavon Cruz fell to his knees, and Alexander realized abruptly what had happened.

On the ground, you piece of shit. Right now. Or I will shoot you.

His father slammed into the ground face-first and didn't move.

Alexander stared down at him for a long, silent moment, his heart a painful stutter in his chest, and tried to absorb it. Then he turned and looked at the man who'd shot his father. *Agent Kent.* Who still held his gun at the ready, old eyes in a young face.

"Are you okay?" the Agent demanded.

Alexander could only blink at him, slightly dumbfounded.

Marlow suddenly rolled, as if to stand, but Sam appeared out of the rain to press his Glock into Marlow's thick jowl.

"I wouldn't," he said, and Alexander's knees went weak.

"Sam." Alexander turned toward him, relief almost making him heady. *"Sam."*

"Down," Sam said to Marlow.

Marlow subsided, and then two Sheriff's deputies descended. Sam stepped back and held up his weapon.

"Sam Steele," he said, and lifted a badge from around his neck that winked brightly in the headlights. "Deputy U.S. Marshal."

Alexander screeched to a halt. Sam looked over to meet his gaze. And Lucia made a harsh sound that made them both turn toward her. She was pushing herself up, her shirt clinging to the blood that washed her; she looked like the victim in a horror movie.

Alexander moved toward her, but suddenly men surrounded them, pushing him aside to get to her. They were lifting her away from the ground, and when she cried out in pain, Alexander yelled, "No," and moved to stop them. But Sam plucked him out of the mix, easily subduing him when he fought.

"No," Alexander said again, trying to break Sam's hold. "They're taking her," he snarled, and tears punched into his chest like a hammer. "We can't let them take her."

"They're paramedics; they're taking her to a hospital." Sam put Alexander down and held onto him with two big hands on Alexander's shoulders. "We'll be right behind her, I promise."

A Deputy U.S. Marshal. The betrayal was like a hot poker. "Where's Ben?"

Sam squeezed his shoulders gently. "He's okay, son.

Everything's going to be okay."

But Alexander shook his head, the tears in his chest turning to stone. "They're taking her," he said again.

"Don't worry," Sam said. "I won't let them keep her."

*****

The young man Isabel had known as Austin Kent had morphed into a predator before her very eyes. As if a switch had flipped, and the darkness within had stepped forward to deal with the darkness without.

Watching the video , she thought, had triggered something within Agent Kent, and her heart silently ached for him, even as she was fascinated by the abrupt transformation.

When he'd fired his weapon, and a neat hole blossomed in Donavon Cruz's forehead, he hadn't even blinked. There was no hesitation, no remorse. And part of Isabel was with him every step of the way, right or wrong.

But there would be serious repercussions.

Added to that was the fact that he still held his weapon at the ready, as if they stood in the middle of a battlefield.

Isabel tried to step toward him, but Tony only squeezed her arm, his hand strong and unyielding as he held her trapped there beside him—*damn him*—and said to Kent, "Put your weapon away, Agent Kent. One man down is enough."

Around them, the rain fell in dense, chilled sheets, and thunder rumbled like a giant stirring. Kent looked down at the fallen form of Donavon Cruz, and Isabel watched a myriad of emotion chase across his features: rage, recognition. A fierce, angry defiance.

"You warned him," Tony continued. "He didn't listen. But now you need to stand down."

Kent looked at him, eyes glittering, and Isabel's chest tightened.

"Just fucking breathe," Tony told him. "It's over."

A shuddering breath rasped from Austin, steaming out into the cold rain; he was pale, his skin sheened by perspiration. He looked like a kid, but the unmoving body of Donavon Cruz belied that presumption, and Isabel knew there was far more to Austin Kent than she'd realized. And that was a mark against her, because she—better than anyone—knew there was always something beneath the surface.

Always.

"Good." Tony held out a hand. "Give me your gun."

Isabel watched, her blood a dull roar in her ears. Kent stared at Tony for a long, silent moment, unmoving, but Tony only stared back, a hard, unbending look as he waited, one that Kent finally bent beneath. He took a deep breath and handed Tony his weapon. Then he stepped back and turned away.

Paramedics suddenly appeared, shoving past them to head to Donavon Cruz's side. Two peeled off and headed toward Lucia. Isabel tried again to take a step toward Agent Kent, but Tony stepped into her path with a sharp shake of his head.

"Knock it off," she growled. "I'm not a dog to be leashed."

He crowded against her until she glared up at him. "I want you safe."

"It's good to want things," she retorted sharply, tossing his own words back at him.

The bastard smiled down at her. "It's better to get them."

Heat flared to life deep within, and she snarled at him. "Get out of my way."

"Baby, no," Tony said softly. He sobered. "Kent just killed a man. Give him a minute."

Isabel stilled. She heard experience in his voice, and she respected that; but she was irritated as hell at him thinking he had the right to cosset or protect her.

No one cossetted or protected her. *No one.*

"I know you can take care of yourself," he continued and took another small step toward her, until his hard frame pressed against her softer one. Before she could move, he ducked his head into the hollow where her neck and shoulder met, and rubbed his bristled chin against her scarred skin, making a sudden shiver ripple through her. "But you're mine to take care of, too."

Damn him. "We are more effective when we work *together.*"

Tony stared down at her, his brows drawn low, his hazel eyes glinting like polished tiger's eye, and Isabel knew that—no matter what he said—Tony would always put himself in front of her when he thought it was necessary. That wasn't something she would ever be able to change.

"Kent was going to fire," he said. "I know that look. Some things you can't stop, honey."

Her throat filled suddenly, sharply. She knew that look, too. She'd seen it, too. And she'd done nothing.

"Is this our fault?" she asked quietly and met Tony's gaze through the thick, endless rain. "Are we responsible for this?"

"We brought forth the truth," he replied after a long moment. "There are always repercussions for the truth."

Yes.

Kent was suddenly walking toward them, his features tight, his eyes dark.

"That piece of shit is still alive," he said.

*****

The hands touching her were cool and efficient.

Lucia's head was spinning, and her mouth was filled with blood. *More blood.*

Marlow's punch had almost knocked her lights out; her head throbbed, her blood a dull, steady roar. Bringing him down had been faintly satisfying, until Donavon Cruz had appeared with her gun in his hand, until Alexander had wedged himself in front of that gun and refused to move.

She remembered...*Sam.* Running toward her through the rain. And then another man—one she didn't know, a man in a suit and a long, dark coat—who'd appeared and...

Shot Donavon Cruz.

Cruz had fallen, landing only a handful of feet from her, on the other side of Marlow, a bloody hole in his forehead, his features slack, and her heart had jolted at the lack of life in his pale gaze.

When she'd pushed up from the ground, it was slippery

with her blood, and her hands almost slid out from under her. But then others were there, paramedics, with their calm competence and unbending determination to deliver treatment, and although she wanted to argue, Lucia knew she was losing too much blood, and she hurt, the pain sharp and vivid, like streaks of sudden, brilliant color in a dark room. So she let them press bandages to her wounds and didn't argue when they tore her shirt away.

"Lucia."

Her eyes opened. Sam was above her, his features sharp, a frown making him scowl down at her.

"We'll be right behind you, sweetheart," he said. "Don't worry."

But she didn't understand what that meant, and when the paramedics pushed him aside, he went, and she tried to sit up and protest. Gentle hands pushed her back down again.

They loaded her into a still, cool place, and she shivered. Her blouse was in shreds, and cold air washed over her damp skin in a chilly wave. Her ears had begun to ring, which she knew wasn't a good sign, and her head continued to throb as though someone had slammed a hard, round stone into her skull.

A dark face suddenly appeared above hers, skin like coal, eyes the bitterest of chocolate. "Who did this?"

"Who then or who now?" Lucia hissed when something cold and wet washed over the wound on her breast. *"Ay, yai, yai."*

The face seemed to glower at her. "Who gave you these wounds? Is that a *bite* mark?"

She shuddered. "He's dead."

"Goddamn, girl." The face disappeared; more cold, wet, burning hellfire eating into one of her wounds.

"*Ay, yai, yai.* That hurts," she growled, wiggling.

Hands returned to her shoulders and stilled her movement. "Take it easy. Your wounds are ripped wide open. I know you know what that means." A pause. "We need to get you closed up."

Lucia remembered her *abuela* sewing her up, gentle hands, whisper-fine thread.

This would be nothing like that.

"I'm going to her," said a different voice.

The hands on her shoulders tightened. Her ears rang like insistent bells.

"No," she said. "I will not fight. I promise. Please, do not sedate me."

A moment of stillness, and she didn't move, the only sound the dull thrush of her blood and that blasted, eternal ringing—

"I'll begin here," said the voice that belonged to the ebony skin and gentle hands. A light touch at the wound on her belly. "When you decide you want the drugs, stop me."

CHAPTER 40

"Cruz is alive. The bullet is lodged in his frontal lobe. The doctors know there's significant brain damage, but not much else. He's intubated, and he hasn't regained consciousness. There's at least a fifty percent chance he never will."

Sam met Tony's gaze; *good riddance.* It was just a shame the fucker was still alive to waste oxygen.

"Other than his heirs, Cruz has no living family," Agent Kent continued, his voice flat. "According to his lawyer, his living will dictates that he's to be kept alive by whatever means necessary. If he dies, some private academy in Belgium is named as the boys' guardian. In the interim, his lawyer, Louis Alcott, is granted temporary guardianship."

"Bullshit," Sam said succinctly from his place beside the door. They had gathered in the shabby, rainbow themed waiting room at St. Joseph's Medical Center, where both Cruz and Lucia were being treated. Tony and Isabel, Agent Kent, and an aging man with a blueberry muffin in hand whom Tony had introduced as Detective Peabody. "The boys stay with me."

Isabel blinked at him. She reminded Sam of a cool, golden bird, sleek and delicate, but her eyes were like dark wells, and within them, Sam saw an echo of something familiar. Tony hovered next to her like her own personal Samurai, protective and—to her open annoyance—territorial. Sam planned on giving him shit about it for the rest of his life.

"You'd better have a good lawyer," she warned softly.

As if in response, Sam's phone vibrated in his pocket. He didn't look. He was pretty certain the wheel he'd pushed was now turning.

"What happened out there?" Tony asked, his hazel gaze narrow.

The boys sat on the opposite side of the room, watching the TV in the corner. *Green Acres*. Daisy was in the truck. Ben leaned heavily against his brother, a sippee cup filled with milk in his lap. They were both exhausted. Sam needed to get them back to the cabin. They needed a break, and they needed to eat. Somewhere safe to sleep.

"I want to see Lucia," he said, ignoring the question. He looked at Kent. "Now."

"No."

Sam's gaze narrowed, and he took an aggressive step toward the young agent. "Would you like to see my badge, Agent Kent? She's as much my prisoner as she is yours, and *I want to see her.*"

Kent blinked. "We both know she was never your prisoner."

Sam took another step, his gaze narrowing. "Is that what we know?"

Kent held Sam's gaze briefly before it broke off, and he looked at Tony, who only arched a brow at him.

"Technically, Lucia Sanchez is in federal custody," Isabel said quietly. "Sam is the federal agent whose been detaining her for the last seventy-two hours; I would say that entitles him to a conversation with her. At the least."

Kent only stared at her, silent.

"She's right," Bob Peabody said, a stray muffin crumb marking his chin. "He's got some play in the game."

"No," Kent denied again.

"Why the fuck not?" Sam leaned down over him. "Where do you think Lucia falls in all this? She took those boys to protect them—and that's a crime—but you shot the son of a bitch in the head. That's attempted murder. So you watch the high horse you've climbed on, kid. Because it's a long way down."

Kent blinked, and color flared brightly in his cheeks. "She's asleep," he said tightly. "They put over a hundred stitches in her."

Sam stilled. *Over a hundred.* He thought about Lucia stitching up his leg, and he fought the urge to simply punch the kid aside. "Now, Special Agent Kent. I want to see her *now.*"

"Don't be a dickhead," Tony added.

"Fine," Kent grated. "But I go with you."

"Fine," Sam growled at him. "But the boys stay with me."

"Fine," Kent retorted. "I'll let you argue with the judge."

"Good." Sam turned and looked at Tony. "Watch them."

Tony nodded, and Sam said, "Let's go."

*****

The ache was deep and steady, but Lucia's skin had been patched, neat, precise lines that spoke to the skill of the person who'd sewn her back together again.

Her head still hurt, and she could hear the intermittent beeps and *hiss* of medical equipment, but when she opened her eyes, she found the room around her to be small and empty. The door was closed, and other than the beeps, it was hushed and still. She could smell antiseptic and alcohol. A saline drip was hooked into her wrist.

She felt like a truck had run her over.

When the door to the small room opened, and Sam walked in followed by someone else—a man in a suit and a long, dark coat—*the man who'd shot Donavon Cruz*—Lucia's heart leapt in painful joy.

Sam went straight to her and leaned over the bed, his hands gentle when he cupped her cheeks. His bright eyes glittered. "You okay, sweetheart?"

Lucia nodded, her throat too thick to speak. To her consternation, tears welled and slid hotly down her cheeks.

Sam turned and looked over his shoulder at the man in the suit. "Get out."

The man flinched slightly; his gaze narrowed on them. "No solitary visitors."

"Fuck off, Kent," Sam said. "Get out. *Now.*"

Lucia reached up and touched his jaw, rubbed her

fingertips against his beard.

"Sam," she said.

His gaze met hers, and she told him, "I do not care about him."

Sam's eyes narrowed, and his jaw hardened beneath her touch, but she said, "No."

His stare burned into hers; he wasn't happy. But she only tugged him closer and whispered, "Kiss me, Sam. While you can."

And then his mouth was on hers, gentle but fierce, and so careful those stupid tears again welled and rolled down her cheeks. Lucia shuddered, and her hands found his hair, and she pulled him closer, nipping his upper lip, flicking her tongue against the lower one. He made a rough, startled sound, and then—

"That's enough," Kent said. "Step away from her."

—and then Sam really kissed her. His hands curved around her jaw and held her to him while he devoured her. The pads of his fingertips were rough; they rasped against her skin as his tongue stroked into her mouth to rub wetly against hers, and Lucia rose against him, awash in drowning heat and sudden, wrenching need. Her wounds protested, and she flinched, but she didn't want to stop kissing him—

Sam broke the kiss and pressed his forehead to hers. His bright eyes gleamed down at her.

"I felt that," he said, his voice low. "I don't want to hurt you." His gaze flickered to the blue and white hospital gown she wore. "Did they do a good job?"

Lucia's breath caught at the look on his face. "Yes. I think so."

His eyes shimmered when they met hers. "I want to see."

Her breath caught.

"Deputy Marshal Steele," Kent said in a tight voice. "This little reunion is over."

"I have the boys," Sam told her. "I'm keeping them for you."

Her heart seemed to stop. "Is he...dead?"

"No, but as good as." Sam smiled suddenly, sharp and deadly. "No living kin. We're it."

"It," she echoed, but Kent suddenly stepped further into the tiny room. Behind him were two suited men with large black guns.

"Goddamn it," Sam said softly.

Lucia pulled him down and kissed him again.

"Take care of them for me," she whispered.

"I know you know this," he said and stroked a careful thumb over her bottom lip. "But I always have a plan."

A startled laugh escaped her, and Sam leaned down and pressed another sweet, lingering kiss to her mouth.

"Faith," he murmured when they parted, and his eyes glinted, and Lucia had never wanted to believe more.

"I've indulged you long enough," Kent said—ground out between clenched teeth—"You need to come with me now. The federal prosecutor can decide whether or not you get to see Miss Sanchez again."

Sam growled softly, but when he leaned down and gave her a brief, possessive kiss, Lucia knew he was going to acquiesce. And she was glad, because his going to jail on her account would do no one any good, and he needed to get the hell out of there so he could take care of the boys. But part of her wanted him to stay, too.

Even if nothing could stop what was to come.

"I'll see you soon," Sam told her, and there was no doubting the promise that shimmered in his gaze.

Lucia hoped it was true, but she wasn't taking anything for granted. So she pulled him back down to her and kissed him like she'd been aching to kiss him; everything she felt poured into the tender, passionate taking of his mouth.

Love.

"Thank you," she whispered against his lips. "I won't forget."

Sam stared down at her. "Soon," he reiterated, his voice deep. "I promise."

CHAPTER 41

Alexander moved to stand next to Sam as soon as Sam returned to the small waiting room. When he'd looked up and discovered Sam gone, his heart had slid into his shoes. The woman who'd remained—*Isabel*—had told Alexander that Sam would be back, but she wasn't anyone he knew or trusted, and he'd paced uneasily before the chair where Ben was sleeping until Sam had stepped back into the room.

Immediately, Sam's gaze arrowed in on him. "What?"

He tried to shrug. "I wasn't sure you were coming back." He looked at Isabel, who watched him with eyes like black coal. "I mean, she said you were, but." Another shrug. "I didn't know."

Sam reached out and clasped Alexander's shoulder warmly. "Well, I'm back. Let's get your brother and go."

Alexander stared at him. "Go where? What about Lucia? You said you wouldn't let them keep her."

Sam squeezed his shoulder. "And I won't. She's safe here, and she'll get a good night's sleep. They sewed her up; she's not going anywhere. I promise."

"We can't leave her," Alexander protested. "I won't."

Sam crouched before him. "Your brother needs a hot meal and a warm bed, and we all need dry clothes. We're going back to the cabin, and like it or not, Lucia is staying here. The docs won't release her, not yet. But she's okay, and she knows we're together."

"Is that where you went?" Alexander demanded. "Did you get to see her?"

"Yes."

"I want to see her."

"They won't let that happen," Sam told him. "As far as they're concerned, she stole you boys. No way they're gonna let you get anywhere near her."

Alexander felt his chest go tight. "Never?"

Sam suddenly reached out and pulled Alexander into a warm, hard hug. "Not never. Just for now. We've got things to sort, bud. It's going to take some time. But she's safe. I promise she's safe."

Alexander stood stiffly in Sam's embrace, his throat too full, the backs of his eyes burning. He pulled away as Isabel and Sam's friend Tony approached, but Sam kept his hand on Alexander's shoulder, and Alexander didn't pull away.

"We're going," Sam said to Tony. "We'll be back in the morning. Keep me in the loop."

Tony's gaze narrowed. Isabel's dark eyes glinted.

"What?" Sam asked.

"You're claiming them?" Isabel asked, and her eyes met Alexander's.

"They're mine now," Sam replied shortly. He turned his focus on Tony. "You're going to get Lucia out of this."

"Have you seen the video?" Isabel asked.

Alexander flinched and knew she saw it. But Sam only

frowned and said, "What video?"

Isabel and Tony shared a look that made Alexander's heart sink.

"Fuck," Sam said. "Now what?"

But to Alexander's intense relief, Tony only shook his head. "Later."

"Fine," Sam growled. "Then we're gone."

*****

The cabin was dark and quiet when they arrived.

Alexander walked Daisy, and when he went in, Sam ran him a hot bath and made both him and Ben get cleaned up. The only clean clothes they had left were their spare pajamas: *Wolverine* for Alexander, *Clifford the Big Red Dog* for Ben. And as they sat on their bed eating the cold club sandwiches Sam had stopped and bought, Daisy watching with avid interest from the floor, Ben said, for the seventy-fifth time, "Are you sure Lu's gonna be okay? Because I think we should go check on her."

"Tomorrow," Sam told him. "We'll check on her tomorrow."

"She's okay, Ben," Alexander said. "She's in the hospital with the doctors. They'll take care of her."

But Ben only shook his head in unhidden, derisive disbelief, and tossed a chunk of his sandwich at Daisy, who caught it mid-air and swallowed it whole.

"Ben," Sam said and sighed.

"What's going to happen now?" Alexander asked. "Is

my father dead?"

Sam sat down on the bed and looked at them for a long, silent moment. Alexander's heart began to beat a steady, terrified tattoo.

"No," Sam said finally. "He's not dead. At least, not entirely." And then Sam explained that his father had been shot in the head, and that machines were keeping him alive. That he *was* dead, for all intents and purposes. And Alexander learned that he had no other living family save Ben, and that people far away had been entrusted with their lives, and that even now someone was coming for them. And his mind spun with the implications of it all, a new kind of terror that kicked the breath from him.

"How would you feel if I filed a petition for guardianship?" Sam asked, and for a moment Alexander only stared stupidly at him. "It'd be temporary in the beginning, but we could make it permanent. If you want. I'd do that."

Alexander felt his face flame. "Why? We're nothing to you."

Sam frowned at him. "You know better than that."

"You should take Ben," Alexander said, and pain cleaved into him, sharp and unexpected. "He deserves a good life."

"What about you?" Sam leaned toward him. "Don't you deserve a good life?"

Alexander felt his shoulders lift and fall. He didn't want to talk about this, he just wanted it to be over. For it to be done. The final blow, swift and sure.

"You're just going to abandon Ben?" Sam asked softly.

"No!" Ben yelled suddenly, and Daisy leapt to her feet and barked sharply, as if to echo him. He glared at Alexander. *"No!"*

Alexander made himself look away, meet Sam's brilliant gaze. "He's better off without me."

"No," Sam said. "You're his brother. He needs you."

Alexander shook his head.

"Yes!" Ben yelled.

Alexander's chest felt as though it was filled with concrete, and his throat ached with all that he kept contained. "I'm…tainted. I'll just taint him, too."

Sam leaned closer. "Is that how you see me?" he asked, his voice sharp. "As tainted?"

Alexander started. "No."

"Why not?"

"It's different," Alexander said, his voice painful in his throat. "You weren't…"

"Zander *stay*," Ben ordered loudly. Another echo by Daisy, a sharp, piercing bark.

Alexander looked away, color burning his cheeks. Tears blurred his gaze. He couldn't finish.

"You aren't what he made you," Sam said. "You're *more*."

"No," Alexander whispered.

That hushed denial seemed to enrage Sam. His hands shot out to wrap Alexander's arms, but unlike his father's bruising grip, Sam's hands were careful not to hurt. They held him immobile, but squeezed him warmly, and Alexander wanted to tear away and run.

But there was nowhere to go, and Ben was there, staring up at him, and Alexander knew he understood far more than any of them realized.

"I'm nothing," he told Sam. "Nothing he needs."

"I know that feeling, like you're shit on someone's shoe. Because that's how he made you feel. How what he did made you feel. Took me a long time to shake that feeling, and sometimes, it comes back. But I know better now. And you'll know better, too. But only if you stick around. Only if you're brave enough to keep going."

"I don't want to be brave," Alexander said. "I want to be *gone*."

Sam's eyes darkened. "I know. But there's a place beyond this one. A better place. *And you will get there.* I fucking promise."

"You can't promise that," Alexander protested, but he watched Sam closely, and hope flared to life, no matter how foolish.

"I just did." Sam's vivid, blue-green gaze bored into him. "You're not alone, son. I'm right here, and I'm not going anywhere. You need to believe in yourself, and you need to believe in me."

Alexander thought about the video—*Sam hadn't seen the video. What would he do when he did? What would he think?*—and the realization made Alexander want to throw up.

"I'm nothing," he repeated, and knew it to be true.

Sam swore softly and pulled him closer, shaking him a little. "You're everything."

Alexander's eyes met his. The certainty he saw in

Sam's gaze was like a punch to the gut, and he gulped against it.

"*Everything*," Sam repeated.

A harsh sound tore through Alexander's chest. He didn't mean for it to escape, but it didn't matter because Sam just hugged him hard, and Ben leaned against his back, his tiny arms stretched wide around them, and Daisy wormed her way between them to sit on him, and they stayed like that for a long, long time.

"One for all and all for one," Ben said suddenly, and Sam leaned back to smile at him.

"You bet," he murmured. He looked down at Alexander. "You in?"

Alexander blinked at him, his heart suddenly beating with frantic intensity. "What about Lucia?"

"Lucia, too," Sam told him seriously. "One for all and all for one."

Don't be stupid. But hope had sprung to life, and it was not so easily derailed.

"Promise?" Alexander heard himself ask.

"Promise," Sam said.

CHAPTER 42

Isabel stood beside the window, staring out at the ferocious storm with brooding midnight eyes, her mouth tight.

"Talk to me," Tony demanded, shrugging out of his sodden coat. He was soaked. Isabel was soaked. Even the carpet of the cabin beneath his feet was damp.

But she only shook her head, silent.

He didn't like that—and it sure as hell wasn't going to fly—but he didn't argue. Instead, he went into the tiny bathroom and turned the shower on, nice and hot. Then he strode over to the window Isabel stood next to and released the wooden blinds, shutting out the storm and the wind, and making her shoot him a narrow look.

"Bring it," he told her.

"Watching the video changed him," she said, her voice pensive. "It woke his demons."

Tony reached out and unzipped the hooded sweatshirt she wore. "Could be." He moved closer to the delicate cinnamon scent of her and tugged the shirt from her arms. She was shivering and covered in goose bumps. Her hair was wet, her feet soaked. He knew. His were, too.

"But, honey, he made the choice to pull that trigger."

Tony stepped back and tossed her hoodie onto the bed behind him. Then he rubbed his palms up the slender, chilled length of her arms, and she trembled in his hold.

He made himself step back. He reached up and pulled at his tie.

"Agent Kent doesn't understand the repercussions," Isabel said, watching Tony's hands with a studiousness that made his skin prickle and his cock stir. "Personally or professionally."

"Maybe." Tony tossed his tie atop her hoodie. "Maybe not." He began to unbutton his shirt. "But it's not your fault that it happened, Isabel. You weren't the catalyst. Cruz set these events in motion, baby. He reaped what he's sown."

Tony slid off his shirt and let it fall onto the pile on the bed. Then he reached out and wrapped his hands around the curve of Isabel's hips.

She stepped back, pulling against his hold. "What are you doing?"

Color flushed her cheeks with rosy color, and her eyes glittered, dark, obsidian pools that watched him warily. He knew she was afraid, but the only way she was going to conquer that fear was by confronting it, so tonight they would move forward.

Lucia was safe, and Alexander and Benjamin Cruz were safe. Sam had claimed them all, which made them no longer Tony's primary concern.

No, Tony's primary concern stood right in front of him.

"Undressing you," he replied simply and slid his hands up beneath her t-shirt, where he found the silken ripple of her scarred back, damp and cold even to his chilled hands.

She inhaled sharply, and her hands lifted to rest hesitantly against his chest, her palms cool where they met his skin. Her gaze roamed over him, lingering on the intricate black tattoo that covered his left arm and bled across his chest. "Why?"

"Because the water's running."

She blinked, and Tony took advantage of her bemusement to pull her t-shirt over her head.

She wore a pale aqua blue bra that was as soaked as her shirt had been, so sheer it was invitation. He looked his fill, appreciating her shape and her scent and the wide, pouting nipple whose color he wanted to see.

Taste.

He saw the scars that shaped her, the exquisitely detailed scenes, every mark a tribute to her strength and perseverance, and there was nothing about them he found offensive. No, he wanted to map them, to discover where she was sensitive. Where she felt less. More.

"You're staring," she whispered, watching him.

"I'm trying to decide where to start first," he admitted and tossed down her shirt.

Color flooded her cheeks. "Start what?"

He wrapped his arms around her and pulled her into the hard plane of his body. So soft and round and inviting, no matter how cold. Her fingers dug into his shoulders.

"My feast," he replied and slid his hands down over the curve of her ass, a heavy touch he knew was primitive and possessive, but he didn't give a fuck. He lifted her from her feet easily, and told her, "Put your legs around me."

"Feast?" she repeated, her voice quiet, throbbing with something that made his cock harden.

"Your legs, baby."

Her fingernails scored him, but she acquiesced and lifted her legs, still covered in denim, and wrapped them around his hips.

"Good girl," he murmured and couldn't help but lean down to press a kiss to the hollow of her throat, where the race of her heart was evident.

Those fingers—slender and strong—speared into his hair and tugged his head up.

"I'll obey for only so long," she warned, her eyes glittering, her cheeks flushed.

"Long enough," he said easily, and when Isabel unexpectedly laughed, he couldn't help but stare. She looked so young; so fresh and so lovely he didn't halt the urge he had, to turn and press her against the wall and put his mouth on her.

She gasped; his tongue nudged her bottom lip, and her mouth opened like the sweetest of flowers, and his tongue licked into her mouth.

So goddamn luscious. She rose against him, her tongue stroking his, a hungry moan vibrating from her. The fingers in his hair clenched, and his cock jerked.

Tony's hands tightened on her. He wanted to push her into the wall and grind himself against her. Taste more of her.

He would be inside her in a heartbeat if she let him.

She shuddered under his hands and arched sweetly into

him, as if reacting to that unspoken thought, and he almost gave into temptation.

But he was not going to fuck her up against the wall.

And that's what was going to happen if they didn't move.

Isabel protested when he broke the kiss, but he rubbed his cheek against hers and said, "You're still shivering."

He half expected her to balk, but she said nothing as he turned toward the bathroom. Tony didn't want to force her into anything she didn't want.

But goddamn if he wouldn't *push*. At least a little.

He wanted to see her. To touch her. *Test her.*

She made a soft, low sound when the cloud of warm steam in the tiny bathroom enveloped them. Tony shut the door behind them and leaned back against it. Isabel gripped him with surprisingly strong thighs, and she was sweetly round in his hands. He didn't want to put her down.

"That feels wonderful," she whispered. Her eyes were closed, and she tilted her head back, and a fine mist shimmered over her skin.

"Just wait," he told her roughly.

Then he slid her down his body to her feet, and when she swayed against him, he caught her and steadied her. He stripped her bra from her before she could protest, and she went still in his hands as he discarded the garment.

"Easy," he murmured, and his gaze met hers, so dark, so still, his heart skipped a beat. She watched him carefully, and her hands lifted to cover herself. That she was self-conscious of the scars was something he accepted; that she was so clearly ashamed of them was not.

"Don't," he whispered and caught her cold, trembling hands in his. "Don't hide from me, Isabel. Please."

Color kissed her cheeks. In his hands, hers fisted. "I know how I look."

"Not to me." He looked down at the proud, pale thrust of her breasts, perfect in every way, no matter her scars. "You have no idea how beautiful I find you."

She stared at him, and Tony could see her fear, her derision, her hope. His chest tightened, and he understood then that he was the first—*the only*—to bear witness to what she'd borne.

The realization humbled him. *A gift.* One he would not squander or ruin.

When his hands went to the button of her jeans, she jerked a little against him, but she didn't protest, and Tony stripped them from her before she could change her mind. Her panties followed, and she jerked again and tried to step back, away from him, but he caught her with gentle hands and lifted her from them.

"Oh," she said. "No—"

Tony ignored her and thrust one hand into the shower to check the temperature of the water.

Perfect.

He swept Isabel from her feet and put her in the shower, then shed the remains of his own clothing and stepped in behind her, shuddering when the hot water slammed into him. He pulled her against him until her body curved into his, and when he realized how cold she truly was, he wrapped himself around her, until she leaned back into him with a shudder, and they stood like that under the hot spray for a good, long while, until she stirred in his arms, tugging until he allowed her to turn in his hold.

Her breasts slid across his chest, and her nipples pressed into him; her soft belly cradled his cock. Tony's hands slid down over her ass again. He couldn't help himself.

She shuddered, and when her gaze met his, it glinted in a way he'd not seen before.

"It's over," she said, and his hands tightened on her.

"Yes." He lifted her against him, just enough he could press the hard length of his cock against her. When she gasped and dug her nails into him, he halted and held her there, locked to him.

"Oh," she said again and trembled against him. "That's…"

"Yes," he repeated and thrust gently against her.

Isabel shuddered again; her nails scored deeper. "What happens now?"

Tony leaned down and flicked his tongue against her pale, rose-tipped breast. "We live happily ever after."

Against him, she stiffened. "Don't make light of such things."

Tony lifted his head and met her gaze. "No joke, baby. We're doing this."

"Doing what?"

He heard her fear, felt the faint tremor of her body. He put her gently back down on her feet and then he sank slowly to his knees before her.

"I'm keeping you," he told her. He leaned forward and

nibbled the delicate skin just above her mons, licking at the water that coursed over her, scratching her lightly with his beard. "We're going home. We can figure the rest out later."

"Home," she echoed, as if the word were foreign. She gripped his hair.

"It's a nice place; it can be our bat cave. You'll like it. And if you don't, we can find something you do." He nipped at her again, and she jumped, but then pressed closer to him. "I'm easy, baby. As long as we're together."

"Together," she repeated and froze against him. "Just like that?"

"How else would it be?" Her scent was making his mouth water. He dipped his head and pressed his cheek against the silky, golden blond curls that covered her and inhaled deeply. Another tremor shook her. "I want to taste you, Isabel."

She stared down at him, her eyes like dark wells, her cheeks flushed. "I can't...I can't be with you."

He only laughed softly, and when that black gaze fired, he dragged her closer, until her thighs cradled his shoulders, and she was served up like the feast of which he'd spoken.

"Tony," she whispered, and he looked up at her.

"I'm...damaged. I can't...I don't have people."

She stared down at him, solemn, *fucking sad.* It infuriated him.

"Poor baby," he said and put his mouth on her.

His slid his arms around her hips and locked her into place, and he stroked the tender bud of her clitoris with his tongue. She was spicy and sweet, and he wanted more. A sharp cry escaped her; she jerked in his hold. The hand in his hair pulled him closer. Her thighs trembled around him. He stroked her once, twice; the third time, her moan rippled into the air between them, and his cock leapt in response.

"Look at me," he demanded, and when her obsidian gaze met his, he said, "I'm going to make you come. And then we're going to eat the food we bought and get some sleep."

"No," she said, but she arched toward him, and her scent filled the air.

"In the morning, I'm going to make you come again," he continued and rubbed his bristled chin against her, and she cried out softly and ground against him, and he couldn't help but stab his tongue into her.

She moaned his name, and her thighs clutched at him, and her nails marked him as they held him close. The taste of her flooded his senses and made him heady.

But there was a method to his madness, and he pulled back, just enough that she clutched at him, that her eyes opened and flew to his.

"Together," he said and dared her to argue.

"That's not fair," she whispered. "Please…"

"I want you to say it," Tony told her. He held her gaze and leaned over and slowly flicked his tongue over her, and when she thrust herself at him, he suckled the tender nub into his mouth, and she gave a hoarse cry and arched against him. Then he pulled back.

"No," she growled at him, and he laughed again, softly.

"Tell me what I want to hear, baby."

Isabel shook her head, as if to clear it. "I don't know that I'm capable of what you're suggesting."

Tony stilled, his hands tightening on her. "You aren't brave enough to try?"

"Damn you." And then, "Of course I'm brave enough."

He smiled and nuzzled her, and she trembled in his arms.

"Say it," he ordered and licked her again, a hard stroke that made her inhale sharply. "I'm hungry."

"Together," she whispered, and Tony growled.

Then he dipped his head and devoured her.

CHAPTER 43

"There's a Facebook page, a Go Fund Me account, and a hashtag: #love4lucia, which is currently trending on Twitter. You are, to put it mildly, a social media megastar—at least, for the moment."

Lucia frowned at the man who sat next to her, rifling through a large expandable file folder. His name was Flynn Abbott; he was slender and tall, with long bones and dark brown eyes. He'd shown up ten minutes ago, and the only reason she'd allowed the Deputy guarding her door to let him in was because he carried a cardboard tray with two cups of steaming, fragrant coffee.

That, and he claimed to be her lawyer.

"I do not understand," she said, watching him. "What are you talking about?"

"The outcry has been deafening." Flynn dropped the file to the chair next to him. Then he removed his eyeglasses and began to clean the lenses with a neatly pressed handkerchief. Sunlight streamed in the window behind him, giving glints of cherry-red life to his dark auburn hair because—at long last—the sun had finally decided to shine. "Once the videos were released—"

"Videos," she interrupted, the memory of Alexander slamming his fists into the TV vivid. "What videos?"

Flynn shot her a surprised look. "You haven't seen them?"

"No."

"The videos were released several days after you disappeared with the boys." He picked up his phone and began to poke it. "They were sent to all of the major news networks. Here. This is the one with...well. You'll see."

Lucia stared at the slender silver device he held toward her; she didn't want to take it. She remembered the brief scene she'd watched at Alexander's side, before Cruz had shown up, and she had no desire to see any more.

No. Which just made her a coward. Alexander had lived through that hell; *the least she could do was watch it.*

But...no. Not yet. Maybe not ever.

"Where did they come from?" she asked, but she wasn't thinking about that. She was thinking about Alexander. About what it would do to him to have the whole world *know*. To have them *see—*

"A hacker infiltrated Cruz's hard drive and released a number of private videos, all of which show him sexually engaged with minors."

"Minors." *More than one.* Fury flared, and bile surged to Lucia's throat. She met Flynn's dark brown gaze. "Including Alexander."

Color touched his cheeks. He put his phone down. "Yes, ma'am. I'm...I'm sorry."

The weight that had lifted yesterday with Sam's brief visit settled heavily in Lucia's heart. *Alexander would never escape what had been done to him.* Not privately, not publically. No matter what became of Donavon Cruz, the boy would never be free. Someone would always remember. Someone—

"Why?" she growled, her hands fisting. "Why would someone do such a thing?"

"I don't know. But I don't think the goal was to hurt Alexander. I think whoever did this was trying to expose Cruz; the boy just became collateral damage. A sacrifice made for the greater good."

Rage made her blood simmer. Who had made that call? What right did they have? To exploit Alexander in such a manner...something he would never be free of...something that had the ability to *destroy* him... Tears stung her eyes; her chest ached. And she wanted to scream at the profound unfairness of it all; so much horror and pain and devastation. How was a child to cope? To survive?

He's just a boy.

"What's going to happen to him?" Her throat squeezed tight around the words; panic flared within her, sharp, painful. Useless.

"Mr. Steele filed a petition for temporary guardianship this morning."

Lucia went still. "He did what?"

"The doctors don't anticipate Donavon Cruz ever regaining consciousness, but because of the language in Mr. Cruz's living will, they are legally obligated to keep him alive. It was Mr. Cruz's direction that his attorney, a man named Louis Alcott, be granted temporary guardianship of his sons until their permanent guardian could collect them. That permanent guardian is a private academy in Belgium. However, both Mr. Alcott and the academy have agreed that

Mr. Steele should be granted temporary guardianship."

"Why?" she asked baldly. "Why would they do that?"

Flynn pushed his glasses back onto his nose and shrugged. "Considering what everyone now knows Donavon Cruz to be guilty of, following his wishes is not first on anyone's list. The boys have no next of kin. They have no pre-existing relationship with either Mr. Alcott or the organization in Belgium, whereas Mr. Steele spent the better part of the last week taking care of them, and they trust him. The fact that he's a decorated former Army Ranger and a U.S. Deputy Marshal doesn't hurt. I don't foresee the judge objecting."

"He's taken responsibility for them both?" Lucia clarified, staring at Flynn suspiciously.

"Yes." Flynn tilted his head. "He's taken responsibility for you, too, but I don't think it will be necessary."

"What does that mean?" she asked carefully and tried valiantly to ignore the sudden, frantic beat of her heart.

"That means that in spite of the many charges that could be brought against you, I don't think any will."

For a moment, time seemed to freeze. "Why not?"

"Because you tried to do things the right away, and every child advocacy organization in the city of Las Vegas failed you. So you did the only thing you could: you took them. I think far more people understand that than you think. And the videos have only served to become your smoking gun. Incontrovertible evidence, so much so that I daresay the federal prosecutor will be loath to waste taxpayers money to punish you for it. Oh, you'll get a slap—because people can't do what you did, not without consequence—but I have a feeling it will be more along the lines of community service than jail time. I could be wrong. I haven't spoken to the prosecutor, although I do have a call into her office. But the support you've garnered, coupled with the truth of Donavon Cruz, will be enough, I think, to grant you a very generous legal boon."

Lucia stared at him, hardly able to breathe. She probably shouldn't listen to him—she didn't know him, hadn't hired him, had only his word that Sam had done so—and he probably didn't know what he was talking about and—

"Take heart, Lucia." Flynn stood. "I think you might be out of the woods." He held out his hand. "It's been a pleasure; I'll be in touch."

Lucia shook his hand—cool, soft, not like Sam's rough, warm skin—and then he was gone.

Community service.

"Preposterous," she muttered. She'd *kidnapped* two children. Driven across state lines.

Buried an ax in a man.

And Flynn Abbott thought she would get community service? He was insane.

But the information that Sam had stepped forward to claim the boys… *I'm keeping them for you.*

A rush of something electric and almost painful arced through Lucia. She'd not expected this, not any of it. She'd been prepared to sacrifice. To die, if that's where it all ended. But Sam had appeared, and everything had changed.

I'm right here.

And he was. *He was.*

"Preposterous," she repeated, and her throat swelled painfully. Outside the window, the sky was so blue it hurt to look at, washed so clean by the violent storms of the last few days that it glittered like finely polished glass. The sunlight was almost blinding. The rays that had flirted with Flynn's dark hair fell across her bed and her arm where it lay atop the sheet, and they were so warm she shivered and shifted her arm so that the rays kissed its entire length.

Sunshine and blue skies and hope

She didn't want to feel it; she wouldn't admit that she did, not even to herself. But as she lay there, forced to rest, to heal, she understood that faith was a choice.

To believe in spite of all evidence to the contrary was a conscious decision. She just had to be brave enough to make it.

*****

Agent Kent stood outlined by the late afternoon sun.

He stared out the window in Nate Thomas' office, his eyes on the jagged, snow-laced mountains that enclosed the small valley, and when Isabel halted behind him, he said, "I'm fine."

"Are you?" she replied calmly.

Is this our fault? Are we responsible for this?

She couldn't get the question out of her head. She *felt* responsible.

"Yes." He turned and looked at her, his features sober, his eyes dark blue slate. "I know what I did, and I can live with it. But I just got here. I'm not ready to go yet."

"It may not come to that," she told him seriously. "Deputy Marshal Steele's statement supports yours, as does the statement of the Sheriff. Tony and I added to that corroboration. There is no question that Donavon Cruz appeared to be threatening the life of his son, Agent Kent. None. You did what any of us should have done in response."

Kent shook his head, his mouth hard. "He was Donavon Cruz."

Anger flickered. "He was a sadistic pig, a pedophile, and a rapist."

"Will that matter?"

Isabel didn't know, so she said nothing. Then, because she couldn't help herself, "You made a choice today."

"Yes." Again, those dark eyes touched hers. "You didn't try to stop me."

"I didn't think you would fire," she told him honestly.

"Tony knew."

She remembered Tony's hand wrapping her arm, pulling her to him. "Should he have tried?"

"It wouldn't have mattered." Kent shook his head again. "He knew that, too."

Cruz set these events in motion, baby. He reaped what he's sown.

But that did not negate the responsibility Isabel bore. For Alexander, for exposing him in her hunt, something she very much understood the repercussions of, something that weighed heavily in her heart, like sharp, tiny stones. And for Austin Kent, who had been unknowingly triggered by that exposure.

Victims. *There were so many.* Sometimes even she forgot.

"One of the other children in Cruz's videos has been identified as a girl who went missing last year in Portland, Oregon," Isabel heard herself say.

Kent only stared at her.

"Another was taken from Dublin two years ago," she continued, "and one of the boys was from a middle class family in Sydney."

"Why are you telling me this?"

The email from Aequitas had arrived that morning, and Isabel had only then understood that Donavon Cruz was just the beginning.

"I'm going to climb the ladder," she replied. "And see what I find."

"The Bureau would take you back in a heartbeat," Kent said. "You're an expert in your field. You have the influence to walk right back in."

"No." Isabel shook her head. "I'm done with the Bureau."

"You're going to go chasing sex traffickers by yourself?"

Not by herself. A first. "I'll be fine, Agent Kent. I'm not without…resources."

"I know." He looked at her for a long, silent moment. "Tony's a lucky guy."

Color rushed into her cheeks, mortifying and unexpected, and she didn't know what to say. *Another first.*

The memory of the night before flooded over her, and her face flamed, but she felt no shame. No, Tony had delivered on his promise, and she'd learned that she knew nothing about sex or intimacy or…love. What he'd shown her scared the hell out of her…and she wanted *more*.

Home, he'd said, and she'd shied. *I don't have people.* A warning, an apology.

Poor baby.

He'd won her surrender, and this morning when she awoken to his hands stroking over her, bold and possessive and greedy, she'd climbed on top of him and ground herself against him until they both came.

She had decided somewhere between last night and this morning; at some point, she'd simply begun to trust him. To believe in his words and the way he looked at her; to revel in the worship of his hands and his mouth and his body. *To jump.*

He would catch her; she was certain. And if he didn't…she was strong.

She would survive.

Life was too short and too painful to hesitate. She was going to take what she wanted.

Tony. And the infinite possibilities he brought. *Opportunities.* The realization was stunning. Intoxicating. So much so Isabel almost felt guilty that something so hopeful had been born of something so malignant.

But that was life; it only moved forward.

"Good luck, Agent Kent," she said finally. "If I can ever be of service, don't hesitate to ask."

"Don't worry. I won't."

CHAPTER 44

Freedom.

He was *free.*

It was not a word Alexander would have ever associated with himself. Not since his father had taught him what it was to be a Cruz, and he'd understood the depravity and sickness that was his family legacy. Because nothing could free him from that.

But the only thing tying him to that legacy lay in a hospital bed, connected to machines that kept him alive. There were no other living Cruz family members, something which should have made Alexander sad, but for which he could only be infinitely grateful.

They were the last of the line. *Good.*

And now they would be free.

The realization was stunning and overwhelming; it seemed like a dream. *A rebirth.* But then he would remember the video, and everything beginning to take root within him would die a sudden, vicious death.

The video.

Alexander didn't know where it began or where it ended; mostly, he didn't want to know. The memory of living through it was enough. *But it was out there.* And he knew that once something was on the web, it was there forever. You didn't get a do-over. And you never, ever escaped its existence.

Sam would see it. And Lucia. Ben—

That thought made Alexander die a little, and inside him despair grew like thick, suffocating ivy, winding tight around his lungs, squeezing his heart, smothering every drop of hope in his soul. The only thing greater than his anguish was his rage.

Free but not free. Marked forever.

Tainted, no matter what Sam said. Soiled and stained and marked. Sometimes Alexander could feel it, a greasy, oily film that covered every inch of his skin and turned his heart black. In his mind he could see it, a living, breathing entity spreading like black, fuzzy mold, covering every facet of his life, bleeding into every moment. *Inescapable.* No matter if his father lived or died.

The damage was done.

How would you feel if I filed a petition for guardianship? It'd be temporary in the beginning, but we could make it permanent. If you want. I'd do that.

Alexander didn't understand why. Regardless of the last few days, Sam was a stranger. Why would he care what happened to them? Why would he want them? And even if he did, once he saw the video...

Lucia might not abandon them—and even that, Alexander didn't know, not for sure—but Sam...Sam was tough and brave and strong. Once he saw how weak Alexander was, he wouldn't want anything to do with him. And Alexander could handle that—no matter how painful—

but Ben...Ben deserved someone like Sam. Ben *needed* Sam. Like he needed Lucia.

So Alexander had agreed when Sam asked about guardianship. Even though part of him had wanted to refuse, to run, to reject Sam before Sam could reject him. He didn't, because of Ben. Because Ben was what mattered now. And even if Sam decided he didn't want Alexander, he might still want Ben and—

"You gonna tell me why you're out here all by yourself?" Sam asked from behind him, startling him. "Or do I have to beat it out of you?"

Alexander stiffened. He sat on the cabin's narrow front porch. The day had dawned quiet and still and cloudless, and the air smelled like sunshine and pine trees. Around him, the trees were still, and tiny, brilliant bluebirds flitted among the thick green boughs. In his lap was the notebook Lucia had found, and beside him, Daisy leaned her slight weight against his leg and shook her tiny tail at Sam.

"Daisy had to go," Alexander muttered.

Sam moved to stand next to him, his shadow so long and broad across the weathered wooden boards that it swallowed all of Alexander. "It's all gonna work out, you know."

A sudden, unexpected swell of fury filled Alexander's throat. "Yeah, sure."

Sam sighed and dropped down to sit next to Alexander, close but not touching. He was a giant, wide and raw boned, and Alexander knew exactly how strong he was. How dangerous. And part of Alexander was terrified by that, because he knew what it was to be at the mercy of someone stronger, someone unbeatable, and even if he didn't really think Sam would hurt him, that part of him—the part that was always ready, always waiting—refused to see Sam as different.

Different than his father.

Which wasn't accurate or fair—Alexander *knew* better—but he didn't have the heart to argue with himself. Because—

"Did you see it?" he burst, unable to contain the question. His heart beat like a huge, hollow drum in his chest, and it hurt.

Sam arched a brow. "See what?"

Alexander's cheeks burned even as ice slid through his veins. "The video."

Beside him, Sam went still. "You know about that?"

"I saw it. Part of it." The words were sharp and jagged. "Yesterday, on the news, before…"

Sam's huge, warm hand suddenly landed on Alexander's shoulder. "I'm sorry. I didn't know that."

Alexander tried to shrug him off. "It doesn't matter."

"Yes, it does." Sam's hold didn't bend. "Tony told me about it this morning."

"Did you see it?" Alexander repeated, aware that Sam hadn't answered his question.

"Do you want me to?" Sam asked, his eyes brilliant in the bright sunlight.

Alexander shrugged, his throat tight. Tears burned his eyes, but he blinked them back, his muscles rigid, his fists clenched around the notebook. "I don't care."

That hard, warm, strong hand squeezed gently. "I

haven't seen it, and I don't plan to—not unless you want me to."

Alexander looked up at him. "Why not?"

Sam met his gaze. "There's nothing there I want to see. Not unless you think it's important."

Alexander blinked. A tear escaped to slide down his cheek, and he swiped it away angrily. "I don't...I don't want Ben to see it."

Sam's arm slid around his shoulders and rested there. "He won't."

"Yes, he will." Alexander shook his head, stiff beneath Sam's hold. "It's inevitable."

"Maybe." Sam shrugged. "We'll deal with it if it happens."

"Everyone knows." The thought was like a knife, cleaving him in two. "Everyone."

Sam's arm tightened around him. "The people who matter won't care."

Alexander wanted to believe that. But he knew better. "I'll never be free."

Sam looked down at him. "Freedom is a choice."

Alexander snorted. "Sure it is."

For a long moment, Sam said nothing. Then, "I carried it for a long time. Everything my pop said, everything he did. Every hurt, every word. Carried it around in my pocket like it was some kind of fucking talisman. So I wouldn't forget. So it wouldn't happen again. And then one day I realized that even though he'd been dead for a decade, my old man still controlled me. Here I thought I was free, but I wasn't. I was in his cage, behind his bars, still listening to his voice." Sam shook his head. "Life's short, bud, and time is a luxury. Don't let him take more than he already has. What you do from here is up to you—no one else. And it can't matter, what other people know or say or do. Only what you do. Being free from all the shit—that *is* a choice. But you're the only one who can make it."

Alexander was silent, Sam's words a vibrant song in his head. He wanted to deny them, but Sam's arm was warm and heavy, and his eyes were serious, and Alexander knew they were enough alike that Sam's words weren't just words, they were experience. And maybe Sam hadn't been through exactly the same thing as Alexander, but he understood, at least a little. *More than anyone else.* And no matter what Alexander had told Sam yesterday, he *did* want to live.

He had dreams, too, even if he never spoke of them.

And now...those dreams, they might come true. There were possibilities today that hadn't existed yesterday. But the video—

What you do from here is up to you—no one else. And it can't matter, what other people know or say or do. Only what you do.

Choices. Life was all about choices. And Alexander was terrified of making the wrong one.

"It's all gonna work out," Sam said again, and squeezed Alexander's shoulders. "You'll see."

Part of him wanted to lash out in denial. But the other part...it wanted desperately to believe.

Another choice.

"What about Lucia?" he asked, his voice hushed. Terror

for her lived ever-present in his chest, a hard, sharp wedge that made it hard to breathe. "What's going to happen to her?"

"I'm working on that," Sam told him.

Alexander nodded. He knew Lucia was going to end up in jail; you couldn't kidnap someone and *not* end up in prison. But he'd hoped—

"The Judge granted me temporary guardianship," Sam continued. "That's what I came out here to tell you. So, that's done. Once Lucia is out—"

"Done?" Alexander repeated and reared back to stare at him.

"Yep, you're stuck with me know."

"You mean…" Alexander blinked. "We're…we're *yours* now?"

"For now. Until I can drag Lucia to the altar. Then you'll belong to both of us."

Alexander stared at Sam, dumbfounded.

"True story," Sam told him. "She's going to take some convincing. I might need some help."

The tears swelled, filling his throat. "She can be stubborn."

"She could give lessons to a mule." Sam snorted. "So, you in?"

Alexander tried not to cry. *So weak.* But Sam wasn't looking at him like he was stupid or weak. Sam was smiling.

"Okay," he squeezed out. "I'm in."

Sam hugged him, hard. "Good. That makes three of

us."

A smile curled Alexander's mouth. He could tell it surprised Sam.

It surprised Alexander even more.

"She won't know what hit her," he said.

And then he hugged Sam back.

CHAPTER 45

Tony stood outside of Lucia's hospital room, the backpack Sam had given him clutched in one hand. He'd asked Sam to let him bring it—along with the news they were cutting her loose—because he owed Lucia an apology the size of Everest, and he was hoping both the clothes—and the news—would prevent her from punching him in the face.

She'd done it before, and even as a kid she'd packed a wallop. Not that he didn't deserve it—then or now—but he wasn't the kind of man to shy from his responsibilities, so he nodded at the Deputy guarding her door and stepped inside.

She sat on her bed, combing through her wet hair, and when her amber gaze met his, he said, "Hey."

Her gaze narrowed, and she stiffened. In the bright, early-afternoon light, the bruises that mottled her skin stood out like dark, angry clouds on a clear horizon. Her lip was split, and there was a mark on her neck that looked like a bite. *A fucking bite.* Sam had told him about Ivan—he'd taken responsibility for the kill—but Tony knew the truth, and looking at her made all of the guilt and anger he felt toward himself swell like a wave cresting.

"Why are you here?" she asked. Her knuckles pressed white against her skin where she held the comb, and her eyes glittered, as sharp as any blade.

For a long moment, Tony only stared at her. All of the things he wanted to say solidified in his throat, and it hurt to swallow past them. To speak.

"I'm sorry," he said quietly, and knew it wasn't enough. "I should have listened."

Her brows rose. She said nothing.

"I thought it was because of Elian," he continued, forcing the words out. "And Donavon Cruz…that name scared the hell out of me."

"Coward," she told him, her voice hard.

"Yes." He nodded. "I should have acted. I failed you—again."

Her lashes flickered. *"Again."*

His gaze met hers and held. "I was a kid. A dumb, selfish, frightened kid who didn't understand the enormity of what Elian had been through. I ran because what he told me scared the fuck out of me. It wasn't right, and it isn't defensible, but there it is. I failed him, and I failed you, and not one day goes by that I don't blame myself."

She looked away, and he took a step forward. His heart beat heavily. Pain and remorse tightened around his chest like cold, steel wire.

"I can't make up for it," he said. "I know that. And when you came to me…history repeated itself. Sometimes I think you were right. It should have been me."

Her gaze flew to his and studied him for a long, silent moment. Then, "No. We were children." She took a deep breath and shook her head. "I have blamed you for too long. Elian, he made a choice. It is not fair to blame you for that."

"I bear responsibility."

"As do we all." She shrugged. "That is why I took them."

"I know."

"I could not stand by and watch." Her voice vibrated, anger and pain and grief that made his own regret resonate with painful clarity. "Not again. I knew what he was doing to Alexander, and you are not wrong—what happened to Elian drove me to foolish lengths—but when everyone refused to help...*I had no choice.*"

Tony flinched. "I know." He steeled himself. "I'm responsible for the video."

Lucia went still. Her hand clenched around the comb. "Why?"

"It was the only way," he told her bluntly. "I obtained it illegally, which meant getting a warrant was next to impossible. The clock was ticking, and that asshole was chasing you, and only a public unmasking was going to stop him. I never wanted to expose the kid like that, but it was either that, or you dead and those boys back under his thumb. It wasn't an easy decision, and I regret the repercussions it will have for him—because I *do* understand what the fuck it will do to him—but I did it to save him. To save you. And I'd do it again."

Lucia stared at him, her eyes opaque. Isabel had wanted to tell her—to take responsibility—but Tony was prepared to take the lumps. They were his due—and he hadn't lied. He *would* do it all again.

"What made you believe me?" she asked quietly, watching him. "Because you did not. You told me I was imagining things."

"Because it was easier that way," he admitted. "To tell myself it was because of then. But after you'd gone, it ate at me. I knew you wouldn't make that accusation unless you believed it to be true. And I knew…I knew you'd come to me because you expected me to know that. To do what I hadn't done before. Then I called DFS and found out you'd tried to report him. I called CPS, and they said the same thing. And I knew it was real. So when the call came in that you'd taken them, I sent Sam."

Color suddenly flushed her cheeks. "He saved us."

She looked away, and Tony thought about what Sam had told him this morning. *I'm going to keep her, so you two had better make your peace.*

It was an unexpected turn of events, but then Tony thought about Isabel, and he understood.

"I'm sorry," he repeated. "I won't let you down again."

Lucia's gaze was dark but steady, and Tony had the feeling she saw far more than he would have liked to share. But there was no half-assing this; he owned it. Better for them all that she understood that.

"What is going to happen to me?" she asked.

"You're free to go."

She blinked. "What?"

"The prosecutor isn't pressing charges—at least, not yet. And considering the outcry, I don't think she will. Something minor, maybe, but I don't think it will be felony kidnapping. Too many people support what you did. Right or wrong, they all saw what *he* did. And they're pissed. People are calling you a hero."

Lucia snorted. "That is ridiculous."

"No," Tony said. "It's not. Not to Alexander and Ben. And not to any of the rest of the kids in those videos."

"Videos," she repeated slowly, remembering what Flynn Abbott had told her. "How many are there?"

"More than a dozen, all different children."

She paled. Her mouth opened and then closed.

"We've been doing some digging," he told her. "All of the kids in the videos are missing children, and they come from all over the world. This wasn't just about Cruz. And it wasn't just about Alexander. You exposed something bigger than anyone realized, and we're going to hunt them all down."

"We?" she echoed, and one of her brows arched.

Heat crept up his neck. "The FBI agent I partnered with is a specialist in the field of human trafficking."

Lucia eyed him. "You will help those children?"

"As many as I can." He nodded. "It's the fucking least I can do."

She only watched him, her expression calm. *Accepting.* And even if he could see the pain that lingered, he knew they'd taken a step.

"From Sam," he said, indicating the pack as he set it down beside her. "He's waiting. If you want to get dressed, I'll take you to him."

She looked at the pack, then up at Tony.

"Get dressed," he told her gently, and turned to leave her to it.

"Tony," she said quietly as he reached the door, and he

turned to look at her.

"Thank you," she said, her gaze steady, and the band around his chest loosened.

"Don't thank me," he replied. "I have too much to make up for."

And he walked out.

*****

"Is she coming yet?"

"Not yet," Sam told Ben, watching the wide, stainless steel elevator doors they were parked next to. The underground parking garage of St. Joseph's was cool and damp, and only a handful of cars occupied the stalls. Sam would have liked to pick Lucia up out front, but the growing mass of reporters—and the crazy number of people who'd camped out in front of the hospital to show their support of her—had made that impossible. He'd actually had to turn his phone off this morning, because everyone and their brother wanted an interview. And he would not be giving any interviews.

Ever.

"I'm sure she's on her way," he said and wondered how Tony was faring. Lucia had been furious with him—and Sam didn't blame her—but he hoped she came around, because Tony was going to be his best man. And having the bride strangle the best man would be a problem.

"Are you sure?" Ben asked from the backseat, his suspicion clear. "Do you promise?"

"I promise," Sam told him. He was aware he was counting his chickens, but he didn't give a shit. He knew Lucia wanted him. She liked him. Maybe even loved him. Because when she looked at him, he saw it: strong and clear and powerful. And he was going to do his level best to exploit the hell out of it.

Mine. A conclusion Sam had grown certain of. Just like the two boys who occupied the Land Rover's backseat. His—for better or worse. And there were no doubts within him. None. Not when it came to them, and not when it came to her. He could only hope he could convince her to *try.*

"Are they really going to let her go?" Alexander asked, and Sam met his gaze in the mirror. He flashed back to the first time he'd looked into that polished glass and crashed into that cold, hard, pale green gaze, and he saw a difference.

Hope. Shadowed by doubt and fear and too goddamn much reality, but it was there.

Sam was going to exploit that, too.

"Yep," he said. "They are." For now. And if the powers that were decided to fuck with her, they would handle it. The overwhelming response of the world to what she'd done had provided powerful leverage, and having one of the best defense attorneys in the country hadn't hurt.

Thanks, kid.

One of these days he was going to have to hunt Honor down; he owed her too much. He'd allowed her to exist in his periphery and told himself she wasn't his responsibility. But she was. She needed him. Because no one should be as alone as she was, something he'd only just realized. *They were family.* And that mattered.

But it could wait. First, Lucia. *Home.*

The future.

The elevator doors slid open, and Tony stepped out, followed by Lucia, who held the back pack he'd given Tony in one hand. She was battered and bruised, clad in worn jeans and Sam's old flannel. The sight of her wrapped in his shirt made something loosen within Sam. When he climbed from the Cruiser, she saw him and smiled, a pure, glorious vision of joy that made his heart leap in his chest.

"You ready to get the hell out of here?" he asked, striding toward them.

"Oh, yes," she said, her eyes gleaming like gold. When he pulled her into his arms, she dropped the pack and went, wrapping her arms around him, and he felt the shudder that moved through her. He eased his grip, conscious of her wounds. Her hair was damp, and she smelled like something fruity and fresh, and when the need to kiss her gripped him, Sam didn't resist. Just a swift, warm press of his mouth to hers.

Just a taste.

Lucia's fingers clenched into his arms, and her mouth opened beneath his, and he wished they were alone. But the sound of the Ben crying, "Lucia!" and the Cruiser doors slamming echoed through the parking garage, and he made himself release her.

Ben appeared a moment later and flung himself into Lucia's legs. Alexander followed, more subdued, and halted a few feet away. Daisy barked from the car, her tiny face pressed against the glass.

"Hello, monkey," Lucia said softly and pulled from Sam's embrace to kneel down and pull Ben carefully into her arms. "I am so very glad to see you."

"I missed you," Ben told her seriously. "Sam made me eat a tomato."

Beside them, Tony laughed softly.

"Tomatoes are good for you," Sam told him.

Lucia held an arm out to Alexander. "*Mijo*."

He hesitated for a long moment, his gaze touching both Sam and Tony, but then he moved forward and stepped into her embrace, and when she hugged him, he hugged her back.

"You should go," Tony said. "The crowd out front is growing."

Sam nodded and accepted the hand his friend offered. Tony pulled him into a rough hug, and Sam slapped him on the back.

"Thank you," he said.

"No," Tony replied. "Thank you."

Sam stepped back and Lucia stood, Ben clinging to her side like an errant shadow. He grabbed the backpack and slid an arm around her and turned her toward the car, but she halted and reached out, hesitantly, to touch Tony's arm.

"I forgive you," she said. "Now, you must forgive yourself."

Sam squeezed her. Tony nodded shortly, his eyes glittering.

"Let's go," she said to Sam, and took Alexander's hand. "We're ready."

He got them all into the Cruiser, and Tony lifted a hand

to wave as they pulled away.

"You okay?" Sam asked her.

"I'm perfect," she said, and when he looked at her, she smiled again.

So fucking gorgeous. No matter how black and blue.

"You are," he told her honestly, and her cheeks bloomed with color.

She shook her head, still smiling, and when the car emerged into the bright sunlight, she turned to look out the window. "The storm is over."

Sam reached over and took her hand in his. "Yes."

Her fingers were cold and tight around his. They circled the hospital, and as they rounded the edge of the building, the large mass of people who'd gathered there came into view. Lucia stared at them, a frown pulling her brows low.

"That's for you," Sam said.

She looked at him in disbelief.

"Really," he insisted.

"But…why?"

"Because you acted. You did the right thing. That inspires people. Gives them hope."

He turned onto the main street and headed away from the crowd. Lucia looked over her shoulder at the collection of people and shook her head.

"That is…crazy," she said.

"That's human beings," Sam replied easily.

She turned back around, her face thoughtful. Sam turned the Cruiser left and headed south.

"Did you get in trouble for the Jeep?" she asked.

He shook his head, smiling. "It's good to be a Deputy Marshal."

"We had blueberry pancakes for breakfast," Ben informed her. "With whipped cream."

"That sounds delicious," Lucia said. "Did you like them?"

"Yeah. But chicken nuggets are better."

Lucia laughed softly. Then she sobered and slid Sam a look. "Where are we going?"

"Home," he said.

"Home?" she repeated.

"Silverbend, Washington. I've got five acres on Blue Ribbon creek." He could feel her stare, so he turned and looked at her. "Why? You got somewhere else to be?"

For an endless moment, she only looked at him, and his heart beat hard at the back of his throat.

"No," she said finally. "I am where I want to be."

Everything within him settled. He glanced into the mirror and again met Alexander's pale gaze. So much uncertainty and doubt and fucking pain. But that was okay.

Time. And love.

Anything was possible.

"Sam," Ben said.

"Yes, Ben?"

"You got a swing set?"

"Not at the moment."

"You should get one."

"Ben," Lucia admonished, but she was laughing again.

"They're mine," Sam told her.

She stilled. Her laughter fell away. "What does that mean?"

"The Judge gave me temporary guardianship. Ninety days. Abbott is drawing up a petition for permanent guardianship. He said there will be a home study, and I'll have to disclose my finances, but nothing that should create a problem."

Lucia stared at him. "You are really going to keep them?"

Sam turned and looked at her. "I'm going to keep all of you."

In his hand, hers trembled. Sam waited for her to argue, but she only squeezed his fingers hard. Then she laughed again, a sound that vibrated with joy and disbelief.

"We did it," she said and turned to look at Alexander. *"We did it."*

The boy stared at her for a moment, and then a small, tremulous smile curved his mouth, and he nodded, and Sam's throat tightened painfully.

Lucia lifted her arms up and crowed, "Woo-hoo!!!!!!!!"

Ben joined her. Daisy began to bark. Alexander watched them, shaking his head, that small smile locked into place.

"I don't see the big deal," Sam said. "I told you I had a plan."

CHAPTER 46

Tony sat in the fraying plaid chair next to the sole window of their rented motel room, staring down at the aging Berber carpet—the same place Isabel had left him twenty minutes earlier, when she'd gone to grab a couple of sandwiches from the sub shop next door.

On the drive down from Blue Ridge to Salt Lake, he'd been quiet. Too quiet. The charming man who smiled so easily and teased her with every breath had withdrawn into a quiet solemnity that disturbed her deeply.

She knew it had to do with Lucia. When Isabel had asked him how things had gone with their talk he'd said only, "It went fine," but—clearly—there was more to it.

The temptation to shake him was strong; he'd dragged her entire history out of her. If he thought she would let him keep secrets, he had another thing coming. But as she stood next to the small round table across from him, she hesitated. Relationship parameters were something she knew little about. She'd never had a relationship—only ever a small handful of friends—and she didn't know if she should push.

Perhaps he would talk when he was ready.

"Food," she said, holding up the bag that held their sandwiches. He only nodded, silent, his gaze unfocused as he stared down at the ugly rug.

Her hand clenched around the bag.

She'd brought down cartels and international sex trafficking rings. She'd testified before Congress and the UN. She'd single-handedly crushed more pedophiles and rapists than she could count, but here and now—in this—she was uncertain.

And Isabel hated being uncertain.

Maybe he's changed his mind. It's over now. Perhaps we were just the thrill of the chase—

"Fuck that," she said out loud. Assumptions were asinine and damaging; if she wanted to know, she needed to *ask.*

So she put down the bag and strode over to him. When he didn't look up, she climbed into his lap and straddled him. His hands immediately wrapped her hips, and that burnished hazel gaze lifted to meet hers.

"Talk to me," she demanded and curled her hands into the thick muscle of his biceps.

The hands around her hips squeezed. His eyes were dark, the line of his jaw hard.

"She said I had to forgive myself." A harsh laugh broke from him. "How the hell am I supposed to do that?"

The anxiety within Isabel fled. "You do something to counteract the guilt."

"I did. I became a cop. It didn't fucking help." His hands squeezed again. "I'm going to carry it forever."

"Scars fade," Isabel told him. "But they never disappear. The best you can do is use them."

His gaze roamed her face. "Is that what you do?"

"I had to make them mean something." Isabel stroked up his arms and down again, petting him. The need to soothe him gripped her. "I was forged in a monster's crucible. I never had any choice in the making, but after…after I had to give them a meaning beyond their origin. I knew if I let them define me, I wouldn't survive. So I use them, a tool like any other."

He shuddered and leaned toward her, his arms sliding around her waist, pulling her into a tight hug. Isabel froze for a moment, and then she wrapped her arms around him and held tight. His heart beat hard and steady against her.

"I'm so fucking proud of you," he muttered and rubbed his bristled cheek against the soft skin of her neck. "My woman is a goddamn miracle."

The rasp of his skin against hers made her shiver, and something within her sighed in such deep pleasure that she stiffened. *This,* she thought, was the danger. Not sharing her scars; not sex. This place where they became one.

This was the risk. And the reward.

"It will always hurt," she murmured. "You just have to use it as fuel. Sometimes all we can do is take the lesson and do our best to make it different the next time. We're all human. We all fail."

"I don't deserve forgiveness."

"Punishing yourself doesn't change anything," she told him. "It only makes you weak."

Against her, he flinched.

"I'm sorry," she whispered.

"No," he said and shook his head, and his bristled cheek stroked her again. "I know I can count on you for the truth."

He pulled back, and his hazel gaze captured hers with a seriousness that made her heart suddenly flutter painfully. "I love you, Isabel."

She went still, her fingers digging into him.

"You don't have to say it back," he said quietly. "I just wanted you to know."

The sudden, overwhelming swell of emotion that filled her throat startled her and made it impossible to speak, and she could only stare at him, stunned.

Love.

How long had it been since she loved someone? *Since someone loved her?*

A lifetime. Would she even know it if she felt it?

"It's okay," Tony said, and the arms around her tightened. "Don't panic on me. No pressure, honey. But I'm not a man to pretend. I love you. I want your babies."

Babies.

Oh, God. Blood rushed to her head. Her heart pounded like an obnoxious dance song. She felt faint.

"You should see the look on your face," he murmured. "Priceless."

"Babies," she gasped, unable to say anything else.

"When we're ready." He leaned forward and pressed a kiss to the hollow of her throat, his tongue flickering against her. Heat immediately flooded her joints, and deep inside, she went soft and damp, and the ache that had plagued her since she'd laid eyes on the man throbbed in hungry demand.

A demand she was going to surrender to, no matter how much of a lunatic he was.

Babies. God help her.

"We've got a lot of bad guys to catch first," Tony continued and nipped at her, and Isabel squirmed on his lap, trying to get closer. "Gotta make the world safer. Then we can fill it with our rugrats."

He *was* a lunatic.

But as his arms pulled her closer and his mouth took hers, Isabel wasn't arguing.

*****

"Zander!"

Alexander looked up from his notebook to see Ben running toward him, Daisy at his heels. His brother was grinning from ear to ear, and for a moment Alexander just watched him.

What would it be like to be that happy?

"Sam said we're gonna go get a swing set!" Ben careened to a halt in front of Alexander and did a little dance. "A swing set!! *With a slide.* Holy cow, holy cow, holy cow, Zander!" Another little dance. "Our very own swing set!"

"Cool," Alexander said, even though he could have cared less about a swing set.

"You wanna come with us?" Ben asked, clapping his hands.

Alexander shrugged. "Nah."

Ben sobered and sat down on the log Alexander occupied. It sat in the middle of Sam's lush green back yard, next to a deep fire pit. A creek wound through the far end of the property, along a line of tall pines, and in the distance, a massive, snow-capped mountain stood like a sentry. Washed in sunshine and filled with tiny, colorful birds, it was a beautiful, peaceful place. Alexander liked it. He liked Sam's big log cabin, too. It was simple and sparse, with just enough room. Charcoal drawings and long, slender fishing poles decorated the walls.

Those are fly fishing poles. We'll get you a shorter one. You can give it a try and see if you like it.

He would've never imagined getting excited about *fishing*. But he knew it wasn't the fishing; it was Sam. Sam, who was…his friend. *Who wanted to spend time with him.* And whose words continue to gnaw at him.

What you do from here is up to you—no one else. And it can't matter, what other people know or say or do. Only what you do.

"I like it here," Ben said. "Do you like it here?"

Alexander looked at him. "Yes."

"Can we…can we stay here?"

The worry Alexander saw in his brother made the fury that never left him stir. "Yes."

"He's not gonna come?"

Alexander shook his head. "No. He's pretty much dead."

"I'm glad," Ben said softly.

"Me, too."

"Are you…is it gonna be okay now?"

Alexander felt his stomach burn. "Yes," he said and

hoped it wasn't a lie.

"Is Lucia gonna stay, too?"

"I don't know."

Ben's lip quivered. "I want her to stay."

"Me, too."

They sat in silence for a long moment.

"Can I...can I call Sam dad?" Ben asked quietly, shooting him an uncertain look.

The idea of that struck Alexander like a physical blow, and he stared at his brother. "I don't know."

"I'm gonna ask."

Dad. Alexander didn't think that word had ever left his lips. He couldn't even imagine saying it. But for Ben it could mean something. For Ben...this could be a whole new beginning.

For us both.

He jerked at that thought. Somewhere between yesterday and today, hope had taken root, and a new, optimistic voice had been born within him. He wasn't certain he liked it.

What if it was wrong?

But then he remembered following Lucia out of his father's cold, ugly house, ducking to get past Ivan, his heart beating with sickening force, certain their escape was a mistake. Everything that had urged him to turn back—*to give up*—had been *wrong.* And he'd almost listened. If he had—

Nothing would have changed.

He'd made the decision to go with Lucia. *He had done*

that. So why couldn't this new life be a beginning? Why couldn't he decide to shed the old and leave it behind like a skin that no longer fit?

It was a wonderful, grand idea. But inside him, a hard, cold lump sat heavy and still, a shadow so dark he didn't think the small seed of hope within him would be able to grow.

"I love you, Zander," Ben said, watching him, and Alexander's heart squeezed, because Ben understood. Even though he was just a little kid, Ben got it.

And loved him anyway.

"I love you, too, Benny," he said, and when Ben opened his arms, Alexander hugged him hard.

"Last call for the swing set store." Sam's voice carried toward them, and Alexander turned to see him striding toward them. Behind him, Lucia stood on the broad wooden porch that encircled the cabin, a steaming coffee mug in hand.

She was smiling.

Alexander *really* hoped she stayed.

"I'm coming!" Ben cried excitedly and leapt to his feet. Daisy barked, her tail slapping Alexander's leg, and he leaned down to give her a pat. "Don't go without me!"

Sam halted before them. "I would never." His gaze landed on Alexander. "Everything okay?"

Alexander nodded. Sam frowned a little, but then Ben flung his arms around Sam's legs and said, "I'm ready!"

"You are, are you?" Sam lifted Ben up and slung him over his shoulders like a sack of potatoes, and Ben squealed in delight. "How about you, Zander? Are you ready?"

Zander. A name only Ben had ever called him. A name that fit him far better than the one he'd been born to. Such a simple, significant thing. Maybe before he'd been Alexander, but now…now he could be Zander.

If he wanted.

He looked over at Lucia. "No," he said. "I'll stay."

Sam nodded. Ben clapped again.

"Alright," Sam said. "We'll be back. C'mon, Daisy dog."

And then he turned and walked back toward the cabin, and Daisy bounced along beside him. Ben waved at Alexander, his smile so sunny it almost hurt to look at. On the porch, Sam halted for a minute to kiss Lucia, and Ben giggled and made kissy faces, and Alexander felt a wedge of something unfamiliar catch in his throat.

Laughter.

It made the hope within him flutter desperately.

After they'd gone, he closed his notebook and walked over to halt at the base of the wide steps that led up to the porch. He made himself look at Lucia and ask, "Are you going to stay?"

"I don't know," she replied. She motioned him closer, toward the wooden porch swing that hung from the overhang. "Come sit by me, *mijo.*"

He didn't want to, especially if she wasn't going to stay. Because that felt like betrayal, and Alexander didn't think he could handle that on top of everything else. But she only watched him and waited, and after a moment, he gave in and moved to sit beside her.

Her bruises had turned a mottled blue-green, and the mark on her neck had a thick scab on it, and he knew she'd already paid too high a price in helping him. It wasn't fair to expect more. *He knew that.* But he did.

"I want you to stay," he heard himself say.

"I have not made any decisions," she said. "But no matter what I do, I will always—*always*—be part of your life. Alexander—."

"Zander," he corrected and felt heat curl into his cheeks.

She tilted her head in question.

"I want to start over," he said. "Be someone new."

Her lashes flickered. "Someone different?"

"The same but different," he said and shrugged feebly.

He couldn't explain it.

"I see," Lucia said. "Are you happy that Sam is your guardian?"

"Yes," he said, because it was true. "I want you to be our guardian, too."

"I do not know if that is possible," she told him. "But I will find out."

Sam's words whispered through him. *She's going to take some convincing. I might need your help.*

"He wants to keep you," Alexander said.

Her cheeks turned pink. "Yes."

"Don't you want to stay?"

She only stared at him, silent. Then, "Everything has happened very quickly, *mijo,* and I...I want to be sure."

"I like him," Alexander admitted. "He's...good."

"Yes," she agreed. "He is."

"You could do worse," Alexander told her, and a surprised laugh broke from her.

"Yes," she said again and sobered. "No matter what, I will be here for you. I promise."

It wasn't what he wanted to hear, but it was more than he had the right to expect, so he only nodded. "Did you...did you see the rest of it?"

"The rest of what?"

The dense, chilling cold within him grew heavier. "The video."

"No," she said softly.

"Are you going to?"

"No."

"It's out there forever," he said, the horror of that realization still fresh. Sometimes—for a minute—he would forget, and then he would remember, and it was like being crushed in an iron fist.

"Yes," Lucia acknowledged. "I am sorry."

"I didn't know he was doing that. Filming us." Alexander hadn't thought he could hate his father any more than he already did.

He'd been wrong.

"The people who found it...they were trying to help," Lucia replied slowly. "It was not about hurting you. It was about exposing him. Stopping him."

I don't care. The rage flared, and when it met the cold, stone thing within him, seemed to crackle and splinter out, and the feeling he'd had after first seeing the video—the storm that had pressed against his skin like an overwhelming tide—returned.

"You were not the only one," she said quietly.

Alexander met her dark amber gaze, his heart suddenly beating furiously. "What?"

"There were other videos," Lucia told him. "Other children."

Alexander stared at her, and a loud, deafening roar filled his ears. "Others?"

"Boys and girls."

For a moment, he couldn't catch his breath. His lungs went tight, his vision blurred, and his heart beat so hard, it hurt. Something within him snapped, like a dry twig beneath a booted foot, and he jerked physically in response. Tears filled his throat and pressed against his chest; his eyes burned.

"You were not alone," she whispered, and a horrible, broken sound escaped him, one he couldn't stop. She reached for him, and he reared back, but Lucia only dragged him into her lap, and wrapped her arms tightly around him, even as he fought. "You were not the only one, *mijo*."

A cry of fury choked him; he pushed against her, but she held firm, and another crack echoed within him, loud, like a gunshot. The wall that stood between him and the world—the one he'd built brick by painful brick—shuddered in effort to stand, and he did everything he could to push it all away, back into that place where it lived—*where he could live with it*—but he could see their faces—those boys and girls—and he could feel their rage and pain and hate.

He could hear their screams.

All of the sacrifices he'd made—to make sure he was the only one, to protect Ben—were worthless. It hadn't mattered.

Not any of it.

He jerked again, and the wall crumbled, and a sharp, piercing cry tore into the air. Huge, gulping sobs shook his shoulders, so violent and deep his cells vibrated, and he couldn't stop, couldn't speak. *Couldn't think.* Tears slid down his cheeks, and jagged, ugly sounds worked in his throat, and he shook like a brittle leaf in a strong wind.

Lucia's arms tightened; she cradled him like a child. "I am sorry," she said into his ear and rocked him, which only made him cry harder. "It will be okay, *mijo*. You will heal. I promise you will. It just takes time."

Alexander didn't know how long he cried. Every time the eruption slowed, more pain rose and shot forth like a geyser, scalding and unstoppable. When it was over, he lay still in Lucia's arms, shuddering in effort to breath, his nose running, his head throbbing. He felt…lighter, somehow, and…tired. *So tired.* That hard, cold stone still sat within him, but the wrenching pain was gone. And the hope…it was waking and stretching and filling the space where only fury had existed. He was still mad, but…

It was bearable.

"You are very important," Lucia murmured, and Alexander blinked up at her and realized she was crying, too, tears sliding down her chin in wet streaks. "I know you do not believe it, but it is true. You are important to me, to Benjamin. To Sam. So very, very important; I wish I could make you understand. And now, now you are *free*. You can be anything, *mijo*. Do anything. There are no limits any longer."

"It hurts," he rasped, unable to summon the cold, disaffected mask he'd worn for so long.

"*Sí*," Lucia said. "It always will. But it does not have to decide for you. Not anymore. Now, you decide."

Alexander stared up at her, and the naked love he saw made another wave of emotion tighten his throat.

"I love you," he whispered.

She squeezed him, hard. "I know."

CHAPTER 47

Boy snores filled the house.

Ben sprawled across his bed, arms flung out as though he dreamed of flight. Beside him, Daisy lay on her back, legs in the air, paws quivering as tiny growls murmured from her. In the other bed, Alexander was out cold, deep, heavy breaths rumbling from him, and between the three of them, it sounded like a pack of wild boars had invaded the cabin and were running amok.

Lucia pulled the bedroom door shut and made her way down to the kitchen. Sam's cabin was simple and solid, and clearly a single man's domain. They'd arrived the night before in the wee hours, and she hadn't looked around much before falling into bed fully clothed and surrendering to sleep, but today she'd spent much of the day exploring it. She'd found no earthshattering revelations; if anything, it only confirmed what she already knew: with Sam, what you saw was what you got.

There was no clutter, no bric-a-brac, no frilly curtains or colorful throw pillows. A few pictures—Sam and Tony outfitted in fatigues, surrounded by sand, their faces serious, their weapons ready; a teenaged Sam and an older man who squinted into the sun and wore a battered gray Stetson. Magnus, she thought, and silently thanked the man for all he'd done.

Fishing poles decorated the walls. The furniture was all lodge pole pine, rough-hewn and solid. There was nothing to soften the blunt lines, but she was comfortable with that. It was warm and welcoming and *safe.*

A blessed relief from the past few days.

She pulled a beer from the refrigerator and made her way out into the back yard, where Sam was tightening the numerous bolts that held together the swing set he'd bought. It was dark, so he was using a flashlight, and she halted on the porch, watching the ray of light cut through the darkness as he moved from one to the next.

He's...good.

Yes. He was. A fine man, one whom she'd done nothing to deserve, and for whom she was infinitely grateful.

I want to keep you.

The memory of those words—but more, the look on his face when he'd said them, those brilliant eyes of his steady and serious and unflinching—made her shiver. She'd tried hard not to think about them, because they had far too much influence, and there were things they needed to discuss.

So she went down the steps and crossed the thick grass to where he stood, crescent wrench in hand. When he looked up from his task, she smiled and held out the beer.

He stared at it for a moment.

"What?" she asked. *Did he not like beer?* He'd brought it home—

"Fuck," he said and dropped to one knee before her. "You're perfect. Marry me."

Lucia stared at him, her mouth hanging open, her heart fluttering painfully. "You—I—you cannot be serious."

"As a heart attack," he said solemnly. Moonlight washed over him, silvering his hair, making his eyes glint like polished stones. He reached into his pocket and pulled something out. "This was all I could get on short notice. Ben said grape was best."

Lucia stared down at the object he held: a ring pop. The giant candy gem gleamed in the moonlight like dark amethyst, and for a moment all she could do was blink stupidly at it.

"Take a chance," Sam whispered, "and build a life with me."

An immense, overwhelming swell of emotion surged through her, and she wanted badly to shove that ring onto her finger and wrap herself around him.

Do it.

But—

"I want them to have…normal," she said haltingly, her throat so full she could barely speak. "I come from chaos and violence and pain. I do not know how to be normal—"

Sam was pulling her down to the ground with him before she could get all of the words out, catching her weight so that she kneeled gently before him.

"Normal," he murmured, his hands possessive and heavy on her hips, "is just an idea. No one is normal, and anyone who tells you different is trying to sell you something."

He smelled like sunshine and sweat and *Sam,* and she wrapped her hands around his thickly corded forearms and clung, unable to help herself. "When my family died, I told myself never again."

"Time passes. We heal." He leaned close, his expression grave. "Do you think Alexander will ever know normal?"

"No," she whispered, a painful truth.

"He needs us both, sweetheart."

Yes. But that did not require—

"I love you, Lucia."

Everything within her went still. Her heart pounded hard at the back of her throat; blood roared in her ears. *Love.* Something she had tried very hard not to think about for a very long time, especially in relation to Sam because—

"They might come for me," she said, her words tripping over themselves. "They might take me away and—"

"And we will deal with it."

Hope warred with terror, and her hands trembled on him. "We are strangers."

Sam scowled. "Really?"

No. She felt like she'd known him forever. And she couldn't deny it: she wanted him.

She wanted to marry him.

"*Ay, yai, yai,*" she whispered. "This is…*muy loco.*"

"I don't care." A muscle leapt in his jaw. His hands tightened on her. "I want you. And I want to do it right. I've never done a fucking thing right in my life, and I'm not screwing this up. You, me, and the boys, together. A family. Come what may."

The vision that rose in her head made her dizzy. *A future.*

One in which she desperately wanted to believe. "I…"

"We're halfway between Yakima and Tacoma. Both have top-rate med schools. You can finish your schooling. I know it's important to you, and I don't want you to give anything up. I can take a desk job at the Service; I'm sick of chasing assholes anyway. We can put the boys in public school and go to Disney World on vacation and just fucking *be*."

She opened her mouth to speak. Closed it.

"Just say yes," he murmured. "The rest will work itself out."

She stared at him, trembling. She thought of all the years she'd spent nursing her pain and her rage; how many things—*people*—she'd given up on. Was that who she wanted to be? That angry, bitter, deeply unhappy woman?

No.

She'd learned that there were no guarantees long, long ago. There were only choices. If she turned Sam aside, she would never know what could have been. She would know she hadn't been brave enough to *try*. And she would regret it every day for the rest of her life.

Taking the boys had been the biggest risk she'd ever taken, and it had paid off. *It had been worth it.* It had changed everything. As this would. Sam was strong and stubborn and proud; he would only bend when she made him. But she was equally strong, stubborn and proud. She could handle him. *She wanted to handle him.* And if it didn't work out…the world would not end.

Life would go on. And the realization that something might end was not justification for never allowing it to begin.

Ivan had shown her how short and precious her life was. How valuable. She would not forget that lesson.

A rush of wild happiness burst in her chest. *She could do this.* Just one more leap of faith. So she leaned over and said softly, "*Sí,* Sam. *Sí.* I will marry you."

For a moment, he didn't move. And then he was shoving the ring pop onto her finger and she was laughing at the sheer weight of it when his mouth found hers.

His tongue pushed into her mouth and stroked along hers, and lust surged through her. All of her fear burned away, and when he pulled her to him, she went, wrapping her arms around the hard, broad width of him, clenching her fingers into the thick, golden pelt of his hair. His hands were gentle as he caught her against him, careful of her injuries, but even though her wounds ached, Lucia didn't care. Her nipples prickled, and she moaned and squirmed to get closer.

"I want you," he grated into her ear, his breath hot, his teeth sharp when he nipped her earlobe.

"*Sí,*" she whispered.

"Now," he added, and his hands swept up her waist to boldly cup her breasts, careful of the bruises that covered her, the wounds that traced her shape. He rubbed her nipples, gentle but relentless, making her cry out. When pinched them lightly, she snarled and pulled his mouth back to hers,

Somehow, Sam stood, lifting her with him. Lucia held on as he devoured her, giving as good as she got. The pain of her wounds faded beneath the onslaught of hunger she felt for this man. Pain simply meant *she'd survived.* And she was going to celebrate that.

Sam lifted her higher, and she wrapped her legs around him, and the hard press of his cock made her womb clench. A scorching, restless fire streamed through her veins, and their kiss grew wild, a passionate tangle of tongues and teeth and wet, raw sex.

Sam made a low, rough sound, and the vibration rippled through her. She was vaguely aware that they were moving, but she didn't care, lost in the heat and the hunger and him.

"Hold on," he growled, hefting her higher, and then they were climbing the stairs, shoving through the door, across the living room into his bedroom. The door shut with a thud and then he was lowering them to the bed, and when he came down on top of her, the weight of him made her moan.

"Naked," he rasped. *"Now."*

Her t-shirt was gone in an instant. He stripped her bra away and stilled. The moonlight was bright through the large windows, and his eyes were glittering brilliantly as they raked over her, searing her flesh, making her nipples swell and throb and ache for his touch. His gaze lingered on the mark left by Ivan's mouth, and Lucia lifted a hand to cup his jaw, his beard rough against her palm.

"See me," she whispered. "Not him."

Sam made a low, rough sound. He cupped her breasts, his skin rough and hot; he thumbed her nipples, small circles that made her breath catch.

"You make me fucking weak," he muttered. Then he leaned down and put his mouth on her, flicking his tongue over their tips, rubbing her until she writhed beneath him.

"Please," she whispered.

"Patience," he murmured and suckled her.

Lucia arched toward him with a sharp cry. An arrow of white heat shot to her core, and the pull of his mouth made the need throbbing within her flare hotter, brighter, more wildly out of control. His teeth scraped her, and she ground herself against him in desperation.

"Please," she said again, and he bit her, a sharp nip that made her entire body clench in need.

"Fucking perfect," he rasped and rubbed his cheek against her, and the rough bristle of his chin made her throat swell with sudden, unexpected emotion. But then his hands went to the button of her jeans and tore it open, and the need took control.

Lucia tugged at his shirt, but he ignored her, stripping her jeans and underwear away.

"You, too," she told him, and he acquiesced and pulled off his shirt. His skin shimmered in the moonlight, the muscle that roped him rippling as he moved above her, and the sheer beauty and power of him locked her breath in her throat. She stroked her hands over his tattoos and scars and touched the gleaming silver rings that pierced his nipples.

He made another low, hungry sound, and she reached for the button of his jeans. His hand shot out and captured hers, and he shuddered, stilling above her.

"We can wait," he said raggedly. "I know you're hurting. This can wait."

Lucia growled at him. "I want you inside me."

His gaze captured hers. "Be very sure, sweetheart. Because once I'm inside, you're mine. There's no going back."

Mine. It was a warning, she knew. But deep within her, something answered. *Yes. Please.*

"I will be yours, and you will be mine," she whispered. "Now come inside me."

His hand flexed around hers.

"Sam."

His jeans were open a heartbeat later, and he was climbing from her to strip them away, and the sight of him naked in the moonlight, so much raw power and sleek male beauty, made her clench her thighs together. The Ringpop snagged the sheets, the sugared gem twisting on her finger, and she was very aware of it. Of the promise it signified, the leap she'd taken. Everything she'd ever allowed herself to dream in her most private moments sat on her finger, and her hand clenched in effort to keep it from sliding off.

Rough hands slid along her inner thighs, pushing them open, and for a moment she resisted. Such vulnerability…but this was *Sam.* Who she trusted. *Who she loved.* So she opened herself to him. When he cupped the aching hollow between her thighs and rubbed knowing fingers through the wetness there, she shuddered and spread herself wider.

It was ecstasy. *But it wasn't enough.*

"So wet," he muttered, his eyes heavy-lidded and pale in the light. He thrust a finger into her, and she arched, a cry locked in her chest. "Christ, you're tight. Going to fit me like a glove. *Fucking perfect.*"

Lucia didn't respond; she couldn't. Every fiber of her being was locked on the hand between her thighs, the thrust of his finger into her. When he pushed a second finger in, a low moan tore from her.

"Just like that," he breathed and leaned down and suckled her again, and she almost came.

"Now," she cried. "Please, Sam. I need…"

His head lifted. His hand worked between her legs, and the pleasure rolled through her like a wave breaking. "What, sweetheart? What do you need?"

Her eyes met his, and her fingers dug into the supple muscle of him. "You," she whispered. "I need you."

A muscle leapt in his jaw; veins stood out in his neck, at his temple. And she realized the control he was exerting over himself, and she wanted that control *gone.* She wanted him as wild as she felt.

"I want you inside of me *right now*," she snarled and wrapped her hand around his cock. So buttery soft, yet like heated steel. The feel of him made her womb clench again. He growled and thrust himself into her hand, and she squeezed him hard, gratified by the shudder that shook him, the clench of his fingers into her, the pleasure that seized his features.

"Now," she said again.

And he pushed between her legs, his heavy, muscled thighs spreading her wider, their rough surface abrading her own soft skin. Then he was poised at the entrance of her body, and she burned and throbbed and tried desperately to get closer.

His hands clamped around her hips and stilled her, and she looked into those shimmering eyes again, and almost begged.

"Are you ready?" he whispered, and his hands flexed

around the curve of her hips.

"Oh yes," she breathed and smiled at him. "Bring it."

"*Fucking weak*," he growled, and the low, deep tone of his voice rasped against her skin like a physical touch, and when he began to push inside her, her breath snagged in her throat, and her body burned like the brightest flame.

She moaned as he thrust through the tight tissue, a slow, wet glide that made her tremble.

"Like a fucking glove," he said and shuddered. "Christ."

"It's been…" She tried to catch her breath. "A long time."

Those glittering eyes met hers. "Good."

And then he thrust hard, shoving all the way into her, and her body clamped down on him like a vise. A ragged sound tore from him, and he thrust again, and the friction bore a pleasure both mindless and consuming. Her nails dug deep into the skin of his biceps.

"We're going to do this every day," he snarled and thrust harder.

His body rippled with power, his abs flexing, the muscle she gripped tense, and her body clenched around him again, so tight she couldn't breath. He hissed and surged into her, each thrust stronger, harder, his control leaking away like water from a spilled glass. Lucia gloried in the loss, lifting herself to his thrusts, her thoughts imploding and scattering.

There was only him. Only this.

Another snarl tore from him, and then the control was gone, and he was pounding into her so hard the bed shuddered in effort to hold them. A sharp, wild cry broke from her, and he took her mouth, his tongue thrusting into her mouth, matching the rhythm of his cock. Lucia moaned, the ache within her curling tighter and tighter, every stroke taking her higher, *closer.*

Then he tore his mouth away, and his breath touched her ear, and he grated, "*Come,*" and she did with another harsh cry, brilliant lights glinting behind her eyelids, her body milking his, the pleasure so intense and shattering she could only hold on for the ride. The sound he made when he came gave life to something ancient and primitive within her, and she came a second time, shuddering around him, her skin vibrating, every muscle quivering.

He rolled them over, and she sprawled on top of him, her body trembling around his, his arms locked tight around her. The faint tremor that moved through him made her deeply satisfied, and for long, quiet moments they simply lay silent, basking in the afterglow. One strong, rough hand rubbed the length of her back, long, soothing strokes that made her boneless.

Sam pressed a kiss to her head, and Lucia felt her heart squeeze with sudden, unexpected fierceness. She looked up at him.

"I love you, too," she told him softly.

His eyes narrowed. "I know."

Arrogant, willful man. She laughed and shook her head and rubbed her cheek against the thick muscle that padded his chest. His hand slid down her back to her butt and rested there, heavy, possessive, and she felt herself stir, that hunger ever-present, urging her to take more.

"I will have to go back," she said. "There are things I

need. Things that are precious to me."

"Then we'll go get them." He paused. "Do you live alone?"

"No. I rent a room in a house."

"Will they be worried?"

"No. We all go our own way."

"We'll go in a few days. Give the boys some time to settle before we drag them around again."

"Thank you," she said.

"Anything you need," he replied quietly. "I'm there."

Tears filled her throat, and Lucia blinked in effort to contain them. What had she done to be gifted with this man? She didn't know; she didn't really care.

She had him now, and no one was taking him from her. *Not even herself.*

"We can do anything," he murmured. "As long as we're together."

She pushed herself up until she straddled him. He was supple and toned beneath her hands, and within her, his cock stirred, making her breath catch. She met the bright, luminesce gaze that watched her with such steady, unwavering intensity.

"I love you," she said again, barely able to contain it.

He hardened within her, and his hands lifted to cup her breasts.

"Show me," he said.

So she did.

EPILOGUE

Webster had two definitions for murder.

One: *the crime of deliberately killing a person.*

And two: *something that is very difficult or unpleasant.*

Well, two was out. There was nothing difficult or unpleasant involved. But number one…

Bingo.

She knew that, and it didn't trouble her for a New York minute.

No, the only reason she hesitated was because he would know it'd been her, and while she harbored no illusions when it came to him—he understood exactly who she was—she knew he would worry. He always had, even if he let her go her own way.

Your ass is gonna get caught. And then what?

Perhaps. But she was very, very good at what she did, and very, very careful. He knew that, too.

"Damned if you do, damned if you don't," she told herself. His favorite saying.

The monitor to her left, which displayed the diagnostics of the machines she'd hacked into, sat silent, awaiting her decision. It was a simple thing, to reach out and push the button that should shut down the ventilator. And she'd made certain to disable the alarms that would sound in the event it stopped functioning.

She wasn't a moron. Many things, perhaps, but not that.

No, all it would take was the stroke of a key, and Donavon Cruz would die, quietly, without fanfare, and by the time anyone realized he was gone, he'd already be burning.

At least, she hoped he would. Because people like Cruz deserved the hell the Christian Bible described.

He deserved worse.

She'd spent the last day working to put the pieces together, connecting him to the much larger organization he'd participated in, one that stole children and sold them to the worst humanity had to offer. And one by one, they would fall.

She would make certain.

But first, there was this. This choice she had to make. And part of her wondered why she was hesitating; at any other time she would simply act. And she knew her hesitation was a sign that she still retained—if only in part—her own humanity. *Her soul.*

A hindrance at times. And at others…her driving force.

An odd paradox.

And yet, it existed. As did she.

"Why am I hesitating?" she asked the second monitor, staring at the slack, unmoving features of Donavon Cruz. The camera was angled so that she could see his face and part of the window behind him. It was night in Boise, and lights flickered beyond him, tiny pinpricks of light that winked through the glass.

It must be done. For the greater good. For Alexander and Benjamin Cruz; for Lucia Sanchez. For all of the children Donavon Cruz had raped and tortured and, she was certain, murdered.

So that those who'd done business with Cruz would know she was coming for them.

To her right, the third monitor suddenly lit, and across the black screen, small white letters appeared.

What are you doing, a rúnsearc?

"Fuck off," she told the screen, annoyed. "Goddamn it."

Lazarus.

Unwelcome and unwanted, and as persistent as the sunrise. Every time he found her, she was forced to scrub her tech. Every piece utterly destroyed, necessitating the purchase of new equipment and the reworking of her entire network.

It was getting profoundly irritating.

Because no matter how many times she told him to go fuck himself, he would somehow find his way back—which infuriated her, because she couldn't figure out how, because it *should* have been impossible—and poke at her. He pushed buttons and teased her and acted like he *knew* her.

But he didn't. He never would.

More letters appeared: *Talk to me.*

She'd made that mistake once, thanks to a bottle of Boone's Farm strawberry wine and her temper. But once had been enough, and now he wouldn't stop. That he could find her seemingly at will disturbed her deeply, because she was a ghost, and he shouldn't have been able to see her. At first, she'd thought he was NSA. FBI, CIA, MI-6... But the things he said made her question that assumption. And in the end, it simply didn't matter who he was.

Light flickered. *I ken you're there.*

Well, since she was *always* there, that was not surprising. *Asshole.* She wanted him to go away. The trail she blazed was forged alone. She liked it that way. It was safe that way.

And safe was important. More important than anything else.

I'm not going away, lass.

I'm here to stay.

"Oh, shut up," she said and turned off the monitor.

Her heart beat hard, and she hated him for that. She had no use for emotion. Emotion was the enemy. It only confused the issue and made everything more difficult.

Case in point: the dispatching of Donavon Cruz.

There was no question he needed to die. Her hesitation was due to consideration of the repercussion.

But the one she worried about wouldn't judge her; he never had. And she knew he was well aware of some of the things she'd done, things that went against every tenant of the badge he wore. He knew exactly who she was—who she *really* was.

Aequitas.

And he understood that sometimes there was only one choice, like the one he'd made with her, one he'd never made with anyone else. That was why they belonged to each other, why he was the only person on earth to whom she held herself responsible. The one she would protect at any cost.

Family.

Her one, her only. What he thought mattered.

But she also knew, if it had been him, and he'd seen of Donavon Cruz what she had seen, he wouldn't hesitate to pull the trigger.

Some animals simply needed to be put down.

Because even if Cruz was—for all intents and purposes—dead and could no longer hurt anyone, he was taking up space. Breathing *her* air. And that was simply unacceptable.

Only one choice.

Yes. He might disagree, but—

"Fuck it," she said, and pushed the button.

The End…Until Next Time

***

Thank you for reading.

If you enjoyed *The Getaway*, please consider leaving a review. Reviews are critical to the exposure and success of independently published works. Thank you!

For a sneak peek at In Plain Sight, keep reading…

IN PLAIN SIGHT

Chapter
-1-

"I need your help."

Someone call Scientific American. Because those four small words—tight, tense, edgy little syllables—were unequivocal proof of a parallel universe.

Or maybe the world really *was* ending, just like Athena the All Knowing insisted.

"Fiona? Are you there?"

In spite of the desperation she heard—or perhaps because of it—Fiona Dresden didn't immediately reply. Maxwell Morrison Prescott the *III* wasn't her favorite person. Never mind that he was her brother—or step-brother, if you wanted to get technical, which she did—or that a decade had passed since their last brief conversation, which had taken place at the foot of their collective parents' freshly dug graves. In her lifetime, there were only two things Fiona had ever gotten from Max: a missing front tooth (care of a Tonka truck he'd beamed her with when she was ten) and a broken heart.

Neither of which she cared to revisit.

"*Fiona.*" He sounded like someone had just totaled his car. Which she had, when she was fourteen. He'd driven a burly Jeep the last time she'd seen him; much better safety features.

"Don't have a cow," she told him. "What do you want?"

Did that sound ungracious? Well, tough tittie. She felt ungracious.

"I told you," he grated, impatience crackling like dry wood catching flame. "I need your help."

"Moi?"

"Don't make this harder than it already is."

"Because I should make it easy?" She laughed, a harsh bark of derision. *She'd learned well.* Would he notice? "What possible use could you have for me *now*, big brother?"

Silence. Heavy, thick, leaden with something she had no desire to contemplate. It had taken years to regrow the skin he'd peeled from her; she refused to reopen that wound.

And yet, she didn't disconnect. She didn't toss her phone to the ground and stomp on it. No, instead she waited for his response, her heart a painful drum in her chest. Frozen and furious and damning herself for trying.

Again.

"I need you, Fi."

The quiet intensity of his tone caused dread to suddenly ripple down her spine, a chilled fingertip that made her skin prickle in ominous warning. Because Max was omnipotent; he didn't need anyone. Certainly not her. His last words to her on that dreary day a decade ago still danced ghoulishly through her darkest dreams.

I don't want anything to do with you, Fiona. We aren't family; we never were.

Ugly words, branded into her soul. He should have just

kicked her in the face with one of his sharp-toed cowboy boots. It would've hurt less.

"You don't want anything to do with me," she reminded him coolly. "Remember?"

More silence. For one endless moment, Fiona thought she'd lost him. And part of her thought: *good. Full circle, brother. Karma's a bitch.* But the child she'd been, the one who'd so foolishly believed that they *were* family—and still did, no matter the reality—waited, breathless with hope.

Goddamn hope.

"I was a dickhead," he said finally, his tone gruff. "I was angry. I'm sorry."

Which froze her, motionless, into place. *The world really was ending.* Because that was not what she'd expected to hear. Honesty; humility. *A freaking apology.*

"Who are you and what have you done with Max?" she demanded.

"I'm not a kid anymore," he retorted. "Cut me some fucking slack."

Another ugly laugh broke from her.

"Fiona."

"You threw me away," she told him flatly, and her throat suddenly filled, and the memory of his desertion stabbed through her like a hot blade. "I owe you nothing."

More silence. *Hang up, you stupid fool.* But she didn't.

"I can't change it," he muttered, and he sounded...weary. As if all of the arrogance and angst he'd always worn like a shield had drained away, leaving only fatigue behind.

Not that she cared. *Dickhead.* On that, they could agree.

Still, how curious that he should…need her. "What do you want?"

"Are you alone?"

An odd question that made her look around. Nothing had changed since the last time she'd looked: the rain was still a cold, steady deluge that left her standing in half an inch of water.

The carnival midway was waterlogged, the ride jocks covered in mud and grass as they struggled to set up the tilt-a-whirl in what was quickly becoming swampland. The games weren't faring much better, the trailers sinking into the ruts formed last night when they'd pulled in. Even her balloon game, built of wood and lightweight PVC pipe, was slowly settling into the wet ground. Just across the midway, the popcorn wagon sat in two deep puddles that would only get worse once she went to work inside.

Thunder rolled overhead, and someone was listening to Tom Petty. In the row of games across from her everyone was working, setting up their stock and flashing their stands, no matter the storm, because tomorrow was opening day, and there was no "called on account of rain" when three days was all you had to make bank.

"Alone enough," she told him, and continued to clean the .22 she held. One down, three to go, and the short-range game would be ready to go.

"You're in Cedar Hills?" Max asked. "At Our Lady of Hope?"

She stilled. "How do you know that?"

"Hatchet. Until Sunday?"

"Hatchet?"

"Stay with me here, Fi. Cedar Hills is only a three day run, right?"

"Right," she growled, annoyed, and glared at the clouds, smoky gray and deep violet, churning like class four rapids as they rolled in. Stinking rain. "What does that have to do with—"

"I have a witness."

"A what?"

"A witness. I need some place to stash her. Some place safe."

Fiona shook her head. Opened her mouth, closed it.

"Some place no one will think to look," Max added grimly.

"Have you lost your freaking mind?" Because clearly he had. "You're not getting me involved in your FBI bullshit. No freaking way."

"Fiona."

"No," she repeated. "I'm not the Witness Protection program! I'm a *carny*. It's what you despise most about me. Remember?"

"No," he said, his voice hard, and she snorted.

"Liar."

"I don't despise you," he said evenly. "I never despised you."

"Did you get hit in the head?" she wanted to know. "Are you concussed?"

"Jesus Christ, Fiona. Was I really such a prick?"

"Really, *really* such a prick. Like the king of all pricks on a big old dickhead throne." Another snort escaped her. *Was he serious?* "You abandoned me, Max. I was *fifteen,* and you were all I had, and you fucking left. Why the hell should I help you with anything?"

For a long moment he said nothing, and Fiona clenched her cellphone. Part of her wanted to hurl it across the midway—or, better, at his head—but another part—that idiotic, foolish child who lived on in quiet, stubborn determination—wanted to *believe.*

"Please," he said. A quiet, solemn word, one he'd never before said to her.

One that sounded sincere. *One that dumbfounded her.*

"Screw you," she rasped, her throat painfully thick, her eyes burning. "You hurt me, Max. I thought we were family."

"We are family," he snarled.

"Since when?" A tear slid down her cheek, and she swiped it away, fury and pain and that sick, twisted hope churning within her. *She didn't want this.* To believe again, to trust, *to want,* only to have him grind her beneath his heel. He would betray her, just like before.

But she was not the child she'd been, not for a long time.

"I'm sorry," he said softly. *Again.*

The dickhead.

Was he manipulating her? Because he was not above that. But neither was he a man to sacrifice his pride—not for any reason. So if he was saying it, he probably meant it. And he sounded...desperate. *Desperate.*

As if, for once, she held all the cards.

Stunned, she tried to digest that earthshattering realization. Had she somehow tripped over the extension cord and knocked herself unconscious?

Alternate universe for friggin' sure.

"Fi." Max's voice was tight. "Listen, I know there's shit we need to hash out, but there's no time. Not right now. Right now, I need your help. I've got a kid in trouble, and if I don't get her somewhere safe, she's dead."

Dead. *A kid.*

Hang up, Fiona thought. He deserved all of her hate. All of her derision and disappointment and disgust.

But the kid... The kid didn't. The kid was innocent. Alone. And in trouble.

Something to which Fiona could relate.

"Craptastic." She sighed. "This is insane."

"No. This is perfect."

"Only for you."

"I can compensate you," Max said in a hard tone. "If that—"

"You're being a dickhead again," she told him. "There's an entire midway full of people here, Max. Innocent people. Your witness—just by virtue of her presence—will endanger all of them."

"I've got that covered."

"You can't possibly," she protested.

"You have to trust me."

Another harsh laugh rasped up her throat. "You burned

that bridge a long time ago, brother."

"Then give me a chance to rebuild it."

Her stupid, foolish heart leapt, and she reached up to rub the back of her neck, more than a little unnerved. This was certifiable.

"The show is the perfect hiding place," Max insisted. "People rarely look too close. It will work."

Goddamn it, she wasn't really considering this, was she? *You dumb shit.*

"Why?" she demanded. "What's going on that you can't keep her in a safe house? Has your precious Bureau been infiltrated?"

Again he said nothing, and the chill winding its way through her veins spread like an ugly stain.

"Awesome," she said sarcastically.

"Just for a few weeks," he promised quietly.

It was one thing to endanger herself; it was quite another to endanger her help and everyone on the show. What the hell was she thinking?

"She's fourteen years old, Fi. Two nights ago she watched her entire family get capped. I have to keep her safe. I'm all she has."

You were all I had, too. Yet he'd walked away without a backward glance.

And now here he was—because he knew she was hard only on the outside, an inconvenient and often painful truth she did her best to protect, and he was not above using that knowledge—the dickhead—which was spectacularly disappointing, if not surprising. That alone should have been enough to send him packing. But this decision...it wasn't about Max. It was about an unknown fourteen-year-old kid, who was little more than a child, who—even faceless—Fiona could relate to. She knew what it was to be alone.

So now what? What are you going to do? Who are you going to be?

Who you want to be, or who you should be?

Goddamn it.

"Three weeks, no more," she said, her voice hard. "And I'm putting her to work."

"Deal," Max said quickly. "We'll be there tomorrow, before noon."

He ended the call with an abrupt disconnect, and thunder rumbled overhead, a violent drumbeat that resonated through Fiona's bones. She squinted up at the darkening sky, her head whirling with the sudden turn of events.

She needed her head examined. To trust Max again, even after he'd proven so unworthy of that trust. And to bring the kind of danger that came with him here... No matter what he'd said about having things covered, all bets were off.

No one would be safe.

Which was on her. Entirely. Because she was cursed with a soft heart, and no matter how much she hated Max, she loved him, too.

Always had, always would.

In her hand, her cell *dinged.* "Yeah?"

"Thank you," Max said into her ear and hung up.

"Shit," she said. Because...*thank you.*

Another thing he'd never bothered with.

"Shit," she said again, angry. At him. Herself. *Life.*

What had happened, to change him so drastically?

And that right there was exactly why she should've said no. Because she didn't know squat about him. The last time she'd seen him, he'd been on leave from Afghanistan to attend their parents' funeral. She had no clue where he'd been in the decade that followed, not who he'd been, not what he'd been doing. She only knew he was FBI because Hatchet mentioned it once in passing.

Hatchet. Who was the closest thing to family she had, and who'd clearly kept in much closer contact with Max than she'd ever realized.

What the hell was going on?

A federal agent turning to his carny stepsister to keep his witness safe? *Please, fool.* That's what the U.S. Marshals were for, no? Men with badges and guns; trained men, armed men. Men with license to do whatever was necessary to protect those they served. Was it not their very job to babysit federal witnesses?

Yes. Yes, it was.

So why would Max turn to her for help—and not them? There had to be a pretty significant reason, and it could be nothing good.

Thunder boomed down again, startling her. The sky had grown dark, and rain was falling in earnest now, heavy sheets that washed down the midway toward the unlit Ferris wheel, where it sat like a giant headstone, looming over the bright array of games, rides and concession trailers. She rubbed at her arms, chilled.

Nice visual.

God willing, it wasn't prophecy.

About the Author

Hope Anika is an indie writer living in the Greater Yellowstone area. She can be reached via Facebook, Instagram, www.hopeanika.com or hope@hopeanika.com.

Made in the USA
Coppell, TX
17 December 2019